# BECOMING VALLEY FORGE

A NOVEL BY

## SHEILAH VANCE

ELEVATOR GROUP
• PUBLISHING •

Helping People Rise Above™

*BECOMING VALLEY FORGE*

Published by

The Elevator Group
Paoli, Pennsylvania

Copyright © 2016 by Sheilah Vance

Trade paperback ISBN 978-09824945-9-2

E-book ISBN: 978-0-9824945-8-5

Jacket and interior design by Stephanie Vance-Patience

Published in the United States by The Elevator Group.

To order additional copies of this book, contact:

The Elevator Group
PO Box 207
Paoli, PA 19301
610-296-4966 (p)
610-644-4436 (f)

www.TheElevatorGroup.com
info@TheElevatorGroup.com

Cover painting: *The March to Valley Forge* by William Trego

Also by Sheilah Vance:

*Chasing the 400*

*Land Mines*

*Journaling Through the Land Mines*

*Creativity for Christians: How to Tell Your Story and Stories of Overcoming by the Members of One Special Church* (with Reverend Felicia Howard)

*Six Days in December: General George Washington's and the Continental Army's Encampment on Rebel Hill, December 13 - 19, 1777*
(an ebook prequel to Becoming Valley Forge)


Sheilah Vance is available for lectures on the topics and themes
in *Becoming Valley Forge*.  Please contact her at
svance@TheElevatorGroup.com or 610-296-4966.
Read about upcoming lectures, book signings and other events at
www.becomingvalleyforge.com, www.sheilahvance.com,
or www.TheElevatorGroup.com.

*Dedication*

*To my children, Hope and Vance, who make me a proud mother every day.*

*And to my mother, the late Ruth Roberts Vance Thomas,*
*whose pride about the historical significance of our home*
*on Rebel Hill was the spark that led me to write this book.*

# CONTENTS

# CHAPTER 1
# SEPTEMBER 11, 1777
# BRANDYWINE

Fred and Allen Roberts slept side-by-side every night, if they could. They were born only seventeen months apart and looked so much alike that most people thought that they were twins. When they didn't have to work on the family farm and were able to go to school, they sat side-by-side in the one-room schoolhouse down the hill from their farm, right next to General Anthony Wayne's estate, Waynesborough.

Some brothers fight when they are too close, but not Fred and Allen. One always seemed to be an extension of the other. They got along so well that their parents, until just a few years ago, thought that they had the perfect brood of children. Connie's running away to Philadelphia and becoming a prostitute shattered that illusion. But, in many ways, it made their parents cling even more to the perfection of the three remaining—Betsey, Fred and Allen.

And now that they were proudly serving as rebel patriots in the 5th Pennsylvania Regiment, 2$^{nd}$ Pennsylvania Brigade, under the leadership of their esteemed neighbor, General Anthony Wayne, the brothers clung even tighter to each other. Even though they only signed up a few months ago, having just turned seventeen and eighteen, and even though they had just been in training and had never been in battle, they had admitted to each other—yet of course to no one else—that they were scared. Scared that they would never marry. Scared that they would never have children.

Scared that they would never see their family again. Scared that they would be maimed in war, yet still have to live.

Yet, as much as they were scared, they were excited. And, they were committed. They hated the British. They hated the way that the British forced their parents and their neighbors to pay their hard-earned money in taxes to support a King and a Queen and a people thousands of miles away. They hated the way that their brothers in spirit, patriots in Massachusetts, Connecticut, and the other New England colonies, were persecuted, tortured, shot, and killed for standing up for themselves and for wanting the liberty and freedom that is every man's right.

So, when General Wayne went from farm to farm looking for Paoli's and Pennsylvania's finest, Fred and Allen signed up, along with most of the local boys they knew. No, Paoli wasn't a place for loyalists although they knew there were some in towns nearby.

Christine Roberts, known to all as Teenie, cried when she saw General Wayne ride up, dismount his white horse and head toward their house. She knew why he was there. Although she was as much a patriot as anyone else, those boys were still her babies. The war had now come to her doorstep. She knew General Wayne from growing up with him and running the rolling hills of Paoli and Easttown Township together as a child. She respected his military genius, although she didn't like his fiery temper that caused people in derision and in respect to call him "Mad" before calling him his given name.

Although proud that her boys were standing up for their convictions and wanted to fight for their new country, she cried even more when, after sitting around the hearth with General Wayne, Fred, Allen, and her husband, Orland, Fred and Allen signed up on the dotted line. They were now officially soldiers in the Continental Army. A few weeks later, a courier came to their house and dropped off orders for Fred and Allen, signed by General George Washington himself.

"And now, this 31st day of July, 1777, you, are hereby commissioned as a private infantryman in the Continental Army, Fifth Pennsylvania Brigade, under the command of General Anthony Wayne, and ordered to report for duty to halt the advancement of the British Army at Brandywine, Chester County, Commonwealth of Pennsylvania. Signed, General George Washington, Commander in Chief, Continental Army, United States of America."

Those orders were tucked safely in a pouch that each of them carried on their belts from the time they marched out of Paoli, down the Darby-Paoli Road, and then down the Baltimore Pike until they came to the lush Brandywine Valley and the river that flowed right through it.

JIMMY SISCO, who lived down the street from the Roberts in Paoli, blew his bugle loudly, signaling to the Fifth Pennsylvania that it was time to wake up. Allen opened his eyes, and then he closed them. Daytime came around all too quickly, whether you had worked the night watch, like he did, or not. The ground that he slept on was always hard, despite using whatever pallet he could put down to soften it. How he longed for the softness of his bed at home, the one he made with his own hands, from the tall tulip poplar trees that grew in their back yard.

Jimmy blew his bugle loudly again.

This time Fred opened his eyes. And he kept them open. He stretched and then hit Allen, lightly.

"Wake up little brother," Fred said.

"Do I have to?" asked Allen.

"Beats the alternative," said Fred, laughing.

"I guess you're right about that," said Allen, as he stretched and threw off the thin blanket that covered him. Although the daytime temperatures soared into the nineties, he always felt a little cool sleeping outside on the dewy grass.

The bugle sounded again.

Fred and Allen knew that they had about ten minutes left, at the most, before they had to line up with the rest of the Fifth Pennsylvania for morning inspection and breakfast. Morning inspection wasn't as grueling as some of the others. It was more like the attendance line ups that they had in school. A count to see who was present. To see how many were left. To see if any had deserted in the night. Luckily, though, the Fifth Pennsylvania were a loyal bunch so far. They didn't have the desertion problems that some of the other regiments did. Most of the brigade knew each other from their small towns, and they knew their commander, so their loyalty ran deep.

Fred and Allen grabbed their rifles and headed towards the open field where the other soldiers began to assemble. They had long gotten used to walking, standing, and paying attention when they were hungry. Food was not in the greatest supply at camp, even though they were surrounded by farms on every side. There were more loyalists down in that part of Chester County. If their home folk from Paoli weren't able to bring down food that week, sometimes there wasn't enough, especially meat, to go around.

"Hey Josh," Fred said to the soldier walking next to him. "Heard from the family?"

"Not for a few weeks," Josh said.

Allen called out, "Tommy! Wait up!" Tommy Wilson, who attended church with him, stopped and turned around. They put their heads together and were in animated conversation as they headed towards the open field.

Waiting for them, fully dressed, in all of his regalia, looking every bit the commander, was their own, General Anthony Wayne.

CHAPTER 2
# SEPTEMBER 11, 1777
# PAOLI

 "**C**aw! Caw!"

The roosters, always loud, sounded a bit more agitated today, thought Betsey Roberts as she turned over in bed.  Maybe they were fighting again.  Or in heat.

"Caw! Caw!"

A female rooster running away from a male one, possibly.  No desire to get pregnant.  Something that Betsey could understand.  No desire to have sex even.  No, Betsey thought.  That was not for her.  She saw what that desire did to her sister, Connie, leading her to leave their small farm in the country in Paoli for the anonymous big city of Philadelphia, where she could fulfill her sexual desires in the most base way—selling her body to any dandy with a quid.  Connie made a living, a good one from what Betsey had heard, but Betsey couldn't understand how Connie could do it.  How she could let her body be used that way.

No matter, Betsey thought. I still miss her.  She's still my sister.

The past two years were hard enough on Betsey, having to listen to her parents criticize and just about disown Connie.  Teenie Roberts prayed every day that her daughter would give up her wicked ways and return.  Orland Roberts openly worried about how to hide the shame of her "profession" if she did. "Caw! Caw!" the roosters crowed again.

"Alright, alright" Betsey said as she threw the covers off her and swung her legs over the side of the bed. She put on the open lattice work shoes that she had made for herself so that her feet would stay as cool as they could on these hot Indian Summer days.

She slid a red gingham robe off the hook next to her bed and covered up her sleeping gown, not that she wanted to—she was hot enough from the 80 plus degrees heat and humidity. Her father insisted on modesty at all times in the household, no bare arms, no bare legs showing. Betsey was a woman, he kept saying. She didn't much feel like a woman most of the time. She had to do the men's work around the farm on top of the women's work that she was already doing since her brothers left with the 5th Pennsylvania Brigade, along with most of her male friends and classmates from Paoli, Malvern, and all over Chester County.

She looked down at her hands, made rough from plowing, picking, and chopping, and wondered when this awful war would end. Not that she didn't think the cause was worthy, because she did. The Roberts were patriots, born and bred. Awful because people died and lives were disrupted. Awful because all of the patriots knew that their army didn't have the money, the training, and, all too often, the men, that the invading British armies had. Awful because people couldn't be free in their own land and were ruled by a king and a queen who lived far away and who knew nothing of the lives that the people led.

But, all that was as it was. Complaining about it wasn't going to change a thing, especially her rough hands. So, she opened an earthen crock on the wooden table by her bed and dipped out a small handful of the fat that they used to soothe the cow's udders. She rubbed it on her rough hands before heading into the kitchen, where the unmistakable smell of bacon was coming from.

"Good morning, mother," Betsey said. She walked over to the hearth where the bacon fried on a skittle suspended over the open flame. "That bacon looks as delicious as it smells," Betsey said.

"I know you need to eat a bit more hardy breakfast than oats and milk since you're doing your brother's work, too," said Teenie. And it's a darn shame that you have to do it, too, thought Teenie, as she turned the bacon on the other side.

"Go on and sit down. This is almost ready," said Teenie. "And the eggs are already done and keeping warm," she said, fanning herself with one hand as she pointed to the other skittle resting in the warming spot in the wall around the hearth.

Betsey pulled her chair up, eagerly awaiting a full meal. Yes, her mom was right. More than a few times she felt faint when breakfast was only oats and cream. Luckily, some of their hogs had fattened up enough to become ham and bacon. They gave the boys all the grown hogs they had when they marched off with General Wayne. Betsey knew that they needed every scrap of food that they could find, so she didn't mind, but she also was happy to be able to eat some good pig meat again.

Teenie piled Betsey's plate high with bacon, fried eggs, and powder biscuits. Hot as it was, Betsey ate every bit.

"Dad gone already?" Betsey asked as she chewed another piece of bacon.

"As usual," said Teenie. "He's out there harvesting the squash. Says it's time to get them to the Tavern."

"Good," said Betsey. "Looks like we might have to make a trip over to the Tavern tonight." The tavern was the Paoli Tavern, local gathering and drinking place for men in the area, soldiers, both British and Patriots, passing through, not at the same time, of course, and for a few women in Connie's profession, or close to it. The tavern was one of the Roberts' farm's main customers, and it should have been, seeing how it was owned by Orland Roberts' brother, Norman. Norman bought as many of Orland's fresh vegetables and meats as they could get for use in their busy food service. He also bought the farm's barley and hops and used it to make the Tavern's famous beer, as much of that hidden from British eyes as possible, because Norman didn't want to pay the dreaded tax.

"Well, I'd better get going," Betsey said as she jumped up and put the dishes in the earthen pan filled with water for soaking and washing.

She went back in her bedroom, pulled on long work pants made out of rough homespun and a long-sleeved shirt made out of slightly less rough and itchy material. She took off her nice cool lattice sandals, and put on her rough leather work boots, the leather worn down to a nice patina from almost daily use. She ran back into the kitchen and filled a small jug with lukewarm water. She poured just a bit into the saucer on her dresser, put a soft cloth in it, and wiped her face down. The refreshing, slightly warm water cleansed her face and opened her pores. She reveled in the soothing feeling of the warm water, and she looked forward to Saturday night, when she would get her monthly bath. Most people thought she overdid it by bathing her whole body that often, washing away all of that protection from sickness, but she didn't think so. She liked the feel of the warm water sliding over and supporting her body. In a life now without many pleasures, with her sister and brothers gone, with her work tripled, soaking in a hot tub of water filled with lavender flowers, cinnamon sticks, and other herbs and flowers that were in bloom in the garden was one pleasure that she looked forward to.

She shook her head, wiped the cloth on her hands, and grabbed a large-brimmed straw hat off a hook by her bed. She walked to the dining area, gave her mother a kiss, and said, "See you later tonight, Mom."

"Have a good day," said Teenie. "Don't work too hard Betsey," Teenie said, knowing all the while that Betsey would be working harder than a girl her age ought to.

# CHAPTER 3
# SEPTEMBER 11, 1777
# GERMANTOWN, PHILADELPHIA

Connie opened her eyes, rubbed them, stretched her arms to one side and her legs to the other. Her feet, toenails painted red with the latest lacquer from England, slipped out from under the thin cotton cover that laid over her long, lean legs. Never one to linger over anything, she swung her feet over the side of the bed, grabbed a silk robe off the hook next to her bed, tied it around her, and slipped her feet into a matching pair of silk slippers. Both silk garments were given to her by a merchant who often sailed the Orient as a tip for extra service one night. Connie usually insisted on cash, but she allowed herself to be swayed by the beautiful colors in the robe and slippers. She reminded herself never to be swayed again. She walked a few steps over to the large picture window and looked out at the traffic that was making its way back and forth down the hill, at a distance, on the road by the Wissahickon River that led to Philadelphia.

Some on horses, some in carriages—fine and run down in equal number, and many on foot.

The amount of traffic was unusual for early morning, even though more people came out in the morning because the weather was so hot and humid.

All of Philadelphia was on high alert, based on talk around her house by loyalists and patriots alike. The loyalists bragged that the King's Army was making its way towards Philadelphia after successful campaigns in New York. They said that they were going to drive the treasonous founders of their new country out of their capital city of Philadelphia in a blaze of gunfire and a show of force. The patriots said that they were preparing to give the Redcoats a shellacking like none they had ever experienced, holding them back from the seat of liberty and driving them back to the Schuylkill River and across the Atlantic.

Connie tried to remain passionless as she heard such talk. Her livelihood depended on servicing both patriots and loyalists, and, if the British Army came to Philadelphia, she would not be above servicing them as well. Her family would be horrified, she knew, because they were passionate patriots. But, her family was so horrified by so many of her actions for what seemed to her to be her entire lifetime, that the thought of their reaction only gave her momentary pause. They didn't understand why she threw away a quiet, honest, clean life in Paoli for a life of debauchery in Philadelphia. And she couldn't explain it to them. Since leaving home two years ago, she was even more sure that she had made the right decision. It was tough at first, trying to make money on her own, as a woman without a sponsor and without much of an education. But she quickly learned that she could make money fast and in sufficient quantities to support herself if she traded on what she had that people, especially men with money, wanted—long legs, big bosom, long chestnut-colored hair, delicate hands, full lips, and eyes framed by long and lush eyelashes.

All of that earned her a clean bed and a small room to call her own when she went to see Madame Celine at her brothel in the heart of Philadelphia, not far from where the Continental Congress met every day one very hot summer. Connie quickly became a favorite of several of the delegates as they spent months away from home and their wives, drafting the Declaration of Independence and creating a new country. Madame Celine was a patriot, and her brothel was a favorite informal meeting place. Connie enjoyed hearing about daily deliberations and how to form a united states out of a loose collection of colonies and all things political when the delegates came to visit at the end of the day or during the middle of the day when they needed a break from especially rancorous debate. Many days she thought about her Mom and Dad and how excited they would be to know that she met and intimately knew many of the men who debated and signed the Declaration of Independence and now were guiding their new country through this terrible war.

During that summer alone, Connie earned enough money to start saving some. And, one of those important men was her backer. Since he was already married, he could not marry her to provide for her. Connie didn't even want that. She suggested to him that he help her establish her own business, a brothel of her own, not downtown in competition with Madame Celine, to whom she would always be grateful, but on the outskirts of the city, in an area where client privacy could be more protected and assured. The heat was maddening that summer, so she thought about setting up shop somewhere that would be much cooler. There was nothing worse than having a large, smelly man sweating on top of you in a room with no air.

She told her benefactor, who came from one of the Southern colonies and didn't know much about the City of Philadelphia, about a lovely part of the city where Germans settled when they came to Philadelphia and where wealthy city dwellers, like Benjamin Chew, bought second homes to escape to when the heat of the city became too much. It was called Germantown. And, since it was outside of the crowded and cramped streets of central Philadelphia, the homes were larger.

One evening, this Southern patriot paid Madame Celine for Connie's time, rented a carriage, and took Connie for a ride to Germantown. He loved the green trees, large houses, and cool air. He said it reminded him of South Carolina. As they drove around, they saw a large stone home set back on a slight hill off of the main drive into Philadelphia. All that was missing were the slaves, he said. Connie assured him that some of the people around there had slaves. She told him, in her sweetest voice, that she didn't believe in the practice herself, but that she wasn't going to hold it against him because he did. She thought that if one human being was going to use another, at least the one being used should be paid for it, like she was. It had a back entrance that was slightly hidden by trees, with plenty of room for carriages. Connie thought that it would be perfect for a brothel, providing the right amount of privacy for clients. Its strategic position overlooking the river drive into the city on the back and fronting on the Germantown Road, would also allow her to see anyone who approached the home from Philadelphia..

Her benefactor loved the size of the house, as it reminded him of his large plantation house. Once they returned to Philadelphia, he made inquiries around town as to who the owner was and whether he would be willing to sell. It just so happened that the owner was a patriot, despite the many loyalist Quakers in the area. And, the owner was planning to enlist in Washington's Army and move his family back into the city to await his return, so the large house would be too much of burden on his wife alone with their young children. When the owner found out the identity of the person who wanted to buy the house, he became even more interested. The purchase was wrapped up within the week. Connie moved in with a few of the other women from Madame Celine's about two weeks later, with Madame Celine's blessing. If one of her girls was ready to move on, Madame Celine would rather they did it out of town than be in direct competition. With what Connie and her girls were selling, the men from Philadelphia considered the trip to Germantown just a very minor inconvenience indeed.

And now, the people came and went on the river drive and the Germantown Road. They had all heard that the British were coming from the south, from Maryland, and the Continental Army was amassing in Brandywine, Chester County, to stop them.

# CHAPTER 4
# SEPTEMBER 11
# PAOLI

B etsey dropped the tiller just inside of the door to the tool barn and ran all the way to her house. Dusty, sweating, feet aching from running, and arms aching from pushing the tiller, Betsey kept running until she got to the front door.

"Mom. Dad," she yelled out. But all was quiet.

She walked towards their bedroom just to be sure that there wasn't another reason why the rest of the house was quiet. The door was open, and then she collected her wits. Of course, her mother and father weren't at home. If they were, they would have yelled out for her to come home once they realized what they heard was gunfire, and even rode one of their horses down to the field to scoop her up and carry her home.

She was alone in the house. She ran outside as another cannon exploded. Not knowing where her parents were frightened her because she didn't know if they had, earlier in the day, traveled down the Darby Road to visit friends or tend to business. They didn't always tell each other where they were going. They assumed that they'd go and then return. That was the way it always was. The war had never come to their doorstep before.

She ran around to the back of the house, looking in all the outlying buildings, calling their names. Certain that she was alone and thinking that each blast that she heard seemed closer, Betsey ran back inside the house. Dad always kept his musket right by the front door. "Never know who might be wandering around out here in the dark," he said. "Especially now that I've got a house full of women," he said after the boys left.

Betsey grabbed the musket and looked out the front door. She turned all around, looking to the east, west, north and south. Certain that she didn't see mother or father, she closed the door, swung the heavy iron bolt across it, top and bottom, and waited, hoping that the next voice she'd hear would be her mother and father, and not someone whose coming meant her nothing but harm.

AFTER WHAT seemed like an eternity, she heard a commotion outside. She heard horse hoofs flying over the hard, dry dirt. She ran to the window and peeped outside. It was dark by then. Betsey checked her musket one more time, loaded it with powder and buckshot, and crouched to the side of the front door—a spot where she could see anyone coming in before they could see her.

With her heart beating almost as loud as the gunfire, she heard those familiar voices. "Betsey! Betsey!" yelled Teenie.

Then that masculine voice that she so longed to hear. "Betsey! Honey! Are you in there?"

"Yes, I'm here! I'm here!" she yelled as loud as she could, excitedly.

Betsey gently laid the gun down. She moved away from the door, also moving away the table and chairs that she had pulled in front of it to keep out any intruders.

"Mom! Dad!" she yelled. "I'm here!"

She heard them trying the door knob, so she yelled out, "I locked myself in here because I didn't know where you were or what was going on," she said, almost crying. "I'm trying to take the bolts off now. Hold on!"

Orland called back in a comforting voice, "Take your time, honey. We're here now."

Betsey flung off the first bolt and then the second. Then she flung open the door and fell in to her parent's waiting arms.

"Don't worry now, honey," Orland said. "You're safe now."

Betsey finally let herself cry. Between sniffles, she managed to get out, "What's going on, Dad? What's happening out there?"

Orland ushered her back in the house, sat her down on the nearest bench while he put her head on his shoulder and patted her on the head.

"War, honey." Looking at Teenie with eyes full of sadness, he said it again. "War."

## CHAPTER 5
# SEPTEMBER 11, 1777
# GERMANTOWN

Connie had just finished surveying the activity on the second floor and was not pleased. Only two of the four bedrooms were in use. She was losing money. Some of her best customers had already fled from Philadelphia with their wives and children. If the British were coming to invade Philadelphia, as everyone said they were, she wished that they would hurry up and get here. Thousands of soldiers thousands of miles away from their wives was good for business.

She grabbed the end of her skirt, pulled it up a few inches, held on to the gleaming wooden rail, and started to descend the spiral staircase with her head held high and her chin up. She looked every bit as regal as a queen. Even though she was slightly worried about the drop in her income, she could not let her girls or her clients see that. The first floor was somewhat quiet, with a few clients lingering, talking and drinking with a few of her girls.

Time to call it a night, Connie said to herself, as she began preparations to close for the night. It must have been close to midnight. Time to close the door. If you were here by now, you got to stay. If you weren't, too late. Come back tomorrow. Connie didn't like to have her clients and girls interrupted too late. The only activity she liked in her house after a certain hour was the activity that took place in a bedroom, between a man and a woman. She tried to run a high class house, one where men did not come and go at every hour of the night—just the hours that she designated.

Connie picked up one of the red candles in the window and blew it out, symbolizing that the house was closed for the evening. She walked closer to the window by the entry door, which was the door leading to the carriage driveway in the back, to do the same with another.

Suddenly, there was a loud bang at the door. Connie was so startled that she almost dropped the still lit candle. She blew the candle out and flung open the hand-sized part of the door that was solid wood on the inside but had a peep hole on the other side to see who had the nerve to visit so late and bang so loudly.

She peeped out and saw standing there Mr. Charles Dunmore, one of her old customers from when she serviced clients at Madam Celine's. He looked dreadful. Sweaty, jumpy, hair matted, eyes wild. Connie opened the door.

"Mr. Dunmore?" she asked, wanting to be sure that it was him.

"Yes," he said, almost stammering. "Connie. They told me I'd find you here," he said, wiping his brow.

"What are you doing here at this hour?" Connie asked. "Did they tell you, whoever they are, that I am the owner of this establishment? And that I no longer see clients? And that I run a respectable house? And that we do not allow men to come here at all hours of the night, like this hour?" she asked, perturbed.

"Yes, yes. They did," said Dunmore. "And, I'm sorry to come so late." He hung his head and wrung his hands.

"But I had to," he said. "I had to find a little comfort." Now he started pacing around the small landing. "It's madness in the city. People running everywhere. The streets full." He kept pacing. "Forgive me," he said, almost pleading. "I went to Madam Celine's looking for comfort, but all the girls were occupied. I was not the only man in Philadelphia tonight looking for that type of release."

"I practically begged Celine to do something to accommodate me, being a long-standing customer and all," he went on. "She said that she could not. The girls were already occupied and had two to three waiting for them. She suggested that I get out of town, if I could, and go to see you, at your place."

Connie looked at him, eyes wide and puzzled. Indeed, what was going on?

She grabbed him by the arm and pulled him inside. "Come in," she said. "I can't have you standing out here babbling like that." She looked around to make sure no one had seen him before shutting the door. But, she didn't let him go upstairs right away.

"What are you talking about? Why is the city so full of activity? Has something happened down there that we don't know about?" Connie asked.

Dunmore shook his head violently. "No, no. Not in the city," he said. "Outside of it. About 35 miles down the road. By the Brandywine River. All day, all afternoon, all night. You don't know? You didn't hear?" he said pacing. "Oh, I guess you are too far away up here."

He went on. "Terrible, terrible. Fighting. All day. Cannons, muskets, smoke. And death."

Connie had enough of his blubbering. She grabbed his arms and shook him. "What are you saying? What happened?"

"Brandywine. The British. They beat our boys and forced them to retreat. The British are on their way to Philadelphia," he said.

Connie looked at him, her mouth open, in shock. She had heard that it was going to happen. And now, here it was. She was a patriot, but she was also a businesswoman. She looked at Dunmore, blubbering, shaking, almost crying. "Get a hold of yourself," she said, almost sternly, to make him snap out of his condition. Then, her kind side surfaced. "I won't send you back out there," she said as she rubbed his arm. "Come," she said, "stand up," as she gently pulled him up. She walked in to the parlor where she saw one of her girls with a client.

"Joann," she said to the girl. "Is your friend here coming or going?"

Joann patted her bosom as a sign that it was full of money, smiled and said, "He was just leaving."

"Alright," said Connie in a sweet voice. "Can you take care of Mr. Dunmore here? He'll be our guest for the evening," Connie said, touching her bosom lightly, which all the girls understood meant that he was a good paying client.

"Absolutely," said Joanna, with a broad smile on her face. "Mr. Dunmore, you come right here with me," she said as she led him up the stairs.

Connie watched them go upstairs. She took Joanna's other client by the hand and said, "You know I'm the proprietor of this establishment," she said, as she led him to the back door.

She patted his arm and said, "Thank you. Come again."

She bolted the door behind him and went into the kitchen and poured herself a small glass of wine.

"God help us," she said, as she lifted her glass to the heavens, made a toast and then drank it down quickly.

# CHAPTER 6

# SEPTEMBER 11
# REBEL HILL, GULPH MILLS

James used the last few remaining hours of day light to clean off his tools and get ready for tomorrow. The war was in full swing in the colonies and the mill at the bottom of the hill was running extra long hours to make gunpowder for the Continental Army. Their tools and equipment wore out faster now, so the blacksmith shop where James worked with his neighbor Daniel was extra busy, too. James worked as much as he could; he needed every bit of wages to buy Ruth's freedom. As close as he got to the amount he needed, it was never close enough.

He cleaned off the last few tools and packed them in the leather satchel that he kept just inside the door. He pulled off his gloves and work boots and his shirt and pants, as hot and humid as it was. No need for modesty. No one would see him until the morning.

Sleep came easy to James after so many years of hard labor. When he was a slave, sleep was a luxury, because your time, your life, not even when you slept, was your own. You never knew when the master or one of his boys would come, wake you up, and have you do something for them. He lost just sleep many a night, but it was even worse for the women. Their sleep wasn't their own, and neither were their bodies. Many a night James lay awake, wanting to get up, but knowing that if he did, he would kill the master or one of his boys who would make their way down any night they felt like it to the women's cottage and have their way with them. James had nightmares about the cries that he heard coming from women in his family and women who were like family.  He thought about Ruth often, and prayed to his God for her safety.

But, tonight, he shook his head to get those thoughts to leave. He closed his eyes again.  Sleep came, and it came hard.

JAMES JUMPED up in bed, startled at the banging at his door.

Bang, bang, bang!  Again!

He picked up the musket that he kept right next to his bed and rushed over to the door, not thinking that he was only wearing enough to protect his privates, and swung the door open.

As soon as he did, the banging stopped.  A sweaty, dirty, and bloody man collapsed in his arms.

James dragged the man over to his bed and laid him down.  He rushed back to the door, musket in hand, ready to fire, pointing ahead of him, trying to make sense of what was going on.

Everything else was quiet.  He didn't see anyone else and didn't hear anything, except the foxes, which sounded like babies crying if you didn't know the difference.  But he knew the difference.  No babies were crying.  No other men were out here walking.

Had the war come to the Hill that soon?  James thought.  He knew that Washington was taking the Pennsylvania regiments from the area down by the Brandywine River to defend against the British, because he saw the orders that the General gave to James' friend and church member Ned Hector saying just that.

He ran back over to his bed where the man lay bleeding.  James calmed down and collected himself.  He looked at the man who looked at him.

"Are you James the blacksmith?" he whimpered.

"That I am," said James.  "Why are you asking, sir, and who are you, and what is going on?"

The man coughed, rubbed the dirt on his face, and said, "I'm from down by the Swedes Ford, and I'm trying to get back there."

He winced as he rubbed his shoulder.

"I'm a deserter now," he whispered. "I rode for hours, as fast as I could. The General told us to retreat to Chester, but after what I saw on that battlefield," he said, "I pitched my horse in the direction of Swedes Ford and never looked back."

James looked at him and frowned. "Battlefield?" he asked.

The wounded stranger said, "Yes. By the Brandywine. The Redcoats got us, and the General ordered retreat." Then he grabbed James' arm. "But I can't go back," he said, shaking his head. "I can't."

He started crying. "I'm not cut out for this. I'm a patriot and all, but I'm also a father. And a husband," he said. "And I can't do it."

James looked at him. "So why are you here to see me, sir? You know you are on Rebel Hill, and Swedes Ford is about a 15 minute ride."

"I know. I know," he said. "But I can't make it any longer. I'm wounded, and my horse needs shoes. I know of your work as a blacksmith from Thomas, who lives down the road from our home."

He grabbed James' arm again, and said, "Please. Help me," before his grip loosened and he passed out.

James looked up to heaven, sighed, and said, "God help us."

# CHAPTER 7

# SEPTEMBER 11, 1777
# PAOLI, PM

Betsey and her Mom and Dad listened to the muskets and cannons all night and saw the smoke on the horizon all night. They sat at the door, largely in silence, and prayed for their boys and all the other boys from the neighborhood. The sounds and the powder cloud didn't get any closer before they both stopped.

When he was sure the lull was not temporary, Orland said, "Go on inside, you two. Get something to eat. Rest. I'll stay out here for a while."

Betsey patted her father on the shoulder. "We'll bring you a plate," she said, as she followed her mother inside.

"I'm so tired, mother," Betsey said. "Tired and worried," she said.

"Yes, Betsey," Teenie said. "I hope that God has answered our prayers," she said as she went about making a quick meal.

"In any event," Teenie said, wiping her hands on her apron, folding them together into a prayer and looking up at the sky, "God help us."

## CHAPTER 8
# SEPTEMBER 11, 1777
# CHESTER

Sounds of "stand down," "stand down," "stand down" rippled through the air.

Allen stopped moving one leaden, aching foot in front of the other, laid down his musket, and collapsed on the hard ground of the Chester Common. Fred did the same. And so did the hundreds of worn out soldiers who surrounded them.

Allen took off his hat and rubbed his hand over his aching eyes and dirt-filled face. He looked over at his brother next to him.

Fred took his hat off, threw it on the ground, shook his head from side-to-side and sighed. After taking a few, short, painful breaths, Fred looked at Allen again, lowered his eyes, and said, "God help us."

## CHAPTER 9
# SEPTEMBER 12
# REBEL HILL

James woke up tired. He hardly slept the night before. Anything could have happened to him, having a white man in his home. There was no telling if that man who found his way to James' doorstep, battered, wounded, and exhausted, was telling the truth. He could have been chased by a mob of white men who wanted him for some crime, whether the men were locals or British. And if they found him in the home of a black man, freed or not, it was very likely that he would suffer the consequences along with the man. Slave bounty hunters were still around, and some of them didn't wait to ask first whether you were free or slave. For some of them, even if you were free, you weren't considered to be a whole man with rights, like them.

James spent half the night sleeping and half the night keeping watch. In the half time that he was awake, he spent half of that time checking on his wounded visitor, hoping that he was still alive. James couldn't stop him from falling off to sleep exhausted or passing out from his wounds. Once he did that, though, James determined which wounds were bloodying his visitor's uniform, cleaned those wounds, and dressed them as best as he could. His visitor barely moved, but he moaned softly with almost every breath.

Several times James asked the man how he was feeling, but if he heard anything, it was the mumbling of the delirious. The man had a fever, so

James fixed a poultice for his head, tying it tight so that it wouldn't come off with all of the man's twisting and turning, but not so tight as to cause him more pain.

James walked outside to see what was going on. Something happened last night, and he had to find out what. At some point, late afternoon into early evening, he thought he heard cannon fire. The war for independence was being fought in New York, he had heard, and not near his home. Although, with his wounded visitor, now he wasn't so sure.

STANDING OUTSIDE his cabin, James didn't see anything different. He saw a few people out in their fields, far away, just within eyesight, over the horizon. Nothing looked different.

The soldier's horse looked as exhausted as he was. It lay in the grass where the soldier had left him. James drew some water from his well and laid the bucket right by the horse. When it was ready to drink, it would. Until then, James figured, the horse needed as much rest as his rider did.

He patted the horse and then abruptly stopped. He turned his head towards the direction of the mill down at the bottom of the hill. It sounded louder than usual down there. There was a commotion that was easily heard, over the usual sound of the mill water spilling over its huge wheels.

James stood up straight and walked over to the edge of the hill. Looking down, he saw more horses hitched up out front than usual and more people coming and going. Some of them were unloading supplies and others were talking animatedly. Since one of the things the mill produced was gunpowder and bullets, maybe the war really had come to his doorstep.

The only thought that occurred to him with that realization was that he had better be ready. Maybe his ailing visitor could help him.

James went back into the cabin where the injured patriot still slept. James thought that as much as he'd like to let him rest, he couldn't afford to. He had to find out what was going on besides the little that the man told him last night.

James readied another cool poultice and laid it on the soldier's cheek first, hoping that would wake him. When it didn't, James shook him a little. He had to get him up.

The soldier stirred some, moving a leg slightly, and an arm even more slightly.

James touched the poultice to his other cheek, hoping that would finish the job of waking him. It did not, so he shook him again.

This time he opened his eyes. As soon as he did, he closed them.

James shook him again. "Friend," he said. "I know you need to rest, but I must wake you. I must know your name. And I must know what has happened to you." He paused for a moment. "What has happened to us all," he said.

The visitor opened his eyes, lifted the arm that was not covered in blood, and touched his head. He felt the poultice and winced. He looked at his bloody arm and his bloody leg, and tears welled in his eyes.

"Don't worry," James said. "I will take care of you and get you to where you need to go, as safely as I can."

The man wiped his tears away with his dirty hand. "Jacob is my name," he said, just loud enough for James to hear him. "Jacob Stafford. Of Swedes Ford."

James smiled, glad to know his name. "Yes. Well glad to meet you Jacob Stafford of Swedes Ford. My name is James Weldon. Of Rebel Hill."

"Yes," said Jacob. "I know your reputation well. Fred Pesto speaks well of you. I hadn't personally brought our horses to you, but I know of your work."

Jacob winced as he tried to sit up. James leaned over to help him, putting a pillow behind him, propping him up.

"I know of your work, and I need to get home," Jacob said.

James drew him a cup of water and let him fully wake up as he drank it.

When he seemed to come more to life, James said, "You said last night that you were in a battle and that you couldn't take it anymore and wanted to get home to your wife and children."

Jacob looked puzzled, "Did I?"

James smiled and said, "Yes."

James pulled up a stool next to the bed and sat down. "Please, Jacob. Tell me what happened. Then tell me exactly where your wounds are so we can tend to them and get you on your way. You know that I go to Swedes Ford every day to work with Daniel. And I will take you there. But first, please, what happened?"

Jacob sighed and looked lost.

"A battle," he said. "We fought the British down in the Brandywine Valley, down at the edge of Chester County, they say."

Now, it was all James could do to keep the tears from his eyes. The war was getting closer.

"We fought them, but we didn't win," Jacob said. "We retreated. We ran. They surprised us," Jacob said. "We weren't ready. We stood our ground as best we could, and we fought back with our strength and our might, but it wasn't enough. We were outnumbered." He shook his head as he went on. "Men were shot right in front of me. When we got orders to retreat toward the direction of the City of Chester, I took advantage of the confusion and stole away in the other direction. And I wasn't alone," he said. "Some men went one way, and some men went the other."

He sighed again. "I'm not a coward, you know."

James looked at him sincerely, "I am not saying that you are. Who am I to judge," he said. "Our Lord and Savior Jesus Christ tells us not to judge."

"I thought of my wife. My kids. I have two daughters and a son," said
Jacob. "I'm a patriot. I'm as fed up with the British as anyone. And I love
this new country we've created. But as I saw men getting killed right in
front of me, I wondered if it was worth it."

James shook his head. He wasn't going to disagree, and he wasn't going
to judge. He knew that he and Daniel and many others hadn't volunteered
for the Patriot army because they needed their wages. Daniel signed up
for the Pennsylvania Militia, like all white men over age 18 were ordered
to do. But, he had a family to support—his mother and handicapped
sister, since his father died a few years ago. Daniel didn't feel like he could
go off to fight, even if he wanted to, which he didn't. He paid the fine
instead and felt satisfied that he added to Pennsylvania's coffers.

James had no interest in joining the Pennsylvania Militia, the
Continental Army, or any unit that was fighting in the rebellion against
the British Crown. James supported the patriots generally, but he thought
that this whole fight for freedom was hypocritical. It was for the freedom
of white people against white people who came from another country.
That was nothing like the freedom that true slaves, those of African
descent, were denied every day. James was fortunate that he was able to
save enough money, by working for freed slaves and anti-slavery white
folks in what little free time his master gave him, over a year ago to buy
his freedom from the Hannah plantation. Now, he needed his wages from
working with Daniel to save enough money to buy the freedom of Ruth,
his fiancée still bound up as a slave at the same plantation. He wanted to
buy her freedom the same as he bought his own.

As long as the war didn't come right to them, both Daniel and James
felt like they didn't have to choose. They had better things to do.

James said, "I understand." He looked at Jacob intently and said, "Now
show me where your wounds are so we can treat them. Or," he said,
motioning to his cook stove, "would you like something to eat."

Jacob said, "Please. Treat my wounds first. Then I'd love to eat. I'm starving."

# CHAPTER 10
# SEPTEMBER 12
# PAOLI

Betsey Roberts could hardly contain herself as she peeled another potato. She wanted to run down to the Paoli Tavern and find out what was going on. She was willing to risk her mother's wrath once again and ask her one more time if she could go down there and meet her father. Just as she got ready to open her mouth, the door opened.

Orland Roberts walked in and took off his torn and fraying straw hat. Betsey dropped the potato peeler and ran over to him. So did Teenie. Orland wrapped his muscular and strong suntanned and sunburnt arms around them both.

"What happened, Daddy?" asked Betsey.

He squeezed them both, hard, before pulling away.

"It seems like our boys were fighting the British down by the Brandywine Creek," he said, somberly. "And it didn't go well. It seems like about a thousand of our boys got shot and killed. And then they had to retreat."

He laid his hat down on the side table and sat down, holding on to the side of the table. Betsey thought that he had to sit down to keep from falling down because he collapsed in the chair in a heap.

"Our boys were down there," Orland said, rubbing his neck. "Fred and Allen and all our local boys in Wayne's Regiment."

Teenie gasped and put her hand in front of her mouth.

Betsey just looked at him, eyebrows raised with concern.

"Our boys retreated to Chester City," he said. "But the British went on the march up here." He waved an arm in the air. "The Tavern is full of them. Even at this early hour. And so is the Darby Road.," he said.

He got up again, mad, and restless. "The sight of them makes me sick," he said. "Wayne sent one of our boys up this way to warn us that the British were coming. He couldn't tell us about casualties or which of our boys made it because when the order came to retreat, there was so much smoke and confusion that nobody could make heads nor tails of what was happening,"

Orland put an arm around his wife. "He told us that Wayne was going to send someone else up today with more news, once he got a handle on our local boys," he said. "And then, he said, Wayne said that they were going to come up here themselves and kick some British tail before they sent what was left of their stinking red coats back across the Atlantic."

Now Teenie sat down, holding the table with one hand as she lowered herself. Betsey saw the tear in Teenie's eyes, and she fought hard to keep them out of hers. She didn't want her father to see that she was scared or afraid or too sad to think. She wanted him to think that she could help.

"Dad," said Betsey, "What can we do to help our boys now?"

Orland said, "We're working on that now. We can't meet at the Tavern because it's so overrun. We're going to meet at the barn at Waynesborough, thinking that those damn redcoats wouldn't dare go there."

"But what about my work at the Tavern?" Betsey asked. "Should I still go there and help out?"

Teenie said, "Absolutely not. It's too dangerous."

Orland said, "Now hold on, mother."

Teenie screamed. "Orland! You can't be serious! We can't let Betsey go there now with all of those British murderers!" Teenie started pacing the floor. "It's bad enough that she's working in the tavern at all. I know that family is family and that your brother needs help and that they watch over her when she's there as best as they can, but they can't see everything and stop every drunk who wants to put their hands on my daughter under normal circumstances, but the British? Absolutely not."

Betsey stood up, hands on hip. "Mom! I can take care of myself! You know I can! I'm not serving all the time. If things get too bad in there, they pull me out of the main room and I help out in the kitchen. You know that!"

"Even so," Teenie said. "It's different now."

Orland grabbed his wife's hand. "Now hold on now, honey," he said. "Norman and Rochelle watch over Betsey like she's their own. The same blood that runs through her veins runs through Norman's, and he's not going to let anything happen to her. He'll kill a man first if he messes with his niece, and you know that."

Teenie said even louder now, "Huh! He's not everywhere all the time. Where was he when Connie was working there? What happened then?"

Betsey hung her head. That was a sore point. Mom still blamed Connie's working at the Tavern for the reason that she turned away from all of the good Christian morals that she was brought up with and ran off to Philadelphia a few years ago.

Orland stomped his foot hard. "Don't start that again, honey," he said. "You know that Norman and Rochelle and the Tavern had nothing to do with Connie's running off. It was that damn boy who came into town from New York City and his crowd, taking advantage of her country ways and filling her head with all kinds of dreams and promises of the fancy life in the big city."

Teenie started crying. Orland put his arm around her to comfort her. "I'm sorry, honey," he said. "I know how much you miss her." He stroked her hair and let her tears soak into his shirt. "I miss her, too. But there's not much we can do for her now, given what we hear."

He looked over at Betsey. "But Betsey's not like her." He shot Betsey a smile.

"And now we need Betsey in the Tavern more than ever," he said. "We've got to do our part in this war," he said. "More than we ever did before."

Orland pulled back from Teenie and held her face in his hands. "The war has come here. The redcoats are right in our own backyard, literally. They're all over the Tavern. They're all over the Darby Road and the Lancaster Road. Pretty soon, they'll be at our door and in our fields, looking for food, for clothes, and maybe even for shelter."

"If there's one thing that we have to do," he said, "that is to help our boys as much as we can. They're going to need information, and we can give it to them. You know how people talk when they've had a few too many drinks. We've got to have eyes and ears everywhere, without letting them know that we do. We're going to need everybody around here who  believes in our cause to step up, help General Wayne and General Washington and whatever other Generals find their way here."

"The one place where we know they'll be and where we know they'll be talking is the Tavern," he said. "I don't want to put our daughter in harm's way anymore than you do, Mother. But Betsey's right. She's not Connie, and she can take care of herself. She can work as hard in the field as any man when she has to, and since our boys joined up with General Wayne, she has to work a lot harder than I'd like her to, being a young lady and all."

Orland took one arm away from his wife and put it around Betsey. "I would never let anything happen to you, Betsey. And I also know that as stubborn and patriotic as you are, we couldn't keep you away from the Tavern if we tried to."

Betsey shook her head on that one.

"Just make sure that you keep a pistol near, a close eye, and keen hearing," Orland said. "We don't want any of our boys' blood shed in Paoli."

# CHAPTER 11
# SEPTEMBER 12
# GERMANTOWN

Connie sat in her kitchen, drinking coffee out of a silver mug. She had been awake all night. If the war was coming her way, whether it be British soldiers or patriots, someone at the house needed to be awake and in possession of their faculties if they showed up on her doorstep. Her livelihood depended on it. She had to protect her house, and she knew that she could talk her way out of anything, or into anything, depending on the circumstance.

All of her girls and their guests were asleep. Someone had to stay awake. And that someone was her. Ever since she arrived in Philadelphia a few years ago and got hoodwinked and double-crossed by her no-good, slickster, dandy, so-called fiancé from New York City, her preservation was left up to her. Although she let those instincts down for him, once he hurt her and left her out there on the street, those instincts came back with a force.

They served her well last night. The sound of cannons, the smell of gunpowder, and the ever-increasing traffic on the main road by the Wissahickon meant what she thought it meant—the war was coming to Germantown.

She nibbled on a few delicacies that one of her clients brought for the girls. Her thoughts drifted to her two younger brothers, Fred and Allen. Her whole family was full of rabid patriots. Fiercely independent, yet loyal, she had no doubt that her brothers were now in harm's way.

Anthony Wayne had always been a rebel-rouser, getting local boys to pretend that they were in battle the same as they played a game of stick ball. Her brothers eagerly joined in those pretend battles, helping the older boys build redoubts in the fields as they readied to face each other in battle. Her Dad regularly met with Wayne and his associates as they discussed and planned Chester County's response to the new nation's call for each county to take a stand in the fight for independence and draw up a militia to kick the British out of their newly formed country. The boys were too young to join when she left, being about four and six years younger than she was, but she was certain that they joined as soon as they were able. With last night's battle being down by the Brandywine Creek in Chester County, she was sure that two of Chester County's finest, her brothers, were there.

She had built quite a business with the patriots, those from the Philadelphia area and especially those who travelled here from all over the colonies for the Continental Congresses, like her benefactor. But she knew that they were going to high-tail it out of Philadelphia if the British invaded. They planned to take the Liberty Bell and all of their business with them. The local trade would fill in somewhat, but somewhat wasn't enough to keep her house going and give her enough money to pay the girls and put some away for the rainy days that she knew would come as she grew older and her body and beauty was bound to fade. Thousands of British soldiers thousands of miles away from home would be good for business—if they didn't destroy Germantown and Philadelphia first.

She continued sipping and nibbling until she heard the first stirrings upstairs. The girls were getting up now, and as soon as Prudence, her most responsible one, came down, she could go upstairs for a few hours nap, but only for a few hours. She knew it was going to be a long day, of lots of clients coming and going, and stories to gather as to just how far away the war was from her doorstep. Not that far away. That she knew.

## CHAPTER 12

# SEPTEMBER 12
# CHESTER

Fred heard the trumpets first. The sound was faint at first as he gathered his wits about him. But, as he slowly came to and sharpened his senses, he thought that the trumpets were especially loud. He jostled Allen to wake him.

Allen quickly opened his eyes and reached for his bayonet.

"Hold on, now," Fred said, holding Allen's arm back with one hand. "It's just me. Fred," he said. "It's time to get up."

Allen slapped his forehead with the palm of his hand. "Good Lord, man," he said. "You're 'bout to get yourself hurt."

Fred sat up straight now. "Not me, brother," he said. "Save it for the redcoats."

He pointed to where the sound of the trumpets was coming from. "By the sound of those horns, we're about to be on the march again."

Allen looked around. Hundreds of patriot soldiers were lying down and still asleep, or standing up and milling around, or somewhere in between. The dirty, ragtag collection of men was even a sight for him. Up ahead, he could see that some soldiers had already been called for breakfast and were lining up for what was being spooned out; others were still sitting, as their food was passed down the line.

The men around them were not from their regiment. Their uniforms were different. Allen knew that they all fought together down by the Brandywine, but beyond that, there didn't appear to be much order. As body after body woke up and either sat or stood straight, the trumpets changed their tunes. They started the melody to call the men to order.

Allen could see the commanding officers way up ahead, on the highest point in town, on their horses. Criers started calling out the officers' names and regiment numbers. What was called out up front was repeated back through the crowd so the soldiers could go and line up in their regiments.

"General Lord Stirling's troops", one shouted. "To the right of the Town Hall."

Hundreds of men got up and moved forward.

"General Wayne's troops," one said. "By the church near the Town Hall."

Fred and Allen stood up slowly, grabbed their rifles and sacks of whatever gear they managed to salvage during the battle, and headed towards their General. Hundreds of other boys did the same, friends of theirs since they were in short pants.

"We've got to be on the move with nothing to eat?" Fred said to Allen, asking a question that he already knew the answer to.

"Maybe our General has something for us," Allen said. "Surely he can't expect us to be on the march after that battle with nothing to eat?"

Fred looked at Allen and rolled his eyes. "Time's is different now, brother," he said, as they took the long slow march up the hill to where their neighbor general stood waiting.

As the boys moved closer to their general, the regiment came together. As one soldier recognized another familiar face, there were pats on the back all around.

Fred didn't want to think that some of his friends didn't survive last night. He preferred to think that they just hadn't seen each other yet when a name flashed across his head and he hadn't seen him yet.

When the Regiment came together, it was a smaller group than before. All of the soldiers whispered that to themselves as they moved into formation, straight lines, facing forward.

General Wayne sat ramrod straight on his large and magnificent white horse, in full clean uniform. Wayne believed that it was important that all soldiers be properly outfitted, especially their general. He believed that proper dress was part of proper discipline and was another psychologically important aspect of a well-disciplined army.

Fred could see that look on General Wayne's face as he counted each soldier who came forward. His head nodded ever so slightly, and Fred could see him mouthing words, better yet, numbers.

When the flow of men to their spot slowed to one or two every few minutes, General Wayne spoke.

"Men," he said, in a voice still hoarse from shouting orders the day before. "I thank God that you are here. Those Redcoats surprised us yesterday with their force and their skill. But thanks to the warning that my good friend Squire Cheyney of Thornbury Township gave to General Washington, we had time to scramble and reorganize ourselves to meet their numbers."

He waved his arms around. "You can look around and see that some of our numbers are smaller. You know that we had some deaths because some of you saw your friends shot down right before your eyes." He paused for a few seconds. "That always hurts. I pray that you use their deaths to strengthen your resolve, not to weaken it."

"Give the names of your known dead to our secretary," he continued. "We will honor them as soon as we can and notify their next of kin as well."

He waved his arms again and said with a scowl on his face, "But some of those who are missing today are not dead. Or wounded." He leaned closer to his soldiers. "They've deserted. They left their country and their compatriots at our hour of need."

He paused a minute to let those words sink in. "I spit on them," he said, as he strongly and violently spat on the ground. "But you," he said, as he waved his arms again. "You stayed. You fought. You fought valiantly, and with all the muster of the strong, strapping country boys that you are." He let that sink in, too.

"And, I'm grateful. And your Commanding Officer General Washington is grateful. And your country is grateful," he continued. "And we must carry on." He paused again. "We must."

The men clapped and cheered. As tired and hungry as they were, their love for country and their patriotism wore out. They were men after all, not cowards.

"Yes," said General Wayne. "Cheer yourselves on! Because we are going to need all of your strength and enthusiasm."

He leaned forward again, serious. "The British are after our great capital of Philadelphia. We believe that the British are on their way to attack our supply chains at the Valley Forge. We believe that their aim is to cut off the supply of goods into Philadelphia and cripple that city."

Wayne pursed his lips. "We all know that the most direct route to the Valley Forge and the Delaware Valley from the Brandywine Creek is straight up the Newtown Road and to the Darby Road, straight through Paoli and Tredyffrin."

Gasps and grumbles rose up from the crowd.

"Yes, that's right," said Wayne. "They're coming to our back yard. They're coming to our farms." He leaned closer. "They're coming to the women and children that we've all left behind."

"Not if I can help it," one of the soldiers yelled out.

"That's right," Wayne said. "Not if you can help it. And that's what we're going to do." He raised his rifle in the air as if in victory.

"We're headed home boys," he said, raising his voice, "to stop those Redcoats in our own backyards!"

Almost in unison, the soldiers under Wayne's command raised their rifles, too, and shouted their victory cry of "Huzzah!"

Wayne let them whoop and holler for a few minutes and get the excitement of going back home out of and in to their systems. But they had to get moving. And he knew it was better if they moved with some food in their stomachs rather than not.

He waved his hands up and down to settle them down. "Ok, Ok, boys," he said. "Let's quiet down." He gave them some time to do so.

"We've got to be on the march as soon as possible," he said, "but I know you haven't eaten since yesterday." He hated to remind them of their hunger, but he knew that they'd feel it again as soon as the excitement of this upcoming assignment faded. "The good people of Chester here have gotten us some food."

The men's faces grew more serious when they heard the word "food". The reality that they hadn't eaten in almost a day had struck them.

"Eat up quickly, men," he said. "Then we're on the march."

## CHAPTER 13
# SEPTEMBER 12
# REBEL HILL, GULPH MILLS

James dressed Jacob's wounds with the skill of someone who knew that his patient's life depended on it. Many slaves, former and current, had that skill. If a slave was injured and couldn't work, he might be left to die. Another slave would take his place. Slaveholders didn't care about exchanging one slave for another. They could always go out and buy another slave, which they often did, because the slaves made the plantations and farms that they worked on very profitable for their owners. No, a slave's life didn't mean much. James knew that. So the slaves had to learn how to take care of each other, dress the wounds, heal them and hide them as best as they could so that the slave could get back to work. House nigger or field nigger—it didn't much matter. They were niggers just the same.

After Jacob ate, James let him lie down while he tended to his horse. The horse was lying down, too. And no wonder. When James went over to take a look, he saw a sharp stone lodged in one shoe. And its other shoes were so thin that they were starting to dig into its hoofs. James coaxed the horse to stand up by holding some hay in his hand for him. Even while he stood up, the horse held that foot up in the air.

James added more fire to the outdoor oven, which he always kept on a slow burn and where he always kept a few sets of horseshoes warm for whoever might need them at whatever hour of the day. He'd work around the clock if he could to get enough money to free Ruth from the shackles of the Hannah plantation.

James patted the horse. "Good girl," he said, as he calmed her down with the strokes of his hand. "I'm going to get new shoes on you, and you'll be on your way back home."

He lifted one hoof and then another as he deftly took off the old shoes and put on the new ones. Every so often he'd hear loud noises coming up from the mill at the bottom of the hill, and he'd stop. As long as the voices weren't angry, he figured that he was alright.

"There you go, girl," James said, patting the horse. He took a chunk of sugar out of his pocket and gave it to the horse as a reward. "Just for you, honey," he said. He patted her again and said, "We'll be on our way soon."

James wiped his tools down as he did any time he used them, and then wiped his hands on his apron. He went back in his cabin where Jacob had fallen asleep again.

"I hate to wake you," said James to himself. "But I've got to get you out of here and on your way."

He walked over to the bed and gave Jacob a few good shakes. Jacob opened his eyes, slowed and dazed. Then he wiped his eyes, and a flash of recognition came over his face. He smiled at James.

"I fell off again, huh?" Jacob asked.

James smiled back. "I reckon you're going to be doing a heap of sleeping these next few days," he said. He stretched out his arm to Jacob and said, "Here. Let's get you up from here and in my wagon so I can get you home."

Jacob sat up straight and held on to James arm as he tried to stand up. He rose a few inches from the bed and then fell back down.

James said, "I have another idea. Here. I'll put my arm around you, and you lean on me. Looks like you can't put any weight on that leg where you got shot."

Jacob reached down to touch it. "Yes. You're right. And it hurts like hell, too."

"That'll pass," said James. "Part of that is those herbs I rubbed into your wound to kill the poison." He laughed. "If it's hurting, it's working."

Jacob smiled at him and said, "Well, it's working mighty good then."

James put his arm around Jacob and said, "When I count to three, you stand up, and then lean on me so you don't put any pressure on that leg. The wagon's right outside the door. You don't have to walk far."

Jacob shook his head. "OK."

"One, two, three," said James, as he lifted Jacob up, and Jacob pushed himself off the bed. Jacob leaned on James, hard, trying not to put too much weight on his bad leg. He had to put some weight on it though, and then his foot touched the ground.

"Ooww," he screamed.

"Hold on now, Jacob," said James. "You'll feel better soon. Your leg's not broken, though," James said.

"Yea, it's just the herbs working," said Jacob, as he winced.

"Working good, too," said James.

Jacob hobbled forward on one leg, leaning on James' arm, until Jacob fell into the wagon right outside the door,

"There you go," said James, as he picked up Jacob's legs and eased them and him into the wagon.

"I put new shoes on your horse," said James. "She should give you a great ride now."

James went over and unhitched Jacob's horse. He held tight to the reins as he jumped on to his horse, which was hitched to the wagon.

"If my wife has any money, I'll pay you as soon as we get home." Jacob said.

"I'd appreciate that mighty," said James.

"That's the least I can do," Jacob yelled, as James kicked his horse to take off.

That's the truth, thought James, as he headed down the hill, holding the reins of his horse and Jacob's, too.

# CHAPTER 14
# PAOLI

Betsey gathered up a few more flowers from the garden in the back. "They'll think I'm too delicate to fill my pretty head with war if they see me with these," she said out loud to no one because she was in the garden alone.

Teenie had finally given in. Betsey was allowed to work at the Tavern. Orland had convinced Teenie that Betsey's ears and eyes could be very helpful to the patriot's war effort. With the British teeming around Paoli with designs on the Valley Forge and the great city of Philadelphia, our boys are going to need all the information they can get, Orland had said to Teenie between Teenie's heaving cries.

Betsey knew that she was up to the task, even though the thought of serving all of those British redcoats filled her with rage. Her family had long since passed the point where they thought of themselves as sovereigns of the British crown. They thought of themselves as ants, held under the British thumb, forced to labor hard and give their fruits to someone/something else. They were simple, hardworking people, independent in their labor and in their thoughts. Their ancestors left England many years ago with a desire to practice their religion and to live a life where your future was not automatically determined by the social position of the family that you were born into. No one in her family wanted a fight, but they were never ones to run from one. None of them—the boys as well as the girls.

She wrapped the stems of the flowers in a piece of burlap, hoping to not disturb the blooms before she reached the Tavern. Once she got there, she would take the burlap off so that any redcoats would see her fawning over the flowers as if she really cared.

Orland was going with her this run. "Too many of them are around right now," he said a little while earlier. "I want to make sure that you and our produce get to the Tavern safely. Once you're there, Norman and Rochelle will look after you."

Betsey walked around to the side of the house where Orland was loading a barrel of potatoes.

"I'm ready, Dad," said Betsey, her voice a slight pitch higher because of the excitement of what lied ahead for her.

Teenie turned around and walked over to Betsey with her arms outstretched. She hugged her and stroked her hair. "You be careful now," she said, as she pulled back to take another look at her.

"You know I will, Mother," Betsey said. "You be careful, too. You'll be here alone."

Teenie laughed. "Not hardly," she said. She pointed to the front door. "I've got one rifle right there and two more inside." She patted Betsey on the back. "And you know I'm a good shot. Better than most men."

Betsey nodded. That was true, her mom had shot many a pheasant from yards away and then skinned it and roasted it perfectly.

Orland climbed on the wagon and said, "Come on, Betsey. Let's get down there."

Betsey hitched up her skirt and climbed up in the seat next to her Dad. She tipped her hat at Teenie and waved.

"Don't worry, Mom," she said. "I'll be fine."

You better be, Teenie thought to herself as she blew her a kiss and waved a goodbye. I don't want have to come down there, she thought.

ORLAND DROVE the wagon down the long dirt road from their farm house to another dirt road that connected with the Darby Road. As soon as they turned the corner off of their own property, they saw them. The white from their coats brilliant in the sunshine against the vivid red. About ten of them heading up the road towards the other end of Paoli.

Betsey audibly exclaimed at the sight of them. "Oh my God," she said, as she put a hand in front of her mouth. She immediately turned towards her Dad. "Sorry that I'm taking the Lord's name in vain, Dad. I'm just shocked to see them so soon."

"That's what I told you, dear," he said softly as he steadied the wagons and tipped his hat at the passing scum and then at his neighbors, who were deliberately walking and riding up and down the area roads more so than usual, to keep a close eye. Betsey was worried about her mother, but Orland knew that he had told some of his friends to deliberately walk by their farmhouse a few times a day, while he was gone, to keep an eye on her. He knew that the Redcoats were also looking for food, buying it from local farms if they had the money or the inclination, and taking it if they didn't. He had warned Teenie already and told her to just give them what they wanted if they came by. Betsey didn't need to know anything about that now, he reasoned. Not yet. And if they tried to take what was in his wagon, well, he hoped that between his rifle and the guns that his neighbors were carrying, they would think better of it.

Betsey tried not to show her father any of the fear that she felt now. Those Redcoats seemed so imposing, so jarring on these usually peaceful roads. She waved to everyone else on the road, and tried not to even look in their direction as they saw increasing numbers of British soldiers.

They turned on to the Darby Road, and even Orland had to exclaim, "God help us."

What looked to be regiment after regiment was marching down the road, lifting their legs in precision. Their muskets were on full display, and the steel bayonets on each of them glistened in the sun. Some of the regiments played their marching music.

Orland stopped the wagon so that a few of the Regiments could march by. His load was well covered up, but he didn't want to get in the middle of them and give them any ideas.

Betsey started to count as they passed by. There were four men in a row, and six rows in each group. Parts of the road looked like dust storms because so many people were passing by. She shuddered at the thought of what went on down there by the Brandywine Creek. If the British had been hurt, they sure didn't look like it. That didn't portend well for the Patriot Army, she thought. She said a silent prayer for her brothers and everybody else she knew who she was sure was down there fighting.

As the last group of regiments passed by, Orland said, "Giddy up now!", and jiggled the reins to get the horse going. The cloud of dust coming from further down the Darby Road meant that more British were coming. But, they were far enough away so that he could get to the Tavern without interruption.

He jiggled the reins to get the horse to go faster. "Hold on, honey," he said to Betsey.

"Looks like they're going to need all of this food down at the Tavern."

Betsey held on to the rail with her right hand as the horse took off down the road. She thought that she had seen a lot of redcoats on the Darby Road, but that was before the wagon turned left and onto the Lancaster Road. Betsey's hand flew up to her mouth to hide her fright.

"Oh, Daddy," she said, as she saw row after row of Redcoats marching on foot, riding on horseback, drawing wagons—each with a gun. She had never seen so many guns. Guns of all shapes and sizes. Long rifles held with two hands. Short pistols dangling from belt loops. Some soldiers' faces were fixed straight ahead with stern expressions. Others were talking and laughing with each other.

Some wagons were full of food, but so many of them were loaded with cannons and even more guns. Betsey had never seen a war cannon up close, so the site of so many of them literally made her shudder. She couldn't imagine having one of those shot into her, and she didn't want to image it being shot into anyone she knew, especially her brothers.

Thank God the tavern is right here at the intersection of the Darby and Lancaster Roads, she thought. She figured it would take them all day to get their wagon up the Lancaster Road with all of the British blocking it, yet alone all of the usual traffic.

Orland waited patiently as the troops passed by, trying to keep an unrevealing poker face. When he saw an opening, he took it, drove the few feet to the Tavern's back entrance, and turned the wagon in. He figured that the British wouldn't bother his load there because men who visited taverns for drink also liked to have food there so they didn't get so drunk so fast.

In any event, he waited until the meanest looking group of them marched by. That was a group with tall, drum-like hats with a band of black feathers at the top. Most of them coming up or down the Lancaster Road from either direction turned down the Darby Road towards the Valley Forge.   But many of them kept going straight up the Lancaster Road. Orland figured that they weren't going too far if their goal really was to take the Valley Forge. But he also knew that if Philadelphia was their goal, going east on the Lancaster Road would lead them straight to their capital city.

Orland looked over at Betsey. "You all right honey?" he asked.

Betsey lied and said, "I'm fine, Dad."

He patted her arm. "I know the sight of them is a shock," he said.

"It sure is, Daddy," she said. "To hear talk of them is one thing, but to see them, and so many of them, with your very own eyes is another thing."

"I know, honey," he said. "I know."

He hopped down from the wagon. "Let's get these things inside."

Betsey hopped down, and they started unloading.

Orland grabbed a bushel of vegetables. "You stay here, honey, until one of us comes back out for the rest of the things," he said. He walked over toward the back entrance. He called out, "Norman! We're here!" before pushing the door open and walking in.

Betsey waited by the wagon. Normally, she would have started carrying things in herself because none of their neighbors were going to bother the wagon and take anything that wasn't theirs. But now that the British were here, they had to protect what was theirs.

So she stood there and watched the parade of war go by the Lancaster Road.

Her thoughts weren't good ones. She was happy when they were interrupted.

"There she is," yelled Norman Roberts as he came over towards Betsey, arms outstretched. He was a big man with a big voice and a big personality. His black hair shone in the sun, and his sun-tanned complexion was the perfect accent.

Norman wrapped his arms around Betsey, who smiled at his big hug like she did her whole life. "Hi, Uncle," she said, as she wrapped her arms tight around him. How could mother ever think that this big, wonderful man would ever let anything happen to her while she was under his watch. She felt safe. If only for the moment.

"Nice to see you, little girl," Norman said with a voice as animated as he was. "Let's get these things inside," he said, then, in a whisper, "before those British realize what's going on here," he said, poking her in the side with his elbow, like they had a secret between them.

"Absolutely," Betsey said as she handed him some things to carry in.

Orland came back out, too, and he and Norman worked quickly to unload.

When everything was in, Orland said, "All righty, honey. Let's go on in."
He locked down the wagon with extra rope and an actual lock. A good
wagon was a valuable asset to an army, and he didn't want his going to the
British. He put a bell on part of the rope so that if someone tried to untie
it, the bell would ring. Hopefully, he could hear it and come out in time.
But as he looked at the stream of soldiers that continued to walk up and
down the two roads, he doubted it. But, it was worth a try.

BETSY HURRIED inside and saw her Aunt Rochelle wiping off tables in the
main room.

"Aunt Rochelle," she yelled.

Rochelle put her rag down and wiped her hand on her apron. "Betsey,
girl," she said, as she walked over, too, arms outstretched. Rochelle's dark
hair was piled high on her head in a bun. She was tall and big like her
husband. Betsey thought they made a perfect pair. Norman was loud,
and so was Rochelle. She had to be to be heard.

"So nice to see you," she said. "And we're so glad that you're going to be
working with us." She patted her on the back. "We need you, honey. Now
more than ever."

Betsey nodded. "I understand," she said. "I'm glad Mom let me help."

"Ah," said Rochelle. "I know your Mom. She's as much a patriot as any
of us. If she heard that our cause needed you, there was no way she was
going to say no, I said to Norman."

Rochelle looked straight at Betsey. "And, you know that nobody's going
to bother you here," she said. "They'd have to get through me and Norman
first, and that is never going to happen," she said. "You can bet on that
one."

"I know," said Betsey. "I feel safe here," she said, lying just a bit.

"Good," said Rochelle, "because, by the looks of what's been going on out there today, we're going to have a busy night. Or days. Or months." Then she shook her head. "Or years."

She finished wiping one more table and said, "Come on, honey. Come help me in the kitchen."

Betsey straightened up the chairs at the table where she was standing and followed her aunt into the kitchen.

# CHAPTER 15
# CHESTER

"Fall in," yelled General Wayne.

The men in his regiment hurried and gulped down what little food and drink they had.

A wagon driven by a black man pulled up next to the General. Wayne got down off his horse and shook the man's hand.

"Men," he yelled out. "I'd like you to meet Private Ned Hector."

Fred looked at Allen. Fred said, "Well that answers that. He must be a freed man."

"This man here," said Wayne, sweeping his arms in a grand gesture, "risked life and limb yesterday on the Brandywine Battlefield." He put his arm around Hector. "He retreated with our boys, yes, he did," said Wayne. "But then, he performed a most heroic act. He is a part of Proctor's 3$^{rd}$ Pennsylvania Artillery. His job is an ammunition wagon driver. When Captain Courtney ordered them to retreat, Private Hector retreated with the rest of his line. But, then he decided, no. He wasn't going to do it. He wasn't going to let those Redcoats get his wagon full of artillery. So what did he do, men?" Wayne asked rhetorically. "He snuck back. Those redcoats fired, but Private Hector didn't care. All along the way he picked up guns and ammunition from our fallen brothers. He reached his wagon, he got in it, and he drove it all the way back here to Chester."

The men broke out in spontaneous approval. "Huzzah. Huzzah."

"Thanks to Private Hector and to Captain Courtney, we can replenish the guns and the ammunition that we lost yesterday," said Wayne proudly, as he tipped his hat to Hector.

"Everyone who needs a rifle or a gun, line up. Come up and get one, thanks to Private Hector," he said. "And, when every last one of you is armed, we are on the march. Back home."

The men cheered again.

# CHAPTER 16
# REBEL HILL, GULPH MILLS

The farther away James traveled from his home on the hill, the more peaceful it became. The usual neighbors were stirring on the hill, doing their work on their farms, getting ready to bring in the harvest. That was until he got down closer to the road that led to the Swede's Ford, near where Jacob lived and near where James worked with his friend Daniel.

More horses and wagons than usual were on the road, and the faces of the riders and their passengers looked more drawn, more worried. The pace of the horses and carriages was faster, too. Everyone seemed to be in more of a hurry. James sped up a little bit. He didn't want to go so slow that he'd be run to the side of the road as others tried to pass him by, but he couldn't go too fast, either, because as best as he tended to him, he knew that Jacob's injuries were fragile, at best.

There were a few patriots in uniform on the road. That didn't worry James any because there always were a few boys going in and coming out. They didn't look any worse the wear to James, so he figured that they weren't in the battle down near the Brandywine Creek with Jacob.

But it seemed like everybody else heard what James figured was going to happen sooner or later—the war was headed on up here to their doorsteps.

Everybody already knew that the British wanted the patriot's capital city, Philadelphia. What better place to capture to show them a lesson and stop the uprising.

That was another reason that James liked it up on the Hill, away from all of the people and confusion in the city. That, and the fact that the air was clearer there. And he was closer to his beloved Ruth, down there still enslaved a few miles away.

When the Quakers took a stand against slavery, the Quaker owner of their plantation only freed about half of their slaves. They realized that they needed the others, and they didn't care whether they were going to be thrown out of Meeting for it, which they were. But, at least the owner allowed James to work to buy her freedom. Some days that made him happy; some days that made him sad. The amount of money that he had to earn seemed like a fortune to him, but, he knew the same as one day led to another that he'd keep working and saving his money until he could get her out of there. Seemed like hundreds of former slaves in Philadelphia did or were doing it. And they didn't mind telling other freed slaves how to go about it. They even had a little network of banks where people could put their money until they needed it. In any event, if the war came to James' doorstep, he hoped that it would pass on by and let him get back to work and free his woman.

James stopped by Daniel's Smithy Shop first. Jacob was fading in and out of sleep, despite James giving him some good strong coffee to keep him awake. Jacob was in no condition to give the directions to his home to James.

The Smithy Shop sat on the same side of the road as the river. It was big enough for the kiln and for two men to work comfortably and safely inside. There was plenty of room for the men to walk around the hot fires without getting burned. There was a long hitching post outside for the horses, and a nice sized bench further off to the side where four or five people could sit and wait for their horses and their shoes or for whatever else James and Daniel were working on for them.

Daniel was already there. Smoke was already coming up through the chimney, not at full fire power like it would be in about an hour, but enough to get a little plume going.

James drove the carriage right up to the front so Daniel could see it when he looked up.

Daniel did look up. When he saw the bloody leg of a man in uniform hanging over the side of the wagon, he put his tools down and rushed to the door.

"It's your friend, Jacob, he says," said James. "Got hurt in that battle by the Brandywine Creek yesterday. Figured he'd leave those boys and come home to his family. Dragged himself up to my cabin in the wee hours of the morning. Heard where I was. Knew I worked for you and could shoe his horse and get him home. 'Cept he's so in and out of sleep he can't tell me where home is, so I figured I bring him here first."

Daniel stepped up on to the wagon to see the face that was attached to the leg. He looked over and said, "My God. It is Jacob."

Jacob woke up at the loud sound of his friend. He squeezed Daniel's arm lightly and said, "Daniel. I made it." He smiled slightly.

Daniel patted his friend's arm and said, "Don't worry, Jacob. We'll get you home."

Daniel looked at James and said, "Let me put the safety cover over the fire right quick, and I'll ride over to Jacob's with you." Daniel hopped down, went into the shop, and came out about two minutes later.

"I wish I had someone to watch the shop today, what with all of this traffic out on this road. Let's hope that whoever might want to take something thinks that we're right nearby and will just keep on their way," Daniel said.

Then he looked back at the shop. Then he looked at James. "But nothing is more important than getting Jacob back with his family." He hopped up on the wagon and said, "Let's go."

THEY STARTED down the road outside the shop for a few hundred feet. "Turn right here, and then go straight down this dirt road," Daniel said as he gave James direction. "Turn right by the road by that walnut tree there. Their place is down at the end of the road, near the quarry."

James turned as he was told, thankful that Daniel was with him. He never would have found his way without Daniel.

They came upon a house not unlike just about every other house in that area. Part log cabin, part stone house, held together with plaster. Rough hewn. Surrounded by a lot of love. Flowers and bushes still in bloom. Children size wagons and tools out front. A doll forgotten here, a ball sitting over there.

As they pulled up, the children ran out first. Two girls and a boy. Not one of them looked to be more than 10 years old. Fast on their heels was the mother. Jacob's wife. Ample figure covered with a working apron with pockets bulging with tools and rags. They were all probably out back, right behind the door, working.

They ran closer to the wagon. Daniel called out, "Amy. It's me Daniel Welburn." He jumped down to meet her and the children.

"Stay behind me, children," Amy called out as they all got closer to Daniel.

Daniel practically ran into Amy. He held her arms to steady her and kept her away from the wagon for a minute as she frantically looked over his shoulder at the wagon. That bloody leg in uniform was dangling over the side again.

"We've got Jacob in the wagon," he said.

Amy gasped.

The children screamed happily, "Daddy!" They couldn't see his leg.

"He showed up at my worker, James', cabin last night," Daniel said, nodding his head in James' direction. "He was in a battle down near the Brandywine Creek. Got hurt. Told James that he'd rather be here with you and the children."

Amy screamed again as Daniel held her arms. He wasn't going to let her go until she calmed down. He shook her slightly and said in a conspiratorial voice, just between the two of them, "Let's have the kids stay here while you come over and take a closer look. James patched him up, but he's still hurt bad."

Amy looked Daniel straight in the eye. She said softly, "Yes."

Daniel slowly let Amy's arms go.

Amy turned around to her children. "You children go on inside the house. That's your Dad there, but he's hurt. We've got to move him into the house. You all be good and go in there and sit down so we can get him on to a bed with no trouble." She touched her oldest child on the head. "Jennie, you go around to the well and get some water for boiling. We're going to need that to clean him up."

The children looked at their mother with that inquisitive look that they get when they want to ask questions. But they didn't ask any questions. They waited a moment, took in the seriousness of the scene that was playing out in front of them, turned around and got busy.

Amy looked at Daniel and said, "Let's go."

She hurried over to the wagon. James had jumped down and tied the wagon securely to a post. Amy ran right over to Jacob.

"Darling," she said, as she leaned down and kissed him.

Jacob smiled and grabbed her hand.

Amy tried to stifle her tears, but she couldn't. He looked that bad. Blood was starting to bleed through the bandages.

"While all those bullets and cannon balls were flying by, all I could think of was that I wanted to be with you and the children," Jacob said. "I'm a patriot, but there has to be some other way that I can do my duty," he added, his own tears now starting to fall. "I couldn't see you being a widow and our babies being orphans," he said. "No way."

Amy kissed him again. "That's all right, dear," she said. "I'm proud of you for going. I'm proud of you no matter what you do." She patted his head. "Don't worry. We're going to get you inside and take good care of you." She motioned to Daniel and James to start carrying him on the blanket they had found.

"And you can do your fighting for General Washington and the rest of them right here at home," she said. She caressed his brow with his hand. "You're not the first to leave that god-awful militia, and you won't be the last," she said.

Daniel and James carefully placed Jacob on a blanket and carried him into their house. They laid the blanket on the bed that Jacob and Amy shared. They got him settled down.

Daniel walked outside to the kitchen dependency where Amy was boiling a large pot of water.

"Is there anything we can do for you right now, Amy?" Daniel asked. "Do you need us to bring you anything?"

Amy shook her head. "No. I've got everything I need to heal wounds, broken bones, anything, right here, what with these children running around and us being down here at the end of this road."

Daniel nodded, figuring that Amy would have to have everything that she needed, just as she said, because she had to be independent with no one else around.

"Well, you let us know if you need anything," Daniel said. "Send one of the kids."

He scratched his head. "But if we don't hear from them while there's still daylight, I'll come around and check on you anyway tonight."

Amy nodded her head and said, "Yes."

Daniel looked at her softly. "I don't blame him for leaving that mess and coming back to you and the kids," he said. "That's why I couldn't bring myself to sign up. I didn't want to leave my mom and our sister. I never could figure out how they were going to make it without me." Then he pointed to James. "And he needs his work to buy his girl's freedom from the Hannah Plantation down there in Merion."

He scraped his feet on the ground and looked down. "No, following General Washington all over the colonies isn't for me, and it's not for James. I'm hoping we can get out of this mess some other way."

Amy nodded her head. "Truer words have never been spoken." She dunked some rags in the boiling water. "All I can say is God help us."

"Me, too, Amy," Daniel said. "Me, too."

# CHAPTER 17
# PAOLI

Betsey was in the tavern kitchen with Rochelle peeling vegetables for stew when they both dropped their paring knives and looked towards the main room. There was a commotion of chairs moving, heavy footsteps on the wood floor, and items being thrown on tables.

Rochelle wiped her hands on her apron, looked wide-eyed at Betsey and said, "Wait here."

Rochelle rushed to the swinging wooden door that separated the kitchen from the main room, and pushed it open. Hard.

Betsey followed right behind her.

Rochelle stood frozen, just where her body had cleared the door.

Betsey looked, and she stood frozen, too.

The room was a sea of red. One after the other, British soldiers streamed in, pushing chairs and each other aside, throwing their weapons on the table, taking over.

Betsey quickly looked around the room for her uncle. All she could see were red coats by the bar, but she knew that her Uncle Norman must have been there behind the bar. He had been outside, watching the street, guarding the door, just waiting for the British to come inside, as he knew they would.

"Didn't you hear me gal?" asked one of the redcoats. "I'll have a pint," he said, looking at Betsey with narrow, evil eyes. "Or don't you serve British soldiers in here?" he asked sarcastically.

His harsh remarks jolted Betsey out of her state of frozen shock. "No, no sir," she said, wiping her hands, wet now with worried sweat, on her apron. "We serve everyone, as you can see," she said, pointing towards the bar where the soldiers were standing two and three deep, calling out for the same.

"That's good to know," said the soldier. "We wouldn't want to have to come in and serve ourselves in here." He laughed coldly. "No, you wouldn't want that." He laughed again, and so did the other soldiers at his table.

Betsey forced a smile, and said, "No, sir. We're here to serve, sir." She forced a pleasant smile again. "So, it's a pint you'll be having?" she asked.

"That's what I said," he said, and swept his arms around the table. "And bring one for my friends, here, too."

Betsey wiped her brow, hoping that none of them could see the nervous sweat that she felt starting to pour down her forehead.

"I'll get right on it," she said, as she turned and walked towards the bar.

She didn't want to push the redcoats out of the way to get through, but she wanted to get to Uncle Norman as fast as she could. The sight of red and white uniforms, guns and bayonets, and evil all around her was almost too much to bear.

"Pardon me, kind sirs," she forced herself to say as she gently moved towards the bar. A few soldiers turned quickly around as they felt her pushing behind them. A few looked at her smiling, leering, and jeering.

"Ah, a comely bar wench," one said. "Let her through, let her through," said another.

"Maybe we'll get our drinks faster," added another.

Betsey slid through as best as she could and tried to catch Norman's eye.

He looked up when he heard her voice, following her movements through the bar crowd.

Norman called out, "Yes, kindly let her through, gents. The faster she gets here, the faster you'll get your drinks." He caught Betsey's eye and smiled, hoping that it would calm her and set the tone for what he could only imagine was a frightening experience for her. "We aim to please."

Betsey made it through the crowd at last. Now that she could see, she saw Aunt Rochelle down at one end of the bar, feverishly filling pints and taking money, while Norman did the same at her end.

When Rochelle saw Betsey, she called out loudly, "Pardon me, gents, while I run down here and see what the girl wants. Don't want those gents over there," she said, pointing to the tables, "bringing down the wrath of God on the poor child if she doesn't get their orders right."

They didn't want to hear that. The soldiers at her end started yelling, "Hey, what about us," but Rochelle had moved down to the end of the bar before they could practically finish their sentences. There was no way that she was not going to go speak to and comfort her niece.

Norman saw what was going on and yelled over the commotion, "Don't worry gents. We'll take care of you. Now what can I get you?" as he slid down to the end of the bar where Teenie was just a few seconds ago.

Rochelle moved close to Betsey. She grabbed her arm and turned her face away from the bar, towards the big wooden barrels of beer behind them. She whispered in Betsey's ear, "Steady girl. You know we won't let anything happen to you."

"I know," said Betsey, as she looked straight into Rochelle's eyes, looking for strength that she knew was there.

Rochelle gently rubbed Betsey's back, hoping to transfer some of her strength to Betsey. She gently squeezed Betsey's arm and said, "Now what do they want over there?"

Betsey said, "Six pints. One for everyone at the table."

Rochelle said, "Let me help you with them," as she rubbed Betsey's back again.

Rochelle filled some mugs, and Betsey started filling some, too. When the six pints were on the tray, Rochelle squeezed Betsey's hand again, before she picked up the tray, and said, "Steady, girl."

Betsey looked at her aunt again, smiled bravely and said, "Yes, steady." Then she hoisted the tray up, called out, "Coming through, gents", and moved through the crowd.

BETSEY, NORMAN and Rochelle served pint after pint for hours. The redcoats got louder and more rowdy. They all tried to humor them so no trouble broke out and so the redcoats didn't break anything in the tavern.

Just as the sun started setting, the soldiers, almost in unison, put down their pints and picked up their guns and their bayonets. Betsey heard a few of them saying that it was going to be a hard march back to camp that night given how much ale they drank. They also said that they hoped that the men who had to stay back at camp didn't have anything to drink because they heard that the rebels were headed back here.

That's when Betsey's ears perked up. I hope they get here soon, she thought to herself, and that this is the last night that we have to serve those redcoats.

Norman stood by the door as the soldiers left, saying, "Come again, gents. Hope you had a pleasant time here."

Rochelle and Betsey stood behind the bar, holding hands under the bar, far from the soldiers' evil eyes, watching every soldier pass by Norman, praying that none of them touched him or otherwise did or said anything derogatory to hurt him and start some trouble.

When the last soldier walked out of the door, Norman stood facing them outside, waved and said, "Godspeed. Come again," in a cheery voice.

He watched them ride away, then turned, pushed the door shut, and slid the iron bar against it. He collapsed into a chair by the front door. He had been on his feet, serving and pretending for three hours straight. The weight of his safety and that of Rochelle and Betsey was on his shoulders. The realization that the war had come to Paoli was on his shoulders, too.

Rochelle and Betsey ran over to Norman and they both wrapped their arms around him before they, too, collapsed in two chairs next to him.

Tears started running down Rochelle's and Betsey's eyes. So much so that they couldn't see the ones that were starting to form in Norman's eyes, too.

# CHAPTER 18
# SEPTEMBER
# LOWER MERION TOWNSHIP

The road from Chester to Philadelphia became more crowded as the 5th Pennsylvania Regiment marched through. The first marker they came to read "18M to P." Every few miles they'd reach another marker that marked the distance to Philadelphia. Large expanses of farmland gave way to villages that were more compact and populated until they reached a sign that said, "Welcome to Philadelphia, Pennsylvania."

The Roberts boys didn't like Philadelphia. Its crowded streets, fast pace, and slick men had lured their sister, Connie, away from the quiet and wholesome life that their parents had planned for her in Paoli. They never understood the lure of the smooth-talking city men and the fast life. They didn't understand how Connie could choose that over her family.

Just about the only times they went to Philadelphia was when they went with their father and Uncle Norman a few years ago to help them look for Connie. They were too young then to understand all of the reasons that she ran away or their parents' fears about what she was doing to get along and who she was with. They looked on their trips as adventures, visits to the big city. They were to look around and take it all in, but to keep a watchful eye to see if they spotted Connie anywhere.

Those were the days when their parents believed that there was something that they could do to get Connie to come back home, even if they could find her. From what their parents heard now from whispers around town or word that got back to them from an occasional search party, there was nothing that they could do to pry Connie away from her life in Philadelphia, as sordid as it was to them. Connie had settled into a different way of life and was quite successful at it, they heard.

The boys had hoped that the regiment would stay in Philadelphia long enough for Connie to hear that General Wayne and his Paoli boys were there. Maybe she'd come around to look for them. Maybe she missed her little brothers. At least they hoped so.

But that was not to be.

Word filtered back through the line from the General that they were only going to march through the west of the city of Philadelphia, only until they could get to the Lancaster Road. Then they were going to head up the Lancaster Road towards the Valley Forge to keep the British from getting their hands on that valuable resource, including an iron forge.

To a man, when each one heard that, cheers of happiness rolled through the ranks like a wave. Valley Forge was only a few miles down the road from Paoli. They were almost home.

AS THE regiment marched into Philadelphia, they were greeted mostly with cheers, even though they heard that the city was full of Tories who wanted to keep the British government there because the Tories made a good living under British rule. The non-military patriots cheered, happy to see the soldiers, hoping that they would protect them from the British who they knew were nearby. The Tories didn't dare jeer the soldiers; that was treason against the new United States and punishable by death. No, the Tories kept their sentiments to themselves as they watched, with frowns on their faces, the soldiers passing through.

# CHAPTER 19

# HAVERFORD

The dust on the Lancaster Road kicked up and covered everything. The road was packed from side to side as patriots walked or rode, west towards the Valley Forge. Thousands of patriots joined the regular locals who were also jamming the road, pulling carts stuffed with furniture, tools, and God knows what else as they tried to go about their day, suddenly made much different because of the thousands of soldiers who had descended on them.

"Are you alright there?" Fred asked Allen as they marched on.

Allen coughed a few more times, and finally whispered, "Yes."

Fred didn't believe him. Allen always tried to cover up his trouble breathing for as long as he could. He'd been that way ever since they were children. The doctor had taught everyone in the family how to help Allen if he got to the point where he really couldn't breathe. They all knew to sit him down somewhere quiet, put some menthol drops in the small pot of water that their mother always kept simmering on the fire for just such a purpose, set the pot on a table before Allen, throw a cloth around his head to make a tent so he could breathe in the vapors. The doctor said that would loosen up his windpipes. After about ten minutes, Allen usually felt much better.

But Fred couldn't do that now. He knew that the dust was Allen's enemy.

But, he looked up into the sky and said to Allen, "Stay strong, brother. It looks like it's going to rain." He patted Allen on the back. "I think all of this dust is soon going to turn to mud, and even though it's not the hot mentholated water, maybe the rain and the moisture will help you."

Allen looked up. He saw the clouds, but he also said a prayer. "I hope so," he said, as he coughed to breathe

They marched about a quarter of a mile until they felt the rain hitting them, like little spittles. Then, the drops got bigger. And the soldiers became noisier as they groaned about having to march in the rain—again.

Allen just turned his head back and opened his mouth. He let the cool drops slide down his throat. They all did. They weren't just hungry, they were also thirsty.

Allen needed the water to breathe; the others needed the water to live.

ON AND on the march went. Through the town of Merion, past the Friends Meeting houses, passing one tavern after another, until they came to one called the Buck Tavern. General Wayne ordered the men to stop and camp for the night.

The whole area around the Tavern was surrounded with soldiers. The word passed through the camp that General Washington was already in the Tavern and that he wanted to meet with all of his generals. After they were forced to leave Brandywine and move through Philadelphia, it didn't take a genius to know that Philadelphia was left unprotected from the British. It was critical that the patriots had a plan. That plan was going to be worked out that night at the Buck Tavern.

The sound of a trumpet blowing the wakeup call floated through the air. Allen began to stir. Even though he was sleeping on the wet ground, he had no trouble sleeping. The battle by the Brandywine Creek and the march through Chester, Philadelphia, and up towards the Lancaster Road had worn him out to the point where he could have slept anywhere. As he wiped the sleep out of his eyes and looked around, he knew that his fellow patriots felt the same way. As loud as the morning trumpet was, only a few stirred. The rest slept the good sleep of the exhausted.

As much as he wanted to let them sleep, he knew that they had better wake up. They could be called to be on the march at any time. General Wayne was like that. "Ever ready," he always said.

Allen nudged Fred. Fred opened his eyes and looked around wildly. Anytime you woke a sleeping soldier you had to be prepared for any reaction. The first, and most dangerous one, was that he wanted to fight you. Ever ready for the enemy. Wayne's words had sunk into the entire 5th Pennsylvania Regiment.

"Wake up everyone," Allen yelled. Allen could nudge his brother awake. He knew how to control him and settle him down from way back, from birth. Not so much with those other fellows. One time a man was nudged out of his sleep, got startled, immediately grabbed his bayonet, and pierced the arm of his friend before he could get out the word, "Stop." The deep sleep that was worn out sleep was also good sleep for dreaming. A soldier could dream about his last battle, about bayoneting or shooting a redcoat and take it out on his poor unfortunate friend who only wanted to help him wake up.

The trumpet sounded again. "Wake up, I say," Allen yelled again. This time, more and more of his fellow soldiers woke up and then the soldier next to them. Some of the soldiers shook their heads to get cobwebs out of a mind with too little sleep and not enough food. Some hung their hands in their heads, realizing the state that they were in with little food and little clothing, away from the comforts of home, wondering why they were there and when it was going to end. Some jumped right up, shaking their arms and legs, hurrying to get themselves fully awake. Always ready. Others opened their eyes and then got down on their knees to pray.

Another day and they were still alive. In a war, that's a whole lot to be thankful for.

Allen took a swig of water out of his canteen. He handed it to Fred, who took another.

"I wonder if we're going to get any food this morning," Allen said.

Fred pursed his lips and shook his head. "I sure hope so," as he looked around.

"Maybe there was some food in that tavern when the generals took over," he said.

Allen laughed. "Yeah, let's hope so." He slid his hand from the top of his head, through his hair, and stroked his chin. "And let's hope that the generals didn't decide to eat it all themselves."

Fred laughed. "Some of them, maybe," he said, "but you know General Wayne would take care of us."

Allen nodded his head. "Yeah, I do know that."

General Wayne had a special affinity for the 5th Pennsylvania. Those were his neighbors, his neighbors' children, his people. He tried to make sure that they had what they needed, even if he had to take the money out of his own pocket to do so. He didn't always have anything to give them, because many a night and day the 5th Pennsylvania went hungry and was cold, like just about every other regiment, but it wasn't for lack of trying.

Fred and Allen sat there, waiting. Waiting until someone let them know what the day ahead of them was going to look like—whether they were going to have anything to eat, whether they were going to get back to being on the move, whether they had to stay put for some reason, or whether they we going to have to fight. Allen thought that at least if they had to fight today, they could eat breakfast.

Only a few moments later, they heard Major James Taylor call out. "There's food today, boys." Weak cries of "Yeah," rang out, because there wasn't much food yesterday. They ate a good breakfast while they were surrounded by the farms in the City of Chester, but there was no food as they marched through Philadelphia and on up the Lancaster Road. Other regiments had gone before them, and the places where they might normally find food, like the many taverns lining the Lancaster Road, or the houses nearby, had already been picked clean.

"It's not a banquet," yelled the Major, "but it's hardy." Behind him, the food detail was dragging in large metal kettles that were precariously perched on flat wagons. He pointed to the kettles behind him. "Line up and step up."

Fred and Allen stood up and unhinged the metal bowl that was attached to their sashes. They stood silently in line, looking over at those who had already gotten their bowls filled, hoping to get a glimpse of just what this hearty breakfast was.

"Maybe there's some meat in it," Allen said.

"Now that would be wonderful," said Fred.

As they moved closer to the front, they smiled. The porridge, the gruel, the oatmeal that they usually had was often lumpy, but not as lumpy as it appeared to be today. Those lumps had to be meat.

The smiles on the faces of the men ahead of them confirmed that.

Allen put his bowl out there. "Tell me there's meat in there," he said to the man who was pouring it into the bowls.

The man smiled, knowing how desperate they all were. "That there is," he said. "That there is."

He added, "Can't tell you exactly what kind."

Allen smiled and said, "Can't tell you that I rightly care!"

They both laughed as smiles started forming on the faces of all of the men around them.

SOME MEN gobbled the food down so fast that they were now laying back, rubbing their stomachs. Others savored every spoonful, trying to make it last. Allen and Fred were somewhere in between.

"Down here at the Buck Tavern, we're not that far from home," Fred said.

"Maybe 10 miles?" said Allen.

"That sounds about right," said Fred.

They smiled again, the type of half smile that some might call a smirk, but this was a smile of sincerity, not one of sarcasm.

"Maybe we'll get to Paoli today," Allen said.

Fred shook his head. "God, I hope so. Just to see Mom and Dad and Betsey and everybody. Just to see how they are. And God knows I hope they kept some food hidden for us, and for them."

"I pray that those redcoats have not literally robbed us out of house and home," said Allen. "For their sakes. If they hurt anyone that I love, they better watch out. Orders or no orders, I'm coming for them," he said, making the motion of a bayonet being thrust into its target.

"Just the thought of seeing them again, of being on familiar ground," said Fred. "Whatever we have to do to drive the British out from our Great Valley, I hope we sure get to it."

"Me, too," said Allen. "Me, too."

JUST THEN, the bugle sounded again. Three times, the same blow. That meant that General Wayne was coming to address the troops. They would soon be on the move, they hoped.

Whether they had finished eating or were still gulping down their food, all eyes turned in the direction of the bugle player. A few seconds later, General Wayne rode up on his horse.

He took off his hat in salute to his men and then placed it back on his head. "Men," he yelled. "Today is a momentous day for us." He paused. "When I give the order, we will march up the Lancaster Road, home. Home to Paoli. Home to defend the Valley Forge. Home to our wives and

children and parents and friends and neighbors. Home to the land that
we are fighting for."

The Regiment was silent, hanging on his every word.

"Now, men. The home that you get to may not be the home that you
left." He paused again. "Our advance scouts have said that the area has
not suffered as much from the horrid redcoat foraging that has hurt so
many of the homes and taverns and shops that we have passed by since we
left Chester." Wayne hung his head. "But there has been some suffering.
Some British advance parties have hit our treasured ground, taking from
our people here and there." He looked at his men and clenched his fist.

"Men. If you find that your home has been affected, God help those
redcoats. I know you will want to run out, find them and take revenge," he
said. He swept his arms around the crowd before he said, "But, you can't.
You must wait. You can't do it alone. We must do it together. And we
must do it on General Washington's orders only."

"Please," Wayne said, almost praying. "As hard as I know it will be for
you, you have to contain yourself. You still have to have discipline." He
shook his fingers at them. "Know that we will get them. Know that we
will take revenge. But we must do it together," he said.

"Our scouts tell us that the redcoats have been in our fine hamlet,
overtaking our roads, pushing their way into our taverns and shops,
taking what they want," said Wayne.

Cries wafted up from the crowd. "No." "Bastards."

Wayne held up his hand to quiet them.

"Wait, wait," he said. "But our scouts have told us that they have
retreated now. That they have taken crops, grain, meat, cows, tools and
just about anything else they could get their limey hands on, and taken it
with them back to the Valley Forge, where they lie encamped now."

"Let's go get them," yelled someone.

Wayne held up his hand again to silence them. "We will. We will," he said. "We will attack them and send them back across the sea to where they came from.

Shouts of "Yeah" rang out.

"Men," Wayne yelled. "We will be marching up this Lancaster Road to encamp on our home ground, to protect our friends and neighbors and families. To recapture the Valley Forge, our treasured forge, so important to our effort."

More shouts of "Yeah."

Wayne held his hands up again to silence them. "Men," he said. "When we get to our home, I know you will want to break camp and see your families. I want to see my family, too," he said. "There will be time for that. We will send out a scout, a soldier, an advance, to ride from home to home and let our people know that we are back and where we are," he said. "Your families will come to you," Wayne said. "You cannot go to them."

There was some grumbling.

He held up his hands again, shaking his head, and said, "You are soldiers! Disciplined! Men of order! We must stay together. We will have a camp site, and we must not, we cannot break camp. Even though we return as their defenders, we still must stay together," he said. "That is how we will stay safe." He looked out over the troops. "That is how we will do what we must do."

He waved his arms like he was scooping up something. "Together. And safe. United. And protected." He pointed to his head. "Smart and cunning."

Then he held his musket up in the air and yelled, "Ever ready."

"Yeah," yelled the men as the hoisted their weapons in to the air. "Ever ready!"

Wayne took a few moments to take it all in, to look out over his troops, now on their feet and energized, just like he wanted them to be for the task ahead.

"Now, men," he said. "Fall in! Let us march! Let us go home."

A great yell rose out of the crowd almost in unison.

Fred and Allen looked at each other.

"Yeah, brother," Allen said, as he patted Fred on the back. "We're going home."

# CHAPTER 20
## PAOLI

Orland opened the front door and yelled in, "They're gone." Betsey and Teenie looked up. "The British are gone," he said, running over to his girls and hugging them both, as they laid on the pallet near the fire, keeping each other warm and as safe as they could, knowing that the enemy was no more than a quarter of a mile away.

"After they left the Tavern, they marched all the way down the road near Howellville and put up a line around the Valley Forge," he said.

"But that's not that far away," said Mom.

"I know," said Dad, "but they're not here. They're not in Paoli."

"And," he said, smiling from ear to ear, "our network says that our boys are on their way back here, General Wayne, and all of them."

Teenie shot straight up now. She looked at Orland with shock.

"Yes, dear," he said. "That means Fred and Allen, too. They're coming home!"

"Yeah," yelled Betsey.

"Praise God," said Teenie, as tears welled up in her eyes.

"When are they going to get here?" asked Betsey. "Where are they now?"

Orland sat down in the chair. "From what we hear, they spent the night about ten miles away from here down near the Buck Lodge on the Lancaster Road in Haverford," he said. "They were to march out this morning as soon as they ate."

He smiled broadly. "The boys should be here before supper time, I figure."

"Oh my God," said Teenie, as she put her hand to her mouth. "I can't believe it. God has answered my prayers," she said. "He's bringing my boys home safe and sound."

Betsey was dancing around the room.

Orland said, "They're coming home, honey, but they're still in the army." He cautioned them, "We'll get to see them, by all accounts, but they're still in service."

"That's good enough for me," said Teenie. "As long as I can look on their faces, bring them some food, touch their hair," she said, her voice drifting off softly.

"Well, let's hope that's the case," said Orland. "Anything can happen between there and here."

GENERAL WAYNE'S regiment was allowed to lead the march up the Lancaster Road to Paoli. General Washington knew the boys would be anxious to get home, and General Wayne told him that you couldn't hold them back in the line. If they were further back, they'd be marching so fast that they'd move the other soldiers out of the way anyway, so they might as well be assigned a spot in the front.

Fueled by a breakfast with meat and a desire to get home, the 5th Pennsylvania proudly led the way. General Wayne, on his white horse, led his men up the Lancaster Road. The General rode straight and tall, proud to be back among his people. Proud to show them that although they might not have won the battle down by the Brandywine Creek, which he was sure they all knew about, they were still fine, fit and ready for battle.

The 5th Pennsylvania marched past familiar sites—the taverns, the shops, the churches. Men, women and children ran out all along the way to greet them and thrust into their hands an apple here, a crust of bread here, some dried meat there, all along the way.

A beautiful young woman with long curly black hair and long black eyelashes rushed to Allen and held out a ladle full of water for him.

He looked at her, smiled, and said, "Thank you very much, miss," as he gulped it down and kept marching.

An older gentleman with a straw hat and worn overalls gave Fred a crust of bread with some cheese in it. Even though Fred had just eaten more breakfast than he'd had in a long time, it still wasn't as much as he usually had back home on the farm, so he took that bread and cheese and ate it hungrily.

They were in friendly territory now, as they passed by the Radnor Meeting House and the paper mills in Devon. Cheers rose up as they marched into Tredyffrin Township and Easttown Township, near Howellville.

They practically ran the distance from Berwyn, up the road towards Paoli. It was only a few miles. When Wayne's Paoli boys saw the Paoli Tavern down the road, the cheers continued, loud, as they continued running. House and shop doors flew open as their neighbors realized what was going on. Hundreds of people started to line the roads, people who they knew. People who were looking to find their sons, their husbands, their fathers. Every so often, one of the people on the sidelines would point, call out a name, and run over. They'd hug and kiss as the rest of the line passed by.

"There it is," Fred said to Allen.

"I can't wait to see them," Allen said back, smiling from ear to ear.

Just as they finished talking, they saw them. Betsey, Teenie, Orland, Norman, and Rochelle—all of them. Standing at the edge of the road, holding their hands over their eyes to help them see, Betsey jumping up and down.

Allen yelled out, "Mom! Dad!" but everyone else was yelling Mom and Dad, too. The road was lined with Moms and Dads.

Fred yelled, "Betsey! Uncle Norman! Aunt Rochelle!" and it worked. They turned around almost in unison.

Fred thrust his gun up in the air so they could see him more clearly. "Over here, Betsey," he yelled. "Over here, Uncle Norman."

As soon as Betsey heard her big brother, she bolted away from the family and ran down the road. The rest of the family followed suit.

Betsey got to the boys first. She pushed a few soldiers aside running to her brothers, but the soldiers didn't care. They knew her, and they were happy to be pushed as their families were running over, too.

When the Regiment, led by Wayne on his horse, reached the intersection of the Lancaster Road and the Darby Road, Wayne held up his gun and called out to his men, "At ease, men. At ease. 5th Pennsylvania Regiment, take ten minutes to greet your families. Then we will resume our march."

The men broke and ran to the sides of the road with their families. The other regiments marched on as the local boys stopped for ten minutes to lift their spirits.

"Mom," yelled Allen, as he grabbed Teenie, picked her up off the ground, and spun her around.

Betsey had already grabbed Fred and was hugging him tightly as Orland rushed over and said, "Son," holding him just as tightly.

Tears ran down both boys' eyes as their aunt and uncle came over and joined in. Norman and Rochelle had brought over a bag of food for their boys and for all of the boys.

"Here," said Rochelle. "We don't want you to starve."

Allen said, "Thank you Aunt Rochelle," as tears came to his eyes. "You don't know how hard it's been."

Rochelle rubbed his arms and said, "Yes I do, son. Yes I do."

When they heard the boys were coming, Norman and Rochelle sent word to everyone they knew to come to the Tavern and help them fill the barrels with drink for the men and to pull out whatever food they had left. Those redcoats ate and drank so much that night before that there wasn't much food left in the Tavern, but Norman and Rochelle always kept a hidden stash. When the Redcoats left and they heard that their boys were on their way, they pulled the stash up out of the hidden room in the basement. They didn't let the neighbors know exactly where the hidden room was; it was enough for them to know that they had it.

So, the grounds around the Tavern were full of barrels of ale, crackers, bread, cheese, smoked and pickled meats. As the families told their boys about the food, the grounds around the Tavern looked like the grounds of the old church picnic—there were that many people sitting around eating.

The regiments from around the colonies marched past, looking over. Everyone knew they wished they could break ranks and get some food, but they knew that they dare not. This was the local boys' homecoming. They either would have their own or had their own; they knew how it went. And, they hoped and knew that the local boys would bring them some food and drink if there was any left. They would have to feed on the cheers they got as they marched by, which, as a matter of fact, they did. It was always good to be in friendly territory.

"HOW IS it boys?" Orland said to his sons as he drank them in fully with his eyes. "You were down in the battle by the Brandywine Creek?"

Allen shook his head, "Yes, we were," he said. "I'm not afraid to tell you that I was scared," he said, with a whisper, so no one outside of his circle would hear him.

"It was hell, Dad," said Fred. "Seeing your friends getting shot. People getting killed. We were lucky that we got out of there with our lives," he added. "When General Wayne gave the order to retreat, I can't tell you how fast I ran!"

"I pray for you all the time," said Teenie.

Allen hugged his mother again. "Keep those prayers coming, Mom," he said. "They didn't send us back here for nothing. We hear that the British are over at the Valley Forge, and that's a pretty valuable property, what with the iron making and all."

"Yeah," said Fred. "I'm sure we were sent up here to drive them out and take it back." He looked at his Mom and gave her a weak smile. "And doing that is going to take a lot more than praying, as powerful as your prayers are Mom."

Teenie took his hand. "I know, son. I'll just have to double up for a while."

Fred hugged her and said, "Thanks, Mom."

THEY ATE and drank and talked as much as they could in those ten minutes.

General Wayne rode out into the middle of the Lancaster Road and held his gun up in the air, again.

"Fifth Pennsylvania Regiment," he yelled. "Fall in!"

Wives kissed their husbands, children kissed their fathers, parents kissed their children.

One by one, the men tore themselves away from their families, which started to line the road in a combination of crying faces, happy faces, and contented faces.

"Fall in, men," General Wayne yelled again. "We need to make camp before dark," he said, knowing full well that they had plenty of time to get to camp before dark because camp was only a few miles up the road in Malvern. Despite what looked like a town full of patriots now, Wayne knew that there were Tories and spies everywhere they went, and that he couldn't let them know exactly where the campsite was.

THE PAOLI boys marched straight up the Lancaster Road, falling in behind those regiments that were going to keep moving on past Paoli and up towards Reading to protect the Continental Army's supply depot. Those regiments would move on up the Lancaster Road and on to Reading while General Wayne's regiments would stay in Paoli and defend the Valley Forge against the British.

A group of soldiers took up position on the rear, basically marching backwards. Their job was to make sure that the army wasn't followed by the enemy, those in red coats, and those without. Anyone who got too close was ordered to get back and then state his business. Even though this was home country, the usual precautions still had to be followed.

When Wayne's regiment came close to the General Warren Inn, a known Tory hangout in the next village, Malvern, they avoided it by turning left off the Lancaster Road. After marching for a mile, maybe two, they came to a large open field with wooden fences around it, marking off the nearby farmer's lands.

Wayne held his musket in the air and called out, "This is it boys. At ease and set up camp."

"Yeah," the boys yelled. Time to rest. They were never sure how long they were going to stay anywhere, but they were always happy to stay anywhere.

"I can't believe it," said Fred. "We're so close to home."

Allen laid his heavy back pack on the ground and said, "This is perfect. Mom and Dad and Betsey and everyone can come up and see us."

"I wonder how long we'll be here?" Fred asked Allen, not expecting an answer, but hoping the answer was "a long time."

"Who knows," said Allen. "I hope they don't move us closer to the Valley Forge when we have to go take out the British." He looked around cautiously, like he was telling a secret, even though the only people around him were soldiers in his regiment. But, he knew that he could never be too cautious.

"I heard that we're going to have to wait here a few days for reinforcements from Maryland to get here before we attack," Allen said.

"Well, that's good then," said Fred. "Then we can spend more time with the family."

He patted Allen on the back.

The Roberts boys went to setting up camp like the others. They raised tents. They cleaned and inspected their weapons. The cooks went to cooking. The quartermasters tended to the horses. The livery group repaired the wagons.

Allen didn't have a job to do right then except to get his own tent set up. He did that in no time. Then he laid his blanket out on the ground and closed his eyes.

By the time Fred had finished his duty of checking the gun powder supplies and condition and returned to the tent, Allen was asleep.

I'll wake him up when dinner's ready, thought Fred.

BETSEY HAD stayed back at the Tavern to help Norman and Rochelle clean up. Orland and Teenie went back home to start doing whatever they could to help the boys. Two soldiers had come to the Tavern to tell the locals where the boys were camped. He told them to spread the word among their people. The whole town of Paoli was a beehive of activity. Anybody who had any food was cooking it, and any crops in the field that were ready were pulled up, brought inside, and cooked. Any cows or sheep that the British hadn't stolen were prepared for slaughter. Smoked meats that were hidden were taken out of hiding and then hid on wagons and in bags to be taken up to the boys' campsite.

The ladies had already been sewing clothes and knitting socks and hats and gloves and scarves and whatever else they could anyway, hoping that they could get them to their boys. Now was their time. All over town, they gathered up what they had already made and finished up what they were working on.

At the Tavern, Rochelle, Norman, and Betsey filled barrel after barrel with ale and whiskey and loaded the barrels on the many wagons that came by. Just one barrel per wagon, in case the British were out there foraging and stealing food from wagons.

Paoli wasn't like those other towns they had heard of where most of the people didn't support the patriots. This was General Wayne's backyard; these were his people; these were his supporters.

"Is that it then?" Betsey asked Rochelle as she put the lid on another barrel. She fidgeted from side to side, rubbing her hands anxiously.

Rochelle looked at Betsey and smiled. "I know what you want to do, girl," Rochelle said.

Betsey jumped around and smiled, too. "How do you know?"

"Cause I do, too" said Rochelle as she gave Betsey a hug.

She waved her arms. "Shoo," she said as she kept waving. "Go on and get out of here. Get on up there and see your brothers."

Betsey smiled and jumped up. "Thank you, Aunt Rochelle."

Rochelle kissed her on the forehead and said, "You're welcome."

Betsey bolted towards the door.

"But, wait," Rochelle said. "Go home first. Let your Mom and Dad know that you're finished here before you go up there."

Betsey frowned.

"Why? Everyone's going up there! They'll know where I am!" she said.

Rochelle said, "Everyone's not Orland's and Teenie's daughter." She wagged her finger at Betsey.

"You know they're concerned for your safety, no matter if everyone is making a beeline up there," she said.

Rochelle put her hands on her hips. "Promise me you'll go home first before going to that camp, or I'll walk you home myself."

Betsey's eyes got wide. "Aunt Rochelle," she exclaimed. "I'm not a baby. You don't have to walk me home. I can take care of myself."

"Let's hope so," said Rochelle.

Betsey ran back to her. "Fine," she said, this time with her hands on her hips. "I'll go home first." She held Rochelle's hands. "Happy?" she asked.

"Yes, happy," said Teenie. She gave Betsey another kiss, this time on the top of her head.

"Now go on and get out of here before your uncle comes back inside. You think I'm hard on you?"

Betsey smiled and said, "You're right." She ran to the back door and said, "I'll see you tomorrow."

There were so many of her neighbors out that night that it seemed like it was church picnic time or harvest festival time. People were smiling and laughing, happy that their boys were home.

Betsey saw her friend Diane walking with her sister. They were both carrying large sacks.

"Hey Diane," Betsey yelled.

Diane turned around, stopped, and Betsey ran up to her.

"Isn't it great, Diane?" Betsey asked, as she linked her arm in her friend's.

Diane shook her head and said, "Yes. It's wonderful."

"Are you taking that up to your brother?" Betsey asked, pointing to Diane's sack.

"Yes," said Diane. "I can't wait to see him again and sit down and talk with him for even a few minutes," she said.

"I know what you mean," said Betsey. "I'm going up later to see my brothers." She turned around and pointed to the Tavern. "I'd be going up there with you right now if I didn't promise my Aunt Rochelle that I'd go home first and let Mom and Dad know," Betsey said. She shrugged her shoulders, "Like they wouldn't know that's where I'm going." She spread out both arms. "That's where everyone's going," she said, pointing to the crowd.

As they walked, Betsey's house came into view. She pulled away from Diane. "I'll see you up there," she said, as she ran towards the house.

**"I'M HERE,"** Betsey said, as she opened up the door. Teenie stood at the cook stove, stirring a boiling pot.

"Good," said Teenie. "You're home."

"And I want to go right up to see Fred and Allen," Betsey said, "but Aunt Rochelle told me to come home and tell you and Dad first so you wouldn't worry."

"Well," said Rochelle, "your Dad is already up there. He took up some supplies about an hour ago. You know nothing was going to keep him away from his sons, the other boys and General Wayne. His network is getting and giving some valuable information."

"That's what I figured," Betsey said. Her Dad and his friends' information network, as they called it, worked hard to help the patriots in their area and to keep the peace.

"So I can go on up there?"

Teenie looked at her daughter, practically jumping around the room in anticipation.

"Yes, of course," said Teenie, as she wiped her hands on her apron. "And I'm going with you," she added. "You can help me take some of these clothes and this food up there."

Betsey frowned slightly.

"Don't worry. I won't make you wait," Teenie said. "Everything is ready." She pointed to two large sacks by the back room. "Grab those sacks and let's get out of here."

Betsey smiled, and Teenie did, too.

Their family was going to be together again.

**UP AT** the campsite, General Wayne and the other officers did their best to keep proper order and decorum. They still had to keep it tight. They tried at first to only let in a few locals at a time, or at least let them come to the edge of the camp, ask for their boys, have the boys come over, let them spend a few minutes together, and then send them back. But, so many family and friends kept coming that General Wayne decided to set up extra pickets comprised of men who were not from the area. He wanted to make sure that his men and their families were well-protected. No one knew how long the men would be there, so Wayne figured that most families would come visit their boys on their first night in camp. He knew that they would be there at least one or two nights more, waiting for General Smallwood and his regiments to get up from Maryland. He figured that one night with family wouldn't hurt. In fact, it would be very good for the men. They all had more food, and good food at that. They got fresh clothes, blankets and warm clothes. Some even got new shoes, horses and ammunition. Whatever the family had that their boys needed, if they could give it to them, they did. Wayne let his men have their night, no telling what the next night was going to bring.

# CHAPTER 21
# SEPTEMBER 23
# PAOLI

Allen woke up happier than he'd been in a long time. For the first time in a long time, he woke up without a gnawing ache in his stomach, signaling hunger that he could only hope would be satisfied. His stomach was actually full, so much so that it was close to aching from fullness. After eating very little for days and months, he ate to his fill last night, as did just about everyone in their regiment.

A full stomach made him happy, but seeing his family made him happier. Last night was like one big family reunion and harvest party.

As the others in the regiment stirred awake, Allen noticed that he wasn't alone. There were a lot of satisfied smiles on a lot of faces. Smiling and glad-handing. Laughing even. The camp became noisier as the men engaged in happy, animated conversation.

Fred stretched his arms, smiling while his eyes were still closed.

"Good morning brother," Allen said, giving Fred a friendly kick to hasten his awakening.

"Oh, hey, good morning," Fred said.

"Isn't it great not to wake up hungry?" Allen asked.

"Sure is," Fred said, as he rubbed his stomach, just like someone who had a full belly.

Allen poured some water onto a cloth and ran it over his face.

"Wasn't last night great?" he asked.

"Oh my God," said Fred. "It was like dying and going to heaven, seeing everyone." He stretched out his arms and legs and stood up. "Even just being able to have a night to rest, to not have to be on guard. To be with our friends."

"I know," said Allen. "It was great that the General let us local boys kind of have the night off while the rest of them worked."

Fred said, "Definitely."

Allen laughed. "Well, I think we'd better savor that and keep that memory for a long time," he said. He looked around at the regiment now swinging into activity "I doubt whether we'll be so lucky tonight," Allen said.

Fred looked around and shrugged. "You're probably right," he said, "but maybe we'll get lucky."

Allen patted Fred on the back. "Maybe," he said. "Maybe."

THE BOYS lined up for a breakfast even bigger than the one they had the day before by the Buck Tavern. They had eggs, ham, tomatoes, onions, every kind of bread you could imagine, cheese, and fruit. Everybody ate until they were full from their first serving, and then they were allowed to go back for seconds. That was unheard of.

"I guess the General went back to Waynesborough with his family," Fred said.

"Yeah," said Allen. "Well, the Generals get to stay in houses most of the time anyway, so at least he got to sleep in his own bed."

Fred raised his eyebrows, and said, "And with his own wife." He laughed. "Maybe he'll be in a great mood when he comes back."

"Wish I could say the same, brother," said Allen.

Fred laughed "That'll happen soon enough, brother," said Fred. He laid back a bit and said, "When we get out of here, we'll both be able to pick one of those nice girls from the neighborhood and settle down."

Allen said, "I hope that day comes soon." He made a rubbing motion with his hand. "I'm tired of handling it on my own."

Fred rolled his eyes and said, "I hear you, brother. My hands have gotten very tired lately."

Allen poked Fred. "Have you ever thought about trying one of those camp women who follow us?"

"Just about every time I see one of them," Fred said, laughing. "Or one of those women we run into sometimes in the villages."

Fred took a sip of the strong, hot black coffee in his tankard. "But then I think about all those diseases that the guys get down there in their privates after they've been with one of those women, and it's back to the hand. At least that way, my thing won't get diseased and fall off."

Allen's eyes widened at the thought. "That would be horrible, so I guess you're right," he said. "I guess I can wait. I've got my eyes on Betsey's friend, Diane. You know who I mean, right?"

Fred said, "Of course I do. She was here last night with her Mom and Dad visiting....what's her brother's name again?"

"Robert," said Allen.

"Yeah, Robert," said Fred. "Diane's a nice girl. Nice looking, too." He paused for a minute. "And has a nice body, if I remember her right," he said, poking Allen in the side.

Allen smiled. "That's right, brother. A very nice body."

Fred said, "Well, put your bid in."

Allen looked puzzled. "What do you mean?"

Fred looked Allen dead in the eye. "Go tell Robert that you like his sister. And tell him to tell her."

Allen looked at Fred seriously, eyes wide, hanging on his every word.

"Then, the next time she comes up here," Fred said, waving his arms around the camp, "you tell her yourself."

Allen shook his head and looked down at the ground. "I don't know if I could do that, Fred," he said. "You know me. You know I'm shy. You know I don't have much experience with girls."

Fred patted Allen on the back. "That's the beauty of it brother. You don't need much experience with girls," he said. "You now have experience with life. You're a soldier. An experienced fighting man. A man in a uniform. Girls like that."

"Really?" Allen said, eyes wide with hope.

"Absolutely," Fred said. "You're no longer that little kid who was out there playing with his friends in the fields. You're a patriot. A freedom fighter. A defender of God and country and everything that she wants." He patted Allen on the back again, "You're now the man that she wants."

"You think?" Allen asked.

"Yes, and I know," said Fred. "All women want a strong man who can protect and take care of them. Connie told me that early on when I started courting girls. And as a soldier now, you fit the bill."

Allen smiled.

"Listen," Fred said, kind of lowering his voice. "The next time you see her, tell her that it's women like her who we're out here fighting for. The daughters of democracy. The future mothers of our country."

Allen sat up straight. "Ok. And what else?"

Fred said, "And nothing else. That will make her feel good, feel proud, feel special. That will give her something to think about."

All of a sudden Fred sat straight up. He threw his hand up in the air "I know," he said. "Tell her that you'll be thinking about her every day until you come back."

Allen winced, wrinkling up his nose and mouth.

"And tell her that you'll have something special for her when you come back."

"Something special?" Allen asked. "What would that be?"

Fred threw up his hands. He said, "I don't know, brother, but you'll have time to figure it out." He smiled broadly and said, "And besides. Women like mystery."

Allen nodded his head. "Great. That sounds like a good plan, brother."

Fred looked at Allen and laughed, "You can thank me later. Just name your first born after me."

Allen smiled and said, "Maybe I will," as he put his arm around Fred and patted him on the shoulder.

Just then, the coronet sounded. That meant that General Wayne was approaching and the men would get their orders for the day.

"See, all good things must come to an end," said Fred.

"Yup," said Allen, "but now I have a plan," smiling.

They both swallowed the last few bites of food and drank the last few gulps of coffee. They put their tankards and plates back in their backpacks and started checking their equipment. No telling what the day would bring.

GENERAL WAYNE looked resplendent as he rode into the center of the camp. The sun shone down and hit his gun so that it sparkled when he held it up in the air. A night at Waynesborough had obviously done him good. His uniform was clean, white where it should have been white, and freshly pressed and starched. He had a fresh hat with a fresh coronet in it.

"Fall in, men," he said. The men picked up their muskets and gathered around Wayne.

"I hope you all had a great day yesterday and into the evening," he said.

"Yeah," the men yelled back. Then they started clapping.

Wayne held up his hands. "You deserved it. We all need the comfort of our home people every once in a while, and I'm glad that we all had time yesterday to have that." Then he put his hands down. "But we can't have that today."

The men quieted down.

"Today must be different," Wayne said. "As much as I wish we could allow the families to come and visit today, we cannot. We must prepare for our mission. We may have to move at any time."

He continued, "You know the British are over at our Valley Forge, stealing valuable iron and supplies as we speak. You know how important the Valley Forge is to this area here, to our brothers and sisters in Philadelphia, to our brothers in the rest of our Continental Army." He paused to let the men consider what he just said. "Well, we have to get it back. That's our charge men. We have to take back the Valley Forge."

Fred looked around. "With just us?" he said to Allen. "There's only a thousand or more of us here."

"I know," said Allen. "Dad said there were thousands of redcoats over there."

"How the hell are we supposed to pull that off?" Fred said to Allen, not expecting an answer.

But he got one from the General.

"We will be joined in our efforts by some troops coming up from Maryland," Wayne said. "When they arrive, we march out, so be ready men. Be ready."

The General thrust his musket up in the air again. "Ready yourselves, men. Continue to make your people proud."

With that, he turned and rode away.


BETSEY HAD gotten up early to join Teenie and Orland in the fields. They walked row by row, trying to see if any of the vegetables were ready to be harvested. What they already had and what was in their hidden stash, they cooked up yesterday, leaving only a bit for themselves for today. Anything that was ripe and ready, they would bring in and cook up for the boys today, or even give them the fruits and vegetables that would be ripe and ready in a few days so the boys could have it with them wherever they might have to march to next.

"I'll go check the hen house for eggs," Betsey said. She did that every morning anyway, gathering up the eggs they were going to sell and the ones they were going to keep for themselves. This morning, just about all of them would be packed up or cooked up and taken up to the boys.

Betsey gathered up the eggs and gently placed them in crates. She put the crates in the wagon that she kept by the hen house door and headed towards the house. Teenie was pulling another wagon full of apples and squash, and Orland was carrying a bushel basket filled with tomatoes. They put the fruits and vegetables on the wagon by the front door and covered it up with a blanket.

They put half of the eggs in the big wagon they were going to take up to the camp and took the other half inside. Betsey lit the fire as they prepared to hard boil the eggs.

"We'll head up there after the eggs are done," Orland said.

Just then, there was a knock at the door. Orland walked over to open the door.

Dr. John Crocker, their neighbor to the south, said, "Good morning, Orland. Teenie. Betsey," nodding to each as he said their name.

"Good morning, John," Teenie called back, almost in unison with Orland.

"What do you hear, John?" Orland asked.

John was part of Orland's spy network. A doctor making house calls wouldn't arouse anyone's suspicion, so a lot of important information went through Dr. John.

"I hear that the boys are going to be on the move today," John said, "and that they're not letting friends and family up there today like they did yesterday. Wayne is reestablishing some sort of order."

Orland rubbed his beard. "Won't we be able to bring anything up to them? We've already started cooking and loading up the wagon, and you know everyone else around here is probably doing the same."

"They're only going to let a few people bring things up. They don't want that many people up there today. They don't know when they have to move. They just know that they will," Dr. John said. "They're waiting on more troops to come up from Maryland, and they don't know when they'll be here. But, when they get here, they're going to move out."

He continued, "They don't need to have to move a lot of friends and family out of the way before they move on. And you know, the more people up there, the more chance that one of their spies gets in and figures out what's going on."

Orland rubbed his hands together. "I know, I know," he said. "Well, who are they letting through?"

"They have said you, Jeremiah, and Norman, and that's it," John said.

Betsey cried out, "You mean that I can't go back and see Fred and Allen?"

"I'm afraid not, Betsey," Dr. John said.

"No!" Betsey cried. "That's not fair." This time she cried with tears coming down her eyes. "They're my brothers! I want to see them!"

Orland said, "Quiet down now, Betsey." He went over and put his arm around her. "I understand that you want to see your brothers. We want to see them, too, but we also have to follow the orders that we're given. And we have to do what we have to do to also keep them safe."

He held her close and patted her shoulders. "That's how it works, honey," Orland said.

"That stinks, "Betsey said. "So what are we supposed to do all day while they're up there? Can't we do something to help them?"

Orland looked at John.

"I think the best thing to do is to keep doing what you're doing. Get things ready to take up there. Keep cooking the food and gathering up the provisions. Even though everyone can't go up there, the three who can will be able to make as many trips as they can."

"That sounds better," said Orland.

"Yes," John said.

Orland turned towards Teenie. "Teenie, you can finish up cooking here and then you and Betsey can go over to the Tavern and help Rochelle and Norman do some cooking, since they have more cook stoves and pots over there. We can get more food prepared for our boys."

Orland rubbed his chin, "In fact, maybe some of our other people can go over there and cook. That could be like our central loading place, since it basically is already."

Dr. John nodded his head. "Good idea, Orland."

"That settles it," said Orland. "That's what we'll do today." He turned towards John.

"So you'll go spread the word now?"

John nodded his head. "Now that I have orders from you, I'll take care of it."

"Great," said Orland. He walked John to the door and said, "God speed."

"See you tomorrow," said John, as he rode away.

WHEN THE Roberts' family drove the carriage up to the Tavern, they had to park farther from the door than expected. It seemed like everyone in the neighborhood network had gotten their orders from Doc – go to the Tavern and cook up some food. There were almost as many carriages there today as there were the day they welcomed the boys back home.

Orland pulled as close to the back door as he could. They all hopped down and started unloading. Betsey grabbed the eggs she had picked earlier that day and hurried towards the door. She opened the door to the cookhouse out back, and the heat from the cook stoves and the people crowded inside and rushing around hit her like a strong ocean wave.

Rochelle, wiping sweat from her brow, looked up. "Betsey," she called out. "Nice to see you darlin," she said as she turned back to the pot she was stirring. "Come right in."

Rochelle said something to the lady standing beside her who was also stirring her pot, and then said to Betsey, "Are your parents with you?"

"Yes they are. They'll be in in a minute," Betsey said.

Just then, Teenie called out, "Ladies, ladies, ladies. Looks like I'm late."

The ladies laughed. Carol Mullen, her neighbor on the far right side, said, "You're right on time Teenie. I can use your help with these sausages," she said, holding up a sausage casing.

"We don't have a lot of meat to stuff them, but they taste pretty good when you chop the vegetables really fine and fill it in with that."

Teenie said, "You don't even know you're missing the meat."

The ladies all laughed at that because they knew that wasn't true. They and everyone else missed the meat very much. But they knew that they had to make do with what they had, and that they should be happy with that. No one was eating as much as they used to. When they cooked, it was always less than they normally did. They always hid some food because they never knew whether the British might come along and steal it or the Continentals might come along and need it.

And the boys told them that they usually never had enough to eat. Sometimes they went days at a time without eating. Even when they did eat, it wasn't as much as they were used to eating. But, they explained that, over time, they got used to eating less. They were used to eating so little that only a little filled them up.

While the women were in the cookhouse, the men were in the tavern, guarding them and talking about what else they could do to help out. Now that the British were in their area, a few miles to the west, and the boys were back in a camp a few miles to the north, the war had indeed come to their back yard.

"It's just a matter of time before there's a battle," said Ron Toshers, the local carpenter.

"Let's hope not," said Martin Deliverance. "Maybe those Brits will high tail it out of the Forge once they realize that our boys are back."

"How likely is that?" asked John Kender. "Why would they give it up without a fight," he said. "Besides, we all know that's why our boys are here. To go get the Forge back."

Tom Turner said, "Sure, sure, that's what we hear. And that they're up near the Pearce and Bowen fields waiting for reinforcements."

Orland ran his fingers through his hair. He squinted his eyes. "So if we know that, don't you think that they know that, too?"

"Sure they do," said Martin. "So let's hope those reinforcements get here soon."

"And if they don't?" asked John. "We may have to take up arms and help them."

Orland stood up and pointed at them all. "And who here wouldn't do that?"

"Not me," they all murmured.

"So let's be ready," said Orland. "I know you all have your muskets with you now."

"Right," they all said.

"So carry an extra one with you, too, if you can hide it," said Orland. "And extra grapeshot."

He paused for a few seconds. "You never know when we might need it."

Rochelle walked in with a large basket of hard boiled eggs. Norman ran to help get it from her. Rochelle gave him a peck on the lips and said, "Thank you, honey."

"Gentlemen," she said, "can we impose on you to pack these up?"

"No problem," said Martin. "Put it over here."

"Great," said Rochelle. "We've got a lot more things coming."

"That's why we're here," said Orland. "To help you ladies."

"Good," Rochelle said. "Because we need you."

"More than you know darling," said Norman. "More than you know."

SO, FOR the next few hours, the women cooked, and the men packed. Once the men had a few things packed, they loaded up Orland's wagon, and he headed up to the boys' campsite.

"Is that it?" asked Orland, as Martin put another barrel into the just-about-full wagon.

"That's it for now," said Martin. "There's not a lot of hiding space in there, and what there is is packed," he said, patting the hidden floor board.

"Alright," said Orland. "Let me get up there and get on back."

Orland drove the wagon away from the Lancaster Road and towards the back trails. While a few leaves had fallen, the trails were still largely hidden if you didn't know where they were. His network figured that the British didn't find that network of trails in the few days that they had occupied the area. Now, there was little movement on the trails. Most of the men and women who might have traveled on it were down at the Tavern already.

About a half mile away from the camp, Orland heard, "Halt. State your name and your business."

Orland couldn't see the person who was attached to the voice, but that was to be expected. Dr. John had said that Wayne had put soldiers from other colonies on the pickets. He didn't want local boys out there on the front line attracting attention. He put his hands up and said, "Orland Roberts. Local farmer. My boys Fred and Allen are up there with the 5th Pennsylvania Regiment. I'm here with a delivery."

The picket stepped out from behind a group of holly bushes, musket with bayonet pointed straight at Orland. Another one came out of the bushes on Orland's right side.

"Keep your hands up," said the one.

As the first one approached, he looked hard at Orland. He said, "Orland Roberts?"

Orland said, "Yes."

"We were expecting you," he said, smiling, and thrusting out a hand for a handshake.

"And I know your boys, Fred and Allen. They're good men," he said.

Orland smiled and said, "Thank you."

Then two more men walked out of the bushes. One had a wagon and one was leading a horse.

"We'll take what you have and get it up there as soon as we can," one said.

Orland sat in the wagon and let the boys unload. He could see another set of pickets not very far down the trail, guns at the ready. When the last barrel was taken off, the first soldier who greeted him said, "We're all set here. You can head on back."

Orland tipped his hat and said, "Very good. I'll get back and load up again. There's a whole army at the Tavern cooking for you all."

The soldier rubbed his stomach. "We sure appreciate that," he said. "It's not often that we get good home-cooked food anymore."

Orland said, "Well, don't worry about that as long as you're in these parts." He smiled at him and added, "We take care of our own, and now that means all of you, too."

"Thank you, sir," said the soldier, as he nodded.

Orland grabbed the reins of the horse and gave him a gentle tap with his spurs. "Come on now, Sadie," he said. "Let's turn around." He pulled the reins to the left and eased the horse around back in the direction that they came. As he had the wagon faced north and ready to ride back, the pickets who were guarding his back side and the back of the trail parted on either side and waved him through. Orland tipped his hat, shook the reins, and said, "Giddy up." He and Sadie headed back down the trails and on to the road.

ABOUT HALF way back, he ran into Jeremiah Steves headed in the opposite direction, towards camp. Orland just tipped his hat and waved. No need to dawdle and waste time. Everyone wanted to get as much food up there as possible as quickly as possible.

BACK AT the Tavern, a crowd of people were coming and going. Orland hitched the wagon to the post on the side and walked inside the front door that was wide open. Even with that, as soon as he walked inside he felt the heat. As he walked towards a row of baskets already covered and lined up, Betsey saw him.

"Daddy's here," she called out and ran over to him. She wrapped her arms around him, and he did likewise.

"Did you get to see Fred and Allen?" Betsey asked.

Orland shook his head. "No, they didn't let me get that close, just like Doc said." He waved to Teenie who was still bent over one of the boiling kettles. "They're keeping the local boys in camp with the ones from the other colonies on the pickets."

"Darn," said Betsey.

Orland pulled back. "Watch your mouth, girl."

Betsey put her hands on her hips. "I said Darn, Dad. D-A-R-N. Not the other one. The swear word."

Orland frowned as he looked at her. "You better not. Just because everything else around here is turned upside down, doesn't mean that you can forget everything we've taught you about being a lady."

Betsey curtseyed. "Absolutely not, Dad," she said as she bent down and twirled around. "I'm still very much a lady," she said, mockingly, knowing that she didn't have the same ladylike qualities that a lot of her friends did and that her Dad knew it and had called her out about that more than a few times.

"Good," said Orland. "You better be."

Betsey gave his arm a squeeze and smiled.

"And even though you're a young lady, I do need your help in getting these baskets into the wagon," Orland said, smiling.

Betsey curtseyed again. "Yes, sir," she said smiling. "M'lady at your service."

Orland rubbed her head lovingly as he picked up one of the baskets.

Just then, Teenie yelled out, "Orland, dear, come over here for a minute before you head back out," as she kept stirring.

Orland put the basket back down on the table and walked over to Teenie. She stopped stirring and wiped her hands on her apron.

"Did you see the boys?" she asked.

"No, honey," he said, rubbing her back. "They wouldn't let me get that close, just like Doc said this morning."

Teenie frowned in disappointment.

"But the pickets I did run into said that they knew Fred and Allen and that they were fine boys," he said. "So, even though I couldn't see them, that made me proud."

Then he wiped his brow. Whether it was from the heat or from relief at what the pickets had said, Teenie didn't know.

"And it was good to know that they were so protected. They have pickets hiding out in the woods all the way up to the camp, as far as what I could see."

"Good," said Teenie. "If we can't see the boys, at least it's good to know that they're protected."

Orland hugged Teenie. He looked back over her shoulder and saw Norman coming in the back door, carrying a metal pan of roasted pig.

"Hey, brother," Orland said. "That looks mighty good. We're going to have to cover that up especially tight. The smell alone would get those redcoats to come out of hiding."

"Yeah," said Norman. "And then our boys could finish them off."

"From your mouth to God's ears," Orland said.

Norman laid the pan on the table with the rest of the baskets. "What are you doing standing around, Betsey? I thought you were helping your mother."

Before Betsey could say something in protest, Orland said, "I told her to come and help me put these baskets in the wagon." He looked at Betsey and smiled and said, "Even though she is a little lady."

"Oh, Dad," said Betsey, protesting. "You know I could fight just as well as any boy around here," she said, holding her arm out like she was holding a gun and pulling the trigger.

"Well, let's hope it never comes to that," Orland said. "Girls fighting in the army."

"You know they need more fighting men, from what I've heard, between some of these boys getting killed and some of them deserting when things got too rough," he said. "God forbid that General Washington or that Continental Congress doesn't get it in their heads that they should muster these young girls."

"God forbid," said Orland. "They'll come after us old men first."

Norman laughed. "If they had to depend on us, I think we'll be in trouble," he said.

"Well, trouble it might be," said Orland, "if our boys don't finish off those redcoats soon, before we run out of manpower, food and everything else."

Norman looked serious now. "You might be right, brother," he said. "Let's just pray that never happens." He turned to Betsey and said, "And don't worry Betsey. We were just kidding about you girls, even you tomboy girls, joining our fighting boys. We'd never let that happen."

"But there must be something else that we women can do to drive those redcoats back to where they came from than just cook," she said, waving her arms around the room.

"Just cooking is good enough for now," said Orland.

Betsey's eyes got bright, and she said, "Yes, you're right, Dad. For now."

For the balance of the day, the same scene repeated itself. The wagons were loaded at the Tavern, Orland and a few others drove them up to outside the camp, the pickets would surprise them, unload the goods onto their own horses and wagons, and then Orland and a few trusted others would come back to the Tavern and do it all over again.

Orland had just approached the Tavern as the sun was setting. He was tired. After his last trip, one of the pickets told him that would be it for the day. He said that General Wayne didn't want anyone coming toward the camp in the evening, even the trusted few. Orland said that he understood. It was harder to see who was approaching in the dark, and it was easier to conceal trouble.

BACK AT the Tavern, the cooking was still going on. It wasn't as crowded, though. Many of the women had gone home. Norman, Dr. John, and a few of the men who lived near the Tavern were the only men there when Orland arrived. Teenie and Rochelle were cleaning out pots and straightening up the cooking area.

"Hi, Honey," Teenie called out when she saw Orland come in. "Come over and have a seat. You must be as tired as we are," she said.

"I sure am," Orland said, as he pulled up a seat at the bar where Teenie was cleaning. Betsey was folding into an orderly stack the cloths that various women had dropped off during the day to be used for covering the food after it was loaded into the wagon.

"Would you like something to drink, honey?" Teenie asked.

"Would love it," Orland said.

Teenie pulled a mug out from under the bar and filled it to the brim with ale. Orland took a sip, held his head back, closed his eyes, and said, "Aah."

Norman stopped straightening up chairs and walked over to the bar. "I think I'll join you, brother," he said. "It's been a long day."

Dr. John walked over to them and said, "May I join you?"

"Of course," Norman said. "Steve," he called out to the man carrying a basket of apples in, "you come and join us, too."

"Don't mind if I do," he said, as he put the basket down on the assembly line table.

After such a busy day, everyone was happy to be off their feet.

"So everything went as they explained it to me?" Dr. John asked Orland.

"Yes," he said. "Just like clockwork."

"Good," said Dr. John. He took another sip. "We'll see how things go tomorrow."

"Let's hope we have another smooth day," Orland said.

"Why don't we drink to it?" Norman said.

"Here, here," said Steve.

The men raised their glasses, and Norman said, "Here's to a good day tomorrow in our fight for freedom."

"To freedom," Orland said.

"To freedom," they all said in unison.

Teenie saw that Orland's glass was empty. "Would you like another one?"

Orland shook his head and waved his hand. "No," he said. "One's enough. This is not the time for a fuzzy head."

"That's the truth," said Steve.

Rochelle called out, "Then I'll take those mugs and wash them up. " She looked around and saw Betsey. "Betsey, dear, would you go over there and get the mugs for me."

"Sure, Aunt Rochelle," Betsey said, as she put the cloth she was folding neatly in place.

"Then that'll be it for the night," Norman said. "It's getting late, and we all need to get home and get ready for tomorrow."

Just as the men got down off their bar stools, they heard a commotion outside. As they walked towards the doors to see what was going on, they were pushed back inside by a wave of red. Five and six, and seven and eight redcoats with bayonetted muskets pushed them back inside, not touching them with the bayonets, but holding them at such an angle and with such determined looks in their eyes that the men knew that any one of those redcoats would push that bayonet straight into any one of them at the slightest movement.

"What's going on here?" Norman yelled, as he walked gently backwards, as did the rest of them.

"Get back in there," yelled one of the redcoats.

"Go sit down," yelled another.

"Don't move and we won't hurt you," said another.

Betsey, Teenie, and Rochelle screamed in unison.

"Go sit over there ladies," said one of the soldiers. "We're not here to hurt you," said another.

One laughed and said, "Yeah, we're gentlemen."

The men continued walking backwards in unison, hands up, and went and sat at the table where the redcoats were pointing their bayonets. They slowly lowered their hands, pulled out a chair, and sat down.

"What's going on?" Norman yelled again.

One of the soldiers pointed a bayonet just inches from his face. "Shut up," he yelled.

"You don't get to know what's going on." Another soldier put his bayonet down at his side and smacked Norman in the face. Norman's head fell back, and he started to raise his hand to hit back. Orland grabbed it and held him down.

"You'll find out soon enough," said another.

The women looked over at the men, all helpless.

The redcoats who weren't shoving bayonets in their face or standing next to them with bayonets pointing at each of them, were standing two deep at both the front and the back door. The first column faced outside with bayonets drawn, and the second column faced the group inside, with their bayonets drawn. One of the redcoats looked around at the roasted pig, barrel of apples, and other foodstuffs that were sitting out in anticipation of delivery to the Paoli boys tomorrow.

"Don't worry," one said in a snide voice. "All of this food won't go to waste," he laughed. "But it won't be your rebel boys who are eating it."

The rest of the redcoats laughed.

"Yeah," said one. "So thank you very much."

They all laughed.

BETSEY FELT tears welling up in her eyes. Of course, she was scared. She was scared for herself. She was scared for her family there in the Tavern, and she was scared for her brothers. If the redcoats were here, bursting into the tavern, she was sure that they were on the march looking for their boys.

"Are you arresting us?" asked Dr. John.

The redcoats laughed again. "Arresting you? What would we want with you old man, and those other old men in here and these women?"

"We're holding you," said one. "We know you all have been running back and forth to that camp where your rebel boys are, but we're going to make sure that nobody runs up there tonight," he said.

"Yeah," said another. "Nobody's going up there tonight but us."

Another said, "You can go up there tomorrow and see your boys, "he laughed a grotesque laugh. "If there's anything left."

Teenie let out a little scream again, but she quickly put her hand in front of her mouth.

Orland gripped his chair as hard as he could.

Norman wondered which one of these men he could take.

Betsey felt the tears welling up in her eyes, but she refused to let those redcoats see her cry.

As the redcoats stood there, the patriots in the tavern realized that all they could do was wait.

# CHAPTER 22

# GENERAL WAYNE'S CAMP
# AT PAOLI

Fred polished the barrel on his musket and said to Allen, "Can you believe it? Two days in a row with a full stomach."

Allen shook his head. "No, it seems like a dream," he said. "The only thing is I wish was that we were able to see the family today."

"Yeah," said Fred, "But it was nice to hear from our friend in the 2nd Rhode Island that he saw them today."

"At least that's something," said Allen. "Well, maybe tomorrow."

"Yeah," said Fred, "if we're still here. I hear that Smallwood's Army is within a day's march."

Allen laughed. "That's what they said yesterday, and he's not here yet." He cleaned the trigger on his musket. "But, at least we get another day in camp here, so if we can't see the family, at least we know that they're around, and, hopefully, we still get to eat good."

"Thank heaven for small favors," Fred said.


SARGENT SHERWOOD walked over to where Fred and Allen sat with the rest of the Fifth Pennsylvania. "Get some sleep, men," he said. "We will probably be on the march tomorrow."

"Yes, sir," they both said, almost in unison.

Sargent Sherwood said, "Our friends from New Jersey are guarding the perimeter tonight, so I think you can have a nice, sound, sleep. You all know what they did to the redcoats at Trenton."

"We sure do," said Allen. "Strike fast and strike hard."

"Yes, sir," said Fred. "That's the way to do it."

Sherwood said as he walked on. "Have a good evening, boys."

"Same to you sir," said Allen.

ALLEN LAID his musket down beside him. He adjusted the cloth filled with feathers that he used for his pillow, and he laid a light blanket over his body. Fred laid his musket on the other side of Allen, put his makeshift pillow on the ground, and pulled a blanket over him.

The coals from a few campfires were burning around them. In the distance, other campfires were burning at almost full roar where the camp sentries were. With full bellies and contented spirits, sleep came easy.

FRED THOUGHT he was dreaming when he heard it. Blood-curdling screams. Yelling. And then gunshots. Faint at first. Then louder.

"To arms, to arms," he heard. "Get up."

Just then, someone ran by him and hit him in the leg.

"Get up. To arms," the figure yelled. "We're being attacked."

Fred shot straight up, realizing that this very definitely wasn't a dream. Soldiers ran all around him. The screams grew louder. One by one, solders ran by, blood streaming down their clothes.

Allen was still sleeping. He had always been a heavier sleeper than Fred.

The shock of what he saw wearing off, Fred yelled, "Allen, wake up", as he pushed him again and again to rouse him.

"What?" said Allen as he woke from a very sound sleep.

"Get up," yelled Fred, as he grabbed his musket. "We're being attacked."

Fred pushed Allen again. "Get up," he yelled. Then he slapped him in the face and yelled louder. "Get up!"

More soldiers ran past them. "Run this way," they yelled. "Hurry!"

Allen sat up. Fred also grabbed Allen's musket.

"Here," he said, thrusting it into his hand. "Come on. We've got to run."

Allen barely had time to wake up before Fred was on his feet. Fred grabbed Allen's hand and dragged him to his feet. Fred started to run and practically pulled Allen behind him.

Allen looked in horror at the trail of bloody, fallen bodies that was littering the path before them. Then he saw some of his fellow patriots running towards them from the right, some cut and bloody, and others running as fast as they could.

Fred and Allen looked at each other as they raced ahead as fast as they could.

"What the hell is going on?" Fred called out to others as they ran by him.

"Redcoats snuck into camp. Quiet," one soldier yelled.

"Bayonets drawn," yelled another.

"Just run," said another.

Fred and Allen picked up the pace and ran.

The screams behind them grew louder and more blood curdling. Allen turned around.

"Oh my God," he yelled. "I can see them."

Fred turned for a minute and saw a band of red and white coming towards them, sticking their bayonets into anything in a patriot's uniform.

They turned face front and picked up the pace. But what they saw ahead of them caused Fred to cry out. "Shit," he said. Hundreds of patriot soldiers were backed up against wooden fences on three sides. Some of the men were furiously trying to dismantle the fence. Others were just trying to climb over it. Others were forming a human battering ram and trying to push down a large section, large enough for hundreds of them to run through and escape. These were the same fences that General Wayne didn't want them to rip down because he knew the local farmers who had built those fences, and he didn't want to destroy his neighbors' property. Now, those same fences that fenced in the animals fenced in the soldiers, and just like the animals, it looked like the soldiers were about to get slaughtered.

Some of the men realized that they were not going to knock the fences down. Allen and Fred saw that some had turned and now were raising their muskets, standing their ground and firing on the British as their only options. But, in a flash, Allen could see that most men didn't have muskets. The British had caught them off-guard and sleeping.

"This way," yelled Fred, as he grabbed Allen's arm again. He pulled him over to the right because it seemed that if they ran straight ahead, they would be shot by their own men.

The screams behind them grew louder. It sounded like they were coming from right behind them. And they were.

Allen turned around for a minute. He saw a bayonet coming straight towards his stomach. He screamed.

Fred held on tight to Allen's arm and ran faster than he ever thought he could.

At that point, the rebels who had guns and who were standing and firing, started firing to their left. There were gunshots. There were more screams. Fred kept running and pulling Allen. But Allen was slowing down.

They ran closer and closer to the rebel line. Fred looked over at Allen and screamed. "Allen!" Blood was turning his blue uniform to red. Allen staggered. Fred swooped him up just as they reached the rebel line.

"Make way," Fred said, as he pushed through the first line of patriots. "Don't worry, brother," he said, "I've got you."

Fred laid Allen down as gently as he could behind the first line and right next to the fence. He figured that since they couldn't get the fence down and that the fighting was now starting in earnest, Allen would be safe in that spot.

Fred grabbed Allen's musket out of his hands and thrust it into the hands of the nearest unarmed rebel he saw. "Here," he said.

Then, Fred stood up, turned towards the Brits who were still advancing and started firing. Now, the night was no longer quiet and serene. Shots and smoked filled the once peaceful farm. The British, who were so close on their tails, started to retreat. The rebels, now coming to their senses, kept firing. Then behind them, came reinforcements. After what seemed like an eternity, the Redcoats started to retreat. The rebels kept firing until the last redcoat ran away or was shot dead.

As the dust cleared and the confusion settled, rebels ran back towards camp. Fred ran over to Allen. Allen's uniform on the front was now almost totally coated in red.

"Allen!" Fred yelled as he saw him.

Allen's face was white as newly fallen snow. Fred knelt down beside him. He put Allen's head in his lap. "Allen! Allen!" he yelled.

Allen didn't move ever again. He was dead.

## CHAPTER 23
# THE TAVERN
# PAOLI

B etsey refused to cry despite there not being anything else to do at the time but wait. And worry. The redcoats wouldn't let them talk.

"Shut up before I smack you, too," one of them said to Orland, when he asked them if they could at least let the women go.

"Nobody's going anywhere," one said.

"You'll all get out of here soon enough."

So, they sat at the table, hands folded on their laps as instructed.

Little by little, the darkness outside lightened up. Just before it seemed that the sun was going to fully rise, there was another commotion outside. It was the unmistakable sound of an army on the march, with hundreds of shoes on the hard roads and equipment clanging against other equipment.

One of the guards at the front door yelled inside, "Make ready! I see them."

"They're coming," yelled the one at the back door.

"Good," said one of the guards inside.

Soon, a man in a slightly different red coat appeared at the front door. His hat was different than the others. The other redcoats saluted him.

"At ease, men," he said. The men who held muskets put them down by their side.

"Our mission is accomplished," he added, looking at the group being held. "We were able to surprise those rebels without any of their kin running up there to warn them." He walked around the group in a circle.

"Don't' worry," he told the group. "We're not going to hurt you." He paused in front of them and looked straight at them. "We've gotten what we came here for without any problem at all. "

He turned around swiftly on his heels towards the men behind them. "So, fall in now men," he said to the guards inside.

They all, almost in unison, picked up their muskets and headed towards the door. Almost every one of them also carried baskets or totes of food and supplies.

One of the British officers looked at the group and said, "Your boys learned today what happens when you go to war with your Sovereign Crown. Maybe you all will learn the same."

He walked over to Orland and Norman. "Now I'm going to give you some more instructions from your King," he said. "You sit here until you can't hear the sound of the victorious army marching. Then you can run to the door. If you see our rear flanks marching away, you stay in here until you can't see them any longer."

He walked over to Teenie, Rochelle and Betsey. "Then, when you're sure that we're gone, you can run out of here and check on your boys."

Betsey looked at him with squinted eyes full of hate.

He looked back with contempt. "Or your brothers," he said.

Betsey felt her temperature boiling. She wanted to spit on him. She wanted to slap him.

But what she wanted most of all was for him to not know that she was scared of him. So she fixed her eyes on his and stared him down. She thought, I won't be the one to look away.

Colonel Windsor held her gaze for a minute or so and then broke it. "I don't have time for you, young lady," he said. He took his hat off, swept it in front of him and bowed.

"Good day," he said, with a smirk.

With that, he turned and walked out of the door, joining the other men who stood waiting for him. "Fall in," he yelled. The men lifted their muskets off the ground and on to their shoulders. "March!" he yelled. And the footsteps that the patriots inside the tavern were supposed to monitor began.

They all looked at the wide open front and back doors as the redcoats marched away. When the rear of the line marched away, the last redcoat that they could see marched by, Orland and Norman looked at each other and started to get up from their chairs.

"No," said Rochelle.

"Wait," said Teenie as she held her hand up to stop them from getting up. "They can't be out of site yet. Don't get up! Do what they say! We don't need any more trouble."

Orland said, "But they're gone."

Betsey said, "Dad, no. I can still hear them on the march."

Orland looked at her in disbelief.

"You know I have good ears, Dad, and can hear everything," she said.

"We don't need them coming back in here yelling at us that we didn't follow the orders," said Teenie. "No telling what they'd do then," she said, as tears started to build in and fall from her eyes.

"Fine," said Norman, as he sat back down. He looked directly at Betsey. "As soon as you can't hear them, little girl, you let us know. I'm not going to sit here a second more than is necessary," he said.

Betsey sat up straighter in her chair as if that would let her hear better. After a few minutes she said, "That's it. They're gone. I don't hear anything except the birds."

Orland and Norman bolted out of their chairs. One ran to the front door and one ran to the rear.

They both looked around to make sure they didn't see any redcoats.

"See anything?" Orland yelled.

"Nothing," Norman yelled back.

"Then let's get up there," Orland said. Orland ran back inside where Teenie, Rochelle and Betsey were now up on their feet, hugging each other and crying.

Orland ran over to the girls and hugged Teenie and Betsey. Rochelle had run outside to Norman.

"Are you girls alright?" Orland asked.

"Fine now," said Teenie.

He turned towards Betsey. "And you honey?" he asked, as he hugged her and stroked her hair.

"I'm fine, Dad," said Betsey. "Just a little tired, that's all."

Orland rubbed her head. "That's my girl," he said. "You were very brave. I'm so proud of you," he said.

Rochelle ran back in. "Come on, everyone," she said. "Let's go find the boys, if we can."

The Roberts' family ran outside.

Orland said, "We can all get in the wagon and ride up."

Norman looked at him, his eyes narrowing and burning with anger. "They took the wagon. And the horses," he said. Spreading his arms wide as he turned around, "They took everything."

They looked around at nothing but bare ground where their wagons and horses used to be.

"Then we'll have to walk," said Orland. He looked over at Teenie and Betsey. "Are you girls up to that? Can you walk after being up all night?"

Betsey said, "Yes, Dad."

Teenie said, "I may not be able to walk as fast as you, but I'll be right behind you."

Rochelle said, "Me, too."

Orland looked at them all. "All right ladies. Let's go."

The extended Roberts family started walking up the Lancaster Road towards the path where Orland carried supplies up the day before. As they walked along, the men and Betsey in front, the women walking behind, their neighbors started coming out of their houses or joined them on the walk with tales of a night spent like theirs. The redcoats had held other neighbors captive in their houses or shops that night. But now, a steady stream of Paoli residents were on the trail headed towards the site of the last known camp of their Paoli boys.

As they walked closer, they heard screams and cries. Both blood-curdling and anguished.

They could see the picket ahead who stopped and checked everyone as they moved closer. After talking with the picket, the people ran crying and screaming up the rest of the trail.

"What's going on up there, Dad?" Betsey asked.

Orland and Norman looked at each other. The cries and screams were not a good sign. As they reached the front, Orland asked, "What happened?"

The picket said, "It was a surprise attack," still shaking a little. "We got massacred."

Orland said, "What do you mean?"

The picket said, "The redcoats found out where we were camped, and they attacked us in the middle of the night. They came silent, and they stayed silent. They didn't fire one shot. They used their bayonets."

Orland's eyes grew wide.

"And all at close range," the picket said. "And we were penned in by the fences that General Wayne wouldn't let us tear down. " He wiped a tear from his eye. "It's a blood bath up there."

Betsey screamed. All she could think of was her brothers.

The picket looked at Betsey and the other women now coming up behind them. "Sirs, are you sure you want to take the ladies up there with you now? It's quite a gruesome scene up there."

Orland and Norman looked at him with tears welling up in their eyes.

"I have two sons up there," Orland said. He put his arm around Betsey and Teenie, who had now caught up with him. "This is their sister. And this is their mother." Then he pointed to Norman and Rochelle. "And this is their uncle, and this is their aunt." He said firmly, "We're all going up there."

The picket said, "I understand," as he moved to the side to let them pass by.

Orland said, "One of the pickets yesterday said he knew my boys, Fred and Allen Roberts, from Paoli, with General Wayne's 5th Pennsylvania Brigade. Do you know them?"

The picket said, "Can't say that I do, sir, but I pray you find them safe."

Orland looked at him and said, "Thank you, son."

Orland squeezed Teenie and Betsey's shoulders as they began the walk to the camp.

Orland slowed down so they could all walk in together. The closer they got to the camp, the louder the screams became. As they came within about 50 feet of the camp, the scene they saw ahead of them was horrifying.

First, four or five bodies, uniforms full of blood were piled on top of each other on the side of the trail.

Teenie and Rochelle screamed. Betsey stared in silent horror.

"Those must have been the pickets," Norman said.

"Yes," said Orland. "The first causalities."

Then the main camp came into site. They all stopped in their tracks for a few minutes to take in the scene ahead of them.

Dead bodies with uniforms full of blood were everywhere. Live soldiers were pulling what looked like dead ones to the side, checking for signs of life. If they found any, they yelled out, "Doctor", and held their wounded compatriot as they waited. Puddles of blood were everywhere. The scene was one of destruction and confusion.

Orland held his hand up to his mouth in shock. Teenie and Betsey did the same.

Orland stopped a passing soldier.

"Son, can you help us? We're looking for our sons. Fred and Allen Roberts. 5th Pennsylvania Regiment."

The soldier said, "Can't tell you sir. You can check with Colonel Davis over there," he said pointing.

Orland, Teenie and Betsey walked over to the Colonel as fast as they could, which wasn't too fast because bodies and blood laid everywhere underfoot.

"Colonel," said Orland. "We're looking for our boys. They're in the 5th Pennsylvania Regiment."

Colonel Davis said, "The 5th Pennsylvania is over there," pointing, "by that corner in the rear."

Orland said, "Thank you," and turned in that direction.

Colonel Davis put a hand on Orland's shoulder and looked at him with sincerity. "I hope you find them."

"So do we," Orland said.

As the Roberts walked over towards the 2nd Pennsylvania, they walked by neighbor after neighbor who were helping the wounded. They looked at each other in horror as they continued their duties.

As they moved closer to the Regiment, Betsey broke from Orland and started running.

"Betsey," called out Teenie.

"Let her go," said Orland. "Let her go."

Betsey ran up to a cluster of all familiar faces. "Tom!" she called out. "Have you seen Allen and Fred?"

Tom, eyes wide like someone who was in shock, said, "Fred is over there."

Betsey ran in the direction that he was pointing. As she ran by the blood and screams all around her, she saw Fred sitting with a group of local boys, tears streaming down his face.

"Fred!" yelled Betsey.

Fred wiped his eyes at the sight his sister.

"Betsey!" he yelled. "Betsey!" He jumped up and ran towards her.

They ran towards each other and hugged.

"Thank God,"

Betsey said, as she hugged her big brother. "You're alive. You're fine."

They hugged and rocked. After a few seconds, Betsey said, "Where's Allen?"

By that point, the rest of the family had run up.

"Fred!" yelled Teenie. "My son."

"Praise God," yelled Orland.

Norman and Rochelle also yelled out their thanks to God at the sign of their oldest nephew.

They all hugged and cried.

Then Betsey started crying a different kind of cry. "Fred, Where's Allen? Where's Allen?"

The hugging stopped. They all pulled back from Fred and looked at him. Tears flowed full force from Fred again.

"No," screamed Teenie.

"Oh, God," screamed Rochelle.

Orland put both hands on Fred's shoulders and looked him straight in the eyes.

Fred drew his father closer and hugged him tightly. "He's dead, Dad," Fred said, as he started crying, tears streaming down Orland's neck, as Orland's tears started to do the same.

Teenie collapsed on the ground. "God, no," she cried.

"Damn British," yelled Norman.

Betsey ran to her mother and rocked her as she cried, just as her mother had rocked her many times before.

# CHAPTER 24

# GULPH MILLS

James was out on the grounds outside of Daniel's Blacksmith Shop, hammering a shoe for the horse that Peter Curtis brought in earlier that morning, when he heard yelling coming from the direction of the Swede's Ford. He looked up for a minute, but went right back to work. All types of sounds came from the direction of the Ford because all types of people crossed the Ford, toting all types of things.

When he was almost finished with the shoe, he looked up again. The yelling grew louder. And this time it sounded like more than one person yelling. James turned to his left to make sure his musket was right where he usually left it, just in case.

As the yelling grew even louder, James finally made out what it was that several people were yelling. Something about the British. James stood up, at a naturally protective full alert, just in case.

Suddenly, he saw a black horse coming straight down the road outside of the shop.

"The British are coming!" the young man yelled. "They're coming to cross the Swede's Ford!"

He sped by before James could stop him. Another pair of riders came by yelling the same thing. This time Daniel came out of the shop. As the other riders neared the shop, Daniel waved his hands to slow them down.

"What's going on?" he asked.

The pair slowed their horses to explain. "The British are on the march towards the Swedes Ford. They should be there in about an hour. Our people understand that they're going to cross the Swedes Ford and march down into Philadelphia," one said.

Then the other said, "So you better hide whatever you want before they get here."

"But they cross the Swedes Ford a mile away from here," said Daniel. "They wouldn't be coming down here if they're crossing the Swedes Ford."

One of the riders looked at Daniel with wide eyes, like Daniel had said something stupid. "And what if they decide to change their mind and not cross at the Swedes Ford? What if they decide to march down further and cross at the Matson's Ford?" he asked incredulously. "You'd be right in their path."

The other chimed in, "And even if they stick with crossing at the Swedes Ford, they might send a regiment down this way to forage for whatever food and supplies they can. So you better be ready, or be prepared for worse."

Daniel said, "My God. I guess you're right." He nodded at one of the riders, "Thanks for explaining that. I feel like a dummy that I didn't understand."

One of the riders said, "No problem. It's hard to understand what type of destruction might be headed your way if you haven't seen it."

Daniel said, "I guess you're right."

"Well," said a rider, "We've seen the destruction those redcoats can bring. They just spent a few days up by the Valley Forge and at camp in Tredyffrin and Paoli. You should have seen what they did to those people up there."

One of the riders took off his hat and held it against his heart, "Not to mention how they massacred our boys in the Continental Army up there in Paoli."

Both Daniel's and James' eyes widened.

"They snuck up on them in the middle of the night, charged at them with bayonets, and never fired a shot," said one. "There was a trail of blood from the Warren Tavern in Malvern to the few miles down the road to the tavern in Paoli. That's how horrible they are."

James wiped his brow. "Thanks for the warning."

"You're mighty welcome," said one. "Tell anyone else you see," he said, as he grabbed his horses' reins again. "Get ready, and be careful," he said.

"Will do," said Daniel as the pair headed off down the road.

"God speed," he yelled as they rode out of sight.

Daniel turned to James and said, "Less than an hour?"

"That's what they said," said James.

"Then we'd better get moving," said Daniel. "We should pull all the equipment that's too big for us to carry on our horses inside the shop and lock it up as tight as we can. Whatever we can carry to our homes we should and hide that away somewhere."

"That sounds about right," said James.

Daniel patted James on the back and said, "We'll do that as quickly as we can, because, if they decide to go across Matson's Ford, they might decide to march through the Gulph. They'd have to march right by your house, and you need to be able to get back there and hide your things, too."

James said, "That's right. Everything I own is up there."

"I know," said Daniel, "so let's get going."

They were a whirlwind of activity for the next half hour. James threw water on the burning stoves while Daniel pulled other equipment inside the shop. James gathered up as many tools as he could and put them in his saddle bag. When everything was either inside or in the saddle bags, James grabbed the biggest iron bar he could find and put it across the door. Then he secured it with the special iron lock that he had made just a few weeks ago. Daniel walked around the outside to make sure that everything was secure.

"That looks like it," Daniel said. He stuck his hand out to shake James'. "Good work."

"Let's hope it works, and it's all here after they pass by," James said.

"You're right about that," said Daniel. He looked at James and said, "Let's hope those sentries were right, that the Brits are crossing at the Swedes Ford and that they leave us alone down here. Guard your home until you hear that they have passed by."

"Will do," said James. "And you do the same."

Daniel nodded his head. He looked at James and said, "Stay safe, my friend, until we meet again."

James nodded, tipped his hat at Daniel, and said, "I will if you will."

Daniel laughed. "Then I'm sure we'll be back here in a few days."

With that, both men jumped on their horses, saddle bags full, and rode the horses out of there as fast as they could.

# CHAPTER 25

# GERMANTOWN

The world around her seemed to be in chaos. Looking out of her bedroom window, Connie saw a steady stream of people and wagons on the roads leading out of Germantown. People were screaming. Babies were crying. They had all heard that the British were coming, and it seemed like everyone wanted to get out of town before they arrived. For the past two days, sentries rode up and down the street and knocked on doors so everyone understood that the British had set up camp in Tredyffrin, had taken over the Valley Forge, and planned to cross the Swedes Ford to march down through Whitemarsh and Germantown into Philadelphia, where they would capture our capital. They all believed the stories that they heard about the death and destruction the British brought with them, the civilians whose houses were taken over, their food and goods stolen to support the British army, their people tortured, their women raped, or worse.

Just about the only thing that concerned Connie about what she heard was that the British had set up camp in Tredyffrin. That was real close to her family's home in Paoli. She didn't pray much—or not at all—any more, but she said more than a few prayers once she heard that. Prayers for her mother, father, little sister, aunt and uncle. And, since she was praying, she threw in some prayers for her brothers. She knew that they were in the Pennsylvania Line, in the Continental Army, and she had heard that the Pennsylvania Line was somewhere in the area. She had heard that one of their battles had fizzled out the day of that heavy downpour last week and that the Army had moved north. So, if the Continental Army was moving north and the redcoats were moving south, that was fine with her. The battle for Philadelphia would probably be a bloody one, she thought, and her brothers didn't need to be involved in that.

As she watched more and more people fill the roads, there was a knock at her bedroom door.

"Miss Connie, Miss Connie," she heard.

Connie walked over the door and opened it. It was one of her girls, Antoinette.

"What is it Toni?" Connie asked.

"Sorry to disturb you," Toni said, "but we had another neighbor come by just now and tell us that the British were definitely on the march today and that they were headed across the Swedes Ford."

"Were they sure? They've been saying that they were on the march for the past few days now," Connie said.

"Yes, ma'am," said Toni, calling her ma'am even though Connie was only a few years older than her. "They said that one of their group saw them with their own eyes."

"Alright," said Connie, straightening out her robe.

Toni looked sheepish. "Are we going to leave, Ma'am?"

Connie looked at her and laughed. "Leave? Of course not."

Toni said, "But Ma'am, what I've heard about the British is that they won't be very nice to us when they get here."

Connie laughed again. "The British are men, aren't they?"

Toni looked puzzled, but said, "Yes."

"Well, if you know men like I know men, then we have nothing to be afraid of," Connie said. "Especially men who are thousands of miles away from their wives or girlfriends or mistresses or whatever they call them over there in England."

Connie wagged her finger at Toni. "If you know men like I know men, you know that men want sex," she said. "They can come to Germantown and burn down every house around here if they want to, but I guarantee you, they're not going to burn down this house."

"Why?" asked Toni.

Connie shook her head. Toni was not one of her brightest girls, although she might have been one of the prettiest.

"Because they're not going to burn down the house where they know they can get all the sex they want. Even though it is for a fee, which I'll make a smaller fee, just for them," said Connie. She laughed. "No, they won't burn us down."

"How will they know what we do here?" Toni asked.

Connie laughed again. "They'll know because we'll show them."

Toni shrugged and threw up both of her hands. "I don't know what you mean."

Connie said, "You don't have to know. You just have to follow," she said as she went to her closet. "Tell all the other girls to meet me downstairs in about half an hour. And tell them to put on their nicest dress, a dress that shows all of their assets."

"Oh," said Toni, laughing now. "Now I know what you mean."

"Good," said Connie. "Now go on and tell the girls." She touched Toni's dress. "And change that dress. You have better."

Toni said, "You're right. I sure do have better," smiling as she walked out of the door.

CONNIE WAS down on the first floor, finishing her breakfast when she saw the girls coming down the stairs.

"Gather in the front parlor," Connie said.

Toni came down first in a red and black dress that was cut low in the front and pushed her breasts together showing a good four inches of cleavage. Joanna wore a pink dress with white trim that fit tightly around her backside, surely her greatest asset.

Connie finished up her tea and went in the parlor for inspection. "Line up," she said. The girls moved into a line right next to the maple breakfront, the same as they did when any customer came in and wanted to see what girls were available that day.

Connie walked from girl to girl, looking at each closely up and down.

"Good job, Michelle," Connie said. "That yellow sets off your hair nicely."

"Go change, Stephanie," she said. "You need a lower neckline."

One by one, she inspected the girls. Most of them passed, since they already knew what their best assets were after putting them on display every night. Their fortunes depended on their making themselves as appealing as possible. They all knew, in some way, that doing so this day was one of the most important things they would ever do.

"Alright, ladies," said Connie. "You all look great." She walked up and down the row. "You know that most of our neighbors are heading out of town because they are afraid of what the British will do."

The girls nodded, most of them with some fear in their eyes.

"You know I'm not afraid of most things," Connie said, "and I'm not afraid of the British. They're men just like the ones who come in here every day, except they talk differently. And just like the men who come in here every day, they have one thing on their mind at just about all times. And what is that?" she asked.

"Sex," Toni called out.

"You're right, Toni," said Connie, giving her a wink. "Sex. Sex trumps war. Sex trumps just about everything." She kept walking. "And ladies, if there's one thing I know that you're good at, that's sex."

The girls all laughed and nodded their heads.

"Today, I believe that you will have to put on the best lineup of your lives," Connie said. "Our neighbors are running from the British and hope to not be at their homes when they arrive. Our strategy is different. When the British come, I want us to be very much at home. I want us to be on display. I want them to see what they could have." She waved her hands around, "And that is all of you. And maybe even me if there's a General or two that I have to pacify." She smiled.

"So, we're not going to run, ladies. We're going to wait. And we're going to welcome the British army like the ladies that we are," Connie said.

The ladies laughed again.

"So, girls. Take a seat. We have Tom on lookout outside, as usual. When he sees the British approaching, we will go out to welcome them."

The girls stayed inside and had time to eat lunch.

"Just eat a little, girls," said Connie. "And eat like ladies! Don't drop anything on those pretty dresses."

As they were finishing up, Tom ran inside. "They're coming! The sentry just rode by and said they were about ten minutes down the road."

"Ok, girls," said Connie. "Put down that food and get yourself looking your best. Grab some rouge and paint your lips and cheeks again."

The girls swung into action as Connie watched. "Hurry, hurry," she said.

When she was convinced that all the girls looked their best, she said, "Alright, ladies. We are going to go out there to the front porch and line up. You can sit down until we see the first British soldier. But as soon as I see a British soldier, you'll have to get up and stand on the porch, in formation, until every last British soldier marches by. I want some of you standing straight and those of you with the biggest breasts leaning forward on the rail, showing them off. Do you understand?"

The girls nodded that they did. Some of them still looked afraid.

Connie said, "Don't be afraid. Trust me. This will work. We will be safe for this entire war, whether Germantown is occupied by the redcoats or the patriots. I don't care. Men are men, whether their uniforms are red, or blue or green or pink."

She fluffed her skirt and then fluffed her long brown hair. "Now, follow me."

She led the girls out the front door to the front porch. She got them lined up and sitting nicely.

Tom yelled out, "There they are!" as he pointed to the far eastern part of the road. A row of soldiers, seven across, marched down the road. They had on green uniforms with green and white high hats and black feathers sticking out of the top.

"Hessians!" yelled Tom.

"Well, they ought to feel right at home in Germantown since they're Germans, too," said Connie. "I guess the redcoats are coming behind."

She turned around to her girls. "Smile girls, and we'll see if we can't get them to look over here." Then she turned around again, "And stick your chests out."

The Hessians marched by in an orderly and terrifying sight, with cannons and guns held at the ready. As intent as they were on facing front and obviously following orders, Connie noticed that some looked her way.

"Make eye contact if you can," she said to the girls. "Keep and hold their gaze. You know how to seduce."

As she and the girls fixed and locked on a target, she noticed that the orderly Hessians started to break their order. Some of the men looked so hard that they ran into the man beside, in front, or behind them.

"If they come up here, let me do the talking," Connie said, as she smiled from ear to ear.

The disciplined Hessians marched right on by. Then came a sea of red. The redcoats marched in orderly lines.

"Make eye contact," Connie yelled at her girls.

Little by little they saw the same trouble in the ranks that had happened with the Hessians. About twenty rows of redcoats passed by before three regular redcoats and what looked like one of their commanders in a more highly decorated uniform turned off from the march and turned his horse in the direction of Connie's house.

"Here we go, girls," said Connie. "Keep smiling and stick those chests out."

As they all did as instructed, the redcoats rode up to the front door, the commander bringing up the rear. Connie locked the commander in her eyesight as soon as he turned off the road.

When they reached within hearing distance of her door, Connie said, "Welcome to Germantown, sirs."

The redcoats took in a smiling Connie from head to toe, then they looked at the row of girls lined up.

"Say hello girls," Connie said.

The girls smiled, thrusting out their chests and backsides for those who were so endowed, and said, "Hello."

Connie twirled her hair and formed her red lips into a pout. She looked past the regulars and kept her eyes fixed on the man in the resplendent uniform lagging behind. "How can we help you General?" she called out as she moved her chest around. "You are a General, aren't you?"

The commander smiled at her and came closer, only a few inches behind the other redcoats.

He smiled and called out, "Yes, I am a General. General Howe."

"Well, I hope you'll come around and see us when you're in Germantown, General Howe," said Connie. She put her hand on her throat and ran a finger down to her cleavage. "Come and see me anytime," she said. "I'll make you feel right at home here."

The General looked at her and smiled again.

"And bring your friends," Connie said. She swept her hand in front of her girls. "My girls are pretty nice, too."

General Howe looked Connie up and down again and said to one of the other redcoats, "Colonel, make sure our boys understand that the ladies of this house here are friends of the crown and are not to be bothered while we make our camp in this fine city."

Connie just kept making eye contact and smiling. "Thank you, General," she said.

General Howe tipped his hat and said, "You will certainly see me again. And what is your name?"

"Connie," she said, smiling. "Please, General, call on me anytime."

The General nodded his head and said, "I certainly will do that." Then he tipped his hat and said, "Good day," as he turned his horse and rode away.

When the General was out of site, Connie breathed a sigh of relief. So did the other girls.

"See girls," she said, as she stayed looking down the road as the sea of red continued. "We'll be fine."

Under her breath she said, "But I don't know about our boys. I've never seen so many soldiers at one time," as the British invaded Germantown.

Connie and the girls stayed on the porch as the British invasion continued. A sea of redcoats marched by. Then there were a several rows of men in green and white with green and white feathers in their caps.

"Who are they?" asked one of the girls to Connie.

"I don't know myself, "Connie said. She looked at Tom. "Who are they, Tom?"

Tom shook his head and said, "They call them the Black Irish. They're British, but from the Ireland colony." As they continued to march in perfect time, Tom said, "They've got a bad reputation as being a ruthless fighting force."

Connie shivered when he said that. She didn't know why. "They give me the creeps," she said. "Let's hope we don't see what their reputation is all about."

"Very true, Miss," said Tom.

They all sat on the porch as the march continued. Cannons, musicians, wagons, all marched by without interference from anyone. One row marched by, and they waited about ten minutes for the next column to arrive. When fifteen minutes passed, and the invasion seemed over, Connie turned towards her girls. "Good job today, ladies," she said. "Like I said, I think we'll be safe. We got their attention." The girls smiled, and so did Connie.

"But," she said, "now that we have their attention, we have to keep it. I doubt whether we'll have any visitors this evening since I'm sure they have to try to figure out friend from foe here now. So, you can go inside and get some rest."

She ran her hand down her skirt. "But, I predict that we'll have some visitors tomorrow, so I want you to put on your second best dress tomorrow as soon as you wake up," she said. "I want you dressed early, because no telling the last time they've been with a woman, and they might be paying us a visit earlier than we expect. And we have to be ready."

The girls nodded their heads. "I don't want to be dramatic with you girls, but you know I'm going to be honest with you," Connie said. "I'm sure you all understand that our lives depend on your doing a good job for our British friends," Connie said.

The girls nodded and said, "We understand."

"Good," said Connie. "So go on inside and sleep well." She waved her hand as if dismissing them.

The girls went inside one by one. Connie stayed on the front porch with Tom. She had to calm her spirit. She didn't know why, but those Black Irish really got to her. Even from the porch, she saw something sinister and vicious in their eyes, in their march. "Shake it off," she said to herself. She couldn't afford to be afraid of any of them. Her life and her livelihood depended on opening her doors in the friendliest way possible to all men, British or patriot.

She regained her composure and said, "All right, Tom. I think we should call it a night."

"Yes, Ma'am," he said.

All of a sudden, a few shots of a gun erupted. They both looked over in the direction from which it came. It seemed like it was about a half a mile away, over on the road by the Wissahickon.

"Why would they be shooting?" Connie asked. "Who would they be shooting at? It seems like most of the patriots have left Germantown. Only the loyalists would be staying here now."

Tom continued to look over in that direction. "Maybe there were some stragglers," he said. "Or maybe they're just flexing their muscle, announcing to everyone that they're here."

"Anyone with a good pair of eyes would know that they were here," Connie said.

Tom laughed. "You know how men are," he said. "They have to mark their territory."

Connie laughed, too. "Believe me, I know. That's why I expect a visit tomorrow from a certain British General."

"You do know how men are," Tom laughed.

"I wouldn't have all this if I didn't" she said, smiling as she stretched her arms out and swept it over her territory.

Connie walked over to him, touched his arm and turned serious. "Anyway, Tom, will you be alright out here?" she asked. Normally, the thought wouldn't have crossed her mind. Tom slept outside guarding the house during the warm weather, and in the cold weather, he slept inside, with his body right behind the door.

"I'm sure I'll be fine, Miss," he said. "I think you had it right when you told the girls that if there was one house in Germantown that the British were going to leave standing, it was this one."

Connie shook her head. "Yes," she said. "I agree. And we'll just have to wait and see what happens to everything else around here," she said, as a few more shots rang out in the distance.

Connie wiped her eyes. "Get some sleep, Tom," she said. "No telling what tomorrow will bring."

"Right," said Tom. "And you do the same, Miss."

"I will," said Connie, as she turned, lifted up her skirt to step on to the step to the front door, knowing all the while that she was definitely not going to sleep well that evening.

The house came to life early in the morning. Since none of the girls had any customers the night before, the house was quiet for a change, and they all had a good night's sleep. Connie heard the footsteps on the floor above her earlier than usual. It seemed like the girls believed her when she told them that they would be safe, that her plan worked. She, however, wouldn't really believe it until the General came to visit, which she was expecting him to do later that day.

Connie picked out another dress that was cut low in the front and that fitted her tight across the backside. She paused as she sat at her vanity to begin rouging her lips and cheeks, and she hung her head. She sighed, and then looked straight at herself in the mirror. She realized that she was going to have to probably work harder at this profession than she had in a long time. After her southern gentleman bought her the house and she filled it with her own girls, she didn't have to spend all of her working time servicing different men. She was lucky enough to only service one man for the past several years, and she grew to see their times together not as work, but as the normal intimate time between a man and a woman who loved each other, even if he was married to someone else. She was glad that she didn't have a different man, or three or four or five or six different men, every night, as she had for years. She even felt for her girls sometimes when men who she knew to be unsavory just by looking at them came to the house looking for companionship. She always told her girls in those situations to just give the man what he came for and to keep the conversation and the charm to a minimum. The men were already getting more than what they usually did when they came to her house because her house had a reputation for having the best girls in Germantown, or Philadelphia for that matter.

As she looked at herself in the mirror, Connie hoped that she could still pull off the whore's act of making the man you were with feel like he was a king, like he had the biggest penis she had ever seen, and that whatever he was doing to her was satisfying her in a way unlike any other. That was, if he really wasn't any good in bed and if she really didn't enjoy it. Really, she hoped that she enjoyed sex with the general. That would make things easier for her. She wouldn't have to fake it. She actually could get those old feelings back again.

She hoped that her southern gentleman lover wouldn't hear about what she was getting ready to do. Just last week, the Continental Congress did as rumored—they left Philadelphia in advance of the British invasion and took up exile in Lancaster to continue doing the important business of keeping the colonies together and building this new nation. She hoped that her man would be too busy with his duties to have time to think that she might betray him when he was gone. But, if word reached him of

what she was doing, she hoped that he understood. Plenty of people had
to do things in war time that they would never do in peace time.

Connie picked up the small, thin brush next to her and ran it over the
rouge pot. She drew a red bow around her mouth and then filled it in
with the rouge. She picked up a different brush with thicker head and ran
that around the rouge pot. She brushed that on her cheeks.   She picked
up a horsehair brush and ran it through her hair. She looked at herself in
the mirror as she counted 100 strokes. When she finished, she fluffed her
long, dark hair so that is rested just about evenly on each shoulder. She
took another hard look at herself in the mirror and stood up. Time to get
ready for what might be the performance of her life.

# CHAPTER 26
# PAOLI

Betsey sat at the dining table with her parents Orland and Teenie and her Aunt Rochelle and Uncle Norman. All of them were exhausted. All of the other neighbors had left. They drank steaming mugs of hot tea in silence.

Their faces were drawn, haggard, and lined. Their eyes had the puffy dark circles of people who had too little sleep.

Orland wrapped his hands around his mug, letting the warmth soothe him. He looked up from the mug and at his family sitting around the table. They had the sad faces of loss. Allen's death was a terrible blow to all of them, but, they saw so much more death and loss in the past few days. They bore the weight of the loss of 50 to 60 sons. That is how many patriots were butchered, massacred, by General Grey and his British bastards in their neighbors' fields in Paoli. Allen's funeral was today. That was bad enough. But they all also knew that tomorrow, they were going to have to help bury the bodies of the boys who weren't from Paoli or nearby, the bodies of the boys whose families didn't or couldn't come to claim them and give them a proper burial back on their home soil.

Orland looked at the group sitting there and said, "We need better intelligence."

Everyone at the table looked up.

"Yes, I said it. We need better intelligence," he said. "If we knew what those bastards were planning, we could have warned General Wayne and the boys."

"Well, yes, of course," said Norman. "If we knew, we would have warned them, and the redcoats knew that. That's why they kept us all locked up at the Tavern and our neighbors in their houses. But we had a network. And it was working, up until the night of the massacre. They obviously kept their plans especially tight this time."

Orland said, "Yes, of course. But that's what I mean. We need intelligence that will let us know what's happening even if they are trying to keep it tight."

"The only way to do that is to have somebody infiltrate their camp," Norman said.

"That's right," said Orland.

"But, it seems like even our Continental boys had a hard time doing that," Norman said. "And they are supposed to have a good spy network."

"We have to build a better civilian network," said Orland. "We have to be able to get in their camps and get out. We have to be able to get next to their soldiers without them realizing what we're doing."

Teenie spoke up. "How are you going to do that?"

Orland said, "I've been thinking. You know that a lot of times they're out there stealing our food, but, depending on their commanding officer, they are ordered to buy food or provisions. We need to make sure that it's our people who are selling to them, our people who are getting in the camps, or at least close to them."

Norman shook his head and banged his mug on the table. "You know they don't trust us," he said.

Orland pointed at Norman and at himself. "Maybe they won't trust us men," he said. "But maybe they would trust a woman."

"What?" said Teenie, getting agitated.

"Wait," Orland said. "Hear me out. Maybe they wouldn't think that a woman would know what she was looking at or take notice of what she was hearing."

Rochelle said, "But maybe a woman would be in harm's way, and would be taken advantage of by these men who are thousands of miles away from the comforts of home, if you know what I mean."

Orland said, "I know what you mean, but did you see those women who followed our boys? Some of them looked like unsavory women, the types of women who would give the men the comfort they desired."

"Good lord," said Teenie. "I can't believe you're talking about this." She looked over at Betsey. "Especially around Betsey."

Orland looked at Betsey. "Well, I am. Especially around Betsey." He spoke to Betsey directly. "Betsey is old enough to understand."

Betsey chimed in. "That's right. I am." She gently placed her hand on her Dad's. "You know I've always wanted to help out more. And I feel that way even more so now after what they did to Allen," she said, as tears welled up in her eyes, again.

"I know you do, honey," Orland said.

"What do you think we should do, Dad?" Betsey asked.

Orland leaned in closer to everyone and said, "OK. Here's what I have in mind," as he shared his newly thought out plan.

# CHAPTER 27

# GERMANTOWN

Connie sat in the first floor parlor for most of the day. She told the girls to wait upstairs in their rooms. Tom was outside on the porch, their watchman, as usual.

Shortly after dusk, Tom burst in the door. "They're coming," he said to Connie as she sat there, just staring straight ahead, lost in her thoughts.

Connie jumped up. "Who, exactly?"

"It's three redcoats," Tom said.

"Alright," Connie said. "Get back out there and see what they want."

She wondered how the General wanted to play this. Was he sending the three as his advance guard to make sure everything was fine in the house, or was this just three men coming on their own for a good time? Time would tell, she thought to herself, as she fluffed her hair.

As she finished, Tom thrust the door open again, calling out, "Visitors, Miss."

Connie stood up as three redcoats entered her house. "Gentlemen," she said. "Good evening. How can I help you?"

One said, "We're here to search your house, Ma'am."

Connie looked at him wide-eyed.

"We don't mean you any harm. We're here on orders of General Howe," he said.

Connie just kept looking at him wide-eyed like she didn't understand.

"General Howe made your acquaintance yesterday afternoon, as I understand it," the soldier said. "And now he would like to pay you a visit."

Connie looked and nodded.

"But," said the soldier, "we need to search the house first and make sure it is safe."

Connie swept her arm across the room, "Do what you must," Connie said. "There's no one in here but my girls and me."

"Thank you, Ma'am," said one. "We'll go through and then be right out of your way."

"Take your time," Connie said, not meaning it. She was anxious for them to hurry up and search the house and clear it and then for General Howe to arrive.

The men started walking through the first floor.

Connie said, "Gentlemen, can I please just let the ladies know that there are men in the house so they are not startled by your sudden presence?"

"Yes, Ma'am," said one.

Connie walked to the front floor steps and called out, "Ladies. We have gentlemen visitors." Hearing that, the ladies walked out of their rooms and looked over the stair case.

The redcoats looked up, eyes wide. Connie agreed that her girls did look lovely.

She looked back at the redcoats. "Ok, I see that the girls are all decent. Please," she said, waving her hand around the room, "continue your search."

The men walked through the rest of the first floor and then eagerly went up the stairs to the second floor. The girls were all out of their rooms and lined up by now. They smiled widely at the men as Connie had instructed them earlier. The men went from room to room, finding nothing but beds, of course. They came downstairs. Connie stood there waiting for them.

"Are you satisfied?" she asked.

"Yes, Ma'am, we are," said the lead one.

"Good," said Connie. "We are friends of the Crown," she added, not exactly lying.

"That's good to hear Ma'am," said another. "That will make things much easier for you."

Connie nodded politely.

One of the soldiers turned to the other. "Go and get the General," he said.

Connie had to stop herself from smiling. One of the soldiers went outside. A few minutes later, he returned.

He walked into the room first and got Connie's attention. "May I present, General William Howe," said the soldier. Seconds later, in marched the leader of the British army in full dress uniform.

Connie looked at him and smiled. The General took Connie's hand and kissed it.

"I told you I'd be back," he said to Connie.

Connie smiled, thrust her chest out, and said, "I'm glad that you are a man of your word."

The general looked at his troops and said, "At ease, men. Wait outside, please." He kept his eyes on Connie as the men walked outside. When the last one walked out, he closed the door.

Connie continued to look straight at the General's eyes. This time, she stuck her hand out first for the General to take it. "Why don't you come with me, General?" Connie said. "I'm sure you could use some relaxation."

General Howe smiled as Connie led him upstairs to her private boudoir.

# CHAPTER 28
# PAOLI

Fred walked over to line up like the rest of the men in the 5th Pennsylvania. As he looked into their faces, he wondered if he looked as haggard as they did. He figured that he did. They all had been to hell and back a few days earlier on the fields that they used to play in as young boys without a care. But now, having seen their friends guts spilling out from holes made by 18 inch British bayonets, and their skulls broken and bashed in by the nails on the ends of the British rifles, eyes that used to dance with life and grow wide-eyed with enthusiasm and passion were now rimmed with the dark black circles and puffy bags of sad and sleepless nights and the wide-eyed dispassion of shock and horror. Their faces hollow from too little food were caked with dirt, and their uniforms, already dirty from days of march, were caked with now brown blood stains, some from their own blood and much from their fellow soldiers whose bodies had been targets for British bayonets.

For such a large group of men, the air was unusually quiet. Gone was the usual chatter as they walked to line up. The men walked in silence. Fred walked with wide, dead eyes looking down, tired and sad.

It was now three days since Allen and some 50 others were killed by the marauding force of some 5000 British soldiers. And in those three days, they had marched about 40 miles through mud and dirt, in confusion and sadness. Every time Fred lifted his foot, it felt like he was lifting a rock. Everything took so much effort. Even the simple tasks took a long time.

He didn't know how everyone else felt, but part of his problem was that now he was starting to wonder whether all of this was worth it. He only had one brother, and now he was gone.

He looked down at what he was wearing. He was just about covered from head to toe in blood, Allen's blood. He wished that he could take off that uniform or at least wash it out so that it was not a constant reminder that his little brother was dead. But there had been no time for anything, it seemed, but to keep marching, to get away from the British.

As he took his place in line, Fred stared straight ahead. This was his first line up without Allen. Usually, Allen was right next to him. Tears welled up in his eyes, but he didn't cry. Instead, he stared straight ahead, hoping that there was something afoot that would ease the fresh hell that he was living in.

Two Colonels stood in the field waiting for all of the men to line up. The colonels walked up and down the line, inspecting the troops. The colonels looked each man in the eye. Fred looked back, motionless.

Suddenly, Fred looked to his left. In a cloud of dust, General Wayne rode up on his white horse. Normally, the men would have cheered at the site of their general, but there were no cheers this time. Whether it was due to the men's obvious fatigue or to the word that had gotten around camp that General Wayne might have been warned about the British attack with enough time to properly prepare a defense or to retreat but that he did nothing, the line was eerily silent.

"Men," said General Wayne. "I know your hearts are heavy. I know your bodies are tired. I know your minds are sad. I know your minds are worried." He raised his musket in the air. "But, be encouraged. We are going to give you a chance to take revenge on the British for every one of our boys who was killed or wounded. The British have crossed the Schuylkill and entered into Philadelphia. And they have set up a large camp a few miles outside of Philadelphia in Germantown."

The men looked on in silence.

"We are moving towards the Germantown Road to engage them," said Wayne. "We will have a chance to avenge our fallen brothers. And when we confront them, we will return tit for tat. We will give no quarter."

With that, the dead started to live. The silent troops had taken in what they had just heard. After about a minute, one of them yelled out, "No quarter!" Then, man after man repeated it like a chant. "No quarter! No quarter!"

"We will avenge that affair," Wayne called out, raising his gun into the air. "So men, get ready! We march at dusk!"

Fred clapped along with the rest of the men. He could feel life coming back to his eyes, to his limbs. He could feel the fog in his head clear. Instead of confusion and doubt, he now had purpose. He was now clear. He would avenge Allen's death. He would drive his bayonet into a redcoat's body if he got that close, or shoot him dead if he didn't. Now, as he walked back to where he had been sitting, his legs felt lighter. The boulders were gone. The weight had been taken off of him.

When he returned to his spot, Fred grabbed a long metal stick and wrapped it with a piece of cloth that used to be off-white but was now close to black with gun powder stains. He stuck the stick down the barrel of his musket and hurriedly moved it up and down. He held the barrel up to his eyes and looked in to see if there were any obstructions from grapeshot or gunpowder that hadn't fired properly.

Satisfied that he had cleaned everything out from the inside, he began to work on the outside. He took the same cloth and wiped down the outside. He slid the cloth in every nook and cranny until it seemed like every piece of dirt and dust came off and attached to the cloth.

Then he lifted the bayonet from its holster and wiped the cloth over it. He wiped and wiped, trying to get it as clean as he could. He picked up a stone and ran it along the blade. He wanted the bayonet to be as sharp as possible when it went into whatever unfortunate redcoats were in front of him. He wanted to see the pained look on their faces that he saw on Allen's face when the bayonet went into his flesh. He rubbed the stone up and down the bayonet. Then he lightly slid his finger over the blade. His skin broke easily, and warm red blood poured from his finger.

"Good and sharp," he said to himself. He lifted the bayonet by its other edge and gently slid it into its place on the holster. When he was certain that the gun was as clean as he could get it, Fred slid the gun into the holster on his back.

"You all set?" asked Henry, his friend from Paoli who was also in his regiment.

"More than set," said Fred, as he stuffed ammunition into the pouches on either side of him.

# CHAPTER 29
# GERMANTOWN

Connie held General Howe's hand as she led him up the stairs. She opened the door to her boudoir and led him inside. When he had walked through the door, Connie gently closed it behind them. She put both hands on his arms now as she moved closer to him, straightening her back and thrusting out her chest. The General pulled her closer and put his lips on hers. Connie opened her mouth slightly as she pressed her lips against the general's. She moved her tongue around the inside of his mouth as she wrapped her arms around his neck. She let her fingers dance gently on his neck. She would kiss him as long as he wanted. Even though she knew that she would eventually be in charge of this scenario, she would let him appear to be in charge at first, as he was used to being, since he was a general.

When Howe pulled back for air, Connie stepped back a bit and smiled.

Howe smiled back as he took off the sword that hung from his sash. He put the sword by the chair next to the bed.

"Can I get you a drink, General?" Connie asked as she waved her arm towards the bed side table that was laden with an assortment of white and brown liquors in various size cut and etched crystal bottles.

General Howe asked, "Nothing that would cloud my head, is there?"

Connie said, "Not if you don't want it to be. I keep spirits here, of course, but I also keep water and lemonade."

"Good," said the general. "I'll take lemonade. I need to be in command of my faculties at all times."

"Of course you do," said Connie, although she knew that with her, he would very soon lose all the control that he had. She picked up one of her best crystal glasses that she had put in her room for just this occasion, and she poured the General a glass of lemonade.

"Refreshing," he said, as he drank it down quickly.

When he was finished, Connie walked over to her bed. The bed was covered with a blanket in the finest, softest silk, in the bright tomato red color that she knew excited men. She turned the blanket down, revealing matching red silk sheets from the Orient. She walked over to the General, who looked at her wide-eyed and excited, as his crotch bulged. Connie started unbuttoning the small seed pearl buttons in the front of her dress. When she reached the last one, she slid the top part of the dress down her arms and let it drop to the floor. She revealed her finest bustier, made of red and white silk and lace. It pushed her breasts up and out, barely containing them. The bustier hooked in the front with gold hooks. Connie looked over at the general. "General," she said, feigning innocence and inability. "Can you help me with these?" she asked as she slowly started to unhook the first one.

The general walked over, smiling. He placed his big hands on both sides of Connie's breast and began unhooking the bustier. He only unhooked a few when Connie's breasts truly spilled out over the top. He smiled, startled, and then quickly cupped them both in his hands. Then he bent down and put first one nipple in his mouth, swirled his tongue around the nipple and the soft flesh around it, and then did the same with the other.

"Um," said Connie, moaning as if that felt good. Howe unhooked the rest of the bustier and gently laid it on the bed. Connie stood there, back straight. Then she lifted her skirt to reveal black silk stockings held up by red and black silk garters.

"General," she said. "Can you help me with these?" she asked as she ran her hand up her legs, towards her upper thigh.

"Gladly," said the General, as he grabbed Connie's leg.

"Oh," said Connie. She steadied herself on the bed post. "I forgot about my shoes," she said, as she lifted up one foot and pointed her high-heeled black silk shoes towards the general.

He deftly unbuttoned and unlaced the shoes until he gently lifted them off Connie's delicate feet. Then he quickly slid his hand up Connie's thigh to the top of her garter.

I hope he's taking a good look at all that I have to offer down there, thought Connie, as she felt the General's hands loosen the garter. Then she thought, as much as he was smiling, he must have seen it.

Howe slid the garter down Connie's leg. Then he unrolled her silk stockings. As soon as the stocking was off her leg, he pulled her closer and put his lips on her thigh. He kissed her thigh, first tenderly, then eagerly. Connie ran her fingers through his hair as he did.

"Can you take off the other one?" she asked softly. The general complied.

When both stockings were off, Connie turned her back towards him. "Can you unbutton this?" she said, pointing to the cummerbund style waist around the skirt.

The general came up behind her, first cupping his hands on her breasts. Then he slid his hands down to the cummerbund and began unfastening the six or seven pearl buttons that held up her skirt. He unbuttoned the last one, and Connie turned around. She shimmied her hips from side to side a bit as she slid the skirt to the floor. The only piece of clothing that she had left on her body was a thin silk panty covering her private area. Of course, it was red.

As General Howe looked on, Connie put both hands on either side of the panty.

"Help me out of this, will you?" she asked, as she lustily looked at the general, lips slightly parted and wet after her having licked them. She gently took the general's hands and placed one on either side of the panty. Then she moved his hands down as the panty slid down her legs and to the floor. Connie lifted one foot and then another as she stepped out of her panties, now completely naked. She stepped back and lay down on the bed.

She stretched out her arms and legs, like a cat stretching itself awake or asleep. She looked straight into Howe's wide eyes. "Join me, General," she said, as she moved her arm over the space next to her.

Howe quickly began the process of taking off his uniform. Connie didn't rise to help him this time. She wanted him to keep his eyes focused on her. To keep his thoughts focused on what he was going to get when he joined her in the bed. Connie licked and bit her lips as if in great anticipation. When Howe was down to his underpants, Connie looked straight at his crotch. She had hoped that the bulge that she had seen in his pants was going to be big enough so that she would at least enjoy herself, if only slightly, while he was her client. The bigger it was, the more she enjoyed it, and the less she had to act. As he stepped out of his briefs, Connie smiled, genuinely this time. It looked like this wasn't going to be as bad as she thought.

Howe moved over towards the bed. Connie put her arms up as she pulled him on top of her. She'd let the General be on top for a while, she thought, until she turned him on his back and took control of the situation using every trick that she had learned from those French whores who had worked with her in Philadelphia.

# CHAPTER 30

# OCTOBER
# GULPH MILLS AND REBEL HILL

James and Daniel were as busy as they'd ever been. They dodged the bullet of having their food and possessions stolen by the British on their march to Philadelphia because they did march into Philadelphia down the Germantown Road and away from Rebel Hill. Little by little, they brought back out things that they needed for daily living, especially working. With the British some 14 miles away in Philadelphia, the mills in the Gulph were back at full activity working for the patriots. James and Daniel had enough orders for horse shoes to keep them busy around the clock. The fires at their shop seemed to burn constantly, just like the fires at the mills all around them.

But James looked forward to tomorrow, which was Sunday. He and Daniel worked almost around the clock six days a week, but Sunday was their day of rest, just like it was the Lord's day of rest. James would go to the slave church down near the Hannah Plantation and spend as much time with Ruth as he could. Daniel went to the white church down at the bottom of the hill with his family.

The sun started to set, making it too difficult for them to keep working. James gathered up the tools and put them inside the shop. He stirred the pot of beans that he was cooking over the main fire. He already knew the answer, but he was too polite not to ask.

"Do you want some Daniel?" James asked.

Daniel said, "No thanks. Mom is cooking a big meal tonight. There's a big supper at church tomorrow, and she's killing two birds with one stone. So, I guess I'll have my pick of some good food when I get home."

"That sounds real nice," said James. "We should have some good food at our church tomorrow, too. It's the first Sunday, and besides taking the Lord's Holy Communion, we try to give thanks that we made it through another month."

Daniel nodded. "That's especially true with everything that's been going on around here. The British killing all of those boys up in Paoli, and then taking over Philadelphia and putting all of those people out of their homes in Germantown if they hadn't left town already."

"That's right," said James. "We're fortunate they didn't come this way." He gave the pot another stir. "And let's hope it stays that way."

"Truer words have never been spoken friend," Daniel said. He hung his gloves on the wall.

James put the lid on the pot of beans and put it into his wagon. "Well, you enjoy your day, and I'll see you on Monday." James took the reins, lightly kicked the horse, and it started off down the road.

WHEN HE reached his cabin, he grabbed a piece of cloth and wound it around the bean pot's handle. It was still red hot. Just the way he liked it. He opened the door to his cabin and put the pot on the wooden table in the middle of the room. He built that table along with just about everything else in the place. His utensils hung on the wall. He walked over and picked up a spoon and dusted it off. Then he sat down to the table to dinner. The dried pork that he had thrown in with the dried beans had filled out and now looked like meat freshly cut and cooked to perfection.

He bowed his head and said, "Dear Lord. Make us thankful for this food we are about to receive. These and all other blessings we ask in Jesus' name. Amen." Even though he was eating alone, he never stopped saying the grace just the way the slaves said it at the plantation whenever they had the opportunity to eat together. They were all truly thankful for an opportunity to sit down together and eat a meal in a civilized manner just like the white folks they served. Too often, they worked at all hours of the day and late into the night making their owners lives comfortable while theirs were miserable. When he was a slave, for six days a week, he usually ate his dinner sitting outside the back door or in the field or on the back of a wagon. Only on Sundays, their day of rest, was he able to eat dinner at a table, surrounded by the other slaves, including the woman he loved, Ruthie. So, yes, he was truly thankful to be a free man, sitting at a table eating a meal. He prayed in the plural, imagining Ruthie sitting right there with him. She would make his "I" into "us."

After he finished eating, James went over to the leather chest he had made. He opened it up and took out his good shirt. He only wore it to church on Sunday or to a funeral, out of respect. When he was finished wearing it, he took it off, heated up a kettle of water, boiled it clean, and hung it up to dry. When it was fully dry, he took it down, folded it, and put it back in the chest.

Then he reached under his bed and pulled out his good pair of shoes. He only wore them on Sundays and to funerals, too. He grabbed a piece of tallow and rubbed it on a cloth. He rubbed it back and forth all over the shoe until he could see his reflection in it. Then, he walked over to the chair by the back door and ran his hand down his good pants. They still had the nice crease that he liked to put in them over at the shop, using one of the tools as an iron. Then he selected a belt from one of the many that were hung on nails on the cabin wall and polished the leather with the tallow and shined the buckle with a bit of polish that he used for the horse shoes.

When he was convinced that everything was in order for Sunday, James went to bed smiling. Tomorrow he would see his Ruthie.

# CHAPTER 31

# LOWER MERION TOWNSHIP

James drove his wagon down Rebel Hill, waving to neighbors as he passed, and on to the Gulph Road. Traffic on the road was light since the mills were closed on Sunday. There were only a few other wagons out. He rode for about thirty minutes until he came to the main entrance to the Hannah Plantation. Massive oak trees lined either side of the wide driveway. It was beautiful anyway, but especially so this time of year as some of the leaves were changing color. The leaves made a tall red, yellow, orange and green canopy. James looked over at the main entrance, but he dare not enter that way. The servant's entrance was in the back, off of the main road. And even though he was no longer a servant, he wasn't exactly an invited guest. Even though he was a free man, you had to have a reason to go on to the Hannah Plantation. Most of the outsiders came to buy the tobacco that was grown there. But Mr. Hannah had let the Methodists set up a church for the slaves in the back of the property. Even though the freed slaves reminded the slaves of their condition, Mr. Thompson didn't mind them going to church together. He didn't mind that seeing the freed ones would make the slaves think of and want their freedom. He had said that the only way he would free his slaves is if they or someone else bought their freedom so, if his slaves wanted freedom bad enough to find someone to buy it for them or to figure out a legal way to buy it for themselves, what did he care? He could always buy more slaves. They were property to be bought and sold, not people who had feelings that mattered.

James rode for a few minutes more down the Gulph Road and turned onto a side road.

After a minute he came upon an entrance that wasn't nearly as grand as the main one. There were trees on either side, but the entrance was unkempt and the bushes and trees on either side of the road were a bit overgrown. James steered the horse down the road until he came to a group of ten or fifteen log cabins. A few children ran around. They stopped when the wagon pulled closer.   James raised his hand and waved. "Good morning, there," he said. The boys looked up. Then they ran over to the wagon and ran by James as he pulled his wagon up next to the fourth cabin.

"He's here," one of them yelled as he ran into the cabin.

James jumped off the horse and tied its reins up to the bar that was out in front.  As he wrapped the reins around for the second time, he heard her.

"James!"

He looked up and smiled. It was Ruthie. Her long black hair was pulled back in to a ponytail, and a yellow ribbon peaked out from behind her head.  She wore a bright yellow long dress with a white apron in front. Her skin, which was the color of the caramels he might have every once in a while as a treat, glistened as if she rubbed it with oil, which she probably did.

Ruthie ran over to James and wrapped her arms around his waist. He wrapped his arms around her shoulder. Then he pulled back and looked her up from head to toe. He smiled at what he saw, pulled her close, and kissed her.

"Oooh, look at them," said the boys as they danced around them and pointed. James might as well have been deaf. He was oblivious to their taunts and jeers. His full attention was focused on Ruthie. He would have stayed kissing her there forever if she hadn't stopped.

"I see you really missed me," Ruthie said as she pulled back.

"I always miss you," said James. He ran his fingers through her ponytail, gently wrapping a curl around his big finger.

"How's it all coming?" Ruthie asked, looking up at him in anticipation.

"It's coming along nicely," he said. "This was a good week. Daniel and I were really busy. With the British in Philadelphia and the Continental Army back out around here, over the Matson's Ford near Whitemarsh, we've been real busy making things for them. Horse shoes, bridles, bits, bullets and even a bayonet or two."

Ruthie smiled.

"If things keep going this way, I should have enough to buy your freedom in about six months," he said. "As long as this is the only part of the war that we see, we'll be fine."

Ruthie squeezed his hand. "I can't wait to be with you," she said. "Some days this place wears on me so," she said, eyes downcast.

James knew that was an understatement. Ruthie worked in the plantation house as a cook. While she wasn't exposed to the elements and the harshness that she would have been exposed to had she been in the field, working in the kitchen was not easy. She was almost always on call, as the masters had to eat breakfast, lunch, and dinner, and entertain late into the night anytime they had a whim to. The kitchen was a hot and steamy place usually. While it was comfortable in winter, it could be unbearably hot in the summer, spring and fall. The large kettles they cooked in were heavy to lift and to move, as she and the other women in the kitchen had to. And, she was still always at the mercy of the men in the house at any time. James knew that Ruthie was good at ducking and dodging and keeping herself busy on other things as much as she could, but she was an attractive woman. It tore James up inside to think that one of the masters had his way with Ruthie, but he didn't delude himself. Just about every slave woman there had had a run in with one of the white men on the plantation, and just about everyone who could have gotten pregnant was or did. Why should Ruthie be any different? When he was still on the plantation, he'd seen her crying every once in a while. When he asked her why, she would never say why. The look in her eyes told him everything he needed to know but didn't want to know. He didn't want to think it, but secretly, he dreaded what he might hear from her on one of his weekly visits. He wanted to be the first man to give her a baby, but he knew that if he wasn't, he would love Ruthie's baby the same as if it was his own. Slave men had been doing that for years. And, she was, after all, still a slave.

James put his arm around Ruthie and walked her towards the cabin. "Come on. We should get going to church. I'm sure you have some food in there that you need me to carry," he said, as they walked inside.

The small cabin was loaded up in one corner with kettles and baskets of food for the first Sunday supper. There was no shortage of food at Hannah. The master was prominent and had connections. He always managed to get whatever they needed, and then some. Plus, as large as the plantation was, there were a lot of places to hide food if any of the armies came foraging.

James pulled the cover back from one basket and saw his favorite—fried chicken. He took one hand and reached in for the wing he saw on top. But he wasn't quick enough. Ruthie smacked his hand.

"You have to wait, honey," she said, smiling.

"You know how hard that is?" James said. "You're the best cook around here."

Ruthie smiled and said, "I know." Then she gave her man a kiss. "Alright then," she said. "Go ahead and take a wing. But just one."

"Thank you darling," said James, as he reached over her shoulder and picked up the biggest wing he could find. He took a bite and said, "Mmm. You sure can cook." He finished off the wing quickly as Ruthie looked on, happy that her man was happy.

"Alright," said James, as he put the wing bones in the waste basket. "Let's get going."

He loaded up two armfuls of food and carried it to his wagon. Then he returned and did it again.

When all the food was loaded, he extended his hand to Ruthie, who stood next to the wagon, looking at him with a happy look on her face.

"Careful now," he said, as she stepped up to sit next to him. The church wasn't all that far away, but it was too far to walk and carry all of the food that they had. They ran into groups of other slaves walking towards the church.

"Ride?" James asked constantly.

There was no sense in these slaves walking when they could be riding, James figured. Some of the slaves were so dead tired and worn down and beat up that it was a wonder they could even walk the short distance to the church. It didn't take long for the back of his wagon to fill up with slaves. Those who got in first held the food on their laps to make room for the others.

In less than a half mile, the wagon pulled up to the church. From the outside, the church looked like two or three cabins put together with a cross on the top. There was a window on each of the three sides. There were late-blooming flowers out front. The slaves had landscaped it so that the little garden in front looked beautiful in every season. They didn't have much that they could call their own that was beautiful, but the church was theirs. No white people were going to be going there. Their preacher was a freed slave who traveled up from Philadelphia every week to bring them the word of God. For a few hours once a week, they could block out the harshness of life and receive some hope.

James hitched the wagon to the post in front. "Hey Paul," he said. "Hello Donald," he said, as he greeted the others. He knew most of them well. They were like family. They were basically the only family that he knew since he was taken away from his family in South Carolina when he was young and sold to a master who moved up north to Pennsylvania. Slaves' families became whatever other slaves were around them; there was no standing on formalities for most of them.

They walked in to the church, greeting everyone. As soon as they crossed the threshold, though, their voices became quieter. The slaves revered the Lord and were happy to be in the house of the Lord one more time. A few of the slaves with banjos took their places at the front of the church. They played music as the others filed in and took their seats. When almost every seat was full, a voice from the back said, "God is in his holy temple. Let us rejoice and be glad in it." The music stopped and everyone stood up. Reverend and Mrs. Johnson appeared at the back of the church. Reverend Johnson held his Bible up in the air, and Mrs. Johnson held on to his arm. He started singing the opening notes of "Great God of Wonder" as the banjo players picked up the medley. The others in the congregation sang along as Rev. and Mrs. Johnson walked to the front of the church. Mrs. Johnson took a seat in the second row on the right, and Rev. Johnson stood in the front.

"Welcome to the House of the Lord," he said.

Choruses of "Amen" and "Praise the Lord" filled the sanctuary.

They sang a few hymns before Rev. Johnson began his sermon.

"Our text for today is Galatians 5:1," he said. He read the verse to the congregation. Most slaves couldn't read and very few had Bibles. "Stand fast therefore in the liberty wherewith Christ hath made us free, and be not entangled again with the yoke of bondage."

"Our word for today is Freedom," the Reverend said. "The Israelites suffered in bondage to Pharaoh. God told Moses to lead the Israelites out of bondage. God did not approve of the suffering that was inflicted on the Israelites. God is a just and delivering God. He does not want his people to suffer."

As Reverend preached this sermon on freedom, the slaves looked around at each other. Every man who was a slave wanted to be free, no doubt. But this was the first time they heard freedom preached in the church.

Reverend continued, "We are now in the midst of a war for freedom. It has affected all of us. The British now occupy Philadelphia trying to stop the colonists from taking their freedom. The Continental Army is camped not far from here, continuing their fight for freedom."

He closed the Bible. "But what freedom is the Continental Army fighting for? Their own? Yes, that's for sure. But are they fighting for your freedom? Do they see the injustice in holding men and women in bondage while they fight against the bondage that the British are holding them in?"

"Has God spoken to them? Do they read the scriptures like I just read them to you?" he said. "They have chaplains who travel with them, who give their soldiers the word of God as they sit in camps, waiting to engage the enemy. They have priests who open their sessions in the Continental Congress as they debate about what type of new country this will be."

"But still, men and women are in bondage," Reverend said as he walked from one end of the church to the other. "Let us pray that God speaks to these men—General George Washington and all of his generals, John Adams, Benjamin Franklin, Thomas Jefferson, Mr. Widener—as he spoke to Moses."

Then he closed his Bible. "Let my people go means let all of the people be free," Reverend said. "Amen."

The slaves said, "Amen" as was customary, but they looked at each other with wide, surprised eyes.

The rest of the service continued as usual. At the end, Reverend walked over towards Mrs. Johnson and held out his arm. She rose, took his arm, and they walked down the aisle toward the back of the church. The rest of the congregation rose and walked out in relative silence.

James held Ruthie's hand as they walked down the aisle. He reached down to whisper in her ear, "Did I just hear Reverend Johnson criticize the patriots and preach against slavery?"

Ruthie said in a whisper, "Yes. I can't believe it."

"I can't either," said James. He looked at his male friends as they walked out. They weren't used to hearing their slavery being compared to Egyptian slavery and the patriots being compared to Pharaoh. The masters might let them go to church, but this was certainly not what they wanted them to hear.

Rev. Johnson waited in a receiving line at the back of the church. When James reached him he echoed what a number of the others had said, "Mighty fine sermon, Reverend." Then he added, as did others before him in a low whisper. "But please be careful."

Reverend Johnson said, "God is on our side, James. And let my people go does mean all people."

James just nodded, but what he wanted to say was "I sure hope so."

AS THE rest of the congregation went outside, conversation grew louder. James walked over to where a group of slave men were talking.

Donald said, "Reverend's word sure has me thinking."

"Me, too," said Paul. "My master talks all the time about freedom, but here I still am. He sure doesn't mean my freedom. I knew that. But Reverend raises the question 'why not'? If he's fighting for his freedom, why isn't he fighting for my freedom?"

"Because that's not the way it is," said Steven.

"Why not?" asked James. "More importantly, why shouldn't it be?"

George said, "You're right about that James. Why shouldn't it be?"

The conversation continued for a few more minutes until one of the women came out and called the men to supper. It was a warm fall day, so they ate outside on benches and tables that the men had built with pride. Everybody was talking about freedom. It was always on the slaves' minds anyway, and now they had a fresh way to talk about it.

After they finished eating, the women started cleaning and packing up. The men kept talking. As the sun set, Ruthie walked over to James. She put her arm on his shoulder. "Looks like I have everything packed up now," she said. She didn't say that she was ready to go because she never was. Not away from James.

James leaned in and rested his head against her body. She hugged him lightly.

"Alright, fellas," he said to the other men at the table. "Seems like it's time to be moving on." James stood up as the other men at the table shouted their goodbyes. He walked hand in hand with Ruthie over to the table with the ladies' baskets and kettles.

"These here," Ruthie said, as she pointed to a pile on the right side.

James picked up all but one or two this time. With no food in them, he wouldn't have to make a second trip. Ruthie picked up one empty basket in each hand and followed him to the wagon. James placed the containers in the back and arranged them so they'd stay upright during the trip. He helped Ruthie up into the front seat.

"Anybody want a ride," he said as he turned around to the people gathered behind him.

"I do," a few of the women called out.

"Well, come on," James said gently. Then devilishly, "Or do you need me to come and get you after eating all of that fine food that you ladies cooked."

Ruthie hit him on the arm. "James, don't say that," she said, smiling.

"They know I love them," James said in a louder voice so the older women who were walking towards him could hear. They obviously heard him because they smiled from ear to ear.

James helped the women up into the back and made sure they were all settled. Then he unhitched the horse, climbed up into the front cab, and started off down the road. One by one, he dropped his few passengers off at their cabins. As he reached Ruthie's cabin, he patted her hand. It was always hard to leave. He pulled the wagon up next to her hitching post and tied up the horse. Then he grabbed the baskets and kettles and walked in behind her. The woman that Ruthie lived with hadn't returned from the church yet. She worked in the kitchen, too, with Ruthie, and she liked to take her time walking on her own accord when she could.

"Reverend Johnson's sermon really made me think, James," she said as she put her baskets on their small wooden table. She turned towards James with anger in her eyes. "Here they are fighting a war for freedom, but I'm still not free. Mr. Hannah is out there supporting the patriots at the same time he's holding all of us here," she said, waving her arms around the tiny cabin.

"I know," said James. "Reverend was right. It doesn't make sense when you put it together like that." He took Ruthie in his arms. "But what can we do about it, honey? You know the white man gets his way. Mr. Hannah said that if you want to be free, you have to pay for it. And that's what I'm trying to do." He held her close and patted her back. "We're nothing to these slaveholders. I'm sure their preachers told them about Moses and Pharaoh and letting my people go. Shoot," he said. "They can pick up the Bible and read it, so they've probably read it, too. But you know they don't really think of us as people, people who think and feel and love just like they do. They think of us like they think of my horse or mule or a cow out in the field. Animals. That they own. "

He went on. "So when they're out there fighting for their freedom, they're not out there fighting for the freedom of their dog or their horse or their cow, are they?"

Ruthie said softly, "No."

"To them, we aren't any different," he said. "So what does it matter? As far as I'm concerned, whoever wins this war doesn't mean half as much to me as how soon can I get you free. If these white folks was to change their mind and say that their side would free all of the slaves, I'd pick up a gun and join General Washington right now, now that they've at least admitted that we're smart enough to shoot a gun and follow some orders and fight just like any man. But I don't hear that." He stopped embracing Ruthie and pulled back to look into her eyes. "So, unless I hear something like that, that war is really no concern of mine."

Ruthie sighed. "I guess so," she said. "But it does make you think."

"For a minute, honey," he said. "Only for a minute. What I think about is the day I'm going to be able to ride you out of here a free woman. Then I'm going to ride you straight to Reverend Johnson and ask him to marry us right then and there. No waiting."

Ruthie looked up and kissed him.

"That's what I'm thinking about," James said, as he kissed her back.

# CHAPTER 32
# GERMANTOWN

Connie entertained General Howe about every other night. The other days, she oversaw a steady stream of British officers who visited her girls. The house was alive again, and money flowed as it did in the days before her best customers started fleeing from Philadelphia and Germantown in advance of the British. Connie wondered what her benefactor was doing now, in exile in Lancaster, but she didn't dwell on it. She had bills to pay and a life to make. Now, she was dependent on the British for that. And, judging by the look of men coming in and out of her door, she was doing just fine.

"Go and tell Thomas to come in here for a minute," Connie said to one of her girls who was eating her breakfast in the kitchen. A few minutes later, Thomas appeared at the kitchen door.

"Ma'am?" he asked. "You called for me?"

"Yes," Connie said. "We've got to get some more food in here."

Thomas said, "That's not going to be easy right now. There's thousands of redcoats out here eating up anything they can get their hands on. There's no market anymore, you know, and they've taken over the empty houses that might have had some food stored in them. There's nothing here in Germantown."

Connie's brow furrowed with concern. "Nothing?" she asked. "Thomas you know everyone and everything up here, and if there's food to be found, you know where to find it. Are you telling me that there's no secret stash, no secret market that we can get to up here?"

Thomas shook his head. "No, not up here. I'm telling you that," he said.

"Well how is this British Army feeding itself?" Connie asked. "They have to get food from somewhere."

"The only place where they are getting their food right now is Philadelphia, and it's scarce down there, too. The Continentals have the port blocked so supply ships can't get in or out. If the food wasn't in the city a few weeks ago or if people aren't bringing it down from west, east or north of here, it's not getting in."

Connie threw her hands up in the air. "So you're telling me that if I want to buy any food I've got to go into Philadelphia, and probably pay way more for it than it's worth?"

Thomas shook his head up and down. "That's about the truth of it."

"But with all of these soldiers out here? I know it must not be that easy to move around. And, I'm sure they're checking wagons in and out of Germantown and Philadelphia for that matter."

"Yes," said Thomas. "There are some checkpoints."

"Well, we've got to get through," Connie said. "And then we've got to keep what we've got."

"We'd need an armed guard for that," Thomas said.

Connie held one finger to her head. "And I know just the man who can give us one," she said.

Thomas smiled and said, "Oh, your friend! He's the one who could do it for us."

Connie raised her index finger and waved it from side to side. "No, I'm the one who can do it for us. He's the one who's going to make it happen."

Thomas rubbed his hands together and smiled.

LATER THAT evening, General Howe showed up. Connie treated him to his usual respite from the war.

"You are nothing short of amazing," Howe said, as he stroked Connie's long, dark hair as she rested her head on his chest.

Connie had pulled out a few more things from her sexual bag of tricks. She had planned to roll them out later, but she really had to get food for her house, and she needed her full arsenal of pleasure. Connie looked up at the general with the wide, doe eyes of an adoring woman.

"You are the one who's amazing," Connie said, as she stroked his chin with her hand. "You keep making me think of ways to please you," she said, only half lying.

General Howe smiled. What man didn't like to be told that he was the greatest?

"I just hope I can keep it up," Connie said. She frowned slightly and said, "I have to be well-fed to keep up with you, and my house is just about running out of food."

The General looked at her. "Really?" he asked.

"Really, "Connie said somberly.

"Well we can't have that now, can we?" he said.

"I hope not," she said. "But we only have enough left for a few days," she said, as she stroked his face and looked softly and lovingly into his.

"I like a little meat on the bone," he said, squeezing her buttocks. "It gives you curves in all the right places."

"That's right," Connie said, as she ran her fingers down his chest. "Me and my girls. Your officers seem to be having a good time, too."

"Yes, they are," said the General. "We all need this type of comfort."

"And we want to keep providing it for you, but we can't if we're hungry," Connie said, as she moved her fingers down to his crotch. "I need to eat more than this," she said, as she wrapped her fingers around his penis, "although it is truly one of the finest delicacies I have ever had."

The General moaned as she squeezed harder.

"Yes," he said.

"Can you help me?" Connie said, as she put one finger in her mouth to wet it and then moved it down to his penis, where she moved that finger in a circular motion around the tip of the penis.

"Definitely," said the General as he closed his eyes with pleasure.

"Let me tell you what I need," said Connie as she squeezed her fingers together and moved them up and down the General's now very hard penis.

THE NEXT morning, Connie woke up and put on a traveling dress—nothing fancy that would get too dirty on the dirt roads, just comfortable. Serviceable. She had one of her girls help her gather all of the baskets, kettles and totes that they could find in the house. They sat them on the kitchen table. When Connie was convinced she had everything in the house, she had one of the girls go get Thomas.

"Thomas, we're going into the city today," she said. "To market. With a guard."

Thomas' eyes widened. He looked at the collection of containers assembled on the table.

"Really?" he asked.

"Really," said Connie. "He should be here any minute, with orders from General Howe to anyone to let us pass unmolested. Orders that state that if anyone dares to take anything out of our cart once we've left market, he will be shot without a trial."

"True?" asked Thomas.

"True," said Connie. "So come and get these containers in to the cart. We can fill up everything we could find."

Thomas clapped his hands together and smiled. He picked up several baskets and cloth totes and headed out of the back door towards the carriage. Once they loaded all of the containers, a redcoat appeared.

"Mrs. Roberts?" he asked as he approached Connie.

"Yes, sir," she said. "And you are right on time. Nine o'clock am, as promised."

"Yes, Ma'am," said the guard. "I dare not be late."

"I imagine that's right," said Connie, as she thought about the wrath that General Howe would bring down on his poor soldier if he stood in the way between the General and a well-fed woman, full of curves, ready to give him some of the best sexual experiences of his life.

The soldier climbed into the cab of the wagon. Tom helped Connie up to the seat next to the soldier, and Tom climbed in the back. The soldier started down the Germantown Road. Their wagon blended right in with the others around them. Most of them were driven by redcoats, too. They carried food or animals or cannons or guns or men. Connie thought that Germantown looked like a colony full of red ants, there were so many redcoats clogging the road. The doors of many of the other well-kept mansions on the Germantown Road were open, with red coated soldiers walking in and out. Red coated soldiers lolled along the front yards in such numbers that front yards looked red and white rather than the green that should be dominating at this time of year. At some houses, horses had worn down the grass by eating it or just by walking around. Besides the redcoats, Germantown was largely deserted.

The crowded Germantown Road led to crowded roads all the way down to Philadelphia. Yet, besides, the redcoats, Connie saw very few regular folks on the roads or off of them. Many houses had porches in the front where, at this time of year, with the warm and sunny Indian summer days, men, women and children would sit, fanning themselves, having a meal, or just enjoying the weather in advance of the cold that was sure to come. Now, there were redcoats everywhere, crowding the porches and the lawns.

Every mile or so, there was a roadblock for seemingly anyone who wasn't in the King's Army. All of the horses and carriages would be lined up on one side of the road, and people on foot would be lined up on the other side. The redcoats would search the bodies and the belongings of those on foot and the insides of the carriages. Beside each stop was a pile of goods. If the redcoat doing the searching liked what he found, he took it and added it to the pile. Connie could hear cries of protest from those who had their goods seized and see them waving their arms or stomping their feet in protest. But, at each roadblock, the redcoat driving the wagon with Connie and Tom would be waved around and allowed to continue down the road with the rest of the redcoats. Connie was glad she thought up what she did. If she had managed to get into the city herself and find food for her house, the redcoats probably would have seized it and added it to their pile.

The pedestrian crowds walking the streets grew more plentiful as they rode in to the main part of Philadelphia. Connie was amazed that there were still so few people than were normally on the streets, and as she looked at those going by, she caught herself looking into faces to see if any of them were of Peg or any of the girls from the old house where she worked and first got her start.

"Which market are you taking us to?" Connie asked.

"We're going down to the one near 2nd and Market," the soldier said. "That's the one that's feeding the King's Army here. You can't find a lot of food all in one place anywhere else."

"I'm sure that's right," said Connie, as she looked at what seemed to her to be an unusually large number of ragged men, women and children holding out their hands, begging for food. Their drawn, gaunt faces were the result of too little food, too little sleep, and too much worrying. For a minute, Connie felt sorry for them, but she realized that was futile. It was obviously survival of the fittest time, and she was nothing if not a survivor.

A line of redcoats with guns drawn stood outside the market at 2$^{nd}$ and Market Streets. There was another line of beggars and plain folk standing there shouting, "Let us in! Please let us in!" The redcoats guarding the food frowned at the poor crowd or at least looked at them with no emotion. If anyone came too close, a redcoat would point the gun at the person and thrust forward, like he was ready to use his bayonet. "We're hungry!" they'd yell, to no effect. No one who wasn't in a red and white uniform got in.

The driver drew the carriage closer. As he did, a redcoat approached. "State your name and your business," he ordered.

The driver said, "My name is Private Wellington, and I'm here on direct orders of General Howe to allow this lady to buy food at the market." Wellington handed the guard the paper with his orders from General Howe.

The guard looked it over and then looked over at Connie. Connie looked at him, holding her head up high, looking him over like she was his superior. She was there on orders of General Howe, so she felt that she didn't have to cow tow to a regular guard.

The guard looked Connie up and down, and then he nodded in acknowledgment, "Ma'am," he said. He looked at Thomas sitting in the back of the cart. "And who's this back here?"

Wellington answered, "This is her boy. She'll need help besides me."

Tom tipped his hat at the guard and smiled.

The guard looked at Tom. Then he looked at Wellington. He said, "Alright then." He pointed to an area right outside the main entrance to the market. "Hitch your wagon up over there." Then he turned to the two guards who stood directly in front him and said, "Let these three pass." The guards nodded and moved to either side as Tom helped Connie out of the carriage. They grabbed an assortment of pouches and a small wagon that Tom could drag behind him to carry their loot in, and the three of them walked inside.

"MY GOD," said Connie as she looked straight ahead. "I see why all of those people were lined up outside trying to get in." There was stall after stall of vegetables, fruit, flour, and dairy. Whole chickens and pigs hung from wooden poles. Milling around each stall was a group of redcoat soldiers two and three deep, shouting out their orders and stuffing their bounty in to their sacks.

Wellington said to Connie," Just let me know what you want, and I'll call out the order for you."

"Fine," said Connie. "Let's start with the meat. I want to get as much of that as we can."

As they walked, soldier after soldier turned in their direction. Besides a few women behind a few of the stalls, there were very few women in the market. Connie was used to being stared at, even where there were plenty of women, but these stares today were different. She was comfortable with lusty stares from men; she knew what to do with that. She was used to hostile stares from women, but she wasn't used to hostile stares from men.

"Why are they looking at me like that?" Connie asked Wellington.

"They don't trust anyone who's not in a red coat at this point," he said. "We haven't been here in Philadelphia that long, and we're still feeling our way. We all know there's not a lot of food in this city, so I guess they might be wondering why you're here getting food."

"Oh," said Connie, as she held her head up, back straight, and walked on as if she had every right to be there just as they did. "Well, they're just going to have to get used to me, because as long as you all are here and our normal markets are closed, I guess they'll see me around here." Still, she held on to Tom's arm and pulled him close.

They stopped at the nearest meat stall. Wellington pushed his way towards the front saying, "Make way. Make way. I'm here on orders of General Howe." The lines parted and Wellington walked to the front, holding his arm out to usher Connie through. Connie held tight to Tom's arm, too, not wanting him to be caught in a hostile crowd that wondered who he was.

The proprietor said, "Help you, sir?" to Wellington.

Wellington said, "Ma'am, tell this shop keep what you want."

Connie looked at what was hanging on poles. "Three pigs and five chickens," she said.

The proprietor looked up at the pole and turned back to Connie. "That would be all that we have, Ma'am," he said.

"Well, good," said Connie. "Because that is what I need for this week."

The proprietor looked at Wellington with a wide-eyed puzzled look.

"All of it, sir?" the proprietor asked.

Wellington looked at Connie as her eyes narrowed in anger at her wishes being questioned. "You heard the lady," he said. And added for effect, "On orders of General Howe, Supreme Commander of His Majesty's Army."

This time, it was the proprietor who got wide-eyed. "General Howe?" he said.

"That's right," said Wellington.

"Well, yes, sir," said the proprietor. "Sorry for the delay."

Connie shot back, "You should be apologizing to me."

The proprietor looked at Connie and said, "Yes, absolutely. Sorry, Ma'am. Whatever you say," as he took down a chicken. Tom moved forward to take the meat as the proprietor wrapped it up. Tom put the bounty in the small wagon and covered it up with a cloth.

They moved quickly from stall to stall, stuffing their pouches and the wagon to the brim with bushels of vegetables and bags of flour and delicious but strange and strong-smelling wedges of cheese. When they absolutely could not carry anything else, Connie said, "Looks like we have enough for now. Let's go."

"Make way," Wellington yelled, as they moved towards the market exit. He turned towards Connie. "Ma'am, because of that crowd out there, I think you should wait here while I pull the big wagon closer."

"I agree," said Connie. Then she looked at Tom and wrapped her arm in his. "You stay here with me," she said with some fear in her eyes.

"Of course," said Tom.

Wellington went to a few of the soldiers in the line guarding the front entrance and had a conversation with them. As he walked towards the wagon, he yelled, "Make way!" The crowd parted slightly to let him get to the wagon. Wellington unhitched the horse and pulled the wagon closer to the door. Then he called a group of four or five soldiers over. They formed a semi-circle around the part of the entrance where Wellington stood. "Hand me the packages, sir," Wellington said to Tom. Tom handed Wellington the packages one by one as the semi-circle of guards pulled closer to stop the crowd from seeing what was being loaded.

The continual yelling of "Let us in!" "We're hungry!" filled Connie's ears. The look of desperation in their eyes touched her heart, but she knew that there was nothing that she could do about it. If she gave any of them so much as a crumb, she was sure there would be a riot.

When the wagon was fully loaded, Wellington covered up everything with several large pieces of cloth. He said to two of his guards, "walk beside us until we get away from this large crowd." The men saluted him and nodded. They moved to either side of the wagon in position.

Wellington climbed up into the wagon, turned behind him and said, "Ma'am, it's safe for you to get in now."

Connie held tight to Tom's arm. Tom walked her to the carriage and helped her in as Wellington and the guards surveyed the crowd. Tom then climbed up on the back of the wagon and got inside. He sat on top of the bounty, spreading his legs and his arms across everything.

Wellington called out, "Ready?"

The guards answered, "Ready." With that, Wellington said, "Moving out." He hit the horse with the reins and the horse started to move through the crowd. A few people rushed towards the wagon. The guards pushed their guns out in front across their bodies and across the length of the side of the wagon. "Get back!" they yelled, pushing some of the crowd for effect and some for real. This continued for several minutes as Wellington inched the wagon forward. It only stopped when they rode several few blocks away from the market where the crowd thinned out. Wellington turned onto Arch Street, where the number of pedestrians on the street dropped greatly. He stopped the cart. "Guards," he said, "thank you for your service. I believe that we can take it from here. You may return to your posts."

The guards saluted Wellington, turned and headed in the opposite direction. Wellington hit the horse with the reins again and increased the wagon's speed. The roads ahead of them were straight. If anyone rushed the cart, it would be quite easy to speed up and ride away.

# CHAPTER 33
# WHITEMARSH

Fred put one foot in front of the other, oblivious to the length of time or the distance traveled since his regiment left the hills of Chester County. They had been on the march since dusk, and now it was just about dawn. All he knew was that he was soon going to have an opportunity to kill some redcoats. That thought drove him to not even let a thought of complaint enter his head. They picked up food here and there along the way from supporters of the cause who happened to be out on the roads or who had a light burning in their home when the men couldn't stand their hunger any longer.

They walked across a ford that led them closer to the west of Germantown. Once they crossed, they saw what looked like another whole regiment coming up from the south to meet them. General Wayne rode out to meet the commander of the other regiment while the men were ordered to wait at rest. Then General Wayne rode back and gave his men their final orders.

"Men," he said. "We are going to advance up these hills here and past the Wissahickon creek on our way to the Germantown Road. We are going to form the rear left flank and attack the British divisions that are encamped there. This could be the defining battle of this war. This could be the battle that sends the British back across the sea. "

General Wayne took off his hat and held it to his heart. "This is the battle where we can avenge our brothers who died on our home ground."

Then he put his hat back on and held up his musket. "And, in so doing, we will return tit for tat. We will give no quarter. And, just like they did, use your bayonets men."

A cry of "Yeah!" rang out from the 5th Pennsylvania.

"Remember Paoli!" Wayne yelled.

"Remember Paoli!" the men yelled, too.

THE TWO regiments marched closer together until they formed one force marching towards the Germantown Road.

"We're the 5th Pennsylvania," Fred said to the soldier from the other regiment walking next to him.

"We heard all about what happened to you all up there in Paoli," said the soldier.

Fred's eyes narrowed with sadness and with rage. "I lost my brother up there. He was standing right beside me when one of those redcoats stuck a bayonet through his back."

The soldier patted Fred on the back. "Now you have a chance to do the same," he said.

Fred nodded. "Can't wait," he said.

"We'll be right there with you," said the soldier. "Remember Paoli, right?"

Fred said, "Hell, yeah. " Then he yelled, "Remember Paoli", causing others to do the same.

TOM HAD just finished a hearty breakfast of fried bacon, scrambled eggs, hot coffee, and fresh bread. He leaned back on his chair on the front porch of the tiny carriage house where he spent a lot of his time. He was drifting off for a nap when he heard the unmistakable sound of cannon fire. He jumped up out of his chair and looked in the direction the shot came from. There was more distant cannon fire and gunshots. Groups of redcoats ran by.

Tom called out to them, "What's going on?"

"Rebels!" yelled one.

Tom turned and ran back past the carriage house and to the main house. He flung open the door and called out, "Ma'am! Ma'am! Come quick."

Connie was in the kitchen finishing up her second cup of tea when she heard all of the yelling. "What the?" she said. She put down her cup and ran out towards the dining room.

Tom was pacing around the room impatiently. "Tom," Connie called out. "Was that you doing all that yelling?"

Tom ran up to her. "Yes, Ma'am. That was me. There's fighting outside."

"What?" Connie asked not understanding what that meant. "Who's fighting? And outside the house?"

Tom, ringing his hands, said, "It's the rebels and the redcoats. I was out on the carriage house porch and heard some cannon fire and saw a bunch of redcoats running down the Germantown Road. I asked them 'What's going on?' and all they said was 'rebels.'"

"Oh, God," said Connie. "The rebels are headed this way?"

"It seems like that, Ma'am," Tom said. "Come outside with me and see for yourself."

Connie grabbed her shawl off the hook by the front door. She flung it around her shoulders and followed Tom out. As soon as Tom opened the door, Connie heard it. Cannon fire, guns, and people running. They ran to the carriage house and hid on the side as rows and rows of British redcoats ran down the road. The cannon and gun fire came closer.

"We shouldn't be out here," Connie said. "Come on back to the main house." They turned and ran back to the main house.

Connie flung open the door. "Girls!" she yelled out. "Everybody wake up and come down stairs." Tom ran in after her. Connie turned to him frantically. "Go up there and knock on every door and get those girls down here."

While she waited for them to come down, she had to think, and think fast. The rebels coming down to where the redcoats were meant that there would be a battle right here in Germantown. Survival. That was Connie's first thought. Given what she heard and saw, there probably wasn't any time for her to go to General Howe and find out what was going on or plead her case for safety. Just like the British came and occupied Germantown, maybe now it was time for the rebels to do the same. Lining the girls up on the Carriage House porch was fine when there was an orderly march into Germantown, but she realized that she couldn't line the girls up at the Carriage House with rebels shooting cannons and guns right in front of them. But she had to protect her house, her livelihood. She had to let the rebels know what kind of house theirs was to protect it. She went to the door again. Now, besides the loud cannons and guns, she saw smoke coming from up the road. Something was burning. Were the rebels burning houses now? Or the British? It didn't matter. She had to make sure that her house was not one of those that would be burnt.

The girls made a commotion as they ran down the stairs and gathered in the parlor.

"What's happening?" some said as they held their ears, the sound of war coming closer.

"The rebels are coming down the Germantown Road, and I assume they're attacking the British as they come," Connie said. "We saw the redcoats high tailing it down the road from the Carriage House. And, now it appears that they're burning houses, too."

Connie looked at them seriously. "Ladies, we have to protect our house again. I can't chance having you line up on the porch of the carriage house, but we've got to show these rebels what's going on behind these walls the same as we did with the redcoats when they arrived." She wrung her hands. "There's probably no time for you to get dressed up like you did before, but you have to line up outside."

"Outside? With a war going on?" cried one of the girls.

"We could get shot," said another.

"Or you could have this house burn down around you while you're hiding inside," Connie said. "We have to take a chance that the shooting and fighting will take place on Germantown Road and not move back this way. If it does, we'll have to run inside. I'm not so desperate that I'd put you directly in the line of gunfire. But, we have to try to save the house."

Connie put her hands in front of her heart like she was praying. "Girls, I beg you. Please. I've taken care of you fine so far. I won't do anything to hurt you. If I see things getting too close, believe me, I'll tell you all to run inside, get on the floor, and pray. If any of you remember how to do that."

The girls smiled and laughed a bit.

"We're with you," said one girl and then another.

"Good," said Connie. "Now get your shawls, throw them over your shoulders and join me outside." Connie looked at Tom who was standing right by her. "I hope I'm doing the right thing," she said.

"I do, too, Ma'am," said Tom. "I do, too."

Connie pulled her shawl closer and walked out on to the porch. Tom was right behind. And right behind him were her girls. One by one, eyes narrowed with fear, noses crinkled up at the smell of fire now strong through the air. They jumped occasionally at the loud sounds of cannon and gun fire, now getting louder. "Everybody grab a chair and sit down," she said. As afraid as she was, she knew the girls were even more afraid. She didn't need any of them to faint or fall over with fear.

So, Connie, the girls and Tom sat there. For a few long minutes. Tom said, "Ma'am, I hear noise coming from behind the house like marching. I hear the faint sounds of a fife, too.  Let me run back behind the house and see what's going on."

Connie looked at Tom, suddenly fearful for his safety.  "If they're coming this way, from behind, they'll get here soon enough," she said.

"Please, Ma'am.  I'll be careful, and I won't be long.  I just want to know," Tom said.

Connie hesitated for a moment.  "All right," she said.  "Hurry back soon."

Connie sat on her chair and rocked.  As the noise around them grew louder, she thought—what hell have we brought upon us with this quest for freedom?  Were the British really so bad that it should come to this?  She was lost in her thoughts for a minute.

Tom ran back up the side of the house.  He ran up on the porch.  "I was right," he said.  "There's a whole troop of rebels marching this way.  They're down there near the Wissahickon, heading up the hill."

Connie wiped her hand across her face.  "All right," she said.  "So we'll wait."

Connie, Tom and the girls sat there in virtual silence as everything around them grew louder and more agitated.  They all stared straight ahead, in virtual silence.

Suddenly, the noise behind them grew louder.  Something rustled through the trees and bushes behind them.  Two soldiers on horseback emerged from the woods.  They had blue and white uniforms.  They were rebels.

Connie jumped to her feet.  "Sirs," she said, "Welcome.  May we help you?"

The men, puzzled, looked at Connie and the girls.  Then the men looked at each other as they understood the type of women they were looking at.

"Oh," said one of them.  "Working girls."

"Ladies," said Connie with a smile.

"Yes, Ma'am," said the other as he tipped his hat.

"What's going on?" Connie asked, leaning forward.

"We're going to drive those redcoats right back to England," said the soldier. "You ladies ought to be inside, though. There's going to be a lot of shooting out here."

Connie looked at him earnestly. "Thank you for the warning." She looked at his uniform. "Where are you from soldier? "

"5th Pennsylvania Regiment," he said. "Under the command of General Anthony Wayne."

Connie's eyes brightened. "Anthony Wayne of Paoli?" she asked.

"That's right."

Connie said, "So he has boys from Paoli in his regiment?"

"Yes, Ma'am," the soldier said. "That would be the 5th Pennsylvania."

Connie's eyes widened. "Are they with you?"

"Yes they are," said the soldier. "They should be here shortly. We're the advance guard."

Connie grew more agitated. "Fine, fine," she said. "Do you know any of the boys from Paoli?"

The soldier said, "I know some."

Connie said, "Fine, fine." She was practically jumping around. "Do you know Fred and Allen Roberts?"

"No, Ma'am," he said. "There's a lot of boys in that regiment." He looked down at the ground quickly. "Or there used to be until the British attacked us about a week ago right up there in Paoli as a matter of fact and wiped out so many."

Connie put her hand up in front of her mouth as she gasped. "What?" she said. "What happened?"

"Attacked us in the middle of the night with bayonets only. No guns," he said.

"Oh my God," said Connie.

The cannon fire coming from the Germantown Road grew louder.

One soldier said to the other. "Come on." The other looked at him and nodded. He tightened the reins on his horse and said to Connie, "Seriously, if I were you I'd get inside."

Then they rode off.

Connie barely moved. Her brothers were fighting in that Regiment, she was sure of it. If they were headed her way, inside was the last place she was going to be. She turned to the girls. "If you want to go inside, go ahead and get down on the floor," she said.

The girls got up and headed for the door. "You, too, Tom," she said.

"What are you doing to do?" Tom asked.

"I'm going to stay out here and look for my brothers. You heard him. This regiment coming up from behind is from Paoli, my home."

Tom touched her arm. "But it's getting dangerous out here. You heard them, and you can hear for yourself."

Connie looked at him earnestly. "I haven't seen my brothers in all of the years since I left home. I've been outcast from the family. I can't go back and see them. But, if they're coming this way, this might be the only way I can see them. And, I sure would like to see them. They were kind of like babies when I left. They must be fighting men now."

Tom understood. His family had cast him off, too.

"If you're staying, I'm staying," he said.

"Are you coming, Missus?" one of the girls asked.

"No," said Connie. "I'm staying out here. I'm sure that my brothers are in this troop coming up from behind, and I want to see them."

"Your brothers?" said one of the girls. "Then I'm staying with you, too."

"So am I," said another.

"Me, too," said another.

One by one the girls came back outside and sat down.

Tears welled up in Connie's eyes as all the girls in her house walked back outside to sit with her, waiting for her brothers to come by, as the war came closer.

IT DIDN'T take long. The sound of hundreds of boots hitting the ground behind them was unmistakable. Then she saw them. Four men in the patriots' blue and white uniforms walked hurriedly up the side of her house. Their guns were drawn, pointing straight at her as they marched around the corner. They must have sensed the human presence on the porch.

The men stopped, gun barrels pointing straight at Connie.

"We are friends," Connie said quickly. "We are with you."

The men looked at her, and Tom, and eyed the women lined up behind her.

"You a whore?" one of them asked.

Connie said, "We prefer to think of ourselves as working girls."

"A whore," the soldier said. He pointed the gun at the rest of them. "These whores, too?"

"These ladies work for me," Connie said, proudly.

Then he pointed the gun at Tom. "And him?"

"He works for me, too. He's my house boy," she said.

"I guess he's not a whore," said one. He and the other soldier with him laughed.

Then he got serious. "You got any customers in that house?"

Connie said, "No."

"Mind if we search it?" one asked.

"No, of course not," said Connie, as she stood slowly, hoping she didn't get shot.

"We're going to search the house, and then you all should go on and get inside. With what's about to happen here, you shouldn't be sitting out on the porch advertising," said a soldier.

"As a matter of fact," said Connie, "we're sitting out here in hopes of seeing my brothers. Fred and Allen Roberts. From Paoli. That's where I'm from. I saw some sentries ride by, and they told me that your unit was General Wayne's, and I know that the Paoli boys would be with him."

The soldier relaxed his hold on his gun. "You're from Paoli?"

"Yes," Connie said. "My family has a farm there."

"I'm from Tredyffrin, Chester County, myself," said one.

"Home folk," Connie said smiling. "Well, we're glad you're here."

"So you're out here hoping to see your brothers march by?" he asked.

"Yes, sir," she said.

He looked at her seriously. He said, "Well, if they're from Paoli, and they're with General Wayne, they should be coming by here." He added, "We had an awful battle up in Paoli about a week ago. I hope your brothers were among the lucky ones."

Connie looked at him seriously. "I hope so, too."

The two soldiers emerged from the house and said, "It's clean."

"Good," said the one who was talking to Connie. "One of you stay here so anyone else coming along won't have to search this place."

The soldier looked at the beautiful girls around him and said, "I'll stay," and smiled slightly.

The soldier talking to Connie said to him somewhat sternly, "Keep your eyes on what's going on around you, not these lovely ladies here."

"Yes, sir."

He turned to Connie and said, "I know you want to see your brothers, but don't stay out here too long. At some point, there'll be so much shooting and carrying on that you really should be inside."

"I know," said Connie. "And thank you."

"Alright," he said. "Take care, Ma'am."

He and the other soldiers hurried on. The two soldiers left behind stayed on either side of the house so they could be seen. A few minutes later, a rush of men passed by. Connie jumped up out of her chair and stood by the rail. The cannons and gunfire grew louder, but she didn't care. She was glad, again, that her beauty made men look. She naturally attracted attention. The soldiers naturally looked at her. She looked back with eyes that she hoped were welcoming.

"Any of you know my brothers, Fred and Allen Roberts, from Paoli?" she called out.

"Remember Paoli," several soldiers called out in response as they practically ran by.

"Fred and Allen Roberts from Paoli. Do you know them?" she continued to call out as the soldiers marched by.

"Girls, help me," she said, as she waved them to come closer to the porch. "Ask them if they know of Fred and Allen Roberts from Paoli."

The girls moved closer and did as asked. After hundreds of men passed by, one of the girls said, "Miss Connie! He knows your brothers! Come quick!" Connie ran over to the edge of the porch where her girl Thomasina was. Suddenly, several of the girls said, "He knows your brothers." "He does, too."

The soldier said, "I'm from Paoli. Name is Charles Duran."

Connie said, "Duran? I know your family. I'm Connie Roberts. You were a young boy when I left." She went on, "Are my brothers Fred and Allen Roberts with you?"

Charles got wide eyed. "Fred is with us," he said. "He should be coming this way soon."

Connie said, "Yeah!" and smiled and kind of jumped up in the air for joy. Fred and Allen were always together, so she figured that if Fred was coming, Allen was coming, too.

"Thank you, thank you," she said, as the soldier waved good bye and joined the rest of the regiment.

She kept her eyes peeled, looking closely into every face that looked into hers. And she kept calling out, as did the rest of the girls. "Fred Roberts! Allen Roberts!" They all yelled over the increasing noise around them.

Just as she called "Fred", a soldier who was looking straight ahead turned and looked straight at her.

FRED'S MIND was seriously set on the task ahead. Killing redcoats. He was determined to get at least one. Maybe the one who killed his brother. All of a sudden, he heard a commotion, yelling from a house they were getting ready to pass by. In that yelling, he thought he heard his name. His hearing was sharp and so were his other senses. As he came upon the house, he saw a few of his fellow soldiers standing there talking to some women. "Fred" and "Roberts", he heard. He even heard "Allen."

"I'm sure I heard my name," Fred said to himself as he turned, looked straight at the porch. He focused in on a beautiful, dark-haired woman calling his name. He couldn't really make out her face, but he caught the eye of one of his fellow soldiers that he knew, and the soldier was waving his arms wildly, calling him over.

Fred ran over closer to the house and stopped in his tracks as the faces on the porch became closer and clearer in recognition. He stopped in shock as he looked straight into the beautiful face that could only be his sister's.

"FRED!" CONNIE yelled as she ran to the porch steps and ran out towards him. "It's Connie, your sister," she said.

Fred's eyes opened in surprise. He loosened his grip on his musket and let it hang by his side. Then he ran over to his sister.

"CONNIE!" FRED yelled as he ran towards her. He grabbed her arms and held her back so he could get a good look at her. Then he scooped her up in his arms and lifted her off the ground, holding her close.

Connie patted him on the back as she held him tight. Tears fell from her eyes although she was smiling. They broke their grip on each other and leaned back to look at each other again. "Oh my God, Fred, it's so great seeing you. You've grown up so!"

Fred looked at his sister. "Connie, I missed you so much. And nobody knew where you were."

"I've been here for a few years," Connie said. Then she looked around. "Where's Allen? You two were always together."

Fred took Connie's hand. "Allen's dead, Connie."

Connie gasped and held her hand to her mouth.

"We had an awful battle in Paoli about a week ago, and some redcoat stabbed him in the back with his bayonet and pushed it straight through to his stomach," Allen said.

Connie's eyes filled up with tears again.

As soldiers continued to march around him, Fred said, "Connie, I have to go. I have to catch up with my regiment. We're going to give those redcoats just what they gave us." He looked lovingly at her. "But now I know where you are," he said, "and I'll be back."

"I hope so," said Connie. "I miss you all. How's Mom and Pop? And how's Betsey?" she asked through tears for her baby brother Allen.

"They're all doing fine," Fred said. Then he looked at the mass of troops moving behind him. He grabbed Connie's arms again. "I promise you. I'll be back." Then he hugged her. "I don't care what you're doing now or what you've done. You're my sister, and I love you. So does Betsey. So does Mom. And, even though you may not believe it, so does Pop." He ran his fingers through her hair. "Connie, they're missing Allen something awful. They saw his dead and mutilated body left on that field along with the bodies of fifty or so other soldiers. It was horrible. They've lost a son and a brother, and I think they'd like to reclaim a daughter and a sister."

Tears continued to stream down Connie's eyes.

"Let them know where you are, Connie. Go see them," he said. "Life is too short, and we all know that now."

The cannon and gunfire became louder. Fred turned around towards those sounds and then turned back quickly towards Connie. He held both of her arms. "I've got to go," said Fred. "But like I said, I'll be back." Then he looked at the house. "Now you go on and get in there. Get down in your basement and don't come up until it's quiet out here."

Fred kissed her on the cheek. "Go inside. I'll see you later." Fred stood still for a minute as he watched his beloved sister turn and leave him. The he quickly fell in line with the last few lines of the 5th Pennsylvania.

Connie ran back to the porch. "Go inside, now!" she yelled. She didn't have to tell the girls that twice. They ran inside with Tom following on their heels and Connie following on his. Tom bolted the front door behind them.

"Down to the basement," Connie yelled. Tom ran over and opened the door that led to the basement. "It's dark down here," one of them yelled.

"Do you want to live or not?" one of them yelled out as they all hurried down the stairs.

FRED MARCHED past Connie's carriage house and onto the Germantown Road with the rest of his regiment. By now, the sound of guns and cannons was deafening. The weather was foggy, and he couldn't see more than a quarter of a mile ahead of him. He couldn't see far, but he could see far enough to see their leader, General Wayne, ahead of them.

"Men," Wayne yelled. "We are finally here! We can avenge our men who died brutally at the hands of the very same redcoats that you are soon going to face."

"Remember Paoli!" some of the men yelled.

"I know you can't see them now, but they're there, down this road," Wayne said. "And when you see them and get close to them," he said, as he held out his musket with bayonet affixed and thrust it into the air like he was thrusting it into a person, "take your revenge. No quarter."

"No quarter" some of the men yelled.

With that, Wayne turned his horse in the opposite direction, held his musket up in the air, and yelled, "March!"

The men let out a rebel yell as they stormed down the Germantown Road. Fred's hands gripped his bayonetted musket. He was ready.

He ran down the road. The air was covered with fog, so he couldn't exactly see what he was running into.

Suddenly, a group of redcoats appeared before them out of the fog. The redcoats were running down the road in retreat, in front of Wayne's troops, trying to get away.

"Faster!" yelled one of Fred's companions.

The patriots ran faster, all the while yelling "Remember Paoli!"

Fred remembered how fast he and Allen had to run when they were kids to try to catch a rabbit. Just the thought of Allen made him run faster. He could see that he was within striking distance of the redcoats.

"Charge bayonets!" yelled one of his officers.

Fred thrust out his bayonet and kept running. It seemed like he and his fellow soldiers ran upon the redcoats all at once. Fred held his musket tight and rammed his bayonet into the back of the redcoat before him. "Remember Paoli!" he yelled. He twisted the bayonet a few times before pulling it out so that it would do maximum damage. Then he stuck that same soldier with the bayonet again, this time near the shoulder. He gave the bayonet a good turn and pushed the soldier over on to the ground. Fred then tightened his grip on the musket, bayonet sticking straight out, and stuck it into the back of another redcoat. The same scene was repeated all around him.

CONNIE AND the girls laid flat on the floor, listening to the world being destroyed around them. The cannon and gun fire was deafening, even though they were inside the house. The smell of smoke and fire entered the house even though the windows were closed. They laid there what seemed like all day and into the night. If anyone had to go to the bathroom, she had to slither along the ground like a snake, pull herself into the commode, do her business as fast as she could, hoping that no stray bullets came through the window, and slither back to her place on the floor. The noise outside started to die down as the sun did. When it had been dark for a few hours, the noise finally ended.

"Do you think it's over?" Connie asked Tom.

"It's been mighty quiet for a while," Tom said. "It seems like it's over to me. You wait here. I'll go to the door and check." Tom slithered along the floor until he reached the front door. Slowly, he raised up his head and chest far enough so he could peek out the door. The two patriot guards were gone from where they had been standing, so Tom stood upright. He walked softly to stand behind the wooden door and peaked through the windows on the side. They were gone alright. He unlocked all the inside locks that he had set to keep them safe. He gently grasped the doorknob and turned the door. He pulled it open. It was quiet, largely. There was some crying and screaming that he heard but no guns and no cannons. Fires burned in the distance. He walked out on the porch. He walked from one side of the porch to the other. Then he went back to the front door.

"Miss Connie, the guards are gone. It looks like everything has died down," he said. "You're gonna wanna come and see this."

Connie put her hands out in front of her and pushed herself off the floor. She stretched a bit from side to side to ease the crick in her back that came from lying on the floor for most of the day. She wiped her brow with the back of her hand in an act of sheer fatigue, and she walked upstairs to the opened front door where Tom stood.

She looked straight ahead and frowned in disbelief. She could see straight to the Germantown Road from her front porch. The little carriage house had been shot through with cannons so that only a few stones remained where the walls once stood.

Connie gasped and walked towards the front steps, towards what was left of her carriage house.

Tom grabbed her arm. "No, Miss. Don't go over there now. Not yet. It's quiet out here, but I've seen a few soldiers walking by on that road. Stand here a minute and you'll see them, too. We should get back inside, lock this door, and wait until morning when we can see what really happened out there. And who might be waiting out there."

Connie stared straight ahead. A few soldiers did walk by on the Germantown Road.

"You're right, Tom," Connie said. "Let's wait until daybreak." She walked back into the house, still holding his arm.

THE NEXT morning, there was very little sound around to wake them up. The roosters at the house out back didn't sound as usual; they had been taken by the Continental Army as they retreated, along with just about every other edible thing they could find in Germantown. Tom woke up first, as he usually did, and he woke Connie. They had a quick and light breakfast of tea and toast. Their main goal for the day was to see what happened around them yesterday, not to have a lavish breakfast.

Connie pulled on a plain brown linen dress. She had a sense that anything else would get unnecessarily dirty, and maybe even destroyed, when she walked outside. She took Tom's arm as he helped her down the front porch steps. The stone path to the carriage house was littered with fallen tree limbs that had been shot off the trees, and a few musket balls had landed there, too. The beautiful lawn in front of her house had been stamped down and torn up so that it looked like a soft, brown muddy mess with a few green patches, like a bad patchwork quilt. The stones that made up the walkway from her house to the carriage house that she had so lovingly picked out at the nearby quarry, had been broken into pieces by the weight of so many soldiers walking on them. It was a slow walk to the carriage house.

As they came closer to the carriage house, Connie saw a few cannon balls that had obviously gone through and knocked down some of the walls. There were stones of all sizes all around her—bigger pieces that remained largely untouched, and small pieces of the stones that suffered a direct hit and were pulverized. She walked up to where one wall used to be and looked inside at what was left of the inside of the carriage house. Pieces of broken wood were everywhere. Only a few pieces of furniture remained standing, and those were small pieces like a stool that was closer to floor level. Shattered pottery and bent metal were everywhere. Connie held her hand to her mouth as she gasped. She maneuvered towards the street on the left side of the house. It seemed like the cannons had been shooting from the left side because the left wall was completely taken out while the right wall was surrounded by large piles of stone with cannon balls on top, on the side, or at the bottom.

She reached what used to be the front of the carriage house and looked back, through the walls, towards her main house. A few of the girls had gone out on the porch. They waved at Connie. She waved back. Tom stood beside her.

"This is what war brings?" she asked Tom.

"Yes, Ma'am," he said. "I think we're lucky that the fighting was contained to the main road."

Connie looked at other girls as they came out on to the porch, waving. "I guess you're right," she said. "I guess you're right."

She pulled her hood over her head and pulled her cape closer as she walked down the few steps to the Germantown Road. "My God," she said, as she stopped and looked up and down the road. She had never seen such a scene of destruction and confusion. Several large houses on the street were mere shells of themselves, much like her carriage house, with walls knocked down, roofs collapsed on top of them, or gaping holes in roofs and walls. Several houses were still on fire, the fire largely having done its damage of essentially destroying the houses. The Germantown Road itself was littered with shoes, pieces of uniforms—both the blue and the red, muskets, broke down wagons, stray horses, and bodies—some in red uniforms, some in blue uniforms, and even some in green uniforms and other colors that Connie was not familiar with.

She walked down the road, stepping around bodies and debris all the while. With some of the bodies, Connie looked more closely. Some had arms, legs or even heads missing. Some had marks on their bodies where you could see the musket ball had gone straight through, leaving a hole that you could look through. Others had the violent, ragged, and often lengthy gashes of an angry bayonet. It seemed like just about all of the people who were left in Germantown were out walking on the street now, surveying the horrible damage that had been done.

"Tom, I can't believe what I'm seeing," Connie said. Just then, a body wearing a redcoat near her feet, who she assumed was dead, moaned and moved. Connie jumped and screamed.

"Help me," the body said.

Tom kneeled down closer to the body, which was largely covered in blood. "Were you shot? Take a bayonet?"

"Both. I think," said the body.

Connie put her hand on Tom's shoulder. "We should help him," she said. She looked all around her. "We should help them all."

"He's a redcoat, Ma'am," Tom said.

"I see that, "Connie said. "But we can't just let all of these people lie in the street if they have a sliver of life left in them. Redcoat or bluecoat. Does it really matter so much right now?

Tom took off his hat and held it in his hand. "Not so much right now, Miss Connie, but remember, your brother is one of those bluecoats fighting these here redcoats. You don't want to help them get back on their feet and then go after your brother and those other boys. And, remember what your brother said. These could be the very same men who killed your little brother at the end of their bayonets." Tom shook his head. "No, you don't want to help these redcoats get back on their feet."

Connie sighed and looked around at all of the bodies around her, up and down the street. Tom had a good point. Why help a redcoat who would kill her other brother just as soon as look at him.

"Alright," she said. "I don't see any living redcoats walking around here like they were just yesterday, and Lord knows where they went to. And, you make a good point. I only have one brother left, so whatever I can do to make sure that he makes it through this war, I'll do. So, fine. We'll take care of our boys."

"I think you made the right decision, Ma'am," Tom said.

Connie poked her lips out in a frown. "I don't know whether it's right, because a man's a man. But, I think it's the most practical decision to make at this time. So, go on back to the house and get some water jugs, some cloth for bandages, and some whiskey for antiseptic. Bring the girls with you. Tell them we have to help our boys get back on their feet."

Tom took off towards the house. Connie walked over to the middle of the Germantown road, put her hand over her eyes to shield them from the sun and help her figure out what she was looking at, and looked over the scene in front of her, looking to spot as many blue uniforms as she could.

# CHAPTER 34

# WHITEMARSH

The 5th Pennsylvania retreated some five miles up the Germantown Road to make camp in Whitemarsh. Even though they were tired from the march back up the hills, General Wayne's troops were jubilant.

"We got 'em!" they yelled as they whooped it up around their camp.

"We got revenge!" they yelled. "No Quarter!"

Other regiments in the next field over yelled, "We remembered Wayne's Affair!"

Fred yelled out the same battle cries time and time again into the night. He was positively giddy. Before they were ordered to retreat, he personally killed six redcoats, all by bayonet. The first one was compensation for Allen; the next five were for somebody else who died on that field in Paoli, he reasoned.

He sat down by the campfire with some of his other friends from the regiment. They shared stories of how many redcoats got the bayonet this time. Fred pulled the bayonet off his gun and held it up in the air, still bloody. "Remember Paoli!" he yelled like a drunken soldier, although he hadn't had whiskey for days.

He lowered his hand and held the bayonet down at his side with one hand. With the other, he poured out some water from his canteen onto a cloth. Then he wiped the bayonet, and wiped, until every trace of blood that he could see was gone. Then he reattached it to his musket and put that, too, down by his side. He stayed up most of the night with his buddies, talking and cheering.  General Wayne had told them that as soon as they reached camp, the plan was to give them a few days' rest, at least, so they could take time to properly enjoy what to them was a victory—bayonetting redcoats—even though they, along with the rest of the Continental Army there, had to retreat.

"It's a victory for us," General Wayne told his troops when they reassembled.  "I've never been more proud of you men."

# CHAPTER 35
# REBEL HILL/THE GULPH

"The army's over there in Whitemarsh," Daniel said to James as they stoked the fire in the furnace. "Heard there was a big battle over in Germantown and that the Continentals drove those redcoats out of Germantown and down to Philadelphia."

"So that was what all that loud noise was coming from west of here a few days ago," James said. "All day and all night, it seemed. Loud as I've ever heard it. And so much smoke. Whether it was from the cannons or the muskets or whatever they were burning over there, didn't you see the smoke rising?"

"I was over at the Pottsford getting some more iron that day," he said.

"Well, you missed something big," James said.

Daniel threw a few more logs on to the fire. "I hope our boys follow them on their heels and drive them out of Philadelphia and put an end to this thing."

James said, "Me, too, but there's not much time left for them to do that before winter sets in and they go to their winter quarters."

"It's only early October," Daniel said. "And it's warm. They have plenty of time to take care of those redcoats before the freeze comes."

"Maybe so," said James as he continued to stoke the fire. "Let's hope they keep it moving southeast that way, towards Philadelphia, and far away from us."

"Yes," said Daniel. "Whitemarsh is too close to us. I sure hope the British don't come up here looking for them. If they do, where do you think our boys will go?" asking a question he already knew the answer too. "They'll go right across the Matson's Ford and come on over here, and that is something that we don't need. We don't' need that war coming any closer to us than it is already."

"That sure is true," said James. "Sure is true."

# CHAPTER 36

# GERMANTOWN

Tom and the girls walked back out to meet Connie, loaded up with water jugs, bandages, and bottles of whisky.

Connie smiled when she saw them and said to her girls, "Tom and I have walked up and down that road, but there's so many bodies out here that there's still so much we haven't covered. So can you girls walk around by the edges and especially down by Mr. Chew's house, where there was a terrible battle? When you come across one of our patriots down, call out to me, or raise your hand and motion to me so I can come over and make sure it's not my brother?"

"Absolutely," said the girls. They fanned out down the road, in the direction of Philadelphia, where a whole lot of bodies and mess laid in the road. Every so often, a girl would call out or raise her hand. So would Tom. Connie would run over there as quickly as she could, bend down and look. Sometimes looking was very gruesome. Bodies had blood everywhere. Gashes in the stomach, throat, head. Holes in their bodies made where the musket balls went straight through flesh. And the day was warming up. The stench rose from everywhere. They tried to reach the patriot bodies before the redcoats, who were now also walking up and down the road, did. More than once, they saw a redcoat bayonet a still living or wounded patriot.

After a few more hours, an exhausted Connie waved her arms, calling her girls and Tom close. "I know we couldn't get to everyone, but thank God, I didn't see my brother."

"That's good," said one of the girls.

"It is," said Connie, "but I can't rest until I know for sure. I have to find out. Just seeing him yesterday made me think of my whole family, which I haven't seen in years."

She turned towards Tom. "I can't stay here. I have to find out what happened to him. "

"I understand, Miss," but how are you going to do that?"

"I have to go home. They tell the families if someone dies in battle, don't they?" she asked.

Tom said, "They do if they can. They'll send a rider with a letter if the soldier's family is nearby, but they have to be organized to do that. Judging by the looks of what we've seen here today, our Continental boys took quite a beating and retreated. They might not be in any shape to start telling families, even though yours is not that far from here."

"Then I'll have to find out myself," she said. "I have to go home and see if they've heard."

"Your home is about 50 miles from here, isn't it?" Tom asked.

"Yes," Connie said.

"Then I'll go with you," Tom said.

"I need you here to protect the house and take care of the girls," she said.

Her best girl Angela spoke up. "I can take care of the house while you're away. I know what to do."

Connie looked at her. "Yes, you do know what to do, but look around. Things aren't like they used to be."

"Well, the British are still in charge around here, aren't they?" Angela asked.

"It looks that way," Connie answered.

"And haven't they been good to us so far?" Angela continued. "If your friend is around, I'm sure he'll look out for us. Maybe he'll even send one of his men over to help."

Connie laughed. "He won't want to help us if he finds out that I'm not here and that I'm gone because I need to find out what happened to my rebel brother."

"So we'll tell him something different," Angela said. "One thing we all know how to do is lie to men." She and the other girls laughed.

"You're right about that," Connie said. "I could send him a note that I have to go see my sick mother, and that Tom went with me for protection, and could he please send one of his men over to the house to watch it while I'm away."

"There you go," laughed Angela. "You haven't lost your touch."

Connie smiled. "All right. That's what I'll do. "

Tom said, "But I'd say you wait a day or two to give everything a chance to settle down. Even though it looks like there's still a lot of redcoats out there, there's not half as many as there were when that battle started. I heard one of them say that the rest had been moved down to Philadelphia, and that most of them were going to follow suit as soon as they got things kind of cleaned up and settled around here. They said your friend went down to Philadelphia to get them settled down there, but that he'd be back."

"Someone's going to have to find him then and get a note to him," Connie said.

"Let us take care of that when the time comes," Angela said. "You know we learned from you how to get these redcoats to do anything for us that we need."

Connie smiled. "That's my girls." She paused for a few seconds. "Ok. Tom, we'll stay in the house tonight. Maybe we'll get some visitors," she said, smiling. "Even if we don't, that will give me time to write my letter and get my things together to go home. "

Tom said, "I'll see how things are in the morning. If I hear that it's safe, and there's not another battle brewing, then we can head out then."

"Great," said Connie. "Now let's head back to the house. We've all got some work ahead of us."

"THINGS HAVE settled down out there," said Tom as he came into the main house. "More of those redcoats have moved down to Philadelphia. I hear that most of them are going to spend the winter there, but they're going to keep some of them here, including your friend. But he's not here now. He's down in Philadelphia, but he'll be back."

"Oh," said Connie. "Alright. Tell Angela. Let her figure out how to get this note to him."

Tom walked back to the kitchen where Angela was waiting. Connie put a few more pieces of fruit, bread and dried meat into her basket. Then she walked back in to the kitchen where Angela and the other girls were gathered.

"OK, ladies. Tom says things are settling down out there, so we're going to be on our way in a few minutes," Connie said. She looked at Angela. "Angela, you're in charge, and you'll get that letter to my friend?"

"Don't worry about a thing, Connie," Angela said. "We'll take care of everything. You go see about your brother and the rest of your family."

Connie smiled.

"OK girls," said Connie. Uncharacteristically emotional, she looked at them all, one by one. She smiled and said, "I love you all."

"We love you, too," they replied.

Then she looked at Tom. "Well, I guess that's it. Let's get the wagon, and we're off to Paoli."

They all walked outside. The girls waved them off, as Tom and Connie drove away. Home. After all of these years, Connie thought. I hope that somebody at that house is happy to see me.

"HERE COMES another one," Tom warned Connie. "Hold on."

Connie's hand flew up to her head as she held her hat. The horse galloped on and the wagon flew up in the air—again. The Germantown Road was normally fairly smooth since it was a main road to Philadelphia from points north and west, but the aftermath of the battle fought all over Germantown a few days ago left the road as pock-marked as many a teenage boy's face. The road was still littered with discarded clothing, spent musket casings, and rut marks left by thousands of heavy boots on damp earth, thousands of horses hooves, and the wheels of hundreds of heavy cannons.

"If I slow down too much, we might not make it to Paoli by nightfall, and we don't need to be out here at night," he said. "No telling who's planning what. Redcoat or patriot," he said.

"You're right," said Connie, "and I hope my family at least offers us a soft bed when we get there because our hind parts are going to be mighty sore."

They both laughed, a welcome moment of levity as they looked at the destruction of a few days ago all around them. They drove mostly in silence as they took in house after house that was burned, still burning, missing walls or pieces of walls. Dirty and dazed people walked up and down the road, shaking their heads and crying. Mother, father or child— it didn't matter. Death and destruction was everywhere. Connie tried not to make eye contact as they drove on. They only had enough food to make it to Paoli and back, in case her family didn't have any food or didn't want to give her any. She couldn't afford to let a charitable thought cause her to give up some of that food, no matter how pitiful the people looked.

They traveled for a few hours up the road. When they reached the outskirts of Germantown, Tom said, "There's a roadblock ahead." A line of four or five wagons, a few riders on horses, and about twenty people on foot were in a line ahead of them.

"What's going on?" Connie asked.

"Not sure," said Tom, "but I reckon it's one of the armies checking to see who's coming through." He stood up in the cab and strained his neck forward to get a better look.

"Still can't tell for sure, but if the redcoats are in Philadelphia and Germantown, our boys are probably out here."

Connie sprang up herself and craned her neck. "Really?" she asked excitedly.

The line moved slowly. Little by little, they got closer.

"Can you see yet?" Connie asked, excitedly looking, turning her head from side to side.

"I think I see blue," Tom said.

"Good," said Connie.

They moved a little further on.

"Yup, definitely. It's our boys up there," Tom said, looking straight ahead.

Connie smiled and said, "Yeah!" She jumped up and said, "Then I wish they'd hurry up. I wonder if my brother is up there with them."

When they reached the front of the line, the soldier said, "What's your business up here?"

Connie said, "We're going to see my family in Paoli. I live in Germantown, and I saw my brother, Fred Roberts, with General Wayne's 5th Pennsylvania Regiment when they marched by my house on their way to the battle in Germantown. I'm going home to see if he's alright."

"How do we know you're telling the truth?" one asked.

"I lost my other brother, Allen Roberts, in the battle in Paoli, and I have to find out if my other brother is safe," she said as tears started to fall from her eyes.

"You lost a brother in Paoli?" the soldier next to Tom asked.

"Yes," she said, as she started crying.

"Alright," said the rebel. "You have my sympathies. That was a horrible affair, from what I heard. But, we gave it to those redcoats good as much as we could at the battle in Germantown. And I heard that General Wayne's boys especially got their revenge."

Connie looked at him puzzled.

"They bayoneted those redcoats just like the redcoats bayoneted them," he said.

The other soldier said, "No quarter."

Tom said, "Good. We weren't sure what happened because by the time we went out there the next day, the redcoats were back out there, shooting any rebel soldiers lying wounded in the road. We tried to get to them first and help them out as much as we could, but we couldn't do much."

Connie said between her tears, "We spent hours looking into the faces of everybody we could find with a blue and white uniform hoping that one of them was not my brother."

Tom patted her on the shoulder to comfort her. He looked at the soldiers. "Luckily, we didn't find him."

"That's good," said one of the soldiers. "We'll let you pass by then."

"Thank you," said Connie, wiping her tears. "Would you know if my brother made it?"

The soldier looked at her and said, "I can't tell you that. All I can say is that most of us did."

The other said, "But listen, you're not going to be able to go down this road much further because we've taken over the area down the hill there. You will have to turn off here and get to Paoli off of that road." He looked at Tom. "Can you find your way to Paoli going that way?"

Tom pulled a compass out of his pocket. "With this, I can find my way anywhere," he said.

"Good," said the soldier. Then he turned to Connie. "Ma'am, I'm sorry about the brother you lost at Paoli. I hope your other brother is at camp with the rest of us. But I'll keep that name in mind. You said Fred in General Wayne's division?"

"Yes, Fred Roberts from Paoli. Fifth Pennsylvania. With General Wayne."

"Ok, Ma'am," he said, tapping his hat. "I have it up here. When I get back to camp, I'll ask around. If I see him, I'll tell him that you were looking for him and that he should let his family know that he's alright."

"And if you don't see him?" Connie asked.

"Well, then, Ma'am, General Wayne would have figured some way to get a note home to your family."

"Thank you," said Connie as she put out her hand to shake his.

"Not at all, Ma'am," he said, as he waved them on by.

TOM DROVE the carriage west, according to his compass. "We have to cross the river up here somewhere to get to Paoli," he said as he saw the Schuylkill River ahead of them. "Matson's Ford should be up here somewhere, or we can go up further and cross at Swede's Ford."

"Let's take the first one we come to," Connie said. "We lost so much time getting up the Germantown Road, and I want to make sure that we reach Paoli well before it gets dark. My family's going to be shocked enough to see me in the daytime. I don't want to frighten them any more when they see a strange person showing up at their door at night time."

Tom laughed. "Alright, Matson's Ford it is. Thank God this wagon is fairly light. It's supposed to be a good, sturdy ford, but I don't like crossing any of them when my wagon is carrying too much."

"I understand," said Connie. "When I was younger and used to go to market with my family, I've seen many a wagon get stuck on a ford that was supposed to carry them across."

Tom continued down the road past the church on the right. They turned right onto the Ridge Road, and then left on the road that led them to the Matson Ford. The Ford was one of the busier ones in that part of the Philadelphia area. It was one of the first sizeable ones from Philadelphia where a wagon of any size could cross. It served people living across the Ford in the area on the other side that was loaded with mills of all types—paper, tools, grain, and even toys. It served the growing population in that part of Philadelphia County, which was occupied by Quakers and people of all religions, Swedes and Germans and people from all countries, and a small but growing community of people of African descent—slave and free.

Tom and Connie's wagon came to the top of the high hill that led down to Matson's Ford. "What a beautiful view," said Connie as they looked out over the forest of trees that was in front of them on the other side of the ford. The leaves were a riotous display of green, yellow, orange, and red. The Schuylkill River below ran full and hard as a result of the recent rains. Wood, stone, and plaster houses lined the road that led down to the ford, a road packed hard and smooth in some parts and rutted and pock-marked in others.

"Hold on, Miss," Tom said. "I'm not going to go fast, but this hill is mighty steep."

"That's an understatement," Connie said, as she grabbed hold of the rail by her right side.

"Alright," she said.

Tom nodded and tightened his grip on the reins. "Easy now, girl," he said to his horse, Daisy Jane.

The wagon proceeded ahead slowly and steadily. Tom steered it from side to side, avoiding as many of the ruts as he could. Other, no doubt heavier, wagons weren't so lucky.

The ruts undoubtedly caused the wagons to shake so violently that item after item was dislodged from the back and sides of the wagons. A steady stream of tin and broken earthenware cups and plates and bags and barrels littered the road, making it even more of an obstacle course.

Tom's deft maneuvering got them to the bottom of the hill safely. He moved their wagon into the line that was waiting to cross the ford. They watched as wagon after wagon crossed safely, not rushing the crossing.

"Things are looking good, Miss," Tom said.

"Yes," said Connie. "It looks like the heaviest wagons either got stuck on the hill or dropped enough of their goods so that they weren't weighed down."

"We should be fine, then, with our weight," Tom said.

"Good," said Connie. "It's starting to get dark."

A few more minutes, and their wagon was next in line. "Hold on again, Ma'am," Tom said, as he moved up into the number one position.

"You don't have to tell me that," Connie said, laughing.

Daisy Jane moved ahead slowly, under Tom's steady hand. As they rode onto the ford, the ruts in the ford came into sharper focus. Unlike the hill, there wasn't much room to maneuver around them. There was no turning back once they started because of the line of people who wanted to get across, too, before darkness descended in full.

"Steady and easy, girl," Tom said, as Daisy Jane moved ahead and the wagon shook from side to side. They plodded on, shaking. As slowly as Tom was intentionally making Daisy go, she slowed down even more. Tom slacked up on the reins, thinking it was he who was causing the slowdown. Daisy plodded ahead, slowly raising one hoof after the other. The Schuylkill River raged on either side of them, closing in on the ford, narrowing its width. Connie held the rails tightly as they slowly moved across.

"Good girl," said Tom, as he patted Daisy's neck while she stepped off the ford and onto the expanse of land on the other side.

"Finally," said Connie, with an air of impatience in her voice.

"Something's wrong," said Tom as he steered Daisy to the side, away from the wagon crossing. "Whoa, girl," he said, as he stopped her. He hopped off the wagon, patting Daisy on the neck the whole time. He walked around and faced Daisy. "What's wrong, girl?" he asked, like she really could answer him. He patted her again. "Don't worry, I'll find out," he said.

Tom patted Daisy with one hand while he lifted her hoof with the other. "Looks fine to me," he said. Then he walked to the hoof on her right side, kept patting her and lifted her right hoof.

"This one, too," he said. He looked up at Connie. "It must be one of the back ones," he said. "I hate to ask you, Miss, but I'm going to need your help. Can you come and keep her quiet while I check? I don't want her to get excited and kick me when I'm back there checking."

Connie opened the rail next to her seat, lifted her skirt, and said, "Help me down." Tom gave her his hand. "It's been a while since I've dealt with a horse," she said, "but I guess that once you learn how to calm a horse, you don't forget. Lord knows I had to do enough of it on our farm." She straightened her skirt as her feet hit the ground. "Let me get an apple or something to keep her occupied." She pulled an apple out of one of the baskets in the back and polished it on her jacket.

"Alright, I'm ready," she said as she walked in front of the horse. "Hey there Miss Daisy Jane," Connie said, as she patted Daisy's neck. "Aren't you a beautiful girl? Well of course you are. All of my girls are beautiful."

Tom laughed and said, "Yes, Miss. That's right," as he reached for Daisy's back leg.

"Look at what I have for you here," said Connie, holding the apple in front of Daisy's eager mouth. "Gotta keep my girls strong and healthy," she said, as she looked into Daisy's big brown eyes. It's been a long time, thought Connie. Ever since she came to Philadelphia, she didn't have to bother with horses. If she wanted to go somewhere, someone else got the horse and wagon together for her. But as she was patting Daisy, her thoughts went back to all of the times in Paoli when she had to feed the horses, apples, grain, or whatever. That part of her horse experience she considered a chore. But what she loved was when she could take the horses for a ride around the farm, the horse's free spirit matching her own, running as fast as they could from one place to another, enjoying the feel of the wind on her skin and through her hair, leaving business as usual behind.

"Ah, here's the problem," Tom said, as he lifted up Daisy's right back hoof. "Her shoe is broken."

"Broken?" Connie asked. "Oh my God."

"She had to be limping on this foot. That's why she was going so slowly," he said.

Connie said, "How on earth are we going to get to Paoli tonight? Daisy can't make it that far on a broken shoe." She patted Daisy's neck, "Can you girl? I know you're strong like all of my girls, but I know you're not that strong."

Tom said, "No, Ma'am, you are absolutely right. We would never make it." He looked around. "There must be a blacksmith around here somewhere."

"Well, we better find him fast, because it's almost dark," Connie said.

"So you stay here with Daisy, Miss, and I'll check in some of those shops over there," he said, nodding towards the street ahead of him.

"Alright," said Connie. She stood next to Daisy as she finished eating the apple from Connie's hand. "Good girl," she said, patting her neck. "Don't you worry. I'll take care of you. I take care of all of my girls." She looked around at the town in which she had just found herself for an extended stay. There was a string of shops right near the shore line. Certainly, there was a blacksmith shop there. Even though it was late in the day, she hoped that one of them would be open.

She spent the next few minutes watching wagons pulled by horses with sturdy shoes riding by. Then, Tom ran back up the road. "Did you find one?" Connie called out as he came closer.

"Yes," Tom said.

"Great," Connie said, clapping her hands. "Let's go."

"Yes, but that shop down there is closed," Tom said. Connie looked at him puzzled.

"But, someone told me that there's another shop not far from here where the blacksmith is actually better."

"How far from here?" Connie asked. "Daisy can't go very far."

"It's not even a mile from here," he said. "Further down here, on the road between here and the Swede's Ford."

"And they're open now?" Connie asked.

"Supposed to be. They stay open later."

"Will Daisy make it that far without hurting herself?" Connie asked.

"She's already in pain, Ma'am, but we can help her if we walk her down there," Tom said.

"Walk?" said Connie, indignantly. "Walk down this dirt road in the dark, or almost dark?"

"You could ride and see how Daisy does," Tom said.

Connie rolled her eyes. "Oh, forget it. I'll walk. I'm not going to hurt Daisy. I would never hurt any of my girls," she said, patting Daisy's neck. Then she looked at Tom. "I've walked much further on the farm. I'm not helpless, you know."

"No, Ma'am," Tom said. "I know that. You are far from helpless."

"Then let's get moving," she said, patting Daisy and handing the reins to Tom. She took off her jacket and put it in the back of the wagon. "It's a little too hot to be walking and wearing this."

They headed off down the river road, Tom leading the way, Daisy limping, and Connie following on the side, stroking Daisy and saying, "There, there, girl. You'll be alright."

The setting sun twinkled behind the orange, gold and green leaves, creating an amazingly beautiful scene. It also shined on the river, giving it a golden sheen.

"Beautiful," said Connie, as they walked along the road. She didn't often take time to stop and enjoy the beauty of nature. In fact, she didn't often take time to stop and enjoy the beauty of anything. She manufactured beauty. Hers and her girls. She manufactured a beautiful experience for the male guests in her house, only if they alone considered it beautiful. The girls considered it to be a job, an acting job at that, most of the time. There were a few who really enjoyed what they were doing, who loved sex as much as they loved cherry pie, but most of her girls did what they did because they couldn't think of anything else to do and make a comfortable living. Running and keeping the house profitable, making sure the girls or the men weren't trying to cheat her, and keeping her benefactor happy when he was around took up enough of her time. There was little time to go sit by the river like she used to do sometimes with her family when they rode down by river by the Valley Forge or by the lake in Newtown Square. When she had the freedom to sit, she usually sat on the porch with Tom, watching the world go by. Even though she was here walking on a dirt road, leading a limping horse, black dress streaked with brown and tan dirt, hair falling over places on her face where she didn't want it to, she felt, for a moment, young, free and happy.

They turned the bend ahead and saw a stone structure with smoke coming out of its chimney. "That must be it," said Tom.

"Good," said Connie.

They slowly led Daisy across the street, and the sign outside the building became visible.

"Smithy" it read. As they walked closer, they also saw the red and yellow flames of the stock fire burning and fueling the black smoke that rose out of the chimney.

"Anybody here?" Tom yelled, as they approached.

Within seconds, a young white man appeared from behind the fire. He held a long metal rod in one hand, and he wiped his brow with his other hand. "May I help you?" he asked.    Sweat dripped down his face, and soot clung to strands of his hair.

"You're the blacksmith, I assume," said Tom.

"You assume right," said Daniel.

"We've got a horse here that needs a new shoe," Tom said. "And we need to get to Paoli before dark."

"I can get you up and running in about an hour, but I doubt whether you'll get to Paoli before it gets dark," he said, looking up at the sky. "That sun will set just about the time that I'm finished."

"Really?" Connie asked. "I thought we had more time."

Daniel looked at her and said, "No Ma'am. Or is it Miss?"

"Miss, if you're being technical," she said. "No, I'm not married."

Daniel laughed. "Must be your choosing then."

Connie looked at him and smiled, "It is," she said.

They locked eyes for a minute until Tom broke in. "So, can we get working on old Daisy here," he said, patting Daisy's neck.

"Sure we can," Sam said. "It will cost you a pound. A Pennsylvania pound, that is."

Tom said, "That's a fair price."

"Especially when you're stranded with no other options.

Daniel leaned the hot steel rod next to the building. "So what are we working with here?" he asked as he walked even closer.

"Left back shoe's split," said Tom. "I didn't realize it until we came down that hill leading to the Matson Ford and crossing over all of those ruts and pits."

"Most people don't," Daniel said as he reached out to pat Daisy's neck. "Isn't that right, girl?" he asked as he looked her in the eyes and patted. When he was sure that he had the horse's trust, he walked around her, keeping one hand on her body, until he came to her left rear. He kept one hand on Daisy's leg as he lifted it with the other. He took a good look at the split shoe and then put her leg back down. "I'll take good care of you, girl," he said, as he patted Daisy and looked at Connie.

Connie looked Daniel straight in the eye, while hers twinkled with a little devilishness, "I hope so," she said.

"I'm a professional," said Daniel, as he continued to look at her.

Connie wanted to say, "So am I," but that wasn't the kind of business she was there to transact, so she said, "And a good one, we heard. So, thank you for what you're about to do for our Daisy here."

Daniel went back inside and came out with a wooden stool. He put the stool on the ground next to Daisy's leg. "Keep patting her for me, would you?" he asked to Tom and Connie, but neither one in particular. He pulled a few tools out of his apron and started removing the broken shoe. It was only split in to two pieces, so that would make it easier to make one with the same measurements. Once he had the shoe off, he gathered the pieces of metal up in his hand and turned back towards his shop. "We have a few chairs inside the shop, right by the front door, if you want to sit there," he said. "It's a little warm in there with the fire and all, but the temperature is dropping a bit, just like the sun."

Connie said, "No thanks. I think I'll sit on your stool out here with Daisy and watch the sunset. It's very pretty around here."

"That it is," said Daniel. "So please, sit down," he said, motioning towards his stool. "Let me get inside and get this shoe so you can be on your way."

As he was inside heating the iron for the new shoe, James rode up on the wagon. He had just made a delivery to one of the families down the road.

"Good afternoon, Ma'am," he said, tipping his hat towards Connie. "Sir," he said, tipping his hat towards Tom. "Is Mr. Daniel helping you?"

"Yes," said Tom.

"Good," said James. "You just sit right there. He'll take real good care of you."

Connie said, "I hope so. We have to get to Paoli before it gets too dark."

"I'm sorry to tell you, Ma'am, but you won't get to Paoli before it gets dark. Do you know the way there?" James asked.

Connie said, "Yes, I grew up there. I haven't been home in a while, but I'm pretty sure I know how to get there. There can't be that many roads between here and the Lancaster Road. And once I get there, it's smooth sailing, or at least it used to be."

James said, "Yes, Ma'am, that's right. So then you know that it gets mighty dark around here once the sun goes down."

"Yes, I'm sure it does," said Connie. "It does everywhere."

"Do you have a lantern with you?"

Tom said, "Yes, we have one, the one we usually have in the wagon."

"That lantern is not big enough to light our way on these back roads with all of the trees blocking out whatever light comes down from the moon," said Connie.

"Yes, Ma'am," said James. "We keep some larger lanterns inside, and we can sell you one. Mr. Daniel can add it to your bill."

"How much?" Tom asked.

"Only two pounds," said James. "And, we should be leaving here as soon as he finishes with your horse. We're going the way you need to go to get to Paoli. You can follow us, and we'll make sure you get on the right road."

"Do you live around here?" Connie asked.

"Yes, Ma'am," said James. "We live on that big hill over there. I live up at the top, by the Gulph Mill, and Daniel lives a little down the road from me."

Connie looked at the massive hill that rose out of the flat ground that she was sitting on. "That's some hill," she said.

James said, "Yes, Ma'am. It is. High and mighty, we call it."

"Alright," said Connie. "If you can help us get on our way and make sure we're on the right road, we'll follow you. And we'll take that lantern."

"Good choice," said James. "I'll go tell Daniel that you'll be needing that lantern."

James hitched his wagon up to the post next to Daisy and went inside the shop. After a few minutes he emerged with a lantern that was about twice the size of the one that hung on Tom and Connie's wagon.

"That ought to help us," Tom said.

"Yes, sir," said James. "I think it will be mighty helpful to you." He handed the lantern to Tom, who secured it to the wagon post with one of the ropes in the back.

Daniel came out about ten minutes later with a perfectly formed, brand new horse shoe. He walked over to where Connie sat and held it up like he was holding up his first born baby.

"Looks good," said Connie, happy that they would finally be on their way.

"Would you just pat her neck while I put this on?" Daniel asked her.

"Certainly," said Connie, as she rose to walk to the front of the horse. Daniel stood close enough to her so that she saw the veins under his heavily muscled, sweat-streaked, and very masculine arms. She always liked a man with strong arms. She felt a little quiver as she looked, but that quickly passed as she realized that there was no point in having any feeling for this man who she would never see again. Instead, he put her hand on Daisy and petted and soothed her like she knew she could pet and soothe Daniel.

Daniel pulled up the stool and got down to the business of nailing the shoe on the horse. After no more than a few minutes, he was finished. He stood up, patted Daisy on her rear thigh, and said, "There you go, girl. You should feel much better now."

"Great," said Connie. "Now what do we owe you for that and for the lantern, again?"

"Three pounds," he said.

"Fine," Connie said. "Let me get my purse out of the back." She walked around him to the back, taking in the sight of his strong, muscled arms again. She pulled out enough Pennsylvania pounds to pay for the horseshoeing, the lantern, and a few coins extra to give him something for seeing them on their way to Paoli.

"Here you go," said Connie.

"Thank you," said Daniel. He looked at the money and quickly counted it in his head. "But there's too much here."

"That little bit extra is for guiding us on our way to make sure that we're taking the right road to the Lancaster Road," Connie said.

"I would never charge you for that," Daniel said. "Consider that a favor."

Connie looked at him and said, seriously, "Not many people do you a favor without expecting something in return."

Daniel looked at her and smiled. "I'm not many people."

Connie smiled, too. "I can see that," she said.

They looked at each other for a few seconds too long and too uncomfortable for Tom.

"I think we better get going," Tom said.

Spell broken, Daniel said, "You're right." He looked over at James. "James, let's close down and get these good people on their way."

Daniel smiled at Connie again and walked back to the shop. He and James doused the fire, put the tools on the wall, and then closed the heavy iron door. James unhitched his horse from the wagon, and Daniel brought his around from the post in the back. Tom reconnected Daisy to the wagon, and Connie climbed into the wagon, sweet talking Daisy the whole time. "Good girl." "Don't worry, girl." "Now we're going to make good time, girl." "Wait until we get to Paoli. We'll have lots of apples there for you in my family's grove."

Tom set a match to the wick in the new lantern, and it lit up the area around them for about three or four feet. Both James and Daniel carried small lanterns in one hand and held the reins in the other.

"Are we all ready?" James asked.

"Ready," said Tom.

"Ready," said Daniel.

"So, let's move 'em out," said James.

James led the group down a small road that led off the river road. Daniel rode beside Connie and Tom's wagon, on Connie's side. He held his lantern high to catch a good look at a face that was beautiful, even under a thin coat of dust and dirt. They proceeded about a quarter of a mile down the flat, small road until they came to a road that ran up that tall hill.

"Hold on now," James said. "This hill is mighty steep."

Connie held on tighter to the bar in front of her. James rode up and up, straight up, it seemed to Connie. As their little party climbed higher, the lights in the houses on the flat roads down beneath them became smaller and smaller. Daisy strained, breathing and snorting harder as she climbed up higher, with her new shoes and load that must have seemed heavier with every step up. Shortly, the road plateaued, and they were on top of that high and mighty hill. Lights shone all around them as families lit their lanterns inside.

"I can see why you stay up here," Connie said, calling out to James. "It's beautiful up here, too."

"Yes, Ma'am," said James. "I like looking down and seeing all of God's creation below me."

"Glad you like our little hill," Daniel said.

"Little?" said Connie, laughing. But then she said seriously, "But what goes up must come down. Do we have to go straight down on the other side?"

"No, "said Daniel. "The road down the back side of the hill into the Gulph isn't so steep. If it was, people would fall right down on the rocks and into the river."

Connie's eyes widened, and she said, "Seriously?"

"Yes," said Daniel. "We had a little problem with that until we cut in a new road."

"Well, thank God for that," Connie said.

They rode for about a mile on the plateau in relative silence. Connie just kept looking at the lights that came on and twinkled like little fallen stars. They came upon a log cabin, already lighted inside.

"This is my house," Daniel said.

Connie noticed the size, too large for just one person, and the lights on inside. "I guess your wife is home," she said.

"My Dad's wife," said Daniel. "My mother. I'm not married."

"Oh," said Connie, secretly glad that he was not what she thought he was for a minute—another married man who hoped that she would fall for his advances.

"Yes, I'd ask you to come in for supper, except I know that you want to get on," Daniel said.

"That's right," said Connie. "Our loss."

"Mine, too," said Daniel, as he looked straight at her.

The caravan made it to his front door. "Well, it looks like that shoe is working out fine for your horse."

"Yes it does," said Connie.

"So, I'll be getting off here. James will stay with you until you get down to the Gulph. Then you follow that road around to the left, and you'll be at the Lancaster Road."

Connie looked at Daniel. "Thank you so much for helping out Daisy here. And thank you for showing us the way."

"My pleasure," said Daniel. He leaned over and extended his hand to Connie. She felt warmth and electricity as she shook it.

"Mine, too," said Connie, as she smiled at him.

Daniel rode to the front and had a few words with James and Tom. Then he rode back to Connie's side. He said softly, "I can say that I hope to see you again, but I doubt whether that would happen."

"I think you're right," said Connie.

"But," said Daniel. "I can dream, can't I?"

Connie laughed. "Sometimes dreams do come true."

"That's what I'm betting on," Daniel said as he grinned. Then he tightened the reins on the horse, turned, and rode straight towards his house.

James called out, "Ready to get going again?"

"Yes," Connie said, as Tom tightened the reins and spurred Daisy on. At about half a mile later, they reached a small log cabin on the side of the narrow road. The only light around that cabin was the light from their lanterns as they approached and passed by. "That's my place," James called out. "It's not a big place, but it's big enough for me. And, when Ruthie and I get married, I'll build on a few more rooms."

"Who's Ruthie?" Connie asked.

"She's my girl. We're engaged to be married," James said. "But I have to buy her freedom first. She's down there on the Hannah Plantation, where I used to be. But I saved my money from doing blacksmithing on the side, and I bought my own freedom. I'm about halfway there with enough money to buy hers."

Connie said, "I don't think one man should enslave another. My family has all that land in Paoli, and we never had slaves, unlike some of the people in our neighborhood."

"That's mighty good of you," James said.

After about a quarter of a mile, the road started sloping. On the right side, it seemed that the earth had opened up. There was a steep gulph of rocks and river with a small road between them. "That's the Gulph," James said. "From up here it looks like God just took a knife and cut the earth open. It goes straight down. But, it's dangerous because there's rocks down there, and a big rock that juts out and hangs over the road. We call it the Hanging Rock. I'll get you down there, though, and point you in the right direction. There's always light coming from the Mill there, so that will help you. And when you pass by that hanging rock, just give your wagon enough room to clear in the rear," he laughed. "Many a wagon has gotten torn up because they didn't give themselves enough room."

They slowly made their way down the hill until they reached what was called the Gulph Road. True to what James said, the Gulph Mill was on their right, light shining through a few of its windows. A healthy creek ran right next to it. And even thought they were about a few hundred feet away from it, they could see a rock that was about 20 feet high jutting out about ten feet into the road.

"You head straight down this Gulph Road here," James said. "Then you keep going straight, and you'll run right into the Lancaster Road. And you said you know your way from there?"

"Yes," said Connie. She put out her hand to shake his. "I can't thank you enough for your help."

James shook her hand and said, "No problem, Ma'am. Glad to do it." Then he looked at Tom. "You'll be all right then, Sir?"

Tom smiled broadly as he nodded. It wasn't often that he was called Sir. He was the one usually calling people sir. "Yes, we'll be fine," he said. "Thank you kindly."

James said, "Alright then. Safe travels." He tipped his hat at Tom and Connie, and even at Daisy Jane, and sent them on their way.

"IT'S JUST like I remember it," said Connie as they rode on towards the Lancaster Road. Mostly wooded, roads packed tight from hundreds of horse hooves and carriage wheels passing over, a log cabin here, a stone house there made from the grey stone of the nearby quarries, interrupted by a mill at every creek. Mostly they saw lights inside the buildings, and an occasional one outside where man, woman or child was leading a horse to a barn, or walking by the side of the road, carrying a sack full of who knows what.

Tom rode Daisy at a fairly rapid pace. It was already dark, and most of the people in these parts went to bed when the sun went down. Connie had said that her family usually stayed up about an hour past dark with devotions, prayers thanking God for the day that was coming to an end and prayers asking him that the day to come be a safe and productive one. Thick woods surrounded them on either side, but as they rode closer to where they knew the Lancaster Road to be, something changed.

"What happened here?" Connie said, not really asking a question because she already knew the answer. The thick woods gave way to clearings on either side where trees were chopped roughly and timber carried off or burned as evidenced by the ashy fire pits visible even in the near dark. There were areas where tree trunks and limbs were fit together in crude lean-tos. Scraps of torn clothing littered some of the areas.

"Looks like our fighting boys have been through here," Tom said, as they drove farther towards the desolation and chaos that war leaves behind. "Your brothers were in that Battle in Paoli," he said," and it looks like they came through here on their way to or from."

"We must be closer to the main road," Connie said, tears welling up in her eyes as she looked at the destruction around her. "Let's hurry up and get out of here."

Tom said, "I don't think it will get any better as we get closer. In fact, I think it will be worse."

"Ugh," yelled Connie. "I'm sick of this war already."

Tom was right. As they rode along, it wasn't just trees that were cut down and burned— it was houses, too. And barns. And just about anything that was standing, it seemed. Fire pits were everywhere, and the smell of smoke filled the air.

"There it is," said Tom as they saw a crossroad ahead of them.

"Thank God," said Connie, not that she had done much thanking to Him or talking to Him for that matter for many years now.

They were close enough to see other carriages passing by on the road. Tom hit Daisy on her thigh to speed her up some. They came to a wooden sign that said Lancaster, 58 m, with an arrow pointing right, and Philadelphia 24 m, with an arrow pointing left, marking the miles to the towns in each direction. Tom turned the wagon to the right. As he did, Connie gasped.

As far as the eye could see, the road was pockmarked and ridged. Trees had been cut down, too, for as far as they could see. Buildings were burnt. Fields that should have been full of corn, squash and all other sorts of crops were stripped and trampled down.

"My God," Connie said, as she looked at what had once been a thriving road, full of commerce, fields bursting with prize-winning vegetables and fruit, and some of the most beautiful homes in the area.

Tom said, "Looks like both sides have been through here."

Connie let the tears that were building up in her eyes fall this time. She rarely cried, thinking that if she let herself go so far as to cry for *one* thing, she'd cry for *every*thing, and the tears would not stop for a long, long time. But she couldn't help herself. The contrast between the Lancaster Road she remembered and the one she saw was horrifying. She let a few tears flow as she wondered what she might find when she reached the Roberts farm. Then, she got hold of herself, as she always did. "Go faster," she said to Tom, in a cold, hard voice.

Tom looked at her, just in time to see her wipe a tear from her eye. "Yes, Ma'am," he said, as he spurred Daisy again and steered her deftly on the rough road.

"We're only about five miles down the road," Connie said. "I'll tell you where to turn."

Connie held tight as Daisy carried them down the road. She gripped her lantern as she looked straight ahead, for the most part, ignoring the destruction on every side. Weakness was not an enviable quality to her, and certainly not for her. She made this trip for a reason; she was on a mission. She'd seen the darker side of life in what she'd been doing in Philadelphia these past few years. She'd seen death, destruction, decay, and disgust. And she had risen above all of it. If she hadn't, she would have drowned in it. She set her face and her feelings like a flint, like she had done so many times before, to get through a bad situation. That was how she survived everything, and that was how she was going to survive this.

After they rode on the Lancaster Rod for a few miles, Norman and Rochelle's tavern came in to view. "We're almost there," Connie said. "We're here. We're in Paoli. That Tavern there? That's my aunt and uncle's place."

"Nice looking place," Tom said.

"When we get past there, we'll turn left at the first road at the top of the hill," said Connie.

The destruction on Lancaster Road to that point was nothing compared to the destruction around the approach to the Paoli Tavern. In what used to be full fields, now there was barely a stalk of corn standing. Everything on either side of the road had been trampled or burned. The Tavern with its strong stone exterior and thick plaster walls stood out like a beacon.

"I guess the soldiers will tear up everything else around them except the Tavern where they can get a pint," said Connie. As they rode closer to it, Connie saw several horses and wagons outside. She thought for a minute about going in and seeing her aunt and uncle who were always there, but she knew that she had to get home before devotions were over. There were a few men standing outside of the Tavern, milling about. They looked at the wagon as they drove by.

"Here, Ma'am?" Tom asked, as they came upon a road on the left.

"Yes, this is it," said Connie, as her normally calm stomach started to fill with butterflies.

The wagon turned to the left, and she gasped. The first farm that they came to belonged to the Howards. Again, places where the corn should be growing tall and the fall squash should be hanging from vines, there was just about nothing. It looked like the locusts that she had learned about in Sunday school had come through. Everything that should have been growing wasn't. It was either cut down or burned down. The fence separating the Howard's land from the Lewis' land was knocked over and incomplete. More of the Lewis' grounds were full of the produce that they should have been full of this time of year than the Howard's farm. Connie figured that was because the Howard's farm was farther away from the Lancaster Road, the main road that the soldiers travelled on. As they came closer to her family's land, there were more clumps of corn and other vegetables remaining, but not a whole lot. It was clear that their land had been cleared, too, and not in the orderly fashion that it was cleared during harvest season. It looked like it was cleared in a hurry, that whatever was there in whatever form was chopped down or picked. In the near distance, the Roberts' house came into view. Not far behind it was their barn. The warm yellow glow of a lantern could be seen through the front windows.

"It's this house here, Tom," Connie said, her voice shaking a bit with emotion.

"Looks like a right nice house, Ma'am," Tom said. "And even in the dark, I can see that the farm is right nice, too."

Connie wiped her palms on her dress. Her hands were sweating. Not much made her nervous anymore, and if it did, she didn't like to show it. But, now, on her own family's land, after all of these years, coming home to a family she left, somewhat in disgrace, but now returning in full disgrace, as far as they were concerned. Betsey would welcome her with open arms; she was still her little sister and she knew that, whatever, Betsey loved her and missed her. She had taught Betsey so much, so much of what it meant to be a girl, a woman, a good woman, not the kind that she was accused of being. And her mother, she was sure that she would welcome her back with open arms. She was her baby, after all. Her first born. Her little girl. That didn't change, no matter what she had done. Her mother would see her as that innocent, beautiful baby that she brought into the world, that little girl that she nursed at her breast until she cooked and mashed and liquefied her food, and fed her with a wooden spoon that her father had made until she was old enough to hold her own spoon and make a mess in their small kitchen as she tried to get the mashed squash and applesauce and wheat cereal into her tiny, eager, and hungry mouth. And she would see her as the little girl whose hair she combed and braided and festooned with ribbons and bows so she could hold her hand and walk her to church or to school. And the girl she taught how to ride a horse side saddle, like a lady, knowing that she would follow behind the father that she adored, and ride it with legs on either side, fast, like he did. Connie figured that her mother would hold back a few seconds because her father would expect her to, but that she couldn't stop herself from holding open her arms and welcoming her prodigal daughter back home.

But her father. That was the problem. Connie knew that he was devastated when she left on the arm or the wagon of a man of whom he did not approve, for a life he did not understand, and that he was destroyed when he heard that man left her and that she took up with a woman whose profession he knew of only too well. He had to see it for himself, he said, when he surprised Connie and confronted her one evening at Madame's home. Orland asked for Connie by name, and when he saw Connie come out, dressed to appeal and made up like a younger, smaller version of Madam, he looked at her with tear-filled eyes, and said, "I just had to see it for myself. And now that I have, I don't want to see you again."

Connie ran back into her room that night and cried so much that she was no good for the rest of the evening. But, when she stopped crying in the morning, she splashed her face with water and vowed never to cry again over a life that she had lost because it was a life that she didn't want.

She vowed never to return to the Roberts farm in Paoli at that time, but she never thought then that there would be a war fought right here, right in their own back yards, involving her own little brothers. She thought like a young person thought then—that her family would always be around and that her parents, yet alone her baby brothers, weren't old enough to die. So, she thought nothing of her grudge and the disconnection that came along with it. Yet, when she heard that there was a battle fought in Paoli, right in her own backyard, a battle that she was sure that her little brothers were involved in, she started to think differently. And then, when she realized that the rebels were coming to Germantown and that those rebels were in General Wayne's regiment and that would, of course, be where her brothers were fighting, she risked her own safety to sit out on her porch and find out what was going on with her brothers.

The sight of her brother Fred filled her with more emotion than she had felt in years. And the knowledge that her little brother Allen had died filled her with emotions that she had stomped down for years before that. The destruction all around her and her house in Germantown deterred her only for a moment. Nothing would have deterred her from finding out what happened to the one brother who had miraculously appeared to her days before. Not even the scorn, the rejection, and the hurt that would come from seeing her father one more time.

So, as the wagon pulled up closer to her childhood home, Connie steeled herself. She was prepared to go in and face whatever her father had for her. She had to know what happened to her brother. She touched Tom's arm gently, "Stop the carriage," she said, softly. "I don't want you to go closer. I don't want them to see us. I can't have my father close the door to us before I find out what happened to my brother, and he might just do that if he sees us coming. So, I want you and Daisy to wait here. I'm going to walk from here and pray that it's my mother or sister who opens the door. And, once they do, and I'm inside, then I'll call for you. Only then," she said.

Tom looked at her with softness and concern in his eyes. "Yes, Ma'am. I understand. Me and Daisy will wait right here."

Connie leaned over and blew on the lantern that she was holding. She gave it to Tom. "I don't even want them to see the light from my lantern, so can you hold this?"

"Of course," he said. "But you be careful."

Connie looked at him as the tears welled in her eyes again. "I've walked this road many times before," she said. "Even in the dark, even with all the time I've been away, I know this road. I know my way home," she said as the tears fell. She wiped them out of her eyes so she could see clearly, held the bar, and stepped down one step and then another. Both feet landed firmly on the sturdy road that she knew only too well. She wiped her sweaty palms on her now thoroughly dirty and dusty dress. She steadied herself, and then she turned towards Tom.

She smiled at him and said, "Wish me luck."

"Good luck, Miss," he said, as he tipped his hat towards her.

"Thank you," said Connie, as the tears welled up again. She turned, lifted her filthy skirt out of habit, and walked down the road home. She walked slowly because, even though she had been down that road hundreds of times, she could only see a few feet in front of her. With every step, more tears came until they overflowed. She pinched herself to try to stop them, but she couldn't. They came, and they kept coming. But she didn't care. She was home. She felt that as soon as her feet touched the ground. She was happy to be home. She was happy to walk on ground that was familiar to her, ground that she walked on when she was innocent. Ground that she walked on when she thought she knew everything. Ground that she walked on now as a woman who knew that she didn't know as much as she thought she did. And with every step, with every tear that fell on that ground, with every tear that streamed down her face, she didn't care that her Dad had said that she didn't want to ever see her again, because she wanted to see him. And she wanted to see her mother. And she wanted to see her sister. She didn't care that she might be yelled at, or rejected, or hurt, or told to get out. She didn't care about any of that. She was home.

As she approached the house, her face was wet, her top was wet, and her skirt was wet with tears. She held her head up, proud and straight. She held her skirt up, mindful that she was a lady, even if some people thought that she was not. She walked straight ahead, softly, and slowly until she reached the front door. She stood there for a minute, crying. Then she raised her hand, grabbed the cast iron door knocker and knocked three times, so there was no doubt that there was someone at the door.

She heard the voices inside. She heard her father say, "Who is it at this hour?" She heard his large feet still encased in heavy shoes walking across the wooden floor. She heard him grab the iron handle from the inside. She heard him slide the latch to the side. The door opened wide, and he looked out. Before he could adjust his eyes to the dark, before he could say anything, she cried, "Daddy!", and threw her arms around him.

ORLAND ROBERTS stood frozen. He looked down at the woman whose tears were wetting his shirt. This woman who threw her arms around him without giving him a chance to say or do anything. Orland Roberts looked down, wide-eyed, at the woman he said he didn't want to see again. Orland Roberts looked down at his daughter.

Teenie Roberts threw her Bible down on the chair and ran over to the door. "Connie!" she called out. She ran over and threw her arms around her daughter, whose arms were still locked around her father. Orland hadn't moved.

Betsey took a minute to realize what was happening, longer than Teenie who would know her daughter anywhere. When she realized that the woman whose head was buried in her father's chest, the woman who had her mother's head buried in her hair, was her big sister Connie come home, Betsey threw her Bible down on the chair and ran over, too. "Connie!" she yelled, as she ran over and threw her arms around her mother, trying to actually touch her sister.

Orland still stood there, looking at these three women whose arms were around him and whose tears were being soaked up by his clothes. He stood there while they cried and cried. He stood there just about motionless. Then Betsey backed up and pulled her arms off her mother. And Teenie backed up to take a good look at Connie. And Connie backed up to take a good look at her father's face.

Orland looked first at Betsey, whose eyes were lit up and whose smile was spread from ear to ear. Then he looked at Teenie, tears streaming down her face, hands clasped together as if in prayer, eyes fixed on his as if her prayer was directed towards him. And then he looked at Connie, tears streaming down her still beautiful face, although worn and older from the last time she saw her, but more beautiful because it wasn't painted up like it was in the parlor of Madam's house, and more beautiful because it had the beauty of maturity. And he thought about his boys, one dead and one who could be dead for all they knew. And he looked at his daughter, his first born, his oldest. He looked into her tear-filled eyes, and his eyes filled with his own tears. And he held his arms out wide, and he smiled, and he said, "Welcome home, Connie." And Connie ran back to him and threw her arms around him, and this time he threw his arms around her and held on to her for a very long time.

AFTER ALL the tears that any of them had stored up inside of themselves fell, the Roberts family—minus the boys—sat in the main room of their house. Connie felt comfortable with just about everything. Even though she had been away for several years, the room hadn't changed that much. There were a few chairs, made when Orland chopped down the trees in the back, and a table, made out of the walnut trees that lined the border of their farm and the Miller's. Embers still glowed in the cook stove, surrounded by the iron pots that the boys made when they apprenticed with Mr. Goodner, the local ironsmith.

Connie sat on a chair next to her mother. Orland's chair faced theirs. Betsey sat at Connie's feet. Connie ran her fingers through Betsey's hair, and Betsey rubbed Connie's leg.

"What brings you back here, Connie?" Orland asked, hoping all the while that whatever it was, she would temper her language and censor herself because even though he and her mother and the boys knew what Connie did, he had hoped that Connie would have the sense not to discuss it around Betsey.

Connie squeezed her mother's hand. "I've come home to find out if you got any word about Fred. He came right by my house a few days ago with the rest of General Wayne's boys when they were on their way to fight the British in Germantown. I was shocked and happy to see him," she said. "He told me that Allen was killed in a battle here a few weeks ago."

"A massacre," Orland said.

"What happened in that battle down there?" Teenie asked.

"I've never heard such noise," Connie said. "Cannons and gunfire all day. We stayed in the house, on the floor and in the basement just about all day. The next day, I went out and almost everything around us was blown up, torn up, and in ruins. There were bodies everywhere. From both sides. Of course I wondered where Fred was. Some of my friends and I walked all up and down the Germantown Road,, where the fighting took place, and looked at every body in a blue uniform. A lot had been killed, but a lot were still alive, but wounded. We looked must have looked at every blue uniform a mile or so down the road where the fighting took place," Connie said, rubbing her eyes at the horrible memory of so much blood, torn skin and broken bones.

She continued, "But nobody saw him. When my friends came upon a man in a blue uniform, I had them call for me and have me look into his face, since they didn't know what Fred looked like. But we didn't see him." Then she rubbed her mother's arm, "And having just seen one brother and finding out that one had been killed, I had to know what happened to the one I had left. The soldiers that they sent to pick up the wounded and any weapons or ammunition they could find said that General Washington was good about making sure that families knew if their boys had been killed. So I decided that I would come on up here and see if anyone had gotten word to you." She looked straight at her Dad. "I know it's been a while, but I hope you don't mind having me here."

Teenie looked at Orland for him to respond. She knew that he had told Connie to never come back home again, but she also knew how different everything was now.

"This is your home, Connie," said Orland. "No matter how long you've been gone." Or what you've done, he wanted to add, but he figured that he didn't have to say that now.

"Thank you Daddy," she said. "Thank you, Mom," she added.

Orland sighed and leaned forward. "Connie, we had heard something about a big battle in Germantown, but we didn't get many details beyond that. We heard it was kind of a draw, casualties on both sides with neither side losing a lot more than the other. But, no, we haven't heard anything about Fred being one of the casualties."

"No news is good news," said Teenie.

Connie nodded, "I guess you're right, Mom. Well, I can tell you that our boys are camped over there in Whitemarsh, further up the Germantown Road. And the British, they've kept a few of their officers and regulars in Germantown, but they sent most of them down into Philadelphia with the others."

"That's good to know," said Orland. "As much information as we can get on those redcoats, the better it will be for our boys. It's been hard to get timely and correct information and information in advance to give our boys the advantage." He lowered his voice. "Your uncle Norman and I are part of a group that collects information and passes it on to our boys. You know a lot of people pass through your Uncle's tavern."

Connie said, "Yes, they always had. I guess the war hasn't changed that. Men want what they want, war or no war, and one thing they want is liquor." The other is sex, Connie thought, but there was no sense in saying that now.

Betsey said, "Are you going to stay here now Connie, since everything was blown up where you were?"

Connie smiled. "Not everything was blown up. I still have my house, and there's still some neighbors who have theirs, not as many, but still some. I just came up to find out if you heard anything about Fred. I have some friends watching my house, but I have to get back soon. It's my house, not theirs, and I'm the one who has to really watch out for it."

Orland frowned. "Isn't it dangerous down there, with the redcoats around?"

Connie said, "No, Daddy. I know how to take care of myself. I know how to make friends with all types of people, or at least have them thinking that I'm their friend. It's about survival at this point."

"I understand," Orland said. "It sounds like you know how to work both sides of the fence."

"I do," said Connie. "I have to. I have to take care of myself."

"Sounds like you'd make a good addition to our network," Orland said.

Betsey looked at her father. "No fair, Dad. You won't let me work with your network, but you want Connie to?"

Orland looked at Betsey, and said, "Hush. Connie's grown and knows how to take care of herself. You're still a little girl."

"I'm not so little," Betsey said. "I'm almost 17."

Connie furrowed her brow in a thoughtful look. She had as much contact with the British in Philadelphia as anyone, and she had favor with officers of all ranks. She could have access to all types of information.

"Daddy, are you serious about me becoming a part of your network?" Connie asked.

Orland said, "You know, I hadn't thought of it before, but you could really be a help to us. We need as many eyes and ears on our side as possible."

Connie said, "I know a lot of the British officers, high and low, and their soldiers. I run into them all the time. It would be very easy for me and my friends to find out information. But how would we pass it on?"

"We'd work that out," Orland said. "We'd find someone we trust to meet up with you and get the information."

Betsey jumped up. "How about me? Why can't I go get the information from Connie?"

Teenie said, "Because you're way too young. We can't have you going into the city on your own to see your sister and get information."

"Well why don't you come with me?" Betsey asked.

Teenie's eyes got wide. She never thought about that.

Orland said, "She's got a point there, honey. Me and most of the other men can't travel that freely into and out of the city. But you," he said, pointing at Teenie and Betsey, "a mother and daughter travelling to the city? That might work."

Connie said, "I know where we could meet." Then she looked at Orland. "Not at my house," she said, assuring him that Betsey would be kept away from Connie's profession, "but at the market in Philadelphia. You could bring your goods in to sell. God knows, there is a need for food, with the blockades and all of those soldiers to feed. You could bring in your crops in the fall and spring, and bring in some wool goods in the winter, you know those scarves and hats you and your friends are always knitting."

"Yes!" said Betsey, excitedly.

"And we can exchange information when I buy your goods at the market," Connie said excitedly. "No one will ever know"

Orland shook his finger. "You hope no one will ever know. You still have to be careful."

"We will," said Connie. "I'll be looking out for them. "

"And I'll be looking out for Betsey," said Teenie.

Orland stroked his beard. "You know this just might work."

"It will work," said Betsey, with all of the confidence of a teenager.

"We'll make it work," said Connie, as she squeezed Teenie's hand and patted Betsey on the head.

# CHAPTER 37
# WHITEMARSH

The hours stretched on. Waiting, and for what? Another battle for sure. The only question was where and when. Fred pushed the same dirty cloth that he used every day down his musket to make sure that there was nothing in it to clog the gunpowder that was going to be put in there. Whenever they were called to battle, he was going to be ready. The Battle of Germantown showed him and the rest of General Wayne's boys that they could beat the redcoats in a fair fight, like the one at Germantown, and not in a blindside massacre, like the one in Paoli. In Germantown, they fought fair and square for the most part. Their line facing the British line. Firepower to firepower. And then, just like the British did to them in Paoli—bayonet to flesh. Hand to hand combat, bayonet to bayonet—no quarter, no prisoners. The other divisions that fought in Germantown might have sustained heavy losses and retreated without accomplishing their objective, but not General Wayne's boys. "Remember Paoli" was their battle cry, and they were going to give the redcoats as good as they got. Before they retreated, the Paoli boys chased down the same redcoat division that massacred so many of them in Paoli and left the redcoats even redder with their own blood this time. Left the street of Germantown littered with British dead and dying. Left the streets of Germantown victorious with their muskets and bayonets held high in the air, shouting slogans of victory.

But all of that energy was fading somewhat as day after day passed in Whitemarsh with no movement, no knowledge of when they might next meet the British and practice their more finely-honed skills on them. Fred still thought about Allen every day and imagined that he would for the rest of his life. Fred thought about the look on Allen's face as he realized that the bayonet went through him and the blood was draining out of him, taking his life with it. That was a look that Fred would never forget.

Every day in Whitemarsh seemed to be like the one before it. They woke up to the sound of a trumpeter's reveille, they ate a sparse breakfast, they did a few drills, they cleaned their weapons, the bakers baked bread, they ate again, General Wayne roused them with patriotic words, they lit campfires and sang or told stories, they did sentry or picket post duty when their turn came, and they slept on pallets that were never soft enough. And the next day they did it all again.

They heard that the British had retreated to Philadelphia for the winter, early, after the Battle of Germantown. They knew that they too were going to winter quarters soon, but they didn't know where. They just hoped that there was some food wherever they were going. There wasn't much where they were now. The British had been there at Whitemarsh before the patriots, taking whatever food they could find on their march into Germantown and Philadelphia last month. All the patriots had left to eat were fruits and vegetables that were too unripe to eat when the British marched through. They ate apples of every variety, prepared in every way possible—mashed, boiled, fried, baked, and just eaten fresh. Squash was just coming of age, so they had that, too, in every form, just like an apple, except they didn't eat the squash raw. Every few days a foraging party would return with a cow or some chickens that they got off some farmer supporter farther and farther away from camp. The meat was cut into as small pieces as possible so that it went as far as possible. Sometimes it seemed that the porridge just had meat juice in it, as opposed to actual pieces.

One day, Fred noticed a few of the divisions marching out. "Looks like we're going to get some action," he said, as he saw them marching off, about a quarter a mile away. Fred and the rest of the Paoli boys cleaned their guns extra well that day, tightened up their packs, and prepared to march out to battle. They anxiously sat and stood around waiting. In the distance, they saw General Wayne riding in, musket held high.

"Men," he said, as he rode closer. "Our brothers in the Connecticut and New Jersey regiments are going off to blockade the British, to take over the waterways going into Philadelphia, to stop their provisions of ammunition, food and what have you from getting to Philadelphia to keep them during their winter quarters. I know you want to join them. I know you want to fight after your spectacular showing in the Battle of Germantown,"

The men yelled positively in response. General Wayne lifted both hands to quiet them. "But this is not our fight, men," he said.

Groans arose from the rebel regulars.

"No, this is not our fight," said General Wayne. "At least not now. Not today. Our fight will soon be known. Your orders will soon come. Believe me. General Washington and I are meeting with the other Generals every day. The British will winter in Philadelphia, and we have to find a location that works to our advantage in every way. We haven't done that yet. So, in the meantime, please take this time to rest, to grow stronger, to become an even stronger fighting force than you showed yourself to be at Germantown. We will need you soon."

Fred joined the rest of Wayne's division in cheering for him, as they always did when he spoke to the troops. They had devotion unlike other troops. The regulars called General Wayne "Mad Anthony" because of his temperament—he was always up for a fight, and never one to shy away from battle. His men respected him for that and, if they weren't like that when they enlisted and started on this journey with their commander, they soon became very much like him. Wayne's division had a reputation, especially after Germantown, as being a fierce, forceful, fearless fighting force.

"This project to block the seaport is a sea battle, men," Wayne said. "The men who are going down now are sailors more than fighters. General Washington needs men with sea skills for this project, so even though he knows of your superior fighting ability, he said to me personally, 'General Wayne, we must save your men for another time when fierce ground fighters, not sea fighters, are needed.'"

Wayne raised his musket up in the air, and his men cheered.

"So, rest men. Your time will come," he said. Then he raised his musket in the air one more time, "Remember Paoli!" he yelled.

"Remember Paoli!" the men yelled back.

# CHAPTER 38
# PAOLI

Connie slept in Betsey's bed, arms wrapped around Betsey like she was a lover she wanted to pull closer. Betsey nestled her head in Connie's chest like she was a man seeking comfort after a long day in the bosom of his woman.

They slept like that the night before, too, as Connie let the fatigue and excitement of the two days previous come down on her. She slept most of her first full day back home. So did Tom, who, despite the movement in the living room, slept and snored loudly.

The rest of the day, Connie stayed in the house, helping Teenie cook, recalling the skills she once had as a younger girl, talking to Betsey about what it was like to live in the city, while hiding exactly what she did in the city, talking to her Dad about the spy network, and planning a schedule of trips for Teenie and Betsey to the city market. She even spent some time at the tavern, visiting with Aunt Rochelle and Uncle Norman. Dad told them that Connie was now going to be part of the network, and they regaled her with tales of how they had been operating before. Even Doctor John came by to welcome Connie into the network.

Aunt Rochelle and Uncle Norman had another local couple take care of things at the tavern for a few hours so they could have a welcome back dinner with Connie at the Roberts' home. Several of the neighbors dropped by, having been warned by Orland to not talk about what they all knew that Connie did.

The day could not have gone any better, as far as Connie was concerned. Everyone welcomed her back with open arms. Tom had a good time, too, not having to work, and just enjoying the food, wine, and conversation. He enjoyed his two days of relative leisure, as Orland wouldn't let him do any work and treated him like a guest in his home, which he was, instead of as Connie's handyman, which he was also.

On the third day, Connie woke up relatively early, right with the cocks crowing. She dressed quickly, as did Betsey who woke up when Connie did. Teenie hurried into the kitchen to fix a big breakfast to send Connie and Tom on their way—scrambled eggs with cheese, fried tomatoes, fresh bacon, home fried white potatoes, fresh baked biscuits. Connie ate two helpings, as did Tom. The conversation at the table was light and happy.

"Well," said Connie wiping her mouth with Teenie's best cloth napkin, "we'd better get going."

Teenie said, "I wish you didn't have to go." She frowned and shrugged her shoulders. "But I understand."

Connie took her hands in hers and said, "I know. But it won't be so bad this time. I'll see you in a few weeks, instead of a few years."

Teenie smiled and said, "Yes. That's much better."

Betsey said, "I can't wait to get to the market to see you again", and she ran over and hugged Connie.

"I'll miss you, too, Betsey," said Connie, "and I'll be so happy to see you."

Then Connie looked over at her Dad. She walked to him and threw her arms around his neck while he was still sitting at the table. Orland put both arms up and rubbed Connie's arms.

"You're still my little girl," he said, whispering into her ear.

"Always," said Connie, as she squeezed him tighter

"I'm glad you came home, and I'm glad you'll be working with us," he said.

"Me, too, Daddy. Anything to help."

Connie loosened her grip and looked over at Tom. "Are we ready?"

"Yes, Ma'am," he said.

"Alright," said Connie. "One more big hug for everyone, and then we'll be on our way. I've got to find out what those redcoats are doing now."

Everyone laughed, came over and hugged her, walked her to the front door, and then waved, as she and Tom drove down the lane, out of sight and back to Germantown.

# CHAPTER 39
# NOVEMBER
# GERMANTOWN

"You must join us," the General said to Connie, as he put first one leg and then the other into his white pants. "The best people in Philadelphia will be there, or so we've been promised."

The best Tories, Connie thought.

"I always did like a good party," she said, smiling, and twirling the curls in her long brown hair. "And any excuse to really dress up in my finest is certainly welcome. There's been so much desolation and depression around this city."

The General responded enthusiastically. "Exactly," he said, slapping his thigh with one hand. "Winter is just starting, and we'll be quartered here for a while. There won't be any fighting. That's not the gentlemanly thing to do, and even though I detest him, I understand that General Washington is a gentleman."

"So I hear," said Connie, when she had heard no such thing. She heard from her Dad and everyone else that the General was one of the most fearless fighting men and one who had been blessed by the Gods with protection from being harmed in battle. His survival against all manner of Indian arrows in the French Indian war was legendary. And his men hardly went into battle without him leading them, even though that was not proper military protocol, as she understood it. She had heard that he was also a brilliant strategist, only defeated in any battle in this war due to a series of unfortunate events, like weather or miscommunication on the part of his generals.

"So, shall I send a carriage for you?" he asked, now putting his sash on over his red coat.

"I would appreciate that," Connie said, "then Tom can stay here and watch things."

The General clapped his hands together. "Perfect," he said. "Day after tomorrow. Thursday. I'll send it for you around six so you arrive on time."

Connie stood now, ready to walk him down stairs, happy for this stroke of good luck to have access to so many British officers and Tories in one room.

The General grabbed her around the waist and pulled her close. "I want to show you off," he whispered in her ear.

"Me?" Connie asked. "Won't some of those society ladies be suspicious of who I am?"

"I don't care about them," the General said. "I'm not ashamed of you. You're a beautiful woman and any man in his right mind should be happy to have you around."

Connie looked at him, eyes narrowed, suspicious. "Most men don't want to be seen with me," she said. "At least outside of this house."

"That's because most men are afraid their wives will find out. But my Mrs. is thousands of miles and an entire ocean away, and as far as I'm concerned, what she doesn't know won't hurt her," he said. "And she's not naïve enough to believe that I'm over here fighting this war with no female companionship and comfort."

Connie pulled back slightly, and looked him straight in the eye. "Then she's a smart woman," she said, with a smile.

The General, eyes wide with a bit of a shock at the statement, looked at Connie and said, "I guess you're right." Then he picked up his hat and said, "Enough about her" and headed towards the door.

Connie followed right behind him and walked him down the stairs and out the side door. He didn't want to enter in the front door anymore because, as he said, as commander of these troops, he couldn't fraternize with them, and certainly not in a whore house—in so many words.

Connie obliged him by letting him come in and out of the side door because, given her new position, the one thing she wanted the General to keep doing was coming to visit her.

When they reached the door, the General put on his hat, and then tipped it towards her. "Until Thursday, then," he said.

"Until Thursday," Connie said, as she blew him a kiss.

CONNIE BEGAN dressing on Thursday around three. First, she took a bath with lavender scented oils to calm herself down. Then she expertly applied her makeup—the new cheek rouge that the General smuggled in for her and the various powders and creams that she already had and used just about every day, because she had long ago decided that she wanted to look her best every day. The only thing she did differently today was to apply some extra dabs of the perfumed oils she made for herself and the girls. Her oils lasted longer than any oils that you could buy because she and her girls needed perfume that would stay on, no matter how much they sweated or rolled around in sheets or on top of or underneath men. She pulled out her finest jewelry—large white pearls surrounded by large sparkling diamonds that hung around her neck, with the largest pearl pointing straight down her cleavage and nestling comfortably no more than an inch above where the cleavage began. She clipped on matching ear bobs. Her ears would be on display because she was going to twist her hair artfully into a curvy chignon. She lid on a bracelet that matched the necklace and ear bobs. For rings, she wore a large diamond, two carats, on her right hand, and a glossy pearl surrounded by inlaid diamonds on her right. Her shoes were white with gold threads, with one large pearl in the center and smaller pearls lining the edges.

Once she put on her jewelry, it was time for the dress. She called one of the other girls to come and fasten the row of delicate pearl buttons that ran the length of the dress' corset in the back. The foundation fabric was a white silk. It was overlaid with gold chiffon. The bodice was gathered into row after row of pleats, each no more than a quarter of an inch wide.

"All done," said Suzie, as she buttoned the last button. Connie turned around. "You look absolutely beautiful," Suzie said.

"Thank you," said Connie as she ran her hands down the sides of the skirt. She looked at the clock across the room. "And a few minutes to spare." Connie walked over to the chair next to her bed and picked up a small purse. The base of it was rectangular. It was covered in ivory pearls, white silk, and rhinestones. The clasp was a large pearl. The cord was gleaming, ivory satin.

"Now, I'm ready," she said, as she turned back towards Suzie.

"The other girls are going to want to see you, you know," Suzie said.

"Oh, I guess you're right," Connie said. "Aren't they working now?" she asked.

Suzie said, "Yes, some of them have clients, but you know they can put them on hold. And, for you, they'd want to."

Connie shook her head. "Alright."

Suzie clapped her hands. "Good! I'll go get them. I'll have them out of those rooms in a few minutes and downstairs to see you. You'll be in the back room?"

"Yes," Connie said.

"Great," said Suzie. "Let me start knocking on these doors, and we'll meet you downstairs."

"That's fine," Connie said, as she headed towards the door and out in the hall.

NOT MORE than a few minutes after she reached the back room, one by one, all the girls had come down. After they "oohed" and "aahed" over her, Connie gave them each a big hug and sent them back upstairs. The General's carriage arrived right on time at 6 pm. The footman smiled widely at the sight of her. "You look lovely ma'am," was about all he was permitted to say.

"Thank you," said Connie, as he helped her into the carriage. The carriage was one of the General's best. It wasn't beaten up and scarred like a lot of the carriages you see out on the street these days. No, on this one, the brass was shined, the wood was polished, and the leather cushions were firmly stuffed. The dirt had been wiped off and the windows cleaned. The footman closed the door, which protected Connie from the dust and dirt on the outside road.

The Germantown Road was largely deserted at this hour. It was already dark. Most people stayed inside their houses now. British sympathizers or not, people stayed home to hold on to what they had. There still was a fear that redcoats would turn up at their doors looking for food, furniture for fires, clothes or whatever. Connie rode comfortably in silence, thinking of the depravation that her family and just about everyone else that she knew was facing. She assuaged her guilt with the thought that the comforts that she had at her house were not just ill-gotten gain. Now there was a purpose to the comfort besides survival—-the purpose was information. She had to keep her relationship with the General and her girls' relationships with the other British officers going because that was the only way to keep the information flowing. And, while most women were dressed in homespun rags and she in a white and gold silk gown, she held the thought that she needed to wear that gown to get information to help that lady in homespun have a better life for herself.

The carriage finally reached the City of Philadelphia, with its narrow streets and street lamps on every corner. Here, there were more people finely dressed, but there were also more people hardly dressed at all. The footman called out, "We're almost there, Ma'am," and Connie sat up slightly. She pulled a small looking glass with tortoise shell backing out of her tiny purse and checked her reflection. "Perfect," she said, and put it back in. The carriage pulled up to a grand house right in the center of the main part of the city. It was brick with a stone wall on the street and a circular driveway that was lined with carriages. Her carriage fell in line. She leaned close to the window and watched the others alight from their carriages. She couldn't see everyone all that well, but she was glad she choose the gown that she did. It seems that every woman who was getting out of a carriage had picked her finest dress. Even so, Connie didn't consider them competition and didn't shy away from understanding how she would compare to the rest of them. She would stand out. She always did.

Her carriage was next in line. She knew that the General would be standing right inside the door, greeting the guests as the commander-in-chief of the British army. He would welcome all of the guests with the other generals and then, when all the guests would have or should have arrived, he would break from formalities and find her and dance the night away with her. At least that's what he told her.

The footman came around and opened the door. He handed the man next to him the card that had Connie's name written on it. The footman extended his hand and helped Connie down from the carriage. The man next to her extended his arm for Connie to hold it and stood with her at the opened doorway. He said, loudly to the generals lined up there, "Presenting Miss Constance Roberts of Germantown."

Connie smiled at the line of generals who were all smiling at her, eyes dancing. Four generals down the line was her General, who was beaming as he smiled at her. The man who announced her presented her to the first general, who bowed and extended his hand, eyes undressing her the whole time. Connie smiled her most gracious and seductive smile, extended her hand, and allowed him to kiss it, gently.

"General Surrey. A pleasure to meet you," he said.

Connie nodded. "The pleasure is all mine."

He passed her hand down to the next general, who quickly took Connie's hand in his.

"General Cotswold," he said. "A pleasure."

"Likewise," said Connie.

Then her hand was passed to her General Howe. He looked her up and down with wide eyes and an even wider smile.

"Welcome, Miss Roberts," he said.

"Thank you, General," she said, as he kissed her hand.

"You look like an angel," he said.

Connie smiled and whispered to him, "Well, we know I'm not that."

The general laughed. "Thank God for that, Miss Roberts," he said, still holding her hand.

"I should be finished here shortly, and then I won't leave your side for the rest of the evening."

"Promise?" Connie asked, looking him straight in the eyes.

"Promise," said the General.

"Good," said Connie. "I'm looking forward to it."

The General broke the trance and looked at the line of people behind Connie waiting to shake his hand. Then, Connie looked over her shoulder.

"I'll see you inside," she said, as she slowly pulled her hand away from his and walked inside the main room.

The main room was awash in people, food, light, taffeta, silk, gold, silver, laughing, and dancing. Connie hadn't seen such a merry scene in a long time. She was used to death, destruction, ruin, depravation, brown, grey, black, crying, screaming, and bits and pieces. She actually smiled at what she was looking at.  No one would ever know that the men in this room were in the middle of a war.  They and their uniforms gleamed in this sea of plenty.  She walked over to one of the polished wooden banquet tables that was stacked and loaded with seemingly every type of food that they could get their hands on.  The blockade didn't affect them tonight.  She wondered how many British regulars were going without so that the generals and officers and their sympathizers could have this party.  But she forced herself to put such thoughts out of her mind.  She was to be gay, unaffected, and a perfect companion for the general.  She could not wear guilt.  That would wear her down, and nothing should wear her down tonight.

# CHAPTER 40

# DECEMBER WHITEMARSH

"We're moving out today, men," General Wayne announced to Fred and the rest of his troops assembled. "We're going down the hill and over the Matson Ford to the Gulph, where we're going to camp. We should be fine, but be every ready. We know that the British have been riding up and down our countryside on foraging parties, stealing food from our people and goods from their homes. But you know what to do if you encounter any of them, don't you?" he asked.

"Yeah," they yelled back. "The bayonet!" someone yelled. "Shoot first and ask questions later," someone else yelled out.

"That sounds about right," said General Wayne, raising his musket in the air. "So grab your gear. We'll be lining up and following General Lee's troops from New England. Now fall out."

The men kept shouting, "Yeah!" and "Finally!" and slapping each other on the back. They were going to be on the move. They had spent several weeks at the camp at Whitemarsh, and they all knew that wasn't winter quarters. They all knew they were going to have to march somewhere else, and the waiting, the boredom, was getting to them all. Matson's Ford and the Gulph wasn't that far from Whitemarsh, but at least it was movement. And movement before it started getting too cold for too long. Fred remembered that he had crossed the Matson Ford many times with his father as they drove into Philadelphia and Germantown to sell their produce, meat and other goods. He remembered the Gulph as a break in the earth that left one massive hill on one side with a huge rock hanging out over the road by the stream and another large hill on the other side. That huge rock pointed straight out like an arrow and was a landmark for anyone who came by. "The Hanging Rock", they called it, because it hung over the road so much. That hill is so high that it would give us a good look out point to see the British if they came out from Philadelphia, Fred thought. If the Continental Army wintered there, at least they could have some shelter, he thought, too. Either way, he would be happy to get out of that Whitemarsh camp. After a month, nearly everything around them was stripped bare, and even though they had to clean up after themselves, the camp wasn't the most sanitary place; in fact, it was kind of a mess.

## CHAPTER 41
# GERMANTOWN

Connie was in the parlor, adding more holiday decorations. Christmas was about three weeks away, and, even in war, the house had to be decorated.  She had already put some evergreens in a garland fashion over the fireplace, and now she added red ribbons.  Tom had collected a few baskets of pine cones, and she was placing them just right among the evergreens.  So much in her parlor was already decorated red, and the greens always made a great contrast.  Just as she grabbed another pine cone, the front door opened, and Tom rushed in.

"The redcoats are marching up the road," he yelled, excitedly.

Connie dropped the pine cone back in the basket, eyes wide, and said, "Where? What road?"  Some spy she was; she hadn't heard anything about the British being on the move.  They were supposed to be ensconced in winter quarters in Philadelphia, with a small group of them in Germantown.

"The road out here.  The Germantown Road," Tom said.

"What?" Connie asked, excitedly.  "What's going on?"

"Don't know, Ma'am," Tom said, "but the first columns just marched by, and it looks like the rest of the army is coming up the road after them. That's all you can see coming down the road.  And they're running into houses, knocking down the doors, and I'm smelling smoke, so it seems like they're burning, too."

"Oh my God," said Connie as she ran to the front door. She ran out on to the porch. Then she picked up her skirt like she was going to run out to the road and see for herself.

Tom grabbed her arm. "No, Miss. Don't go out there. They're looking mighty fierce today."

Her face suddenly went pale. "Our boys are further up the road, in Whitemarsh." Her eyes became large for a few seconds. "And my brother is there. If he's still alive."

"I know, Ma'am. I know," said Tom. "But right now, we have to take care of our own."

Connie had momentarily forgotten herself. Survival. That was her game. She turned to Tom, "You're right. Go get the girls, and tell them to get down here. Half the British army has been over to this house, but we still have to be on guard against the half that hasn't."

"Yes, Ma'am," Tom said. He turned and ran into the house.

Connie stayed outside on the porch. "That bastard," she said out loud, thinking of the General. "The least he could have done was warned me." But he didn't, she thought. So, game on. If he wasn't going to warn her when his army was potentially coming right to her doorstep, any guilt she might have felt about spying on him flew out of the window.

The girls started coming out of their rooms and going outside. Connie turned around at the noise of their footsteps—a survival habit. "Again?" one of them said as she ran to stand next to Connie.

"Again," said Connie, with anger in her voice.

One by one the other girls came down until they all stood on the porch. As they did, the noise from the Germantown Road grew louder. There was the sound of thousands of boots marching on hard packed dirt roads, large cannons being dragged across those roads, horses being ridden by lines of light dragoons, sporadic gunfire, cannon thunder, and screams from her neighbors whose homes and persons were violated—again.

Connie hung her head as she shook it from side to side. Again. Again. This damn war, again. She thought of her brother and the other boys from Paoli up there at the other end of the road, waiting, known or unknown, for the full force of the occupying British army.

With every minute, the noise from the Germantown Road became louder and louder. From the porch, they saw smoke rising. With every blow of the wind, they coughed.

It's too late now to warn them, Connie thought. There is no way she'd get out ahead of them, even if she went on a back road. She wasn't a woman who prayed, but she lowered her head again. She prayed that her brother was alive first, and second, that he stayed alive in the onslaught that was coming.

# CHAPTER 42
# WHITEMARSH

Fred was sitting around a campfire with other boys from his regiment, when a sentry on horseback rode through. "The British are coming men! Make ready!" The sentry rode down the woods to the next encamped regiment before any of the soldiers near Fred had time to stop him and ask what was going on.

Fred jumped up along with the others and grabbed his musket, which was always beside him. As he did, he heard, "Make ready men! Make ready!" General Wayne was riding in on his horse, musket held up in the air. He was riding so fast that he almost rode straight into the campfire.

"It's time men! The redcoats are marching up the Germantown Road! Make ready! Line up!" he yelled.

The men scrambled as their commander had ordered. They fell into lines.

Fred thought that day after day of cleaning his musket, he was ready. Since they had been camped there for almost a month, or a little over a month, he was rested and had eaten more in the past month than he had eaten almost since he enlisted. He and the other boys who were itching for a fight were going to have one.

FRED FELL into formation with the rest of the front line of his division. Adrenaline flowed through his veins. A line of redcoats intent on killing him stood facing him not 200 yards away. He just hoped that his commander would call for them to fire first. He prayed with his eyes wide open that those redcoats were bad shots. Just then, his commander called. "Make ready." Fred pulled the long iron rod out of his side sash and quickly stuffed it down the barrel of his musket. "Load". He pulled some buckshot out of his leather pouch and shoved it down the metal barrel. "Aim." He raised his musket, steadied it on his shoulder, stared straight ahead at a redcoat across the field, and waited to pull the trigger. In a second, his commander yelled, "Fire." He steadied himself and pulled the trigger. The force of the blast made him lean back slightly, but he didn't fall. Across the field, the redcoat that he aimed at fell backwards as metal hit the side of his face. The redcoats who hadn't fallen pointed their muskets, called Brown Bess, straight at Fred and his friends.

"Fire" was all he heard, as the thunderclap of hundreds of pieces of metal headed straight towards him all at once filled his ears. Blood and pieces of flesh splattered up on his face as his friend next to him was hit in the neck. Fred instinctively bent down and put his hand over his friend's neck to stop the blood, which sprayed out like a fountain. "Make ready," his commander yelled. As much as he wanted to keep his hand in place and prevent his friend from dying, Fred stood straight up, pulled out his rod, and made ready to fire again. He picked another redcoat out of the lineup and aimed straight at him. Then he prayed and steeled himself for return fire. After a few times of this back and forth, more redcoats laid dead on the ground than patriots.

"Bayonets ready", yelled his commander. It was time to move in, kill the remaining British and claim the victory. The Paoli boys still had the massacre on their mind. "Remember Paoli", one of them yelled, and when the commander yelled, "Charge", Fred joined his friends in going after the British with all of their might.

He raced across the field, bayonet first. He picked out a redcoat and went for him. The redcoat saw him coming and came straight for him.

As he ran closer, Fred saw the fear in his eyes. He was afraid, too, but he knew better than to show it. Besides, with his brother dead, he had more desire for revenge than feeling of fear. No dead redcoat could bring back his brother nor truly avenge him, but if anything could give him even a little comfort, that could. Fred picked up his speed as he ran closer to the redcoat. He rammed the bayonet into his stomach first, to disable him and slow him down, then he ripped it out and rammed it again straight into his heart to kill him. The redcoat gave a bloodcurdling scream as he realized that his life was over. Fred didn't dwell on it too much. He blocked with one hand the redcoat who came up on the side now, trying to kill him. That redcoat lost his footing and fell. Fred rammed the bayonet straight into the heart this time since the red coat was already disabled on the ground. Just to be sure, he pulled it out and rammed it into his throat, right where the Adam's apple was.

Fred pulled out the bayonet again, just as he heard the British yelling "retreat." Then all he saw was the back of the redcoats as they turned and ran back from whence they came. Fred ran after them, as did the rest of the Paoli boys, catching the unfortunate ones and either killing them with their bayonets or the knives they all had hanging off their sashes. After several minutes, the redcoats were either lying on the ground dead or close to it, or they had run off.

Fred whooped and yelled in celebration with the rest of the Paoli boys. As they were celebrating, General Wayne rode in to the front of the line.

"Huzzah, men!" he yelled, holding his musket up in the air, while he turned his horse around in a circle so everyone could see it. "Great job!"

The men whooped and hollered "Huzzah" and "Remember Paoli!" patting themselves on the back and reveling in the adrenaline of victory. They were happy to be alive.

After a few minutes of celebrating, General Wayne said, "Some of our men have fallen, men. We must survey the field and tend to those we can."

With that, the Paoli boys settled down, turned back to the battlefield, looking for the wounded and dying, and collecting the dead. Reality settled in as they headed back to camp. The adrenaline spike gave way to shock and to sheer exhaustion. The fatigue of a hard fought battle came crashing down on them. Fred headed back to camp happy with their victory in this battle, but hoping that this would be the last of the season as they went into winter quarters.

FRED LAY on his pallet, feeling energized, satisfied, and tired at the same time. They beat off the British attack, showing that they were a good fighting army. The Paoli boys had again shown their mettle and the fact that they were a fierce fighting force. Their causalities were minor, but they knew that the redcoats they engaged couldn't say the same. The British were forced to go back to Philadelphia with their tails between their legs. Hopefully, they had learned their lesson and would stay there. If the British couldn't beat the patriots now while the roads weren't as frozen, snow-covered, and pock-marked as they were going to be in a few days or weeks, they surely couldn't beat them with all of that in the way. As long as the patriots stayed strong. As long as they had enough food to eat and enough clothes to cover them. A well-fed, well-dressed, well-sheltered army fighting for freedom had to beat a bunch of career soldiers only doing their jobs and not fighting for a cause. At least that's what Fred and the other boys told themselves, day after anxious day.

# CHAPTER 43

# THE GULPH

J ames and Daniel smelled the smoke before they saw it. They both stopped, sniffed, and looked up.

"Something's burning," said James.

"Sure is," said Daniel. They looked out across the bridge and saw it. It was coming from the other side of the river, not far from the Matson Ford. Then they heard it. Cannons like thunder. Gun shots. They knew that the Continental Army was camped over in Whitemarsh for the past month. Everybody in the area did. Groups of patriots left camp on foraging parties, and those who supported them, as James and Daniel did, gladly gave them the half of their crops or meats that they asked for. Since they were blacksmiths, the soldiers even brought over a few horses to shoe. Besides, the patriots kept them busy making tools and musket balls with their spare and scrap iron. And the patriots paid James and Daniel—in Continentals, the currency of the new United States. Some blacksmiths didn't take Continentals because they thought the money was worthless, backed by nothing but a new nation's hopes and dreams. But James and Daniels took it. And gladly. Who knew? The Continentals just might win the war.

"Looks like the British have found our boys," Daniel said.

"Sounds like it," James said.

"Well, I hope our boys beat them back and hold the line. We don't need the British over here," Daniel said.

"You're right about that," said James.

But the noise from across the river grew louder and the smoke smell grew stronger. Then, the flames rose, shooting high up in the air. James and Daniel stopped what they were working on and just looked.

"Maybe we ought to get home," said Daniel.

"Maybe we ought to," said James. "Sounds like the fighting is getting closer."

They launched into their end-of- the-day routine—dousing the flames, locking up the tools, battening down the hatches. When everything was secure, they climbed on their respective horses and headed home. As they rode down the river road, everyone around them was closing up their shops or homes, bringing things inside, running, preparing to go inside and hold their own, or hide so that the British didn't find them. The road was a jumble of activity. As they rode closer to the Matson Ford, they saw a long line of people on the other side in line waiting to cross over, away from whatever battle was behind them. James and Daniel turned their horses down the road away from the Matson Ford, hit them on the sides, and rode them fast towards their homes on the hills, just like everyone else around them seemed to be doing.

They reached Daniel's house first.

"Do you want to come in and wait with us?" Daniel asked James.

"Thank you kindly, Daniel," James said, "but I'm alright. I can't leave my home unprotected. If I'm not there, no telling what I would come back to."

"I guess you're right," Daniel said. He pulled his horse towards the hitching post. "Stay safe, and let's check in with each other tomorrow."

"Right," said James. "You stay safe, too."

James turned his horse towards the top of the hill, hit it hard on the thigh, and they took off towards home. The roads to the top of the hill were heavy with traffic of people riding the other way. Those who worked at the Gulph Mill were heading toward their homes, which were located all over the area. As he passed by others, they all exchanged knowing and worried looks. They nodded and waved to each other, but no one spoke. Everyone knew the British were just across the river.

**JAMES DRAGGED** a few more pieces of his scant collection of furniture over to the door to make it harder for the British to break in if the fighting across the river came over to the hill. The cannon and gun fire that cracked in the distance was a steady roar since he left the blacksmith shop. It still sounded distant, but he knew that he could not be sure in the dark. He checked the few windows in the cabin and made sure that the shutters were also secured from the inside.

He pulled some dried beef jerky from the shelf near where he had set up his cooking area. He was hungry for a hot meal, but he dare not light a fire and draw attention to himself. He drank water from the bucket he had drawn from the well earlier that morning and settled down in his most comfortable chair. There was no sleeping in the bed tonight. His body was as restless as his mind at the thought that the British might come during the night. He had to be as prepared, and strong as possible, in mind and in body. He grabbed his chair and sat on it, facing the door, his musket with bayonet attached, and a collection of sharp, long knives that he had made around his feet. He was ready.

**MORNING CAME** and the sound of thundering cannons and gunfire continued to pound in James' ears. James moved his furniture to the side and unlocked the padlocks, one by one. He opened the door and stood there. The smell of gunfire and smoke filled his nostrils. He put his hand over his brow to shield the sun from his eyes. Because the hill was so high, you could see for miles around. Black, white and grey smoke rose over the top of the trees across the river by the Matson Ford.

The only place to be while a battle was going on nearby was home. No one was walking up and down the hill. He walked around the house to the other side to look down at the Gulph Mill. The only thing moving there were the two large wooden water wheels on the outside of the Mill. As long as the water moved down the stream, the water wheels moved, too. The usual collection of people and wagons coming and going was gone. No one would be working as long as the British were nearby. The owner of the Mill was a patriot. Everything there would have been locked down and secured the day before so the British couldn't get anything. A few men stood around the Mill with muskets at their side. No, no flour would be ground today.

James went back around to the front of his cabin. He went inside, picked up his gun and his knifes in one hand and a chair in the other. He pulled the chair outside and sat down. As long as it was daylight and the British had not yet come, he would sit there, protect his home, and listen to the battle being waged just over the river.

# CHAPTER 44

# REBEL HILL

"They're going to have to be on the move sometime soon," James said, "or stay where they are. Winter's here." He pulled his scarf tighter around his neck as the first snow flurries of the season fell.

"That's right," said Daniel. "It doesn't seem like they could stay where they are now. Everybody, including the British, knows where they are. Even though they beat them off in that last battle, I can't believe General Washington would stay in that camp. They'll be like sitting ducks."

"Right," said James. "If I were the General, I'd at least put a river between me and the British." Even as he said it, he looked at Daniel.

"Like this one right here?" Daniel said, knowing that it made good sense.

James shook his head. "Yeah, like this one right here."

"You think they'd really come over here?" Daniel said, again, knowing the answer.

James scratched his head. "Well, they'd get across the river there at the Matson Ford. They could easily post guards there to keep the British from coming across. And, there's no place higher around here than our hill. You know you can see just about clear to Philadelphia, and certainly to Germantown, from the top. You can see anyone coming across the river at the Matson Ford and even up to the Swedes Ford."

"Good God," Daniel said. He shook his head. "We've been lucky to escape the war really coming here this long, since the army was right over the river. You make a lot of sense James. It seems like we're not going to be able to escape much longer."

James said, "I think you're right."

"But how are we going to handle that? How are we going to be able to go on living like we're used to, like we need to, if they come over here? How are we going to be able to keep working for anybody but the army and making any money? We'll be lucky if we can keep working. We'll be lucky if they don't decide to just take over our shop and use it for their army."

Daniel wiped his face as he frowned. "I support our boys and all, but it still stands. I don't want to join up with them. I don't want to go off fighting when my family needs me so."

"And you know I need every cent to buy Ruth." James said.

"It's bad enough that groups of them come over here regularly taking what we have," Daniel said. "Oh, excuse me," he said sarcastically, "They only take half of what we have, which is what General Washington has asked those of us who support him. But it seems like the word didn't reach some of his boys given what they took from us last time they were here."

He wrung his hands. "Maybe we'll have to join those folks who high tailed it away from their homes and on up there near Lancaster and Reading and Bethlehem, away from this mess."

James held his hands up as if to quiet him. "You don't know what's going to happen, Daniel. We've been able to make it so far. We'll have to see what happens. I don't want to leave my land, in fact, can't leave my land, any more than you. I wish this whole thing was over, but it's not, so all we can do is keep saying our prayers."

"And hiding our food," Daniel said, laughing.

"Yeah, that, too," James said.

## CHAPTER 45
# WHITEMARSH

Rumors flew around the camp for days. They were going to be on the move, into winter quarters. The first snowflakes fell a few days ago, and the temperatures dropped every day.

General Wayne rode into camp with a knit scarf flying behind him. He raised his musket in the air as he approached his regiment. "Men," he yelled. "Assemble yourselves. Important news." He stayed on his horse, talking to whoever approached, as the men drew nearer. When it seemed like all the troops had assembled, Wayne began.

"We are going to move out today. The British know where we are, so we have to move on. The good news is that we are not going far. We will be marching across the Matson Ford, and we will occupy the hills there near the Gulph. Some of you know those hills very well. In any event, we will not be too far from home."

He paused for a moment. "I know you may wonder whether these are our winter quarters. You know I can't say that right now. Just take all that you have, and be prepared."

"And men," he said. "I need a small group of you to be in the party that is going to lead this great army across the Ford. I need a small group of you to join with your brothers from the Pennsylvania Militia to lead and protect this great army. You would be our advance guard. Now who would like to lead us on?"

Fred was fortunate that his tent was in the area where General Wayne rode in to, so he was right up front. The General looked straight at him and said, "You." Then he went down those near him and did the same. "You, and you, and you," he said pointing, as the men he pointed at jumped up in the air with pride.

"You men who will be in the advance guard under the command of General Potter of the Pennsylvania Militia. A finer officer I know not. Colonel Johnson will take you men to his camp. So, you go gather your things and meet the Colonel right here as soon as you can." He waved his musket, "The rest of you gather your things and meet me back here. I will lead you on to our next site of victory." The men cheered "Remember Paoli." Wayne cheered back, "Remember Paoli. Always!" He turned and rode away.

Fred took down his tent and packed his things. He rolled his clothes and tent into his backpack and joined the group of nine soldiers waiting for the Colonel. The normally talkative soldiers waited in silence. When the Colonel showed, he said, "Men, it is an honor that you were selected to lead us on to our next camp. Come, let's march."

Fred straightened his hat, which he had accented with a fresh feather, picked up his musket and marched on, proud to be in this small group called to lead the army to winter quarters. They marched about half a mile through the camp where all of the other troops were packing up their things and gathering for the march out. Eleven thousand troops on the move after a month and a battle. They reached a clearing separated from the main army. Small groups of men in different colored uniforms were gathering. Fred wore the blue and white of the 5th Pennsylvania. Other soldiers wore brown and white with touches of green or, it seemed, whatever else they could find. Their hats were different, too. Fred's was black and tri-corner. The group closest to him wore coonskin caps with the coon's tail hanging down. Some just wore what looked like scarves tied around their head.  All had chests proudly straight out and extended—leading the Continental Army on to their next stop.

Fred shook hands with the boys from the Militia and the other Pennsylvania regiments that were called in to assist.

After they had assembled, General James Potter rode in.  His uniform looked like it was freshly washed.  His brass shone in the sunlight, polished to perfection.  He was leading the Continental Army after all, Fred thought.

"Men," he yelled.  "I am General James Potter.  We have the honor of leading this great Army across the Matson Ford and into the hills where we can see any British movement.  We will head across the Matson Ford and into the hills, as the advance guard, assuring that they are safe for our men.  Our scouts have said they are, but we must be cautious and ever vigilant.  Are you good fighting men?"

"Yes," they yelled back.

"Good.  Because if we find any redcoats, we are the front line.  Do you understand?"

"Yes, they yelled back."

"Good," yelled the General.  "Then let's move out."

Fred took his place in the column with the few from the 5th Pennsylvania.  He held his chest out with pride.  He was ready for anything, but he believed that General Washington would not have them move out to territory that was not safe.

The plan was for them to move out, cross the Matson Ford, march straight through to the Gulph Mill, with some regiments fanning out into and on top of the hills while the rest stayed on level ground.

# CHAPTER 46

# REBEL HILL

J ames and Daniel were outside the shop making horse shoes when they
heard a commotion in the direction of the Matson Ford. They looked
and first saw a group of about ten Pennsylvania Militia soldiers at the
Ford, ready to cross. That was not unusual. Small groups of soldiers had
come across in foraging parties since they took up camp in Whitemarsh.
But behind this group was another group of ten, except this group was
making music, the music of the fifes and drums of an army on the march.
And behind this small group, there was a general with gleaming sword
held high, brass shining. Behind him was another group of soldiers, some
dressed in Continental Army uniforms. It looked like they were in groups
of ten across, but there was row after row lining up at the Matson Ford.

Both James and Daniel stood up, eyes wide, horrified.

"They're coming!" Daniel said.

"My God," said James.

The columns started moving as the General led his men across. Rows
of soldiers in perfect formation. Mixed in between them were cannons
and wagons.

James and Daniel looked at each other. "Let's get this fire out and run
down there and see what's going on," said Daniel. They both threw water
on the fire with the buckets they always kept handy in case of a stray
spark, and James ran to the well to pull up some more. He ran inside and
doused the hot coals there.

"Lock up tight," Daniel yelled to James, as if James didn't know to do that already.

They padlocked the doors. Then they unleashed the horses and hightailed it in the direction of the Ford.

ALL ALONG the river road, the curious came out of their houses—standing at the front door, running out into the streets, taking their possessions inside. There was commotion everywhere. Women dragged children and possessions inside while men jumped on their horses and joined James and Daniel as they rode in the direction of the advancing army.

Just as they reached the road that ran perpendicular to the river road that led towards the Gulph Mill, another group of neighbors on horseback approached, almost running into them.

That group was waving their hands and shouting. James and Daniel slowed down to see what they were yelling about.

"The British. The British," some yelled. "They're here, and they're taking everything!"

"What?" Daniel asked.

"The redcoats. There must be a few hundred of them. They're foraging here, over in the Gulph and up in the hills," said Donald Coston, who lived on the hill by James.

"The redcoats here? In the Gulph? Up in the hills?" Daniel yelled.

"Yes," the man said, "and they're taking everything they can find."

Daniel pulled his horse to a standstill and looked in the direction of the Ford. "How can that be? What the? It looks like the Continental Army is down there," he pointed, "crossing the Ford."

"Then we're in for it," Donald said, "because the British are headed this way."

James and Daniel looked at each other, eyes wide and full of fear.

"I've got to go check on Mom and Prudence," Daniel said.

"My cabin," James said. That was all he could say.

They looked down towards the Ford at the patriot army crossing over and then back at each other. They grabbed their horse's reins tight, hit the horses hard, and sped off towards their homes.

The British soldiers were easy to spot. They had no thought of camouflaging themselves in the woods. The bright red and white of their uniforms reflected their arrogance. They didn't need to hide. They were the mighty army of the Crown, or of the King or the Queen or whoever was in power at the time.

"We'll see them before they see us," Daniel yelled at James, "but we still have to be careful."

Neither had come face to face with a British soldier, yet alone hundreds of them on a search, steal and destroy mission. They heard that the officers fancied themselves as gentlemen, but that the regular rank and file soldier fancied himself as one of the finest fighters in the world.

As they rounded the bend in the road, near the turn off they would take to go up the hills to their homes, they saw them. About 20 redcoats about an eighth of a mile away. Soldiers on foot led cattle and sheep, while other soldiers drove wagons full of goods. They both pulled the reins to slow down the horses and rode over to the side behind a clump of trees. The redcoats walked slowly, weighed down by their loot. The ones in front didn't have their guns drawn; they were still in the holsters on their sashes.

"Let's go," Daniel said. "Slowly and quietly until we reach that next clump of trees there on the hill."

"Right," James said. He tapped his horse lightly with his foot to get him to start moving and held the bit tightly so he wouldn't move too fast.

Daniel did the same until they reached the next clump of trees. Being up on the hill, even at that height, gave them a chance to look around. Hundreds of Continental Army regulars were crossing the Ford and marching towards the hill. They were about a quarter mile away from the British. The two armies would come together very shortly.

James said, "Donald said there were hundreds of redcoats, and that doesn't look like hundreds over there."

Daniel looked up. "They must be up in the hills or spread out." He closed his eyes.

"We have to be careful."

"Right," said James. He looked at the redcoats, who were coming closer. "But we've got to get out of here."

Daniel said, "Yes we do." He grabbed his horse's reins and started up the hill.

James grabbed his horses' reins and followed after him.

They rode for a few hundred yards before coming to a neighbor's house. The house was locked up tight; word must have gotten out around that the British were in the neighborhood. As soon as they passed it, they heard horses, marching boots, and wagons. Heard but didn't see. The sound came from the turn in the road by another clump of trees. The curve in the road blocked their vision.

"Must be redcoats," James said.

"Yes," said Daniel. Then he heard the voices. "We need to hide."

"Agreed," said James. They couldn't go back down the road, because that's where the other group of redcoats was and that's where the group ahead of them was no doubt headed. The only place to go was higher, deeper, into the woods, off the road. They jumped off their horses and led them off the road and into the woods, behind a group of trees, bushes and rocks.

After a few minutes, a couple of redcoats rounded the bend on the road. Then a few more. Then about ten more. They approached the house that James and Daniel had just passed. A few went to the front door and started knocking. A few went to the well and started drawing out the water bucket. After a few knocks, Carol Wharton came to the door, her eyes wide and her face full of fear. Carlton Wharton had signed up with the Continental Army earlier that year. She and the redcoat at the door exchanged a few words, and then that redcoat went in, followed by three others. Some of the soldiers outside walked into the gardens and gathered up armfuls of vegetables. Others were stripping the apple tree of apples. A few were unhitching the Wharton's horse. After a few minutes, the soldiers who were inside came outside with arms full of dried foods, pottery, utensils, cloth, and water jugs. Carol Wharton ran out after them, hands flailing, pleading with them to please, not, don't take everything. Then her four children between the ages of three and ten ran out after their mother, pulling at and hiding behind her skirts. Tears streamed down Carol's face as the redcoats smiled and laughed as they loaded their things into wagons and in pouches on horses, impervious to the pain that they were causing that family.

James and Daniel looked in silence until the redcoats marched out of site. They pulled their horses out of hiding and back down to the road. They rode down a few feet to where Carol was now sitting, tears in her eyes, trying to stop her children from crying.

"We saw it all from up there," Daniel said, as he rode closer, "but don't worry. We're not going to leave you with nothing. We'll come back. But now I have to go check on Mom and Prudence, and James has to go check on his cabin."

"I know," Carol said, between sniffles. "They took just about everything we had. What am I going to do? How am I going to take care of these children?"

Daniel hugged her and patted her back. "I'll come back and help you. I swear. You know we take care of each other on the hill."

Carol looked at him. "I know that we did," she said. "But, if that's what they've done to all of us up here, what can we do?"

He patted her again. "Look, the Continental Army has just started to cross over at the Matson's Ford, so I suspect they'll run into those British anytime. They'll take care of us."

Carol wiped her eyes. "I hope so."

"I know so," said Daniel, although he knew no such thing.

"We've got to go now," he said, "so you all get back inside and lock the door. Don't come out until morning, if you can. We'll come back for you tomorrow."

Carol looked at him. "Thank you," she said softly. She gathered the children and headed back inside.

James and Daniel jumped back on their horses and rode down the road, further along the hills, hoping to get to their homes, now thinking that the British had gotten there before they did.


THE FURTHER they rode up in the hills, the more they could see the road to the Matson Ford. There was a steady stream of British soldiers now, on foot and in wagons, surrounded by cattle, sheep, chickens, vegetables, fruit, furniture, dry goods, clothing, tools, and other things they had stolen from the hardworking people on the hill and in the gulph. James and Daniel rode as fast as they could, but they still had to pull over every few hundred feet to hide. They rode by house after house with pig pens with the doors wide open and no pigs, neighbors sitting outside, crying, or inside at the windows looking frightened.

Then they came to their hill. As they rode close enough to see the damage done at Daniel's house, what they saw was no different than what they saw at just about every house they rode by. The horses were gone. The few sheep they had were gone. The vegetable garden was trampled and bare. Branches were broken on the apple tree which now had no apples. The water bucket for the well was on the ground next to it, broken into pieces.

Daniel galloped to the hitching post as fast as he could. He jumped off the horse and ran to the front door.

"Mom! Prudence!" he yelled, banging on the door. "It's me Daniel. Open up!"

He heard furniture being moved away from the door and the heavy iron latches being unlatched. The door flew open, and his mother, Hope, stood there, eyes red. "Mom!" Daniel yelled, as he hugged her. "Are you alright?" he asked.

He broke the hug, stepped back and took a good look at his mother.

"They took everything," she said, waving her arms around the room.

Daniel hit the wall of the house, hard, in anger. "Where's Prudence? How's Prudence?" he asked.

Hope stepped aside as he headed inside. "She's frightened, of course," she said.

Daniel ran in to find his sister sitting on her bed, her crutches on the floor next to her, broken in two. He hugged Prudence, her long blonde hair in pigtails on either side of her face, and said, "Don't worry. I'm here now. Everything will be all right." He picked up one of the broken pieces in his hand and looked over his shoulder at his mother, eyes wide, questioning.

"One of them said that we don't need any more rebels walking around, committing treason against the crown," Hope said.

"What?" Daniel said, loudly and angrily. "Damn them! How cruel! Why would they say something like that?" asking a question but not really expecting an answer.

"Because Prudence said that they could take whatever they wanted now but that we'd get it all back soon enough when the patriots won this war and ran them back across the ocean."

Daniel looked at Prudence. He held her by the shoulders. "You said that?"

Prudence looked at him with all of the purity and innocence of a girl just on the verge of womanhood. With all of her twelve-year-old self she said proudly, "Yes, I did. And I meant it, too."

Daniel looked at her again, burst out laughing, and hugged her. "Well, Prudence," he said. "I mean it, too, when I say things like that, but that's to be said around us only, and especially not around the redcoats."

Prudence looked at him seriously. "Are you mad, Daniel?"

Daniel said, "No. Not at you. Of course not. How could I ever be mad at you?"

Prudence smiled, and he hugged her. Then he looked around at the room they were in.

Just about everything that could be picked up and moved was taken. Furniture was missing. Dried meat and fruit that had hung from the walls and ceiling was missing. Water jugs were missing. The tools that he made with his own hands were all gone. He put his hands on his head and looked down.

Hope walked into the room, and Daniel looked up. "The Continental Army is coming across the Ford, so they're going to run right in to the British," Daniel said. "They might even have run into each other by now and are battling it out."

Hope said, "I guess the war has come to us."

Daniel looked at her with a mixture of anger and fear. "I guess it has."

James walked in. "Excuse me, Daniel. If you don't need me here right now, I want to go check on my cabin."

Daniel looked at him. "Oh my, God, James. I'm sorry. Yes. I can take care of everything here right now."

James asked, "Are you sure?"

Daniel jumped up, walked over and patted James on the back. "I'm sure," he said.

James said, "Fine, then. Let me go check. I don't expect to find much there, but I've got to go see what they've done. Then I can come back and help you all here."

Hope looked at Daniel and said, "Son, you go with James, and see what they did to his place. I can take care of things here until you get back."

"But Mom," Daniel interrupted, "you need a man around here."

Hope held up her hand. "I know Daniel, but I can hold things down here for a while. If you had been here when the British came here, we might have had more of a mess because I'm sure you wouldn't have let them come in, let alone take anything, without a fight, and no telling how that would have turned out. They would have hurt you, I'm sure. At least, they didn't hurt us physically. All the other things they've taken, Prudence is right. We can get it back, maybe not as soon as she thinks, but we can get it back. So go help James."

Daniel looked at his mother, his eyebrows turned up, skeptical. "Are you sure?" he asked.

"I'm sure," Hope said.

Daniel rubbed his head. "Alright, James," he said, turning toward him, "you don't need to go alone. No telling what you might run into. I'll ride down there with you."

"Mom," he said, turning toward his mother and taking her by the shoulders, "I want you to lock this door and put the furniture in front of it again like you did. Our boys could be over there near the Ford fighting with those redcoats even now, and I don't want any redcoats running in here for safety."

His mother smiled. "Yes, Daniel. I'll keep us safe."

Prudence called out, "Me, too."

Daniel ran over to Prudence and kissed her on the head. "I know you do, but you listen to Mom, you hear?"

"Yes," said Prudence, shaking her head.

Daniel turned toward James and said, "Alright then. Let's go." They walked to the front door. Daniel stood on the other side of the door while he heard his mother drag a few pieces of furniture in front of the door and put the heavy locks back in place.

"You all secure in there, Mom?" Daniel asked.

"Yes, dear," Hope said. "We're fine. Now go on before it gets dark."

James was already on his horse. Daniel jumped on his, and off they went up the hill.

THE DOOR to James' cabin was wide open and swinging on its hinges. The tools that he left outside were gone. The few chickens that he had that normally walked around the front were not there. This time, James jumped off his horse without hitching it. Daniel grabbed the reins and hitched both horses at the same time.

James ran inside the cabin. All of his furniture was gone except for the heavy double chair that he had made for himself and his Ruthie. All of his dried food was gone. All of the tools he had inside the cabin were gone. His water jugs, blankets, clothing—all gone. After what he had seen along the way and at Daniel's house, he wasn't surprised that the redcoats had taken everything from him, too. Still, he sighed a sigh of heaviness at his loss. He looked at his now near empty cabin, and the thought that most came to him was whether the place where he hid his money to buy Ruth's freedom was secure enough.

Daniel came in, looked at James and said, "James, I'm sorry."

James said, "It's not your fault, but thank you anyway."

After a few minutes, James said, "You know I've been saving up everything to buy Ruth's freedom, and nobody knows where I've been holding that money except Ruth." He turned towards Daniel. "I put my money in a hole in the ground, and I cover it over real good. Now, I have to go see if they found my hiding place."

Daniel nodded and looked at him. "I'll wait right here."

James nodded and touched his cap. "Thank you kindly."

James pushed the broken door to the side and walked outside. He ran a few hundred feet away from the cabin, around the back. The ground around his hiding spot had been trampled by British soldiers, no doubt. His stomach was in knots. He started sweating. If they had found his money, he didn't know what he would do. He didn't need that much more, and then Ruth would be free. He could start over again because he wasn't that old of a man, but he wasn't that young of one either. He walked over broken branches and fresh footprints in the dirt. Then he reached his spot. The branches that he always put over the spot were trampled on and broken. The question was whether what was under them had been disturbed. James looked all around him to make sure that there was nobody around. The sound of gunfire in the distance startled him. He figured that the patriots and the redcoats had finally met. He kneeled down, moved the branches to the side, and smiled. The earth below the branches was undisturbed. He stood up, looked around again to make sure no one was watching him, and he covered the spot again with branches. It was right in front of a group of trees and rocks that he knew was not going anywhere. It was still safe. More gunfire erupted, this time it seemed closer. He closed his eyes. Yes, the war had come again. More gunfire. Closer still. This time he turned and ran back towards the cabin.

Daniel was standing outside listening to the gunfire, wringing his hands. "Looks like the two armies found each other," Daniel said to James as he came closer.

"Yes, and it seems like they're getting closer to us," James said.

Daniel gestured toward the cabin with the door hanging on its hinges. "You can't stay here James. You can't close your door. We don't know what's going on out there except that it seems that it's getting closer. You're not safe here. You need to come with us."

James sighed. "This is my home."

"I know it is, and it's a fine one, but you can't stay here. Not tonight. Not when we don't know what's going on out there or how long it's going to last. The only thing we know is that the patriots and the redcoats have met up and it seems like they're coming back this way."

More and closer gunfire erupted.

"We've got to go," Daniel said. "Mom and Prudence are alone."

James said, "Yes, you're right. Alright. I'll stay with you tonight and help you protect them."

"Good," said Daniel. "Let's go."

James said, "Wait. One thing. The only piece of furniture that they didn't take was the double chair for me and Ruth, I guess because it was too heavy for them to carry down that hill and back to Philadelphia."

Daniel said, "Yes, I guess you're right about that."

"But," said James, "I can't leave it here. I made that chair for me and Ruth. With my own hands. I spent so many days and nights thinking about me and her sitting in that chair, holding hands, resting at the end of a long day, holding our children, holding our grandchildren. I don't want to leave it here."

"What do you want to do?" Daniel asked.

"I want to take it to your house," James said.

"How?" Daniel asked.

"They might not have known how to move it, but I do. I made it so I could take it apart if we ever had to leave here. Give me a few minutes, and I can pull out a few pins," James said.

"I should have figured as much," Daniel said. "You're as good a furniture maker as a blacksmith." More gunfire. "So, go ahead and do it, but hurry."

James went inside as Daniel stayed outside and kept watch. James came out with several pieces of wood tied up in two bundles with the few pieces of rope that the redcoats didn't take because it was hidden in a shelf in the ceiling. James tied one bundle on his horse and one on Daniel's.

"You know we have to walk them," James said to Daniel, looking up and smiling.

"I see," said Daniel. He smiled, too. Then he said, "Alright. Make it secure because we've got to hurry back down the hill."

"Already did that," James said, smiling.

"I should have known that," Daniel said, grinning.

Gunfire erupted again. "Let's go," said James. They each grabbed their horse's reins and walked swiftly back towards Daniel's home.

JAMES AND Daniel steadied the heavy furniture on the horses as they walked down the steep hill. They tied the horses to the hitching post and unloaded the chairs one by one. They carried them into the house and put one in the alcove where Prudence and Hope slept and one in the main room so there was at least one piece of furniture to sit on.

Just as they finished, Daniel sat on the floor, hard, the weight of the day's excitement pulling him down to the floor like gravity. James sat down, almost fell down, as if someone was standing on his shoulders. They looked at each other, no words necessary, understanding how tired they were. Mom was with Prudence, calming her, quieting her,

"You hungry?" Daniel asked, now having time to feel his hunger.

James nodded and said, "Sure am."

"Mom said the only thing left to eat is was what was buried outside," Daniel said.

"You're not in any shape to go out there and dig it up at this point," James said. He wiped his eyes with his sleeve. "Neither am I."

Daniel, not moving, said, "You're right about that."

After a few seconds, Daniel said, "I'm thirsty, too. Maybe we can at least have some tea."

"That sounds real good," said James.

"Alright," Daniel said. "I'll go out front and get some water." He pointed to the kitchen area. "Look over there near the cooking stove and see if they left us with any tea. I think Mom said that she hid it under that shelf on the right."

Daniel stood up first, slowly, stretching his aching bones and muscles. He held out his hand to James to help him up. Daniel walked out the front door and James walked over to the kitchen area. Just as James slid his hand up under the shelf, the front door flung open.

"They're back," Daniel yelled as he ran in.

James looked up and said, "What? Who's back?"

"The British," Daniel said. "They're coming up the hill now. Hurry." Daniel ran and grabbed his knife. He shoved it into his pants. James ran over to his backpack and took out his knife, too. He put it down in his boots, in hiding. They both grabbed their guns.

Daniel ran to Hope, who was lying down on the floor. She looked up as he ran in.

"Mom, the redcoats are back."

Hope started to sit up.

Daniel put his hand out. "No, don't get up. Stay here with Prudence. James and I will be outside. We'll try to stop them from coming in here by telling them that their men have already been here."

Hope looked at her son with wide-eyed fear in her eyes. "Oh my God," she said. "Be careful." Prudence slept soundly.

"We will," Daniel said.


JAMES WAS already at the front door when Daniel ran out. They could hear the boots marching up the hill. They were loud. They were close. Daniel and James stood in front of the front door, guns in hand.

The first redcoats came in sight. They were close enough to make eye to eye contact.

James and Daniel stood motionless and didn't say a word. An officer more decorated than those behind him was in front. He was flanked by two regulars with muskets drawn, once they saw James and Daniel.

"What is your business here?" Daniel yelled.

The officer said, "We come on behalf of the Crown. The King's Army is in need of food and goods to quash the rebellion."

Daniel said, "Your men have already been here. They have taken food and goods from my mother and sister, who were here alone."

The officer said, "We mean you no harm."

"My sister is crippled, and your men broke her crutches," Daniel said.

"That should not have happened," the officer said. He was close enough now to see Daniel eye-to-eye.

"But it did," Daniel said.

"Well, that won't happen on my watch," the officer said. "So please step aside."

Daniel cocked his head. "I just told you that your men were already here, and they took everything."

The officer leaned back and pursed his lips. "We'll be the judge of that. Now step aside, peacefully. I want to send my men in to make sure that you're not hiding anything from the King's Army and holding it for the rebels."

"We're not," Daniel said. "If we were with the patriots, we would have signed up for the Continental Army by now."

The officer looked them over. "You might have, but your slave would not have. You know General Washington and the rest of those slaveholders wouldn't have let him sign up," he said pointing at James.

"I'm a free man," James said. "I bought my freedom," he said proudly.

The officer laughed. "Oh, pardon me. I was going to offer you freedom if you came right now and joined the King's Army." The officer waved his hands in the air. "No matter," he said. Then he stepped closer to Daniel.

"Now step aside and let us inspect your premises." He squinted his eyes into near slits of anger. "Step aside and you won't get hurt."

Daniel just looked at him.

"I won't say it again," the officer said. He raised his voice, "Step aside or we will move you aside."

Daniel thought about his mother and Prudence more so than himself. "Alright," he said. "But my mother and sister are still inside, and they're asleep."

"We won't hurt them," the officer said. "And if you're telling the truth, they can go back to sleep shortly."

Daniel just looked at the officer and said, "Fine."

The officer said, "Open the door and go in. Both of you," he said, waving at James. "We'll be right behind you."

Daniel and James put their guns down, and Daniel opened the door. As soon as they crossed the threshold, he saw it – James' chairs. The officer saw it, too.

The officer walked over to the chair. "I thought you said that my men took everything?"

With anger in his voice.

"They did," Daniel said.

"Then what's this?" the officer said, running his hand on the smooth wood on the chair.

"That's all that the other men left us," Daniel said, looking at James, who was looking at the chair, trying not to show how much it meant to him.

The officer laughed. "No, that's not what this is." He sat in the chair and ran his hands along the chair's arms. "Now, this is much needed firewood."

James started to move, and Daniel held his hands out to hold him back. Luckily, the officer didn't see that movement because about that time, two other soldiers came back in from the sleeping alcove. "There's another chair in here," they said.

The officer said, "This is a very nicely made chair here," still running his hands on the wood. He stood up and walked over to Daniel and James. "But, the fact is, it's here. You said everything was gone." He looked at Daniel close in the eye. "The fact is that you lied."

Daniel just looked at him.

"And I'm not used to people lying to me," the officer said, "that is unless they are rebels or rebel sympathizers."

Daniel just looked at him, face stone-like, like the one he used when he played cards with his friends, not revealing his hand.

"So you must be one or the other," the officer said.

Daniel looked at him.

"Hold them," the officer said, with a cold, hard voice.

Four redcoats ran over and grabbed Daniel and James by the arms. The officer came close to Daniel, face-to-face. "Private, give me your musket," he said.

Daniel still stood there, face to face. He stifled the urge to spit in the officer's face. He prayed that he wouldn't be shot.

The officer took the musket from the regular and pointed it at Daniel. Then he turned it around so that the butt faced Daniel and thrust it straight and hard into Daniel's stomach. Daniel grunted, bent over, and fell back. He would have fallen over if the soldiers weren't holding him.

James instinctively strained against the soldiers who were holding him.

The officer quickly looked at James. "You want to help your friend, freed man?"

James just looked at him, eyes narrow with anger.

The officer didn't wait for an answer. He shoved the butt of the gun into James' stomach, too.

"That's what you get for lying to the Crown," the officer said. "And you're lucky that you didn't get worse," he said, looking at both of them. "But, the King has said that we are to be somewhat gentle with you rebels because you, after all, are really British subjects. Even you, freed man."

"Hold them tight," the officer said. He motioned to another group of solders standing to the side. "Now one of you come here and chop up this chair into much needed firewood. And one of you go get that other chair, bring it out here, and do the same."

James looked on with anger and sadness as the chairs that he had so lovingly built for himself and for Ruth were chopped into bits.

"Get that rope over there," the officer said, pointing to James and Daniels things, "and tie this up."

As soon as he said that, the front door burst open.

"General," the soldier yelled. "The rebels are here."

The officer looked up, stunned. Then he frowned and looked at his men. "Let them go, and get outside," he yelled.

The redcoats took their hands off of Daniel and James, and they both fell to the floor. The soldiers ran outside.

James and Daniel heard commotion, horses running, men running, guns being fired.

Daniel wrapped one arm around his stomach in pain. He looked towards James. "You okay?"

James held his stomach, too, but he straightened up. It had been years, but he was more used to being beaten than Daniel. Every male slave was, and many women, too.

"I'm fine," James said. This time he held out a hand and helped Daniel get on his feet. Daniel swayed and doubled over in pain. "I'll check on your Mom," James said.

He ran into the sleeping alcove. Hope sat on the side of Prudence's bed, hands outstretched, guarding her like a mother tiger and her cub.

"Did they hurt you?" James asked.

"No, we're fine," Hope said. "And you? And Daniel?"

James looked at her worried anxious eyes and said, "No, we're fine." He didn't consider himself lying because they actually were fine now. "Our boys are here now. That's what you hear outside. So just stay in here until everything passes," James said.

"Yes, I'll do that," Hope said calmly. "But you all be careful out there."

"We will," James said. With that, he ran to see what was going on outside.

JAMES FLUNG open the front door. Daniel was right outside the door, crouched down, close to the ground. The scene in front of them was chaotic.

A group of redcoats ran up the hill as fast as they could. Cows and sheep, stolen from their neighbors, ran around untended as the redcoats retreated. A group of rebel soldiers ran after a group of redcoats in hot pursuit, bayonets leading the way. Another group of patriots was shooting muskets as fast as they could load them. The patriots gave bloodcurdling yells as they ran and caught some of the redcoats, engaging in hand to hand combat, or shooting them dead. The redcoats, except those who were killed or wounded, ran out of site, and the rebels ran quickly after them in hot pursuit. In what seemed like only a few minutes, the last rebel had run by them. Daniel and James stayed crouched on the ground until the battle was over. They knew that the Continentals and the redcoats would meet as the Continentals crossed the Matson Ford and the redcoats headed the other way, but they didn't know that they would meet right in front of their house.

Daniel had ignored the blood that streamed down his head as he watched the rebels and the redcoats battle it out. But, he couldn't any longer. He screamed out in pain. James held one hand against his own head where he was bleeding, but he was stronger than Daniel. He ran over to Daniel and gently grabbed him by the shoulders. He laid him down on a patch of leaves, right there by the front door. He ran inside to the sleeping alcove.

Hope looked at the blood on James and cried out.

"Shh," James said, "It's worse than it looks. I'm alright."

"Where's Daniel?" Hope asked.

"He's at the front door. He's hurt a little more than me," James said, as Hope's hand flew to her face to stifle her scream. "He'll be fine, but I have to stop the bleeding. I need some long strips of cloth. I have to clean and tie up the wound."

Hope pointed to the clothes that she was lying on. "Take them," she said. "They're about all that's left."

"Thank you," said James as he grabbed a pallet-size cloth that she had used for sleeping. He took it into the main room and pulled out his knife. He cut the clothing into four pieces of various shapes and sizes. He ran out to the door and lifted Daniel off the ground. He held his head in his chest as he tied one piece of cloth around the wound, somewhat tightly, to stop the flow of blood. Daniel cried and winced in pain.

"You'll feel better soon," James said, as he tied another strip around the wounds. With the worse of the blood stopped, James put his hands under Daniel's arms and dragged him backwards into the house. He pulled him over to his backpack and laid Daniel's head on it.

"I'll be right back," James said.

He ran outside and groped around in the dark. Soon, he found what he was looking for, a nice size rock. He put the rock at the end of one of the pieces of cloth that he had cut and tied it in there securely. Then he ran over to the well. The first group of foraging redcoats had smashed the well bucket, so they couldn't draw out any water. But James needed water to clean their wounds. The stone secure in the long piece of cloth, James threw that cloth and lowered the cloth into the well. Then he threw in another stone wrapped in cloth. Both cloths were wet from top to bottom, and he pulled them out. He went back into the house, where Hope now sat on the ground, her son's head resting in her lap. James took one wet cloth and handed it to her.

"Use this to clean the wound," James said.

Hope carefully unwrapped the other cloths and began to wrap the wet cloths around Daniel's head. James walked over to where the chairs he had built so lovingly, the chairs that he had so many of his dreams built around, laid in ruins on the floor. The wood might have been in toothpick size pieces, that's how useless it looked to him. He sat down, next to the wood that was now truly the firewood that the officer wanted, sighed, took his wet cloth and began to gently clean his physical wounds.

"REMEMBER PAOLI" Fred yelled, as he ran quickly up the steep hill, in hot pursuit of another group of redcoats. Since they had crossed the Matson Ford, they had run in to one small group of foraging redcoats after another. He and his companions yelled out, ran, bayoneted and shot, leaving a trail of dead and wounded redcoats and left over spoils—cows, sheep, furniture, and food—in their wake. The soldiers from the other regiments proved to be as good fighters as Fred and his group of Paoli boys. General Washington was right to send a group of crack soldiers from each Pennsylvania regiment out first before the rest of the Continental Army came across. Their spies hadn't told them that the British were out this far from Philadelphia on a foraging mission, but these soldiers were ready for anything.

This group of redcoats was no different from any other. They ran, they put up minimal resistance, but, in the end, they retreated. Fred ran up the steep hill with the other Paoli boys until they reached what looked like the top. Then they ran down the steep hill, faster, because it was easier. They came back down to the bottom of the hill where there was a tavern on one side and a mill right across the road. As they came to the bottom, the last of the redcoats ran out of sight into the woods on the road leading away from the Tavern.

"Stand down men," yelled their commander. The command spread back through their ranks, and the rebel soldiers stopped and caught their breaths. "We've turned those redcoats back," shouted General Potter, "but our men say there's at least another thousand in these hills and amassing on the high ridges. We can't risk the main army crossing now because we don't know how many more redcoats are out here or on the way."

The men looked at him anxiously.

Potter continued, "So we're going to retreat despite the fine job you men did in turning those redcoats. We've already sent one of the pickets back to tell the main army to stand down."

Fred sat down on a rock and breathed, for a change. The adrenaline started to leave his body. As usual, he thought of Allen, like he did in every battle since Paoli. Allen would have been proud. He killed two redcoats and wounded five more. He would add the two that he knew were dead to the notches in his gun when they were back at camp. For now, they were still on high alert.

# CHAPTER 47

# REBEL HILL

Daylight at Daniel's' home revealed the destruction of the previous night. Hope stayed on the floor, holding Daniel's head in her lap, stroking his head or hand or arm with every moan, comforting him like a mother should. Daniel slept soundly. So did James. Hope barely slept because, even though she held her son, she was also looking over at her son's friend, now the man who had helped save her son's life. James turned as he slept. Every once in a while, Daniel did the same.

James opened his eyes but didn't move. It felt like his arms and legs had been pulled in every direction and that someone sat on each limb, pushing them down into the thin pallet that he laid on, making all of his limbs exceedingly heavy. He went to lift one arm, but he couldn't. His muscles didn't seem to work. He tried lifting his other arm, too, but the result was the same. His arm was too heavy to lift, and the pain shot through his flesh like a gunshot.

He moaned and decided to lie still until he was fully awake. He stared up at the ceiling as the memory of the night before came fresh to his mind. That's why my arms ache so much, he thought. Then he moved his head, startled. Daniel was beaten, the house was turned upside down, and there was a battle right outside their door.

James summoned every bit of strength that he had and pressed his hands hard into the floor. He used them to push his back off the floor, slowly and painfully, until he sat straight up.

"Mrs. Welburn," he called out, as he saw Hope across the room, still sitting on the floor, holding Daniel.

"How are you feeling James?" she asked.

"Mighty sore," James said.

"Rightfully so," Hope said. "The redcoats held you awfully tight while they beat Daniel," she said, looking down at her son.

James sighed. "Yes, I know," he said. "How's he doing?"

"Just sleeping," Hope said. "And moaning." She stroked his hair. Then she looked straight at James. "But he'd be in an awful way if you hadn't helped him last night after the beating. Holding his head up. Cleaning out his wounds. Wrapping his head to stop the bleeding. And then dragging him in here when you could barely even drag yourself in."

James wiped his eyes. "He would have done the same for me."

Hope shook her head. "Yes, I suppose he would have."

James put his palms face down on the floor again and took a deep breath that he felt in every one of his aching ribs and other bones. He pushed hard on the floor again, steadied himself when he was halfway standing, and then stood up straight. He looked at the chaotic scene around him. His beautiful double interlocking chair was in ruins. Things that used to be neatly stored on shelves or in cabinets were thrown all over or missing. And his best friend was beaten and bloodied.

James told his mind to pick up his leg and move in Daniel's direction. But, his legs felt as heavy as his arms did. He wanted to lift his legs, but he couldn't. He could only push his foot forward, like an old man's shuffle. He pushed one foot forward, then the other, and then he stopped. He did this until he made his way across to floor to Daniel and Hope. As he shuffled closer to Daniel, James said, "Good Lord." The areas on his face where the redcoats hit Daniel with their fists and the butt of their muskets had turned purple as the blood internally and externally gathered and congealed. The cloth that was wrapped around Daniel's head was now black-red in places where it had soaked up Daniel's blood. James slowly raised his hand to feel the cloth that was wrapped around his head. It stuck to his head where the blood had dried, and it hurt as he slowly turned his head from side to side.

"Those bastards," James said. "Excuse my language, Mrs. Welburn."

"That's fine, son," she said. "That's just what they are."

James looked at Daniel and tears came to his eyes. He stopped his eyes from welling up any further. Tears weren't going to help anything, and the salt would just sting the numerous cuts on his face.

James looked at Hope and said, "Can I help you with anything?"

Hope shook her head. "No, not now. I think this is going to be a day where we all just sit here and rest. That is, if the armies leave us alone."

"Right," said James. "Let me get myself together, and I'll go outside and see what happened out there last night. Let's hope our boys chased those redcoats far from here and that they're on their tails right now."

"Yes, let's hope," said Hope.

"I'll go out and see if I can find us some food and some water," James said, as he started to stretch his muscles.

"That'd be good," Hope said. "Prudence will be hungry when she wakes up."

"I'll make up fresh tourniquets and wet one to clean off the rest of the blood. I know you don't want Prudence to see all that," James said.

Hope nodded. "Yes, that's right. No sense in frightening her any more than she will be already."

James shuffled across the floor until he reached the front door. He leaned against it to steady himself. Once he felt that his legs were steady underneath him, he said a silent prayer that he didn't find an outside that was as destroyed as things were inside.

He opened the door slowly and stood there for a minute as he surveyed the scene in front of him. The Welburn's once well-tended and neat yard was destroyed. The bushes and plants were trampled down. Where trees once stood, now there were only stumps, the trees having been chopped down for that night's firewood, no doubt. A few loose, muddy shoes were strewn around the yard. So were the cases that used to hold the Continental soldiers' gunpowder and buckshot. Out on the road, James saw the legs of what looked to be a redcoat by the side of the road. The dried blood on the road was visible from where he stood. He closed the door behind him as quickly as his aching arms would let him and hung his head.

FRED WAS on high alert as he marched back towards the Matson Ford with the rest of his regiment. They had routed the redcoats they had run into on the hills, but intelligence said that there were more around. The steep hills made perfect hiding places. He held his musket in his hands, not in his sash, ready for whatever they encountered.

"The General sure got it right this time," Fred said to the soldier beside him as they walked along.

"Sure did," said the soldier. "Now let's just hope that we get back in time to warn the rest of them not to cross over this way."

"I'm sure we will," Fred said, "seeing how we're the best of our regiments."

"Yes," said the soldier, "but let's hope we don't have to prove it again before we get back."

"Understood," said Fred. They marched on, silent and alert.

They reached the bottom of the Matson Ford and congregated there. Once all of the front lines returned, they formed a circle several men deep. The soldiers on the outside stood with their muskets outstretched, ready to shoot, protecting the soldiers in the interior. Fred knew he was a great shot, so he volunteered to take the outer ring.

General Potter yelled "Ready men? Forward!" The mighty circle started moving across the Ford.

Fred was anxious, yet not afraid. If anything happened at this point, the 10,000 man Continental Army was just across the river, ready to swoop in and rescue them. It took them about fifteen minutes to move across the Ford to reach the dry, solid ground of Whitemarsh.

They stayed in formation for a mile or so across the ford, then they broke into a column of about four or five men across as they more speedily marched back to the Continental Camp.

"Stay here men," General Potter ordered. "Don't return to your normal units. Given your bravery and excellence in battle, I'm sure General Washington will want us to remain together and lead our army forward. Again," he said. Then he rode away.

Fred sat down on a rock with his new regiment and waited.


SNOW BEGAN to fall on the hill as Daniel, James, Hope and Prudence sat on the floor. Daniel was sitting up now, leaning against his mother on one side, while Prudence leaned against her on the other side. They sat in front of a roaring fire. Achy as he was, James had gone outside and gathered up firewood so they wouldn't freeze on that very cold day. He gathered as many broken limbs as he could find and took them back into the house for Mrs. Welburn to burn first. Seeing that that was not enough to last very long, he went back out and slowly, painfully, walked around the woods to find and cut down the dead trees, drag them back to the house, and chop them into firewood. He had to walk farther than usual because either the British or the rebel boys had chopped down the dead trees near the house. As he walked around, he ran into evidence of the battle the night before—discarded shoes, cylinders, cast off holsters, and the most gruesome of all—limbs or other body parts detached from their owners—and dead bodies

They sat mostly in silence. The only person who really had the strength to talk was Prudence, but even she grew tired of talking after a while. Every so often, James would rise and put a few more logs on the fire.

The next day brought renewed energy to their bodies and their minds. Hope had let Daniel sleep flat on a well-padded pallet, instead of on her lap, her holding up his head. She was convinced that the danger of him passing out or dying from his head injuries had passed.

James awakened first, like he was used to. Slaves were never permitted to sleep late, so he was used to waking up earlier than most white people. He fed the fire and even brought in some water from the well with the new bucket that he made the day before. He heated some of the water in a small iron pitcher that he found out on the hill when he was out looking for firewood.

"There's hot water for tea," he said to Hope when she woke up.

"I thought they took all of our tea," Hope said.

"They did," James said, "but I found some." He didn't tell her that he found some in the pockets of a dead redcoat. She didn't have to know that.

Just then, Daniel walked in. "Do you have enough for me?"

James and Hope turned around quickly.

"Praise God," said Hope as she hurried over to where Daniel stood, leaning on a stick that James took out of the woods. "How do you feel, son?"

Daniel sighed and leaned more of his weight on the stick. "I feel like I ran straight into a tree on a sled," he said. "Remember that time?"

Hope smiled, "Yes I do, son," she said, as she wrapped her arms around him gently.

"I must look like it, too," he said looking straight at James.

"Yes, if you say so," James said, smiling. Then getting serious, "They hit you pretty hard, Daniel."

"I know," Daniel said. "I know."

# CHAPTER 48

# WHITEMARSH

General Potter gathered his elite regiment around him. This time, General Washington gave him additional soldiers from some of the other states. "Men," he said, "we're headed back out again. Back to the hills where we routed those redcoats."

Fred frowned. Back to the same hills? Back the way we came?

The General held up his hand. "We're not going across the Matson Ford this time. That was too close to Philadelphia, and we don't want to run into any British that way. They know we are over here on the other side of the Forge, so we have to take a different way in," he said.

"We're going to move a few miles up the road and cross the river at the Swedes Ford. Then we're going to march down to the Gulph and occupy those hills again."

Fred looked at his friend. "Again, General Washington makes good sense. Those hills are the highest for miles. You can see straight down to Philadelphia from there. At least, if the British wanted to head out this way towards Philadelphia, we'd see them and have a chance to crush them before they crossed the Schuylkill."

"So you're from around here?" the soldier asked.

"Yes, about ten miles from here. In Paoli," Fred said. "And you?"

"Connecticut," said the soldier.

"That's a long way from here," Fred said. "What's your name?"

"Joseph," said the soldier. "Joseph Plumb Martin."

"Well, Joseph Plumb Martin," Fred said, "Once we take those hills, we'll be sitting pretty."

Joseph sighed. "I hope so. I hope we can sit anywhere for a few days. I'm getting weaker and weaker every day. This not eating every day or only eating a little bit here and there is starting to wear on me."

Fred laughed. "Starting? I'm hungry all the time."

The General yelled out, "Alright men. Let's move out."

Fred grabbed both ends of his scarf and pulled them tight against each other. He picked up his musket and, hungry as he was, put one foot in front of the other with vigor and determination.

They marched up the road as the snow fell lightly. That snow joined with a covering of about an inch or so that was already on the road. The march to the other Ford was a few miles up and down a few slight hills. When they reached the Ford, General Potter led them across. Fred was with the group that was, once again, on the outer edges. He got in position with a group of soldiers that were surrounding, guarding, a great cannon. The men pulling the cannon slowly dragged it across ground that was frozen and pitted in parts and wet and muddy in other parts. Water lapped against the sides of the Ford, too close in spots, washing over the sides and over the pitted ridges. Other soldiers had to be called in to help as one group pulled the cannon and another group pushed it. Everyone was tired, and everyone was hungry. And, everyone was sleepy. It was the wee hours of the morning, when they would normally be asleep.

After about an hour of steady pushing and pulling, where Fred even had to jump in at one point, their group crossed the Ford. The snow picked up and came down with such force now that it was hard to see even a few feet ahead of them. God hope there's no redcoats around here now, Fred thought, as he held his musket out at the ready, ready to shoot a redcoat, if he could only see him. Waves of nausea and fatigue took turns washing over him. He walked and stumbled as much as the other soldiers around him.  Once they crossed the Ford, their march should have been easier, but because of the new falling snow, it wasn't.  At times, he still had to stop and help push or pull the cannon.

After a few hours, the high hills came into view, even in the blinding snow.  They marched slowly and agonizingly around the back of the hill, he and his compatriots guarding the big cannon.  They marched through the farms of Gulph Mills, past one mill after another, until they came to the great Gulph Mill at the base of the tallest hill of the range that they called the Conshohocken hills.

"Look familiar?" Fred said, jokingly to Joseph, who also had his musket out in the ready.

"Yes, so we're back.  I sure hope we can stop here," Joseph said.

They both stood again, at the ready, on the road by the Gulph Mill and the Inn.  As they did, word passed through the ranks.  The message was— this is it.  We will head up into the hills and find a place to sleep.

"At last," Fred said to joseph.

"Thank the Lord," Joseph said.

"What about the cannon?" Fred asked one of the commanding officers near him.

"We will leave a group here to guard it," the commander said.  "We need you men up in the hills.  We need our best shots up there.  Our men who can shoot a redcoat from a mile away."

Fred managed a laugh.  "Well, that would be me."

"Me, too," said Joseph.

Knowing that they were now at the end of their journey, at least for the night, gave Fred and Joseph renewed energy.  They bid goodbye to their buddies who were left at the bottom guarding the cannon and marched quickly up the hill, looking forward to finding a place to lay their head. Their heads along with the heads of 11,000 other men.

# CHAPTER 49
# REBEL HILL

James slept peacefully until he heard branches breaking outside. A few, at first, but then he heard voices. He jumped up, still sore and in pain, knowing that he was the most fully functioning man in the house. Daniel was recovering, but slowly.

James grabbed the musket that he kept right beside him and went to the window. He moved the red and white gingham curtain to the side and peered through the shutters. There were people out there, marching up the road, marching up the yard, oblivious to the fact that this was someone's home. It took him a minute to adjust to the darkness and see that the soldiers were patriots. Even in a few minutes of looking, what looked like tens of groups of soldiers became hundreds.

Hope ran in. "My God, what's happening now?" she asked.

James turned to face her. "Patriots coming back. Hundreds of them."

Hope walked quickly to the window. She looked out with James. Her hand flew up to her mouth to stifle her gasps.

"What now?" she asked, not really expecting an answer.

"It seems like they're camping out here," James said. He looked at row after row of soldier falling out, laying down, pulling a blanket out of their backpack if they had one, laying the backpack on the ground, and laying their heads on them.

"It's freezing out there," Hope said.

James said, "I know. But look," he said, pointing to an area, "they're lighting fires."

Hope moved closer to the window. The dark early morning air was lit here and there with fire after fire. That gave them both a better idea of how many soldiers were out there, as the soldiers lit even more fires. The narrow road, an area that didn't need clearing of brush, was almost fully covered with soldiers lying on it. Their front yard, too, was covered with men in blue and white coats.

As they looked out of the window, they heard a knock at the front door.

James and Hope looked at each other.

Hope said, "Let's go to the door together."

James was glad to hear that because many white people still thought that any colored person they saw was a slave.

"You stand right beside me," Hope said.

They moved over towards the door, musket firmly in James' one hand. He opened the door with the other hand. Before them stood a patriot with the markings of some type of officer.

"Good morning, Ma'am. Sorry to disturb you. I'm Sargent Chandler, 3rd Virginia Regiment, Continental Army, United States of America," he said.

Hope said, "Yes, Good morning Sargent. What's going on here?"

Sargent Chandler said, "We're going to be camping out here, Ma'am."

"For the night or for how long?" Hope asked.

"Well, Ma'am, I don't rightly know. We'll be here at least for the night. I just don't want you to be alarmed."

Hope nodded and said, "Thanks for letting us know. You and your men are welcome here. Sorry we don't have much to offer you," she said, waving her arm around a room that was bare and in disarray. "The redcoats were here a few days ago and took just about everything we had. They even beat my boy. He's lying in the next room. They would have beaten our neighbor, James, here, if some of your fellow soldiers hadn't come up upon them. So, I'm grateful," she said. "If you and some of your men want to sleep in here, you're welcome to. Like I said, we don't have much, but what we have you're welcome to. "

Sargent Chandler said, "Thank you, Ma'am. Some of our boys are mighty hungry and sick and some don't need to be sleeping out on that ground, in that snow. I do have some I can send in here. Just for tonight, mind you. We don't want to be a bother. If we are going to stay here any longer than one night, we'll have tents up tomorrow and be in better shape to make it through the night. But, I'm afraid that some of our boys won't make it through the night unless they have a warmer place to stay and some shelter from that snow."

"Well, Sargent, you bring them on in. Only thing, I have my little daughter back there in the other room, too. But, we'll make room for some of your boys back there, too," Hope said.

"I'll help you bring them in," James said.

Sargent Chandler looked at him. "Is this your boy, ma'am?"

"I'm a free man," James said proudly.

"Yes," Hope said, "he's a free man. He's our neighbor. His home is up there on the top of the hill. He's here helping us. If it wasn't for James, my son would probably be dead right now."

Sargent Chandler looked at James as hard as James looked at him.

James said, "So if you want the help of a freed man, I'm happy to help."

Chandler looked at James up and down and said, "Yes, I could use your help."

James looked at him, eye to eye, man to man. "Show me where."

For the next half an hour, James, Chandler and various soldiers in the Continental Army carried in other soldiers and gently laid them on the wooden floor. One by one, the small room filled up with cold, hungry, tired, men, coughing almost as much as they were breathing. When they filled up that room, they went back and brought a few more men back into the next room.  Daniel woke up with the commotion and called out, "Mom." Hope came running.

"What's going on?" Daniel asked.

"The patriots are camping here on the hill.  There's hundreds of them outside.  Some are too sick to be out there, so we bought them in here."

Daniel started to sit up. "I'll help you," he said.

"No you won't", said Hope.  "You just stay here and rest."

"Is James helping you?" Daniel asked.

"Of course," said Hope.

"What would we do without him?" Daniel asked.

"Only God knows," said Hope, "but let's hope that we don't have to find out." Then she patted Daniel on the head.  "Now go back to sleep, son. No matter what happens, tomorrow is going to be quite a day."


JAMES SAT up the rest of the night in the main room of the house now full of sick, shivering patriot soldiers.

Hope stayed awake in the other room, watching her sick yet recovering son, her fragile daughter, and the few other sick soldiers in the room.

As sunlight crept in the window, the soldiers stirred.  Hope walked into the main room and towards James.

"Now what?" she asked.

"I'm going to start bringing up some water," James said.

"The little dried meat we have isn't enough to feed all of us, yet alone them," she said, looking out at the soldiers all over her house.

"I know, but maybe they have some food of their own," James said. Then he thought better. "But looking at them, I can see that can't be that much."

"Well, we can at least heat some water and give them something hot to drink.  We still have some of that dried sassafras," Hope said.

"Yup," said James, "and I can always go pick more of that."

He grabbed a pitcher from one corner of the room, gingerly stepping over the men. He opened up the front door and gasped. As far as his eye could see, every bare spot on the hill was filled with soldiers in blue and white. Most were sleeping, but some were starting to stir. Yes, it was going to be some day.

"WHERE ARE you from?" Daniel said to the man lying on the floor next to him.

"Massachusetts," the soldier said.

"How long have you been in the Continental Army?" Daniel asked.

"Just over a year," the soldier said.

"And how's your family doing without you? Do you know?" Daniel asked.

"I don't know, really," the soldier said. "I got a letter a couple of few months back, but that was it." He closed his eyes. "I suspect they'd be doing a whole lot better if I was with them," he said. "But, they understand. They know what I'm fighting for. And, I tried to leave them with as much food and things as I could when we left."

Daniel said, "That must be hard, leaving them like that."

The soldier wiped his eyes. "It is hard. It's really hard. But, it was harder living under those redcoats' thumbs, telling us what to do, taking money for everything that we did or had. No, that was hard." Then he looked at Daniel. "And you?" he asked. "What's going on with you? I see you're not in a Continental Army uniform, but are you militia?"

Daniel shook his head. "No," he said softly. "I'm not actively fighting in the Militia, but I've paid my tax or dues. I've been here helping my mother and sister. My Dad died about five years ago, and they need me."

The soldier's eyes widened. "All of our families need us, man," he said as he turned away from Daniel.

Daniel agreed with him but he didn't get a chance to say so before the soldier turned his back on him.   Here was a man who left his family all the way up in Massachusetts, a good week's ride if the weather was right, especially this time of year, if he remembered his geography class from school, to come down here and fight the British. Right in Daniel's own back yard.  Daniel thought that he always supported the patriots, but since the redcoats were far away, off in other colonies or states, the redcoats always seemed like somebody else's problem, not his.  But now, they were more his problem than he cared to admit.  First of all, they beat him and hurt him badly.  And, if that small band of patriots hadn't intervened, those redcoats would have beat James at least as bad as they beat him. Both of them would likely have died, leaving his mother and sister in a worse situation.  At least now, James was in good enough shape to take care of him while his wounds healed and his bruises went down.

So, Daniel sat up, determined this time to help take care of these men who were now all over his house.  These men who left their own families to fight for their liberty and for his.  He put his hands on the thin pallet on the floor and pushed himself up.  His head ached, and he felt dizzy. He held his head between his hands for a minute.  Then, he bent his leg at the knee and gently kneaded the knee with his hand.  Then he bent the other knee and kneaded that.  He held on to the wall next to him as he pulled himself up straight.  He stepped around and over the men that were all around him.  Some had arms in slings.  Legs in tourniquets.  Heads wrapped in bandages.  Dried blood on blue uniforms.  Fingers, toes, and noses black and blue with frost bite.  He walked in to the main room.  The men in there were stirring, and they looked about as bad as the men in the small room.  Daniel walked over to where Hope was putting sassafras leaves in to a pot full of boiling water.  James was pouring more water into another large pot.

"Mom," Daniel said, as he walked over towards her. He put his arm around her waist from behind and kissed her on top of the head. "I'm back," he said. "I'm feeling better."

Hope smiled and said, "Praise God."

"Yes," Daniel said. "Praise Him. I feel almost like my old self."

"Good," said Hope. "We can use your help."

"Don't worry, Mom," Daniel said. "I'm going to help. I'm going to help a lot." He kissed her on the head again and walked over to where James was. Daniel stuck out his hand.

"Thank you, James," Daniel said.

James put the water barrel down and shook Daniel's hand.

"Glad to see you back on your feet," James said.

"Thanks to you," Daniel said. "I know that."

"You would have done the same for me," James said.

"Right," Daniel said, as he patted James on the back. "Now what can I do?"

James sighed. "I thought there were hundreds of our boys out there, but it looks more like thousands. It looks like the whole Continental Army is here on the hill."

Daniel walked to the front door, opened it, and looked out. He gasped. "My God, it looks like you're right." He took a minute to take it all in. "Once we get these boys set in here, maybe we should go out and walk around and see what else we can do. I'm sure they're looking for food, to figure out what plants and things they can and can't eat, and they may need to know something about how to get around these parts. We can just walk around and talk to them, if we can. Just offer our help."

"That sounds good to me," James said. "Because we owe them. We wouldn't be standing here if they didn't get those redcoats out of this house a few days ago."

"I know," said Daniel. "We've got a favor to repay."

James nodded.

THE SOLDIERS in the house settled, Daniel and James set off. Many of the soldiers they ran into looked as bad as the soldiers inside the house. Soldier after soldier was barefoot, in the snow, in the freezing weather. Some of their shirts and pants were so torn they hung off them, exposing red and raw skin. They saw so many frostbitten fingers and toes that they stopped being shocked at the site. Man after man asked, "Have any food?" "Have any water?" It only took Daniel and James a few feet of walking before they realized that this Continental Army that was supposed to fight off the redcoats was tired, worn out, hungry, exhausted.

"They should be going in to winter quarters soon," Daniel said.

James said, "Yes, I know."

"They'd better get somewhere and rest soon," Daniel said. "This is an army that looks like it needs a break."

"You're right about that," James said.

They walked up and down the hill, and everywhere they walked, there were patriots—sheltered under pine trees, or breaking down branches to build lean-tos to shelter themselves for another night. They looked down at the Gulph Mill, where patriots were swarming around like bees. Soldiers filled containers with water from the parts of the Gulph Creek that weren't frozen and from the big waterwheel that turned constantly on the outside of the mill. Every so often, Daniel and James were stopped.

"Where you from?" they'd ask.

"We live on this hill here," Daniel would answer.

"You're not militia?" was most often the reply.

"No," said Daniel.

"You a Torie?" they'd ask.

"No," Daniel would answer. "We support our patriots."

"Good, or else I'd have to kill you," one said.

"Then you should join the Continental Army," said another.

"Then you should be a part of the Pennsylvania Militia," said another.

Daniel always started explaining about his widowed mother and sick sister, but even he got tired of hearing it. As he heard story after story of hardship from soldiers from the southern states to the northern, he felt immensely grateful for their sacrifice. He realized that his concern for his mother and sister was the same as their concern for their families, except they were committed enough to the patriot cause that they'd leave their families behind. The more he ran into soldiers with one leg, one arm, blood everywhere, but still committed to General George Washington and the United States, the more he realized that these soldiers were not only fighting for their freedom—but that these soldiers had also fought for his life by routing the redcoats out of his house. The fact that he was able to walk back into his home, even though it was a home now full of soldiers, made him feel even more guilty.

ANY FOOD that the Welburns had, even the food that they hid out in the woods away from the British, was fast disappearing. It was barely enough for Daniel, James, Hope, and Prudence. But, to have to stretch it to cover the sick and dying soldiers who now filled their house took all the cooking tricks that Hope had. They had a patch of root vegetables hidden in the woods, but when James and Daniel walked over to that, they saw that the garden had been dug up by some of the thousands of soldiers who now occupied the hill. The soldiers were using the vegetables to make soup with the water they had melted over a fire from the snow that covered the ground. Hope put smaller and smaller pieces of dried meat into the soup she made every day for her household and guests, and she took to hiding the other dried meat between her breasts. No other place was safe, and she figured that not even a starving soldier would search between her breasts.

Daniel and James took turns in leaving the house. As the soldiers who were brought in the first night the Continental Army occupied the hill retained their strength, they moved around more, and Hope needed more help to take care of them—sitting them up to change bandages, holding them up as they softly walked on swollen legs to keep the circulation in them flowing. They all came to know the soldiers who camped inside their house and right outside.

They heard stories of battles that took place all over the colonies—when the revolution started at Bunker Hill in Massachusetts, in Connecticut, when they lost New York to the British, when they triumphantly crossed the Delaware River at Trenton in New Jersey, when they fought thousands of British down by the Brandywine Creek in Chester County, when the British showed no mercy and bayoneted the boys in Paoli, and when they stormed the Chew house in Germantown.

Daniel's guilt grew with each story he was told. But not James'. He felt for the thousands of starving and sick men who were around him as far as he could see, but he didn't feel guilty. His people were still slaves. Like the Virginian officer who came to the door the first night of the encampment, a man with black skin was seen as a slave. The Virginian wasn't fighting this war for the black man's freedom; he was fighting it for white men's freedom. So, no, James didn't feel guilty that he wasn't fighting side by side them and could live in peace when the Continental Army moved on to wherever they were going next.

On one of his walkabouts, James ran into the quartermaster corps. There was a group of scrawny, horses with their ribs showing through their still beautiful shiny coats in one area on the hill. The equally scrawny, threadbare group of soldiers around them was picking up the horses feet, examining their shoes.

"No wonder this one doesn't want to move. Look at these shoes," said one, showing a split shoe to another.

"This one, too," said another.

"This one won't make it much further without a new one," said one soldier.

"But that's going to have to wait," said another. "These tools are about worn out."

James and Daniel walked closer to the group.

"Do you need some help there?" Daniel asked as he approached.

The soldiers looked around. "Sure do," said one. "These tools aren't worth much of anything," one said, holding up a battered and beaten anvil.

Daniel said, "Well, we're blacksmiths," pointing his finger back and forth between him and James. "And we live on this hill."

"You got tools?" one asked.

"Yes," said Daniel.

"You want to help us?" one asked.

"Yes," said Daniel. "We can go get our tools, and we can help you with all of these horses."

"Good," said one soldier who walked closer. "We don't have any money to pay you with right now, but we can go see if the head of our quartermaster corps has anything for you. I think you'll be using up a lot of your iron shoeing these horses."

"Alright," said Daniel, shaking the soldier's hand. "We'll go get our tools and everything, and you go check with your general."

Daniel and James walked back quickly to the Welburn home. They gathered their tools into their hands and set out back up the hill. When they reached the ring of horses, one of the soldiers approached them.

"Major General Thomas Mifflin, head of our Quartermaster Corps, says he can pay you something for helping with these horses. He wants me to take you there once you've done the job," the soldier said.

James looked at Daniel. Daniel said, "under normal circumstances, we'd have to be paid before we start the work, especially for this many horses. But, I understand that this situation is anything but normal, so yes, we'll take care of these horses and then go with you."

"Thank you kindly," said the soldier, shaking Daniel's hand.

The soldiers had already started a roaring fire. Daniel and James walked over and began heating the iron they brought, measuring the horses' hoofs, bending the iron to fit. One by one they went from horse to horse, putting the shoes on expertly, making the horses comfortable again. Soldier after soldier helped them. The soldier who had brought them word from General Mifflin walked with them from horse to horse, inspecting the good and quick work that Daniel and James did. Two hours later, they had put new shoes on or repaired the shoes on some 20 horses.

"You two do good work," said the soldier.

"Thank you," said Daniel. "Some say we're the best in this county."

"I can see why," said the solder. "So, come, let me take you to the General."

They buried their tools in snow to cool them down and walked on to meet the general. They walked a little further down the hill, past the homes of their neighbors, and the soldier stopped them in front of a small house at the top of the hill.

"This is Mr. Jonathan Reese's house," said Daniel.

"Might be," said the soldier, "but this is where our generals are now."

"Our home is full of sick soldiers," Daniel said. "I guess everyone here has taken soldiers in."

A few soldiers guarded the house. The soldier who had been talking to Daniel approached another soldier and told him who he was, while pointing at Daniel and James. Then the soldier walked back towards the two.

"Alright," he said. "Come with me."

"Me, too?" James asked, the memory of the Virginia officer fresh in his mind.

"You, too," said the soldier.

They walked past the soldier guards and went inside the house. When they got inside, the Reeses were nowhere to be seen. What they saw instead was General Mifflin, sitting at a table with what looked like other Generals. They all had clean uniforms, and it looked like they had had enough to eat. They sat at a square wooden table near a roaring fire. There were more soldiers inside guarding the generals.

When they walked in, all the generals looked up. General Mifflin rose from the table and walked towards Daniel and James. The general's hand was outstretched.

"Gentlemen," he said. "I understand you did a great job helping us with our horses," he said, shaking Daniel's hand. "I hear you are the best in this county," he said, extending a hand to James, who, though surprised, shook it as well.

"Thank you General," said Daniel.

"Yes, thank you," said James.

"We appreciate your support of the Continental Army," said the General, "and, as promised, we are going to pay you for your services." He took a few Continental dollars out of his back pocket and handed them to Daniel.

"Thank you," said Daniel, as he looked at them.

"And these are for you," the General said, as he took some out of another pocket and handed them to James.

"Thank you," said James.

The General put his hands behind his back like he was at ease. "We could use men like you to help us with our horses."

"We're happy to help again," said Daniel.

The General smiled and said, "Good. I can sign you up right now for the Continental Army or the Pennsylvania Militia," looking at Daniel. "And," he said, looking at James, "I understand that you are a free man."

James stood a little straighter and proudly said, "Yes."

"Good," General Greene said. "You can join us, too. Not in the Pennsylvania Militia, but in the regular Continental Army. We can use you in the group of blacksmiths that are working directly with the Generals here. Our horses need shoes, too. And, we have a lot of work for an excellent blacksmith to do."

Daniel looked at James and then at the General and said, "With all due respect your honor, we're here on the hill now because our families need us and our wages. We support the patriots, you know that, but it would be very hard for us to leave."

General Mifflin waved his hand. "It's hard for all of us to leave, but leave we must. Gentlemen. We know you support the cause of liberty. Some of us have seen you walking up and down the hill, helping our men, showing them where to find water, showing them which plants are edible and which aren't. We will be in winter quarters soon. We will be rebuilding this great army that has sacrificed so much. We need you to be with us."

Daniel and James just looked at the General.

"If you join us, you will be paid wages. Your families will be taken care of," he said. "Our winter quarters may very well be right here where we are standing. If you are with us, your families would be very close, and you could still get the wages to them. But," he warned, "if you are not with us, you will not be able to do any work for your regular customers or others because this entire area will be home to 10,000 troops as it is now. No one except the people who already live here will be able to get in or out, basically." He smiled at them. "Gentlemen, we know your hearts are with us."

James eyes grew larger as he looked at Daniel.

"Join us," he said.

Daniel and James looked at each other.

General Greene looked at them. "Gentlemen, think it over. We need you. Your country needs you."

Daniel, with a pained looked on his face, said, "General, yes, we support you. But we just can't sign up right now and leave our families. At least without talking to them."

Green laughed. "Yes, the joy of talking with your family. I remember. But yes," he said, patting Daniel on the back. James, too. "Talk with your families. Think it over. Please come back tomorrow and let me know your decision." Then he got serious. "We need you. We need you both," he said, looking at them.

The soldier who accompanied them, nodded, said, "Are we free to go now then General?"

General Mifflin said, "Yes, soldier. Please. See our friends out. But bring them back tomorrow!" he said, confidently.

The soldier walked Daniel and James to the front door. As they walked outside, there was another commotion. Several soldiers rode up to the house on horses that rode like they had good shoes. And riding up right behind the soldiers was a man who was causing all the other soldiers who saw him to cheer, wave and shout.

"General!" "Our commander-in-chief!"

James looked at Daniel. "Commander?" he said, looking at the men cheering. "Is that General Washington?"

Daniel looked, stunned, too. "It must be," he said.

"Wait here until the General passes," said their escort.

But the General didn't pass. He turned his horse into the Reese's yard, right where Daniel and James were standing. Their escort stood at attention. Daniel and James did, too.

One of the soldiers on the ground tied the General's horse up to the hitching post while he stood there regally, waving to the soldiers who continued to cheer him and shout his name. When the horse was securely tied, he dismounted. He walked on the stone pathway, towards where Daniel and James stood. Their escort raised his hands in salute. Daniel and James did, too.  General Washington walked down the pathway and stopped right in front of the trio.  He looked them up and down.

"Good afternoon," he said to the three.

"Good afternoon, General Washington," the escort said.

"Good afternoon, General," Daniel and James said, almost in unison.

"What regiment?" he asked the soldier.

"Second New Jersey," said the escort.

Then the general looked at Daniel.

"And you son?" He didn't comment on his not being in uniform.  Many soldiers clothes were so tattered that it was sometimes hard to tell whether they were in uniform or not.

"I'm not in the army yet, General," Daniel said.  "I live on the hill."

"Not yet?" said the General.  "Are you thinking of joining us?"

"Yes," said Daniel, still saluting.

"Good," said the General.  "We need you."  Then he turned to James.

"And you? Are you free or slave?" the General asked.

"I'm a free man," James said proudly.

The General nodded.  "Then we need you, too."

"Yes, sir," James said.

Then the General saluted them back and walked into the Reese home.

FRED REACHED into his sash and pulled out his ax.  He looked around for a tree that already wasn't surrounded by soldiers cutting down its branches and trunk.  The hill was thick with soldiers now trying to find shelter from the wind and snow.

"No tents tonight, men," his commanding officer had said earlier that day.  "We hear they are stuck somewhere north of here.  So, you know what to do."

Fred walked a few feet until he came to an oak tree that was now never going to grow to its full potential.  He ran his hands around the trunk.  It wasn't too thick to cut down without help. But, he knew that if he needed help, another soldier would be there in a minute. No matter how tired, hungry, or wet they were, the soldiers helped each other out if they could.

Fred started hacking away at the trunk. Chips of wood flew off as the tan interior was exposed. As the trunk became loose, Fred put the ax down, put both hands around the tree, and started shaking it. After a few minutes, it leaned to one side, and he caught it before it fell.

All around him, men were hacking off limbs and deftly positioning them as they built lean-tos. Fred did the same. He built up one wall of branches and then laid others over them so that one end of the limb lay on the branch wall and one wall lay on the ground. His new lean-to was only a few feet tall now, but tall enough for him to lie down inside so he could sleep with at least something covering his head. Some of the branches still had dead and brown leaves sticking to them. He gathered as many of them as he could. They helped fill in the spaces between the bare sticks and keep out the wind and the snow.

The hill came alive now as more soldiers arrived. The grounds were a collection of various colored uniforms as the various state militias with their greens, yellows and browns mixed in with the Continental regulars in their blue and white. What trees weren't used to build lean-tos were used to build fires that now sprung up all over the hill. Some fires burned pure red and yellow with dead, dried out wood—even with the snow— and others smoked black and grey as still living branches and limbs were tossed on. The temperature outside was in the thirties. Freezing men didn't mind a little smoke if it kept them warm.

Fred's lean-to built, he helped another soldier cut down a large dead tree. They chopped it up into firewood and started building a large fire in an open area. A fire that size would heat a lot of men. Once they got that going, Fred helped build another fire that wasn't so large a few feet away. That fire would be used for cooking. They'd gather and melt snow for drinking. If someone had a few loose pieces of tea, they'd throw that into the pot. It wasn't the tea that they were used to drinking at home, but it was hot water that warmed them. And, if anyone came by with a few vegetables, so much the better. They all wanted meat, but they hardly even expected it.

Fred looked around for a rock to sit on. He saw one jutting out of the snow, brushed the snow off, and moved it over to the large fire. Other soldiers were already cooking and, besides, he was tired, and there wasn't much else he could do that day.

"I'LL LEAVE you now," said the escort as he walked James and Daniel back to where the quartermaster unit was. "We'll be over there tomorrow, I think," he said, pointing to the unit. "But don't wait too long to join us. Things change day to day, you know." He stuck his hand out to Daniel. "So, let us know. We really need your help, and I know your family can use the money. Just like mine. Nobody makes much money or does much business after the army comes through, let alone fights a battle in their neighborhood, so think about it." Then he stuck out his hand to Fred. "We need you, too. You heard the General. Freed men are welcome, and to be placed with the generals is quite an honor."

"Yes, I imagine it is," James said, still wary.

With that, the escort walked off.

Daniel looked at James. "Can you believe what just happened?"

James said, "Not really. I never expected to meet any of those generals, let alone General Washington."

"Me either, "said Daniel. "And to have him say that he needs us. That was unbelievable."

"I know," James said, scratching his head.

"They're making this sacrifice for us," said Daniel as they walked along.

"For some of us," said James. "There's still plenty of people like Ruth whose freedom means nothing to them."

"Some of them," said Daniel. "There's men here from all over. Some of the states have outlawed slavery. There's plenty of men here from free states, where Black men are free."

"I guess you're right," James said. "But maybe while they're doing all of this fighting for their own freedom, they'll come to understand that everybody wants to be free and deserves to be free, too."

As they walked down the hill, Daniel said, "Look," pointing to his left.

Coming up the hill was a group of soldiers, Black men, some in regular Continental uniforms, and some in militia. James and Daniel walked closer to them.

When they reached them, James, wide-eyed, said, "Howdy there. Where are you men from?"

"Rhode Island," said one. "We're the 3rd Rhode Island."

"All of you freed men?" James asked.

"Yes," said one. "No slaves can fight in the Continental Army."

James said, "Yes, I know. I just was kind of shocked. I haven't seen so many Black men fighting in this army."

One soldier laughed. "There's a few of us here and there. But this whole regiment here is freed Black men."

"My Lord," said James. He paused a few seconds. "So, let me ask you. Why did you join this here army when there's still so many of our people who are slaves? I know most of these patriots aren't fighting for the slaves' freedom. And, if they could, they'd probably put you and me and every other freed man back into chains."

"Not all of them," said one man in the regiment. "And, don't you like being free?"

James said, "Of course I do. And I'm working hard and saving my money to buy my girl's freedom, too."

"Well, I like being free. And I want to stay that way. I was born free, and I don't want anyone telling me what to do. Living under those British telling us what to do was like living under a kind of slavery. I know it wasn't the same, but it's similar in my mind. And, with everyone now talking about and fighting for freedom, I hope that rubs off on these boys and they see that everyone should be free."

"Hope," said James, sarcastically.

"Yes, hope," said one of the Black soldiers. "What else do we have?"

James nodded. "You've got a point there."

One of the soldiers said, "Listen. If these patriots win, and I expect us to even though there's no evidence of that, they'll look around. If we weren't side by side fighting with them, do you think they'd be inclined to free the rest of our brothers and sisters?"

James shrugged his shoulders.

"I think that if they see us fighting side by side with them, then when this war is over, our people will be as free as they are," said one.

"That's something to think about," James said.

"Yes it is," said one. He spread his arms to his other men. "Every one of us has someone we know who was a slave or is a slave. We know the barbarity. We know the cruelty. And we know that we're fighting as much for them as we are fighting for these new United States of America."

James raised his eyebrows. "I hear you. That makes some sense to me."

One said, "So are you going to join us? There's Pennsylvania regiments all around here."

James said, "Well, my friend here, we're blacksmiths, and we just put shoes on a whole bunch of horses up there in the quartermasters area. And the commanding officer there was so impressed with our work that he took us to his commanding officer who was meeting in our friend's house up there on the top of the hill with a bunch of generals. And they asked us to join them."

"Now isn't that something?" said one of the soldiers.

"And then," said James, "as our escort was walking us out, who comes up there riding on his horse looking all regal, but General George Washington. And he talks to us and asks us to join them, too."

"Ain't that something?" said one of the Rhode Island soldiers. "A personal invitation from General George Washington? How can you turn that down?"

James raised his eyebrows again in surprise and wonder. "Well, I was going to because despite all that, I didn't see this war as being something that a Black man needed to fight in or was wanted to fight in. But, seeing you all and hearing you all, I'm starting to see things differently."

"Good," said one of the men, patting him on the back. "Come on and join us. We need you."

James nodded. "I hear you. "

Daniel looked at James and smiled.

James looked at the Rhode Island soldiers. "Maybe I'll see you soon."

"We hope so," said one, as he stuck out his hand to shake James hand.

Then, one by one, the rest of the Rhode Island soldiers shook James hand as they went by. Daniel stood back and let James have that moment. When the soldiers had all passed by, Daniel looked at James.

"Have you changed your mind, friend?" Daniel asked, patting James on the shoulder.

James looked at Daniel. He said, "If you're going, I'm going."

Daniel smiled. "Oh, so you put it on me." He laughed. "You've known me long enough to know that my mind is made up. I'm going, and I'm glad that you're going with me. We'll do this together. Like we have for years."

James stuck out his hand and shook Daniel's hand.

Daniel sighed. "Let's go tell Mom," he said, as they walked down the hill towards the Welburn home.

HOPE FIRST hugged Daniel. Then she hugged James. She hung her head down as tears dropped down her face. She wiped them off with a hand that was holding a tattered piece of cloth. "I'm sorry to see you both go, but I understand," she said. Then she extended a hand and held both of their hands with one of hers. "And I'm not surprised. I know you've been out and around, up and down the hill, talking with men from all over the states, including those in this house. I know you can't see their sacrifice and not think about making your own.

"Daniel," she said, looking at him. "I know how I raised you with character and dignity and a sense of duty." Then she looked at James. "And James, ever since I've known you, I've seen your sense of dignity, hard work and responsibility. You worked hard for your freedom, and I know you're working hard for Ruth's. I didn't think that you would be able to resist the fight for freedom when it came right to you." She squeezed both men's hands. "I guess this is what happens when the war comes to your back yard."

She wiped her hands on her apron. "Alright. Let's get you two ready."

JAMES, DANIEL and Hope spent the next few days trying to gather supplies for James and Daniel to use in the army and for Hope and Prudence to use when they are left behind. At the same time, they were still caring for an unending stream of Continental Army soldiers who needed special care. A knock on the door interrupted the usual bustle of activity.

"Come in," said Hope, as she showed the Sargent in.

"Thank you, Ma'am," said the soldier. "I'm Sargent Harman. 3rd New York," he said as he saluted Hope. "I'm here at the request of General Washington. He's issued General Orders for today that he wants all soldiers to hear and all civilians on the hill here helping us out."

Hope's eyes grew wide.

"It's nothing bad, Ma'am," the Sgt. Harman said, smiling. "But it's important."

"Alright, Sargent," said Hope. "Let me get everyone." She walked in to the small side room where Daniel and James were packing up their gear. "There's a Sargent here with an announcement," she said. "Something important from General Washington that he wants all the patriots to hear." Daniel went to help Prudence to her feet, and James went to help the other men to theirs.

When they all assembled in the main room, Hope looked around and said, "We're all here Sargent. You can go ahead now."

Sgt. Harman said, "Thank you, Ma'am. What I'm going to read is today's General Orders from General Washington. He wants all of you, every Patriot, to hear this:

## GENERAL ORDERS HEAD QUARTERS, AT THE GULPH, DECEMBER 17, 1777.

The Commander-in-Chief with the highest satisfaction expresses his thanks to the officers and soldiers for the fortitude and patience with which they have sustained the fatigues of the Campaign. Altho' in some instances we unfortunately failed, yet upon the whole Heaven hath smiled on our Arms and crowned them with signal success; and we may upon the best grounds conclude, that by a spirited continuance of the measures necessary for our defence we shall finally obtain the end of our Warfare, Independence, Liberty and Peace. These are blessings worth contending for at every hazard. But we hazard nothing. The power of America alone, duly exerted, would have nothing to dread from the force of Britain. Yet we stand not wholly upon our ground. France yields us every aid we ask, and there are reasons to believe the period is not very distant, when she will take a more active part, by declaring war against the British Crown. Every motive therefore, irresistibly urges us, nay commands us, to a firm and manly perseverance in our opposition to our cruel oppressors, to slight difficulties, endure hardships, and condemn every danger. The General ardently wishes it were now in his power, to conduct the troops into the best winter quarters. But where are these to be found? Should we retire to the interior parts of the State, we should find them crowded with virtuous citizens, who, sacrificing their all, have left Philadelphia, and fled thither for protection. To their distresses humanity forbids us to add. This is not all, we should leave a vast extent of fertile country to be despoiled and ravaged by the enemy, from which they would draw vast supplies, and where many of our firm friends would be exposed to all the miseries of the most insulting and wanton depredation. A train of evils might be enumerated, but these will suffice. These considerations make it indispensibly necessary for the army to take such a position, as will enable it most effectually to prevent distress and to give the most extensive security; and in that position we must make ourselves the best shelter in our power. With activity and diligence Huts may be erected that will be warm and dry. In these the troops will be compact, more secure against surprises than if in a divided state and at hand to protect the country. These cogent reasons have determined the General to take post in the neighbourhood of this camp; and influenced by them, he persuades himself, that the officers and soldiers, with one heart, and one mind, will resolve to surmount every difficulty, with a fortitude and patience, be coming their profession, and the sacred cause in which they are engaged. He himself will share in the hardship, and partake of every inconvenience.

To morrow being the day set apart by the Honorable Congress for public Thanksgiving and Praise; and duty calling us devoutely to express our grateful acknowledgements to God for the manifold blessings he has granted us. The General directs that the army remain in its present quarters, and that the Chaplains perform divine service with their several Corps and brigades. And earnestly exhorts, all officers and soldiers, whose absence is not indispensibly necessary, to attend with reverence the solemnities of the day.

AFTER SGT. Harman finished reading, the room was silent. Tears streamed down the faces of many of those assembled.

Hope wiped the tears from her eyes. She looked straight at Sgt. Harman and said, "Thank you, Sargent. We will be celebrating Thanksgiving here tomorrow with whatever we have, which, at this point, isn't much. But, please know, you are welcome to join us. And, as many patriots as can fit in here, we're happy to have them."

Sgt. Harman nodded at her and said, "Thank you, Ma'am. I'll spread the word."

Hope walked back to where he was standing, reached her arms out, and hugged him.

"God bless you," she said, as the tears welled up again. "And be safe."

"God bless you, too, Ma'am. You're a real patriot," the Sargent said.

"Yes I am," Hope said. "We all are," she said, sweeping her arms around the room.

"I'VE GOT to go talk to Ruth," James said to Daniel as they were packing their things up.

Daniel looked up. "I reckon that you do," he said.

"I'm sure they have her working, getting ready for this Thanksgiving," said James. "I'm sure they have food down there being that Mr. Hannah is so high up in the government."

Daniel laughed. "Well, see if she'll give you some of that food for our celebration. I don't know what Mom will pull out of her hat to feed all of these people."

"Maybe the rations will come in today just like the tents did the other day," James said.

Daniel laughed again. "Yeah, and maybe it will be 90 degrees out there today. Some things just seem unlikely."

"Well, if Ruth can get me anything extra, you know she will," said James.

"I know. Well, good luck. And be careful out there," Daniel said.

James made his way through the collection of soldiers in the house to the front door.

He stepped outside, carefully stepping around the tents in the front yard. He unhitched the horse from the back of the house, put his saddle on her, jumped up, and rode away. He couldn't go as fast as he wanted because of the tents and soldiers everywhere. The men before him were some of the most retched that he'd seen anywhere. Those who were clothed had on clothes that were dirty, torn, and clinging to them because they were wet, or hanging off of them because they were torn. Many men's long pants looked like short pants; long sleeve shirts were now short sleeves or no sleeves. Many a man had nothing on his feet, his frostbitten black toes contrasting sharply with his white skin. Some men had leaves, secured by string, wrapped around their feet for at least some protection. James just rode on.

The Continental Army's tent city stretched out a good ways along the route to the Hannah Plantation. Tents lined the main road. The front entrance to the Hannah Plantation had a group of Continental Soldiers in front. James wondered who was inside the massive main house. He figured that it was another general. He rode on past to the back entrance that was used by the slaves. As he approached, he saw another group of soldiers guarding that back entrance. But he also saw his friend Henry, whose normal spot was to stay at the back door, seeing that things that got delivered got delivered right. As he approached, James saw Henry speaking to one of the soldiers. James slowed his approach, but kept heading towards that back entrance. Henry looked up, waved to James, and motioned for him to keep coming.

"Come on, James," Henry said. "I told them you're a safe man. Used to be a slave here, but now a free man."

James waved back at Henry and came closer. "Hello Henry," he said.

Henry said, "Come on over James, and tie your horse up right here."

James did as Henry said. Henry went over and patted the horse.

"What brings you here?" Henry asked. "And do you have all these soldiers up your way?"

James shook Henry's hand and said, "Yes. The hill is full of soldiers and tents. Has been for days."

"All around here, too," said Henry. "I guess the war is right here."

"Yes it is," James said. Then he took off his hat. "Henry, I'm here to see Ruth. I'm sure they've got her working, getting ready for the Thanksgiving celebration tomorrow. But, I've got to see her."

Henry frowned. "You're right. They've got her working hard, cooking up a feast, or something like it. Even we don't have the food we used to 'cause we've been feeding so many of the soldiers." He frowned his lips and eyes like he was puzzled. "Do you have to see her today? Can it wait until day after tomorrow? The soldiers are moving out then, so things will be getting back to normal around here."

James frowned. "That's just it. When the soldiers move out day after tomorrow, I'm moving out with them."

Henry's eyes widened with surprise. "What? Why? You joining the Continentals? No wait. I know you're not joining the Continentals. General Washington don't allow no Black men holding guns in the Continentals."

James nodded. "You're right about that for slaves. But he asked me personally when he was up at Rebel Hill after I told him that I was a free man. I'm joining one of the Pennsylvania regiments, and I'm going to be assigned to a special blacksmith unit in the Quartermaster Corps that works right under the generals. Me and Daniel. We put new shoes on some horses for them up on the hill, and they asked us to join them. Said they'd pay us wages, too. Said we wouldn't get wages otherwise this winter because the war is here now."

Henry shook his head in disbelief. "So you're joining the Continental Army? On invitation from General Washington himself? You're going to join these white men in fighting for their freedom when they could care less about freedom for the rest of us?"

James held his hands up to silence him. "No, Henry. That's not it. I think those of us who are free have to fight for freedom for you all, too."

Henry shook his head. "I don't understand that. You know those crackers don't want no free niggers."

"A lot of them don't, but a lot of them do," James said. "Times are changing. All this talk of freedom has rubbed off on some of them. And there are some of our people out here fighting for freedom, making sacrifices for all of us. Have you seen them?"

Henry said, "What do you mean 'our people'? Black people?"

James shook his head yes.

Henry said adamantly, voice raised, "No. I haven't seen any of our people out here fighting."

James proceeded to tell him about the Rhode Island regiment and his conversation with them.

Henry laughed. "Well, if you niggers think you can change these white folk's minds by going out there and fighting with them and possibly getting yourself shot up, you go right ahead. If you get my freedom, I'll thank you, but pardon me if I don't hold my breath."

James patted Henry on the back. "Henry, I've known you a long time, so I'm not even mad at what you're saying. You know I understand. But,

I'm going to go. I'm going to try. And, I'm going to get paid for trying. And, if fighting for freedom doesn't bring everyone's freedom, I'll have that much more money saved up to at least buy Ruth's freedom." Then James laughed. "Then maybe I'll start on yours."

Henry threw his head back and laughed, too. "Alright. Alright. I hear you." Then his facial expression got serious. "But seriously, James, you be careful. Don't you go getting on the front lines when those redcoats start shooting. You stay right in the back where they like to keep us. Let those crackers die for freedom, and then the rest of them will see what it feels like and looks like when a man is willing to go to any lengths to be free. Maybe they'll stop sending these slaves who run away back to their masters to be beaten and killed just because they wanted to be free."

James nodded. "I understand."

Henry raised an eyebrow. "Now, you go on and find Ruth, and you better hope that she understands."

James nodded. "I know. I know," he said. He stuck out his hand. "Henry, if I don't see you when I get ready to leave, you take good care of Ruth now, will you?"

Henry nodded. "You know I will." Then he laughed. "And you know I'll see you when I leave. Mr. Hannah hasn't gotten so full of the freedom bug that he'll let you leave through the front door, so you know you'll be walking right out this back door when you get ready to leave."

James laughed. "I think you're right about that," he said, as he patted Henry on the arm.

James walked off towards the kitchen. The area leading up to it was a bustle of activity. Slaves and soldiers carried bushels of vegetables and other food in toward the kitchen. Great fires ran in the cook houses and barbecue areas. A nicely browned pig turned on a spit. What he wouldn't give for a piece of that? Then there was another spit with a cow's torso on it. Pork and beef. Two things he hadn't eaten in over a week. As he walked towards the kitchen, all the slaves shouted greetings and waved. A young girl ran up to him.

"Mr. James! Mr. James!" she yelled. "What are you doing here? It's not Sunday."

"I know," said James, as he picked her up and twirled her around. "Can't I come by here and see my girls any day?" The little girl smiled. He gently put her back on the ground.

"You here to see Miss Ruth, right?" she asked.

"That's right," said James. "You're a mighty smart young lady."

The girl smiled broadly. "I'll run and tell her that you're coming. She's in the kitchen."

"As usual," James said under his breath.

The girl ran into the kitchen, and James walked faster. He knew that if Ruth was allowed to leave the kitchen, it would only be for a minute, and he didn't want to waste any time.

Just as he reached the kitchen back door, Ruth met him, running out.

"James!" she said, excitedly. She ran over to him and wrapped her arms around him. "What are you doing here?"

James squeezed her as he held her tight. He didn't want to let her go, but he knew that he had to. "I'm only here for a minute," he said. "I know you're working, getting ready for Thanksgiving tomorrow." He stepped back and took a good look at her while holding her shoulders. She was as beautiful as ever, even in her plain brown homespun dress and apron.

"Yes," she said. "They're working me harder than ever. We've got so many more mouths to feed with all these soldiers. Do you have them up there on the hill, too?"

"Yup, all over," James said.

"So what's going on?" she asked. "I'm always happy to see you, but why today?"

James held her hands. "Well, you know that the army's moving out to winter quarters the day after the Thanksgiving."

Ruth shook her head yes.

"Well, I've been asked to go with them. To work with the quarter master corps." He told her how he put shoes on the horses, met the General, and how this would help him keep earning wages for her freedom.

Tears came to Ruth's eyes as soon as he said that he was going with them. "I wish you weren't going, but I know why you are." She hugged him. "You're making quite a sacrifice to earn money to buy my freedom."

James squeezed her harder. "You're worth it, Ruth. I'd do almost anything to have you free and with me. If that means I have to go join an army I never wanted to join and fight a war I never wanted to fight because that was the only way I could still earn money to buy your freedom, I'll do it. And, I know that God will be with me. He'll protect me and get me back to you because what I'm doing is the right thing."

Ruth held him tight as she talked. "I know. I know," she said. She hugged him for a few minutes until one of the older slaves on the plantation called her from the back steps.

"Ruth, girl, come on. We've got no time for that. You know we've got all this work to do," the slave yelled. "And, oh yes, hey there James."

"Hey Miss Sue," James called back. Then he pulled back from Ruth.

"Now, don't you worry. I'm coming back for you. I'm going to stay with them for the winter, and then we'll see how that goes. I'll be right down the road at the Valley Forge. Henry and some of the other men know where that is. If you need to send me a message, you get one of them to run it on up to me. I'll be with the blacksmiths. You remember that?"

Ruth nodded and said, "Yes, the blacksmiths. Of course. You're the best."

James kissed her on the head. "That's right." He kept his arm around her as he walked her towards the back step. "I hope they're not too hard on you this winter. And, I hope that by the time winter is over, I'll have the money to get you out of here."

Ruth looked at him lovingly. "I know you will."

James wrapped his arms around her, squeezed her again, stepped back, and kissed her lovingly on the lips. He pulled back, and Ruth touched her lips with her fingers as if she wanted to touch the kiss and take it with her. "I love you, Ruth, and we will be married one day. Soon."

Ruth smiled and said, "I'm counting on it." She stepped back, still holding both of James large hands in her small ones. They stood there looking at each other for about a minute. Tears welled up in both of their eyes. Just then, the back door opened. Miss Sue walked out.

"Ruth and James, I hate to break this up, but the Missus is coming in and out, and she wondered where you were," Sue said. Then she walked closer and put a packet wrapped in paper in James pocket.

"Pork," she said. "I know you could use it with all these soldiers everywhere, and Thanksgiving tomorrow."

"Thank you, Miss Sue," said James as he put one arm around her. As he did, she took another packet out of her apron and slid it in his other pocket.

"Beef," she said as she looked up at him smiling. "Happy Thanksgiving."

James laughed and kissed Miss Sue on the head. "Happy Thanksgiving to you, too."

Then Miss Sue stepped back a few steps. "Come on, honey," she said to Ruth.

James pulled Ruth close and kissed her on the top of the head one more time. "Go on, honey," he said. "I'll be back."

Ruth stepped back and looked him in the eye. "And I'll be waiting." With that, she turned and walked away, collapsing into Miss Sue as she walked her back into the kitchen.

JAMES HID the meat in his boots before he rode back to the hill. Meat was as precious as gold. If he was stopped and searched, he hoped they wouldn't search his boots. Luckily, he wasn't stopped at all. The soldiers he passed by looked too tired to do much of anything.

He reached the Welburn house, hitched the horse, and hurried inside. As he figured, Mrs. Welburn was in the cooking area, making fires, boiling something, bustling, trying to cook something for that evening's dinner. He walked closer, smiling.

"Did you see Ruth?" Hope asked.

"I sure did," James said, smiling.

Hope raised her eyebrow, looking puzzled. "I'd have thought you'd come back here sad, having to be away from your girl."

James said, "Yes, that part does make me sad." Then he looked around, making sure that nobody else was listening or looking at him. The he said, "But Miss Sue there gave me a parting gift." He went right up to Hope's ear and whispered in it, "Pork."

Hope said, "Oh!" excitedly, and she quickly put her hand to her mouth to stifle her excitement and noise.

James laughed a little, and he said, "And beef."

Hope, hand already over her mouth, raised her eyebrows high with excitement.

"Glory be," she said softly, taking her hand down.

"Amen," said James.

"I'll put a little in the soup today, cook more for Thanksgiving tomorrow, and then dry out some so you can take it with you the day after," Hope said.

"And keep some for you and Prudence," James said. "Winter's only just beginning, and you'll need it when we leave."

Hope hugged him. "Thank you James. You're right about that. I hate to think about what will happen when you and Daniel are gone."

James patted her on the back. What could he say? He knew it wasn't going to be easy for them. "The people on the hill pull together. You'll have them to help you."

"That's true," said Hope. "But it won't be the same."

James knew that was right, but he wasn't going to say anything.

"Well, let me get somewhere private and pull off these boots and give you this meat," James said.

ON THANKSGIVING Day, Hope was already up, cooking and baking. She had just put a loaf of bread in the cook stove when Sgt. Harlan appeared again at the door.

"Good morning, Ma'am," he said. "Happy Thanksgiving."

"Nice to see you again," Hope said. "And Happy Thanksgiving to you."

"I wanted to let you know Ma'am and everyone here, too, that our chaplains will be preaching Thanksgiving service this morning. You'll see them all over the hill. They'll start at 10 am, and you are all welcome to attend," said the Sargent.

"That's mighty kind of you," Hope said.

Sgt. Harlan shook his head. "Not me. General Washington," he said.

"Alright," said Hope. "That's mighty kind of General Washington. I'd like to hear the services, and I'm sure many of these men would, too."

Sgt. Harlan left, and Hope went right back to cooking. Daniel walked over.

"I want to hear the sermon, but I can't leave all these men," Hope said.

Daniel looked around. "Some of these men are in no shape to go outside and sit around and listen to a sermon. I bet some of them would be happy to sit in the kitchen while we go out. I'll walk around and find out." Daniel walked to the soldiers who were lame or still obviously weak.

He found three who would rather stay inside than go outside. After the Welburn's generosity and care, they were happy to watch the food and give Hope a break so she could listen to the sermon.

"All set, Mom," Daniel said, as he helped the three into position around the cooking area. One even volunteered to stir the pot at the appropriate time. Another said he'd be responsible for getting the bread in and out of the oven.

"I do thank you, boys," Hope said. "I want to share this important day, this important sermon, with my son and my friend here," she said, pointing to James. Then she pointed to them. "But, when I get back, be ready. We're going to have one last feast before I send you off!"

They all smiled, laughed and cheered, as Hope, Daniel, Prudence, James, and the other soldiers walked outside to find a Thanksgiving sermon.

THE WELBURN group didn't have to go far to find a sermon. The group of soldiers that normally camped in their yard or right outside of it was gathered now all together, closer to the road. All over the hill, soldiers gathered in groups, standing or sitting. James and the Welburns walked over to the group next to their yard.

"Are you gathered for the Thanksgiving sermon?" asked Hope of one poor young man leaning on a cane fashioned out of tree branches.

"Yes," said the young man. "And the food they said we'd get after the sermon was over," he added, smiling.

"Mind if we join you?" Hope asked.

"I don't mind," said the soldier. "But what I say doesn't carry any weight around here." He pointed towards the right. "Our commanding officer is over there. You might want to check with him."

Hope checked in with the commanding officer, and he said that all was fine.

They took their place in the group just as a man dressed in a preacher's stern black and white robes walked down the hill towards the group.

FRED WOKE up slowly. The past five days on the hill were not easy ones for him or for anyone, as far as he could tell. For the first three days, he slept on what could only generously be called a "bed" of leaves under a lean-to made out of branches. The snow fell pretty steadily for the first day and a half, making it harder to light a fire to stay warm. Wet wood and water didn't make a good fire. The only good thing about the snow is that when you did have a fire, you could melt the snow and get water without having to walk down the steep hill to the creek by the Gulph. Food was practically nonexistent those first two days except what they caught or dug up. After the second day, he was reunited with his normal regiment. Thankfully, he and the other Paoli boys knew what plants they could and couldn't eat. And, anything that moved and breathed, they caught and cooked—squirrel, fox, whatever. It didn't matter. They were starving.

The tents arriving after a few days in the Gulph only made things slightly better. By the time they arrived, he was bone chilled, and although the snow had stopped and the sun came out, that wasn't enough to get the bone chill out of him. Yet, even though he was cold and hungry, he welcomed this day with a smile. The generals had decided on winter quarters, and they were going to move out the next day. They were going to spend the winter at the Valley Forge. Fred and the rest of his regiment were overjoyed. That way, they'd only be a few miles away from their families—close enough so that the families could reach them with food and clothing and other provisions to get them through the long winter.

General Wayne had told them that the march to Valley Forge was delayed one day so that the army could celebrate the Thanksgiving that the Continental Congress had proclaimed earlier that year. To the soldiers,

Thanksgiving still meant food. Not the type or amount of food that they were used to back home on Thanksgiving. No one had seen that kind of food for months. But each man was supposed to finally get at least some piece of meat and some whisky. That alone was worth being thankful for. But, Fred was thankful for so much more. He remembered back to the Thanksgiving the year before, at home in Paoli with the rest of the family, with his brother, Allen. He remembered how they had all talked about the war and waited for Allen to turn old enough to enlist. He remembered how excited Allen was to be able to join up with General Wayne when he started a regiment from the area. But, most of all, he remembered Allen's face as the blood drained from his stomach after the redcoat ran a bayonet through him. He remembered the look on Allen's face as all life drained from him. He would remember that forever.

So, Fred slowly stretched his bones that were still cold and his muscles that were still aching and pushed himself off of his bed. He blew his breath into his hands to warm them up. He shook his feet to get the blood flowing down in to them. And then he walked over to the fire near his regiment and waited with the rest of his friends for their commanding officer.

After what seemed like half an hour, General Wayne rode up on his horse. He was followed by another man on a horse, a preacher. Since the men had cut down just about every tree for firewood, dried or not, smoking or not, there was plenty of space for the horses to come through. The crowd of men parted for the two men on horses.

"Happy Thanksgiving, men," General Wayne yelled to his troops. "I know this is not the Thanksgiving that you're used to in your homes, but we have much to thank God for. We are here. We are alive. And we are moving into winter quarters where we will have a respite from war and an opportunity to rebuild." He pointed towards the reverend. "I want to present to you Reverend Israel Evans, Chaplin to General Poor's New

Hampshire Brigade. He will deliver the Thanksgiving sermon to us today. And, after his sermon, the quartermasters will make their way over here, delivering to each man an extra portion of rations today—even some meat."

"Yeah," yelled the men.

"Alright now," said General Wayne. "Sit if you want to sit or stand if you don't want to sit or can't sit. But, let us get our minds on the same page as we prepare to give thanks and continue in this great cause of ours." He held his hand out to Reverend Evans like he shooing him in to a room and said, "Reverend Evans. The men are all yours."

Reverend Evans began his sermon. During it, the men were quiet. In fact, most of the hill was quiet. All you could occasionally hear were other sermons being delivered and cheers at the end. Fred listened intently to Reverend Evans. He thought about the sacrifice that he was making, that Allen made, and that all of these men were making for freedom. Tears came to and rolled down his eyes and the eyes of every soldier that he saw. At the end of his sermon, Reverend Evans said, "Amen." Fred said, "Amen," and then joined his fellow soldiers in letting out a great cheer.

Right on cue, a few soldiers from the quarter masters corps rode and walked over with buckets of food. They went from person to person, handing out a piece of meat, a vegetable, squash, and a potato. Some of the men immediately started building more fires. The quartermasters also dropped off to each regiment one large iron pot that could be used for making one big stew. The regiment's cook immediately sent a group down the hill to fetch water from the Gulph Creek to cook their Thanksgiving feast.

BACK AT the Welburn's, Hope had the cookpots boiling. When they returned home from the Thanksgiving sermon that they listened to, the quartermasters had already visited the house. All of the men had received a food ration. James and Daniel had gathered some firewood as they walked back, and Hope was so happy to have so much meat. She cooked the small pieces that the men had given her and some of what James brought back from seeing Ruth.

At one point, Sargent Wharton came to the door with another soldier. "Happy Thanksgiving, Ma'am," he said.

"Sargent," said Hope, like she was looking at her best friend. "Happy Thanksgiving. So good to see you. What can I do for you today?"

"Well, Ma'am, I know you have a group of men here who need medical care, and before we march out to winter quarters, we thought we'd get them checked out," he said. Then stepping aside, he said, "This here is Dr. Abilene Waldo, Surgeon General of the Continental Army. He will be inspecting the men."

Hope nodded and said, "Absolutely. Welcome Dr. Waldo." She shook his hand. "I've tried my best to take care of these men. Me, my son and his friend. But we're mighty glad to see you here."

"Yes, Ma'am," said Dr. Waldo. "I heard that you've done wonders nursing these men back."

Hope blushed and smiled at the compliment. "Thank you, Doctor," she said. "So you go right ahead and check them out. " Then she said, "I'll just be in the cooking area, cooking up our Thanksgiving feast. Would you like to join us?"

Dr. Waldo hesitated.

Hope said, "We have plenty, Doctor. Please. We would love to have you join us."

Dr. Waldo then smiled and said, "Yes. I'd love to join you."

Hope turned to Sgt. Wharton. "And Sergeant, you, too. You're welcome to stay."

"I'd love to have a final meal here with you, Ma'am. But I've got to get back to my regiment," he said.

"I understand, Sargent," she said. Then she walked closer to him, put her arms out, and hugged him. "You be safe, now," she said as she squeezed him. "I'll be praying for you."

The Sargent hugged her back and squeezed her tight. "Thank you, Ma'am. I'll be praying for you, too. You are one of our angels."

Hope again blushed and smiled. "Just an old woman helping out some fine young men," she said.

"A mighty fine woman," Sargent Wharton said, as he hugged her again. Then he stepped back, saluted her, and walked out.

Dr. Waldo went from man to man, inspecting and treating him. He talked with each man, seeing if he was fit to make the march to the Valley Forge or whether he should be picked up and sent to the hospital in Reading. He declared most of them to be fit enough to make the march. All of the men there wanted to go with their regiments. Only a few would be going to the hospital at this point. All of them sang praises on the care they received from James and the Welburns.

All were in good spirits as they talked about memories of Thanksgivings they had back home. The Welburns and James relayed as much as they could about the essence of the sermon to the men who didn't hear one. Honor, duty, God's grace, God's protection and providence shining down on the Continental Army. Thankful that God was on their side. Thankful that the Army would be going into winter quarters where they could rest and rebuild.

Dr. Waldo filled in, too.

After they ate, the men's stomachs were fuller than they had been in a long time. Satisfied looks came over all of their faces. One by one, they fell asleep.

Daniel and James stayed up until all of the other men fell asleep. Then they walked into the cooking area to help Hope with the last of the cleanup. She looked up as they came in, and tears were already forming. In less than 12 hours, they would be leaving. Daniel and James walked over towards her. She wiped her hands on her apron and opened her arms.

"Come," she said. She took James in one arm and Daniel in another and held them close.

"I'll miss you both," she said. "But I'm so proud of you both."

They each put an arm around Hope and squeezed her.

James stepped back and took a good look at Hope. He said, "Mrs. Welburn, you've been mighty good to me ever since I got my freedom and moved on this hill. If anybody around here had a question about me, you put an end to that. You're a fine woman, and I'll never forget what you've done for me."

Hope smiled. "You're a wonderful man, James. Now everyone around here knows that."

"That's all because of you," James said. Then he smiled at her again. "Now, I'm going to go take my place on the floor and go to sleep. I know the Valley Forge isn't that far from here, but by the looks of this army, as weak as these men look, even with the food we ate today, I think it will take us longer than usual to march there."

He patted Hope on the back. Then he looked at Daniel. "I'll see you in the morning, Daniel," James said.

"Bright and early," Daniel said.

James walked into the other room.

Daniel walked closer to his mother and took her in his arms. "Are you sure you'll be alright here, Mom?"

Hope said, "Of course, son. Don't you worry about us. You know I can take care of Prudence and myself."

"I know you're tough and independent and strong," said Daniel. "But times are different now. Things are harder."

Hope looked up. "You think I haven't lived through hard times before? I have. It was never easy around here. When I was young and before you were born. We had to be tough and strong, being some of the first people on this hill."

"I know, Mom," Daniel said.

"No, you don't," said Hope. "It was much easier when your father was here, sure, but it's never been as hard as it was when we first came to the hill." She patted Daniel's back. "Don't worry son. I'll be fine. And, like you said, you won't be that far away. If I really need you, I'll come get you." She looked up and smiled.

Daniel was still worried about his mother and about Prudence. Although he now had a burning desire to join the Continental Army, he still had doubts about leaving his mother and sister alone. But he knew that he had to stuff down those doubts because his mother had doubts of her own, no matter how strong or tough she made herself seem.

"I suppose you're right, Mom," Daniel said.

"I'm always right," Hope said. "Don't you know that by now?"

Daniel looked at her and smiled bravely, "Yes, I do," he said.

# CHAPTER 50

# DECEMBER 19, 1777
# REBEL HILL

The soldiers on the trumpet called out reveille as soon as the sun came up. Fred woke up feeling better than he had in days. Even though it was cold, he had food in his belly. And, he would be leaving, marching to the Valley Forge, to spend the winter not too far from home. He packed up his tent and took his place around the fire. There was no food that morning, only hot water. Even though the Valley Forge was not far, it wasn't close enough to make the march comfortably without something to eat.

General Wayne came riding in and gave the troops a pep talk. "Men," he said, holding his musket up high, "We're ready to march out. Closer to home. And when we get there, we can rest. So men, pick up your things, and let's march on!"

Fred stood up, pulled his roll off of the ground, put it on his back, and lined up with the rest of the tired, hungry, barely clothed regiment. They started moving out, taking their place behind the line of regiments full of tired, hungry, barely clothed soldiers who had marched out ahead of them.

They walked down the hill towards the Gulph Mill. Hundreds of soldiers had already marched ahead before them. Fred looked down. So much of the white snow was now pink where blood from the barefoot or near barefoot soldiers had already passed. Some spots were red where the shoeless or near shoeless had just passed.  A soft snow fell.  It was going to be a long day, he thought.

DANIEL WIPED the tears from his eyes as he closed the door to his home behind him.  James stood there waiting for him, having already wiped his tears, giving Daniel those last few moments with his mother and sister.

James pursed his lips and looked at Daniel. "Ready?" he asked

Daniel wiped his eyes again.  "Ready," he said, as he put his roll on his back.

They turned, leaving the Welburn home behind them as they walked up the hill to join the rest of the soldiers on their march to the Valley Forge.

# CHAPTER 51

# REBEL HILL

Daniel and James lined up with the 5th Pennsylvania Regiment, where General Mifflin had assigned them to be under the command of the great General Anthony Wayne. They lined up with the rest of the Pennsylvania line.

When the men all over the hill were lined up with their units, General Washington appeared at the top of the hill and called out to the men as loudly as he could. "Ready, men?" The men around him called out, "Ready, General."

"Then move out," the general yelled. A cheer rang out from the men.

As they started walking, it seemed like the cheer took all the strength that the men had because, even though the fife and drum and the officers tried to keep the men marching at a certain pace, it was hard. Men slowed down. Men fell down. Daniel and James had to help up their share of men who fell right in front of them and just couldn't go on any longer.

All of that was easy to understand. Clothing hung off some of the soldiers. Some had no shoes or leaves tied with string around their feet. The snow mixed with blood right in front of them. Some men called out for water, but all they could do was pick up snow that hadn't been trampled on and suck on it. Some men called out for food or complained that they didn't have any. The officers said there would be no food on the march, but that they were expecting there to be some at the Valley Forge when they arrived. For some, that put pep in their step. For some, that caused them to yell out in agony.

But, for the most part, the men—tired, hungry, and cold—marched on, following orders, hoping that once they reached the Valley Forge they would get the rest, the food, and the warmth they so much desired.

# CHAPTER 52

# THE VALLEY FORGE

The 5th Pennsylvania had made it. The fields and woods by the Valley Forge had already been divided up and marked up by regiments by the advance scouts. There were wooden markers stuck in the ground telling the men where they were to live and build their huts. The army marched in and dragged themselves in largely by late afternoon before it became dark. Some men fell out and down right where their divisions were marked. Others threw their gear down on the snowy, frozen ground, pulled out their axes, and went to work cutting down trees. General Washington, in his General Orders a few days before, promised a monetary award to the first division that had all of its huts built, and to the first regiment.

Captain Benjamin Bartholomew gathered Fred and the men in his division.

"Men," he said. "You know that there is a reward for the division and regiment that builds their huts first."

The men nodded as some yelled back "Yeah."

"You heard the dimensions before we left the hills by the Gulph, but I'm going to repeat them now. And, I'm going to give you your hut assignments, so you know who you'll be living with for the rest of this winter," he said. "Now, we told you on the hill that militia, regular Continental Army soldiers, and some special units are going to be mixed in together here so we can all learn together, learn from each other, and

build a better army while we're here for a few months. We're going to
get training to sharpen our skills and turn us into an even better fighting
army."

"So," he said, "since we're going to get trained together, we're going to
live together. Militia, continentals, and specials. One army."

Fred raised his eyebrows. He said to his friend, "From what I hear,
most of those militia need training just to get up to where we are as far as
being skilled fighters."

His friend said, "Yeah, that's what I hear, too."

The captain went on. "One army. One cause. Together." He looked
especially over in the direction of where the Continental regulars were
standing. "The enemy is out there," he said, pointing east towards the way
they had just come, closer to Philadelphia. "Not here," he said, pointing
down towards the frozen ground.

"Alright. When I read your name, come stand over here. General
Washington has ordered that there be twelve soldiers or non-
commissioned officers to a hut. Once you have your group together, you
can go about setting up your hut."

The captain read off the names of the men, a few militias and specials
mixed in with the regulars.

"Fred Roberts. Daniel Welburn. James Weldon. Bruce Lawrence," and
on he went.

Fred walked over towards the captain.

Daniel and James smiled at each other and patted each other on the
back as they picked up their gear and walked towards Fred. "Glad we're
together," Daniel said.

"Me, too," said James, as they walked over together.

Fred approached and stuck out his hand. "Fred Roberts," he said.

"Daniel Welburn," Daniel said shaking Fred's hand.

Fred stuck his hand out to shake James hand.

James stuck his hand out. "James Weldon."

Fred nodded and looked right at James. "Glad to know you." He assumed that Fred was a free man. All of the Continentals knew that slaves weren't allowed to fight in the army for the patriots generally. Any person of African descent had to be a freed man, except in some of those southern state units, where the slave masters who were too cowardly to fight sent their slaves to fight in their place.

Bruce introduced himself, too, to Daniel and James.

Fred looked at the group. They all looked to be in pretty good shape compared to the rest of the people around them. But you never knew.

They walked off to the side and to a plot of ground next to the hut group that the sergeant called before them. They put their bags down.

Fred said, "So, we all look like we're in pretty good shape. Considering."

Daniel said, "James and I just signed up. We live up on the hill by the Gulph."

"Well, welcome," said Fred. "We've been in for about four months. Joined up in August, right before the battle down by the Brandywine. We're both from Paoli," he said, pointing to his friend Bruce.

"So you're not too far from home," Daniel said.

"No," said Fred. "I hope I can somehow get a message to them that I'm over here and not laying in a ditch somewhere or six feet under."

Daniel said, "Right. I hope you can, too. Seems like you should be able to since we'll be here for a few months."

"Yes," said James. "That's one good thing about winter. No fighting."

Bruce said, "You're right about that."

James said, "Have you seen other battles besides the one by the Brandywine?"

Fred nodded. "Yes. We went right from there to the Battle of the Clouds, and then we were both in the Paoli Massacre. That's where I lost my little brother, Allen," he said.

"I'm sorry," said James.

"Yes, me, too. We were very close," Fred said, as he closed his eyes for a few seconds. "But, I got some revenge a few weeks later at the Battle of Germantown when we stuck those redcoats with our bayonets just like they did to our boys that night in Paoli. Then, I had a little action in Whitemarsh and in a skirmish by the Matson Ford before we crossed the Schuylkill to the Gulph."

"So you've seen quite a bit of action," Daniel said.

"Yes," said Fred, "and I'll be glad to have a break."

He looked around a minute at the other soldiers around him. "So, should we get to building our hut? Couldn't we all use that extra money?"

"Sure could," said Daniel. "Are either of you carpenters?"

Bruce raised his hand and said, "Right here."

Daniel smiled. "I'm counting that money already. Where do we start?"

Bruce pointed to a group of trees. "Let's cut down that group over there. Then I can work my magic."

They all laughed, picked up their axes, walked over to the group of trees and started cutting. They had no trouble felling the trees unlike some groups. They did have more strength than others. They dragged the trees over to their hut area rather than split the trunks and branches right there where the trees fell. Even though the uncut tree was heavier, it was less cumbersome and more timesaving than cutting the trees into size and carrying them over to their hut area as some of the weaker men were doing.

Bruce measured the trunks according to General Washington's specifications: fourteen by sixteen each, sides, ends and roofs made with logs, and the roof made tight with split slabs, or in some other way; the sides made tight with clay, fire-place made of wood and secured with clay on the inside eighteen inches thick, this fireplace to be in the rear of the hut; the door to be in the end next the street; the doors to be made of split oak-slabs, unless boards can be procured. Side-walls to be six and a half feet high.

Bruce showed the others how to cut the notches into the trunks so they would fit together more easily. Even though James had built his cabin himself, and Fred and Daniel had helped their fathers build their homes and barns and other structures on their property, Bruce had a few tricks that they didn't know.

As they saw their hut come together faster than the other groups around them, Fred said, "Hey. I think we might just win this."

Bruce said, "That's the plan, friend," as he expertly placed another log on top of another.

The men cut and placed and cut and placed until they had all four sides up. They were farther along than the rest of their division. They expertly cut the roof, following Bruce's direction. When they placed the last log on the top, they all yelled out, "Sergeant! Hey! Over here! We're finished! We're first!"

The Sargent already knew that. He watched all the men build their huts, stopping in and providing help where necessary. He walked over quickly to Fred, Bruce, Daniel, James, and the others assigned to their hut.

"Great, men," he said. "We have a winner!"

The group yelled out and shook each other's hands in congratulation.

"So when is the reward paid?" Fred asked.

"Next pay period. End of the week," Sargent said.

"In Continentals?" Daniel asked.

"Yes, Continentals," said Sargent.

"I guess we'll be able to spend them when we get out of camp," Fred said. People were losing faith in the Continental dollar. It wasn't set against gold like the British pound. And, if the Continentals lost this thing, the Continental dollar would be worth less than it was worth already, which meant it would go from meaning very little to meaning nothing.

"Yes, if we do this thing right, you will be able to spend them when we get out of camp," said the captain.

James just added his portion to what he had saved to buy Ruth's freedom.

THE NEW hut mates pulled their packs into their hut. The sun was starting to set.

"Let's use the wood we have left over to build a fire," said Daniel. "We don't have enough light to build our beds, but we sure need something to warm us for tonight."

"You're right about that," said James. He gathered up some wood, took some flint out of his pack, and lit the fire. The wood caught fire easily. It gave the hut a warm yellow glow and the warmth of a few degrees of heat. James pulled his thin pallet out of his pack, laid it on the floor, and rested his head.

Daniel put his pallet down near James'. "Well, we're here. We're in the army now."

"Yup," said James. "We'll see what the next few months hold."

"Yes," said Daniel. "It could be anything." He looked at James. "Are you a little scared?" he said in a low whisper so James and Bruce couldn't hear him.

"Sure," said James. "Are you?"

"Definitely," said Daniel, laughing. "But, this is what we wanted. And I'm glad we're here."

"Me, too," said James. "Me, too."

They fell asleep with the warm glow and heat of the fire comforting them on their first night as members of the Continental Army.

# CHAPTER 53

# PAOLI

"The Valley Forge?" Betsey asked. "Right down the road? The whole army?"

"Yes. Yes. And yes. At least the 10,000 men who are with General Washington. There's another branch of the army up there in New England and New York, but yes, almost the whole army is over there at Valley Forge," Orland said, as he patted Betsey on the head as if to stop her from jumping around excitedly.

"Then that means Fred, too," Teenie said as she clapped her hands together in excitement.

"Sure," said Orland. "General Wayne is still with General Washington, so, yes, that means Fred, too."

"Great," said Betsey. "Then we can go see him."

Orland rolled his eyes and looked at her. "He might be close but that doesn't mean that we'll just be able to ride up there and see him. They're not going to let just anybody walk through the camp. Just like when the boys were over here in Paoli, there'll be pickets around, stopping you from getting close."

"But what if just like in Paoli we were to bring them food and clothes and things?" Betsey asked. "Then they'd let us get closer," she said, expectantly.

"That's a thought there," Teenie said. She turned towards Orland. "We could do that, couldn't we?"

Orland thought for a moment. "Hmm," he said, stroking his chin. "We could do that. Lord knows they need everything from the reports that we get. They marched over here from the Gulph barely clothed on their body or their feet. They've had a rough few months."

Teenie wiped her hands on her apron. "Then we have to help. If our boys are going to be over there for the winter, we can't just sit here and do nothing."

"That's right," said Betsey.

"Honey," Teenie said to Orland, "your network can get over there and see what they need."

"We could," said Orland.

"And then we can get the women around here to cooking, and sewing and knitting," Teenie said.

Betsey thought. If there were eleven thousand men over there, there weren't enough women in Paoli or around here to help them.

"Why just from around here?" Betsey asked. "There's men there from all over the colonies, right?'

"Yes, of course," said Orland.

"Then there's women left behind in all the colonies who would want to help them if they could. I just know there are," Betsey said.

"Sure," said Orland.

"Then we should get them to help. Nothing they cooked would be in decent shape to eat by the time it got here, but they could sew and knit," she said.

"But how are we going to get things in from the colonies when the British control the port in Philadelphia? Anything coming up from the southern colonies would take forever to get here," Orland said.

"Not necessarily," said Betsey. "If we get word to them now, we can have them start sending things up. Or down. And, if we need to get something up here by sea, maybe Connie can help us get things past the British."

Orland hugged Betsey. "You're getting to be one good little spy and a great contribution to our network,"

Betsey smiled and said, "Thank you, Daddy. But it just makes sense. Connie and I already have a system down pat for getting food past the British. I know we could do the same with clothes and things."

"Isn't that a little more dangerous?" Teenie asked, looking at her little girl.

"Not more dangerous," Betsey said. "It just will require a little more thought to pull off, but I know we can do it. I'll talk to Connie about it the next time I head into the city."

Orland smiled and said, "That's my girl."

# CHAPTER 54

# GERMANTOWN

Connie rolled over from her place on top of the general, where she had been what they called "riding the pony" for the past 15 minutes.

"Ride on," the general called out over and over again as Connie worked him to secure the benefits and access that she needed now, not just for her girls, but for her family.

Sometimes, she even enjoyed it. This wasn't one of those times. This time, it was just work for which she expected to be rewarded for a job well done.

"Marvelous," the general said as he lay back, wiping his brow.

"All for you, darling," Connie said, as she squeezed his hand. The thought of touching him in any other way did not appeal to her anymore.

She pulled her red silk robe off the peg on the bedpost and wrapped it around her.

The British occupation of Philadelphia was wearing on her today because her thoughts were with her brother, Fred. Tom had told her that Washington's army finally went into winter quarters up by the Valley Forge. And, he told her that the army barely had clothes, shoes or food. And here she was, looking into the warm fire in her bedroom fireplace, wondering what she would wear to the Thursday night ball tomorrow. A ball where there would be plenty of food and drink and men who would be happy to kill her brother on site. She shivered at the thought, stood up, and walked over to the wash basin to wash off traces of the general from her skin while he slept soundly.

# CHAPTER 55

# LATE DECEMBER
# PAOLI

O rland loaded the wagon with another bushel of potatoes. Betsey
said, "Are we ready yet, Daddy?"

"Almost," said Orland.

"I'm so ready to go," Betsey whined to her mother. "I want to see Fred."

"In time," said Teenie. She wanted to see Fred, too, of course. If he
was alive. And, as much as she wanted to see him, she didn't want to
know if he wasn't alive. Connie came looking for him after the Battle of
Germantown and left not knowing whether he was dead or alive. And
now, they had heard that there was a skirmish over in the hills above the
Gulph. As long as Fred wasn't confirmed dead, Teenie thought of him
as alive. She thought of him as the strong, vibrant young man that she
gave birth to and sent off to war under the care of their neighbor, General
Wayne. But, if they caught up with Wayne's division at the encampment
at the Valley Forge and they found out that Fred was not with them, it just
might be too much. So, while she was anxious to get to the Valley Forge,
she wasn't as anxious as Betsey. Or as naïve.

"Alright, that's it," Orland said. "We can't get anything else in this
wagon."

He hopped up into the carriage, grabbed the reins, and hit the horse
gently on the thigh.

"Off," he said.

Betsey bounced up and down in the seat beside him.

The wagon rolled onto the Lancaster Road. They joined a string of wagons headed to the Valley Forge. Just like when their boys were at Paoli, the residents were going to do whatever they could to help their boys with food and clothes. There was almost a party atmosphere as excited friends and neighbors passed excited friends and neighbors all on the road to the Valley Forge.

As they approached, just like before, they ran into the pickets. Each wagon was stopped and searched. When the pickets were convinced that the wagons contained patriots with food and clothing, they let them through to the next picket. There were more pickets than on the way to the army in Paoli, but that made sense. There were more soldiers in Valley Forge than in Paoli. Ten thousand or 12,000 as opposed to about 1000. The bulk of the Continental Army instead of a small group of regiments.

As they reached the last picket, when the picket finished searching the wagon, the picket asked, "Are you donating or selling?"

Orland frowned. He was offended that the soldier thought that he would be doing anything but donating. "Donating, soldier," Orland said.

The soldier smiled and said, "Thank you, sir. We have someone who can take those things off your hands."

Orland frowned again. This time for a different reason. "Sir, if you please, I understand that we don't have to go farther if we are donating these goods. But, we'd like to. You see, my son is in the 5th Pennsylvania with General Wayne. And, we know he's been in a few battles since we last saw him when the army was here after the Paoli Massacre. We know he was fighting in Germantown because my other daughter saw him there before the battle began. But we don't know anything about his whereabouts since then." Orland whispered to the soldier so Teenie didn't exactly hear. "We don't know whether he's dead or alive, or injured. His mother back there and his sister here, we need to know. So, if we can, we'd like to take these goods in ourselves, to General Wayne's regiment if we can, and see if he's there."

The soldier looked at Orland. "Alright. You're clean, so I can send you on. Go on to the next picket, and they'll tell you where General Wayne's soldiers are hutted."

Orland stuck out his hand. "Many thanks, young man."

The soldier said, "You're welcome. I'm from Boston, but if we were up there, and my people came looking for me, I'd want someone to let them through." The soldier saluted Orland and waved him on through.

They drove further down the Swedesford Road and slowly rode up a hill. As soon as they reached the top of the hill, Betsey said, "Wow!"

The city that the Valley Forge had become now came into view. What used to be forest and hills was now hut city. Thousands of huts dotted the landscape. Thousands of soldiers were walked around.

"My God," said Teenie.

Orland drove on to the next picket. Once they reached it, Orland explained who he was and who he was looking for.

"General Wayne's regiments are up at the top of that hill there to the right. Just head down that road there, and you'll run right into them at the top of the hill," said the picket.

Orland moved the carriage, faster and faster, up the hill.

"There's so many people!" Betsey said, looking from right to left as the coach went up the hill.

Teenie looked, too. Thousands of men moved about, but thousands more were just sitting down and lying around. They looked tired. They looked thin. They looked hungry. Teenie prayed another prayer that Fred was alright.

When the carriage reached the top of the hill, there was a picket, right where the other picket said there would be. He stood next to a sign –

General Wayne. Pennsylvania Line. 1$^{st}$, 2$^{nd}$, 3$^{rd}$, 4$^{th}$ and 5$^{th}$ Pennsylvania. Pennsylvania Militia.

"Here," Orland yelled, excitedly. Betsey and Rochelle's heads snapped looking to where Orland was pointing.

The picket stopped Orland's wagon and came over. Orland said, "Son, I'm here to deliver these goods to General Wayne's boys. And, my son, Fred Roberts, should be here with you in the 5th Pennsylvania, but we haven't heard anything about his whereabouts since someone saw him before the battle of Germantown, so can you help us, son? Do you know him? Is he here?" Orland said quickly, excited to get it all out.

The picket looked at Orland, eyes wide. "Fred Roberts? Yes, sir. Yes, he's here. His hut won the hutting contest a few days ago. Got their hut up faster than anyone else around here."

Orland clapped his hands together. "Praise God," he said. "Can you get him for us? Can we see him? Do you know where he is?"

The picket said, "Yes, sure. I know where he is. I can't leave my post, but I can send someone to get him."

Betsey jumped up in the seat. "Can I go with him?" she yelled excitedly. "Can I?'

The picket looked at Betsey and said, "I suppose that's fine. You don't have that far to go."

Betsey hopped down off the carriage before the picket finished his sentence. "Let's go," she said, jumping up and down again on the ground.

The picket called another solider over, said something to him, the soldier saluted, and he looked at Betsey. "Come with me, Miss."

Betsey clapped her hands together and ran over to the pickets. She turned and waved to her mother and father before she ran off after the soldier.

Fred was outside talking with Daniel, Fred, Bruce, and a few other soldiers from the next hut over when he heard someone call his name.

"Fred! Fred!" Betsey yelled as she ran over towards him.

Fred turned and looked towards what he was hearing. He squinted. He held his hand up to his eyes to shield the sun to better see who was out there disturbing the calm of an otherwise tranquil day.

"Fred! Fred! It's me! Betsey," she called out.

Fred looked and frowned again. "Betsey?" he said out loud, but to himself. "What the…," he said, his voice trailing off. Then she came into focus. He stopped for a moment and yelled out, "Betsey! Betsey!" His heart skipped and his eyes got as wide as they possibly could. Initial surprise over in a few seconds, Fred came to his other senses and started running towards her. By that time, Betsey was no more than a few hundred yards away.

She ran down the paths between the huts, paths that now looked as worn as any country road.

"Betsey!" he yelled as he wrapped his arms around her and lifted her up into the air.

He spun her around.

"Betsey! Betsey! What are you doing here?" he asked.

"Oh my God," she said. "I'm so happy to see you. Connie told us you were fighting in the Battle in Germantown, and then she went looking for you and even came home to see if we had gotten any word, but we didn't so we didn't know what had happened to you. But we prayed you were alive, and God answered our prayer!"

Fred said, "Oh my God! Connie! Yes, I did see her when we were in Germantown, but then we moved on up the Germantown Road and into camp." He rubbed his brow. "And she came home looking for me? We left that town pretty demolished, so I guess she wondered whether I made it out ok," he said, kind of talking to himself.

Then he took hold of Betsey's shoulders to settle her down. "But Betsey, what are you doing here? How did you get through? Where's Mom and Dad?"

"They're out on the main road by the picket. They've got a wagon full of food and clothes. The picket said he knew you and was going to go get you and bring you to them, but I asked him if I could go with him, too, because I just couldn't wait," she said. "They'll be so happy to see you."

Fred said, "OK. Let me ask my sergeant for permission to leave this area, and I'll walk you back."

"You'll probably need some other help, too," Betsey said. "We have a lot of things for you."

Fred put his arm around Betsey while they walked to his sergeant. All along the way he kept introducing Betsey. "This is my sister. She's here making a delivery," he said to soldiers as he walked closer to the area where his regiment was. As he got closer, some of the Paoli boys recognized Betsey.

"Hey, Betsey! What are you doing here?" one called out.

"Making a delivery," she said, smiling and proud that she was there and being recognized for something important.

When they reached the cabin, Bruce called out, "Hey. It's Betsey! Oh my God! Is everything all right? Are your parents alright?"

James and Daniel looked on.

"Yes, they're fine," Betsey said.

"They're right out on the road," Fred said. "With food and clothing."

"Thank God," said Bruce.

"See, I told you that we were close to home," Fred said to Daniel and James. Then he introduced Betsey.

Daniel stuck out his hand and noticed how beautiful she was. Her dark brown hair fell loosely over her shoulders. Her gingham dress was plain red and white, without embellishments, definitely a dress for working.

But her brown eyes danced as she smiled and shook his hand. Something about her looked beautifully familiar, but he couldn't quite recall what. He knew that he would remember someone as beautiful as her if they had met before. Nevertheless, he felt like he knew her.

"Pleased to meet you," she said to Daniel.

"Likewise," said Daniel as he smiled broadly.

She also shook James hand.

Fred went over the Sargent and asked permission for him and his hut mates to leave. The sergeant granted the permission.

"From what Betsey says, we're going to need help to unload everything. And you two can meet my parents," he said, looking at James and Daniel.

"Sounds good to me," said Daniel.

The quartet walked hurriedly down the path between the huts and up the hill where the Roberts waited. Teenie and Orland stood by the carriage, looking down the hill.

"There they are," Teenie yelled, pointing at the quartet as they came into view. With both hands, she hiked up her skirt and started running down the hill. Fred broke loose of Betsey and ran up to his mother. She didn't have to run far before Fred caught up with her.

"Mom," Fred cried out as tears filled his eyes.

"Son!" Teenie said as Fred lifted her off the ground. Fred hugged her so tightly she could barely breathe. After a few seconds, she broke the hug and stepped back so she could take a good look at him. "You're alive!"

"Yes, Mom. I'm alive," he said.

"Praise God. We didn't know," she said.

"I know," he said. "Betsey told me. And she said Connie even came home looking for me."

"Yes, son. That was a great moment. Your father welcomed her back with open arms. We're one family now. In fact, she's helping us and your father's network get food and supplies through the British blockades."

"What?" Fred asked. "How?"

"Don't ask, son," Teenie said. "Connie has her ways. Always has. But this time she's using those ways to help the cause."

"Good," said Fred. "I'm glad she's back in the family," he said as he ruffled Betsey's hair.

Just then, Orland called out, "Fred! Son! Come on up here!"

"Excuse me Mom," Fred said as he squeezed her arm and ran up the hill to where Orland stood beside the carriage, guarding it actually, making sure that as much food and goods as possible reached Fred and the other Paoli boys.

Fred ran straight into his father's arms. Orland hugged him just about as hard as Fred hugged his mother.

"I'm so glad to see you, son," said Orland. "So glad to know that you're alive."

"Here I am, Dad," said Fred. "And, I'm so glad to see you, too. We heard that the British came back to Paoli after the Massacre, and we didn't hear anything about how our people were doing."

"We did fine, son," Orland said. "They tried to intimidate us, and they definitely took what little food we had left, but we stayed strong. We stayed the course. We stuck together. And we got our network back working. It's working fine now. Betsey's even a part of it now."

"I heard," said Fred. He looked at his father with more tears starting to form in his eyes. "Thank you. We need all the help we can get. The last few battles have been a little rough. After Germantown, I was in a skirmish over in the hills by the Gulph when I was in the front guard. We had to stop the whole army from crossing over the Matson Ford, straight into the redcoats' hands. We never have enough to eat or to wear. I've been doing ok because being from here, I know what to eat and what not to eat and where to find things to eat. But, most men in this army aren't so lucky," he said. "Look around."

Orland said, "I know. I can see that. So many of these boys look like they're on their last legs."

"That's because they are, Dad," Fred said.

Teenie approached them, being led and held steady by Bruce on one side and Betsey on the other. Daniel and James followed.

"Bruce," Orland said. "Glad to see you, too, son." He hugged him. "Your parents are fine. So are your brothers and sisters. I'll let them know that I saw you."

"Thanks, Mr. Roberts," Bruce said. "Tell them to come over, too."

"I'll do that," Orland said. "Yes, indeed. I'll tell the whole neighborhood to get over here if they can get through the pickets. You sure are protected."

"We'd better be," Fred said. "The British Army is really not too far away. They're not supposed to fight us in the winter, but I don't trust them to be men of their word. I guess General Washington doesn't either. And good for him"

He patted his dad on the back. "So what do you have here, Dad?"

Orland started telling him. "As much as we could get you. As much as we could spare. Two bushels of potatoes. Three barrels of apples. Some cured bacon. Some dried beef. About ten loaves of fresh baked bread. Cheese using milk from our best cow that we hid way in the woods when the British came. And some clothes."

"The ladies in the neighborhood got together and have been knitting hats, scarves, sweaters, gloves, and socks." Betsey said.

"General Wayne is going to be mighty happy to see all of this," Fred said.

"The sergeant said for me to get a wagon from that shed there, hitch it to a horse, and drive it back down to where our huts are," Fred said.

"Yes, sir," said Daniel. "We're quartermasters of our division, so we handle the supplies."

"Good," said Orland. "Then I know that these things are going into good hands and for good use."

"Yes, sir," said Daniel.

Fred went and returned with the wagon. James, Daniel, and Bruce started transferring the goods and packages and barrels from one wagon to another. Fred and Orland worked side by side, transferring the goods, while Teenie and Betsey helped, too. When all the goods were moved from one wagon to another, Orland said, "Well, I guess that's it."

Teenie went up to Fred again and hugged him, for a long time this time. They stood silently, arms wrapped tightly around each other. Betsey stood next to Daniel, and they looked on. Soon, Fred opened one arm and motioned for Betsey to come over. Betsey ran over, and Fred put his arm around her, holding her tightly in his bear hug.

Orland walked over and looked Fred straight in the eyes. "Be careful, son," Orland said.

"I will, Dad," said Fred. "The good thing is that we have a few months with no fighting if we're lucky. We all need the time and the rest."

"Good," said Orland. "We'll use the network to round up as much food and goods as we can."

"Good," said Fred. "We'll need it all."

"Alright honey," he said to Teenie, patting her on the back. "We need to get going so we can get home before it gets dark."

Teenie stepped back. She took Fred's face in her hand. She caressed his skin softly and looked deeply into his eyes. "Take care, son. I'll be praying for you every day."

"I know, Mom. You take care of yourself, too," Fred said.

"Don't worry about us," Teenie said.

"I do," said Fred. "And you," he said to Betsey. "You take care of yourself, too. I hear you're in the network now, running back and forth to Philadelphia to see Connie."

"Yes," said Betsey, proudly.

"Be careful Betsey," Fred said. "The British can be brutal."

"I know," said Betsey. "But I am careful. Connie is, too."

"Ok, but know that I'll be praying for you, too," he said.

"Good," Betsey said. "We can always use prayer."

Fred laughed and said. "Yes. Yes, we can."

Then Orland separated them. Tears formed in everyone's eyes. Everyone was worried, more worried than they wanted to admit. They all wondered whether they were leaving each other for the last time. They all wondered whether they would ever again have to wait like they just had to wait to find out whether someone was living or dead. They all worried, but they didn't want to say more, knowing that saying more would just make them worry more and cry more. And they had another three to four months of winter to go before the fighting started up again. At least that's what they hoped.

# CHAPTER 56

# VALLEY FORGE

Daniel, James, Fred, and Bruce sat in front of their hut eating breakfast, warmed by a huge bonfire that radiated much needed heat.  Because the Roberts family had delivered all of that food, along with other families from the area—Paoli, Howellville, Tredyffrin—the soldiers in General Wayne's division actually had pieces of meat—bacon and ham—with their hardtack, unlike the men in the other divisions who just had the hardtack—unappetizing, but filling, sitting on their stomachs like a stone.

"Line up, men" Captain Bartholomew called out.  "General Wayne needs to address us and make assignments."

The four hut mates gobbled down the last of their breakfast, scraped off their plates, and took them inside.  They came back out as a steady stream of men walked towards the open field where General Wayne's division lined up.

"Most of these men look like they can't do much work, if any," Daniel said to James.

"I know," said James.  "They're reed-thin and barely clothed."

"I guess the stronger ones of us will have to make up the difference," Daniel said.

"We always do," said James, remembering how the stronger slaves would do the work for the weaker ones, hiding it from the masters so the weaker ones didn't get whipped.

They walked over to the field and lined up at ease like everyone else around them.

Suddenly, they saw General Wayne on his white horse in the distance, galloping over the hills, the whiteness of the horse's hair blending in beautifully with the glistening white snow that was still on the ground.

The men instinctively stood at attention at the site of their commanding officer.

"Attention!" the Colonel called out.

General Wayne slowed a bit as he rode closer to his men. He stopped at the edge of the gathering.

"Men!" he said. "It is a wonderful site, riding over these hills and seeing my men lined up, ready for service." He tipped his hat towards the group. "And today, we will let you know how you can serve this great Army for the next few months. We need men with all types of skills to support this great encampment city that you have built here. We need carpenters, blacksmiths, cooks, tailors, quartermasters. We need you all. You all have skills."

"So today, your sergeants will divide you up according to your crafts and professions and make assignments. Some of you will work right here with your fellow soldiers in my divisions. Some of you will go help soldiers in other divisions because they are too weak or have a scarcity of the skills that you have. And some of you will go and work with me and the other generals at our headquarters," he said. "While we are here in winter quarters, you will work and you will train. You will drill. You will get stronger. We will march out of Valley Forge stronger, meaner, better, more finely tuned, more able to beat those Redcoats and send them back across the Atlantic."

The men cheered.

"So men, I know that whatever assignment you get, whether here or elsewhere in this great Valley Forge, you will make me proud, whether you are a Continental regular or a Pennsylvania Militia," Wayne said. Then he lifted his musket in the air. "Huzzah!" he said.

"Huzzah!" the men shouted back.

Wayne took his horse's reins in one hand, turned, and galloped away.

"Alright men," said Sargent Crocker. "Let me run through your assignments."

He looked down at a few sheets of paper. "Smith! Cook for the 3rd Pennsylvania. Johnson! Carpenter for General Wayne's Division."

James, Daniel, Fred and Bruce looked straight ahead.

"Roberts! You're one of our best shooters. Your assignment is marksmanship instructor. You'll be working closely with me as we do drills."

"Yes, sir," said Fred, happy with his assignment. By teaching others how to shoot, his already excellent skills would only improve.

"Weldon and Welburn! Blacksmiths assigned to the iron forge by General Washington's headquarters."

Daniel and James looked at each other, smiling. They received a special assignment, just as they were promised.

Sargent Crocker continued to call out names until he said, "That's it men. You will report to the place of your assignments when we break ranks. You will work at the location where you are assigned until the sun sets, then you will return to your huts for the evening. Is that clear?"

"Yes, sir," they all called out in unison.

"So, go and make us proud," he said. "And at ease."

The men relaxed their shoulders and their stances. Daniel and James looked at each other.

"Just like General Mifflin promised," Daniel said.

"Yes," said James. "General Washington's headquarters."

"Then I wasn't dreaming," Daniel said. "That's quite an assignment. That's quite an honor."

"Yes, it seems to be," said James. "But where is it?"

"I don't know," said Daniel. "Nowhere around here, from what I can see," he said, pointing to the regular soldiers huts that covered the landscape as far as the eyes could see.

Just then, Sargent Crocker walked over. "Boys, you have the honor of working at the forge near General Washington's headquarters by special request of General Mifflin to General Wayne. Seeing you work these past few days, we realize that you were the best blacksmiths in this Division, and you already know how to work well together."

"Thank you sir," said Daniel saluting.

"Yes, thank you," said James.

"Make us proud," Sargent said, patting Daniel on the back.

"We will, sir," said Daniel.

Then Crocker stuck his hand out towards James. "And you, too, son," he said.

"Yes, sir," said James.

"Do you know where the General's headquarters are?" Crocker asked.

"No sir," said James.

"Alright," Crocker said. "Go down past the hills over there, to the west, and keep walking down until you get to the river. There will be pickets all the way down that road. Tell them you're going to your assignment at the iron forge at General Washington's headquarters, and then they'll let you through. They'll ask you for a password the closer you get. Use the word, Waynesborough. Once they recognize you as soldiers who work down there, you won't have to use the password again. Understood?"

"Yes, sir," said James.

"Good," said the Sargent. "Head on down there."

"Yes, sir," said James and Daniel, in unison.

JAMES AND Daniel turned to the west and headed down the hill. The new city that was the Valley Forge was rife with activity. Men were walking or standing all over the hills and fields, with a purpose this time. Walking towards or working in groups at their assignments. Standing in groups receiving instructions from their leaders. Some men were making bricks. Others were cooking. More were out cutting down trees to feed the never ending fires that kept them all from freezing. They walked past blacksmiths who were assigned to regiments and greeted them as fellow brothers. But, as often as they passed other blacksmiths, they smiled to each other, knowing that they were among the best in the encampment, with only the best being assigned to General Washington's area.

They reached the first picket. Three men stood before them.

"Password," said one.

"Waynesborough," Daniel and James said in unison.

The men nodded and stepped aside. Daniel and James kept walking. Three more times they gave the password and passed through. After the fourth time, they headed down a hill.

"This must be it," James said.

Ahead of them was a river, the Valley Creek, an undulating body of water that fed commerce wherever it went with forges, mills, docks, and centers of commerce on either side of its banks. The smoke from the forge floated up towards the top of the hill. A few hundred feet from the forge stood four stone houses.

"One of those must be his headquarters," Daniel said.

"Looks that way," said James, as they walked further.

The area in front of them was as busy as any they had just walked past. Blacksmiths stood outside by the roaring fires, hammering iron into all types of shapes. Guards stood stiff in place outside all of the houses. What looked like officers on horses came and went from the general area. But, as they walked closer, James noticed something else. Slaves. Coming and going from a small house, undoubtedly the kitchen, to a larger, well-guarded house, undoubtedly General Washington's headquarters. He watched a few women carrying large pots to the headquarters, bent over, struggling, the pots obviously too heavy for the two women to carry.

Some things don't change, James thought, as he wished that he could run down, grab the pots from the women, and carry them himself. But he knew better. No African would run when there were white men around with guns. Not even here.

He watched the women struggle back and forth as he walked closer. And as he approached, one of the women stood out. She looked to be one of the youngest, and she was helping one of the older women carry the pots. She bent over as she helped one of the older women carry a large pot, but she straightened up faster and easier. Her head was wrapped in a muslin cloth, the same type of muslin that her apron was made out of. Her fingers were long and thin. Her skin was slightly darker than the muslin she wore, a sign that her mother, father, grandmother, grandfather—one of them—was not an African, but was a white person. Most likely the father or grandfather, James thought. And he thought that she must be a house slave, gone outside to help the kitchen slaves bring the noon meal inside. The masters always liked to have the lighter skinned slaves working inside the house, maybe as another visual reminder of their total power and domination over another human being. Light-skinned slaves didn't come over from Africa, and everyone knew there was only one thing that caused light-skinned slaves to look the way that they did.

James literally shook his head to clear his mind and remind himself that he volunteered for this army only for the wages that serving as a soldier would bring him since the other work was drying up with the war coming to their back yard. He allowed a small part of himself to hope that maybe if these generals saw slaves—current and freed—fighting side by side for their freedom, maybe they'd free all slaves once this war was over. But only a small part. In the meantime, he kept his mind on doing the best job that he could as a blacksmith and a soldier, hoping that one day he'd have enough money to free his precious Ruth from this madness and let her taste freedom for the rest of her life.

They reached the last picket right where a path turned off towards the General's Headquarters on one side and the forge by the creek on the other.

"Password," said the guard.

"Waynesborough," said Daniel.

The picket looked at James. He looked him up and down.

"You a soldier?" the guard asked, in that strange accent that people from the southern colonies have, and asking even though James wore the same blue and white Continental Army uniform that he did.

"Yes, sir," said James well aware that this type of person wanted a black person to call him sir, even though he was a regular soldier like him, as far as he could tell from his uniform.

The picket looked James up and down again. He turned to Daniel. "Where are you boys going?" he asked.

"We're assigned as blacksmiths in the forge," Daniel said.

James just stared straight ahead, looking at the picket with a poker face, very nicely concealing the anger and rage that he felt at being disrespected—again.

"Alright," said the picket. "You see the forge down there. Ask for Sargent Banger when you get there."

"Will do," said Daniel.

James said nothing and walked in the direction of the forge with Daniel.

Daniel felt James' anger. Any decent man knows when he comes across one who is not decent.

"What a horse's ass," Daniel said.

James smiled and nodded. "You said it."

They walked silently for a few minutes until they reached the forge by the river.

The water still ran clearly and easily in the river. Winter hadn't been so cold for so long that the river had frozen over. Even so, the extreme heat that the forge generated always kept the air around it many degrees warmer than the surrounding area. All the sites around them were familiar ones—large and hot fires inside and out, the sound of iron hitting iron as men shaped tools and materials of all types, other men carrying in wagons full of wood and others constantly feeding wood into the large fires. A good 20 men were working very hard already.

As they walked closer, they saw a man with sergeant's stripes directing a group of other men.

"That looks like him," said James. He and Daniel walked over in that direction.

As they approached, Daniel called out, "Sargent Banger?"

Sargent Banger turned to fully face them and said, "Yes, at your service."

James and Daniel saluted.

"We're blacksmiths assigned here from General Wayne's division," Daniel said. "I'm Daniel Welburn and this is James Weldon."

"Well, welcome men," said Sgt. Banger.

Daniel said, "We're sorry that we're just getting here, looking at all the other men working already, but it was quite a hike from General Wayne's encampment at the top of that hill over there," he said pointing west.

"You're fine," said the Sargent. "All of the other men from other divisions aren't here either." He patted both of them on the back and said, "But you're here, so let's get you started. You're here because you're the best from your division. You're here down by General Washington's headquarters because, although we don't have much, we want him and his officers down here to have the best of everything. And, once they have everything they need down here at headquarters, we'll be making tools, materials and ammunition for the rest of army. And we want our boys to have the best when we get back on the front lines in the spring."

"Very much understood, sir," Daniel said.

James nodded in assent. Even though Sgt. Banger seemed like a good man, James knew it was best not to say too much to any white man for fear of the repercussions.

They walked over to an area where what looked like a larger version of the blacksmith's shop they had back on Rebel Hill was set up. "You'll be making tools, musket pieces, and any other more complex materials that we need. We have men with lesser skills working closer to their divisions making musket balls and horse shoes."

Both men nodded.

Sgt. Banger waved his arms over his head in a "come this way" gesture. "Let's get you set up," he said.

FRED WALKED with Sgt. Medley up and down a series of hills. On their way to meet with other soldiers and officers who were part of the marksmanship team, they stopped at a stone two-story house with soldiers on guard all the way around it. Fred's favorite and most trusty musket was slung over his shoulder.

Getting closer to the house, the soldiers recognized Sgt. Medley and saluted. They parted to let him and Fred enter. They walked into a small foyer that led directly into a much larger room. It would have been the dining room if this was a normal family home, but it wasn't. There was no dining table in the room. It was only filled with soldiers standing and sitting all around the perimeter and various types of muskets stacked in the middle of the room. There was a smaller table in one corner, one that only had room for four seats. Fred recognized by their stripes three colonels and a general—a general that he didn't know. In his months of fighting in the Continental Army, he only knew two generals besides Washington, of course—General Wayne and General Potter, who led the group from the camp in Whitemarsh across the Matson Ford when they met that band of redcoats.

Fred stood with his sergeant as other men and their sergeants came in, just about filling up the room. Then, the General stood up and walked into the middle of the room. The men who were seated stood up, and the men who were standing saluted.

"Men," said the General," I am Major General Baron de Kalb, Commander of the Massachusetts brigades that started this great war for freedom." He paused for minute to let that sink in as he looked around the room.

"You men are here because you are the best. The best shooters, the best marksmen in our regiments, and I applaud you for that," he said. "And while we are here in winter quarters, I want you to turn every man in this Continental Army and every Militia man who is joining us for the winter into as fine a marksman as you."

Fred nodded along with the other men.

"We've lost too many battles," the General said. "And we've lost too many men. We need more skill, and we need more discipline. We are going to drill, to shoot, to practice, to hit the target, until we are sure that every man in this Continental Army can shoot a redcoat dead between the eyes at 500 feet."

Fred nodded and smiled.

"Now," said the General. "I will train you and your sergeants on how to train others. You will learn new techniques, and you will teach them to others. I will lead this effort and we will have help from our Allies. In the next few months, I will be joined by General Friedrich Von Steuben, sent here personally by Benjamin Franklin at the recommendation of our French supporters and General Washington, of course. He is a master in teaching the techniques of the fine and expert Prussian army, the French army and other fine armies across Europe. And he will teach us."

The General paused. "You are also going to have to become familiar with the various types of weapons that our Continental soldiers use. I want you expert shooters to be able to shoot everything. I know you have your favorite muskets, but you have to be flexible. You have to be able to shoot anything. What happens if you are in the midst of battle and something happens to your favorite gun and your fellow soldier, perhaps from another state, hands you a gun from one of your fallen patriots? What happens if you kill a few redcoats and the only weapons available to you to kill any more are the Brown Bess muskets from the redcoats that you just killed?" He looked around the room.

"You have to be ready for anything," he said. He swept his eyes around the room again. "We all do. So, we're going to go over what each of these weapons is, how to use them, how to shoot them expertly. And, if any of you have another type of weapon that's not like those assembled here, come show us now. Come and stand here by me and tell us what you have."

The men on the sidelines came in a little closer to look over the cache of weapons spread out of the floor. One by one, a few men stepped forward and stood by the general.

When there were about four or five men, the General turned to the first one. "Son," he said. "Explain to us what you're holding."

The soldier held his musket out in front of him and began, "This here is a French rifle. General Lafayette was able to get some of them for us in the Third Division, and now everyone in this group will get one, too. It's lighter, and you can shoot it faster than the muskets you're used to."

Fred moved a little closer to so he could see every detail of what was pointed out on the gun that he wanted to know just as well as he knew his own.

# CHAPTER 57

# JANUARY 1778
# GERMANTOWN

"**D**on't you think it would work?" Betsey asked Connie as they drove down the Germantown Road towards the market in Philadelphia. Once a month, Betsey and her mother drove their empty wagon from Paoli to the Gulph, across the Matson Ford, into Whitemarsh, and down the Germantown Road to Connie's. They never went inside— Connie wouldn't let them. They always went on the seventh day of the month. Lucky seven, said Teenie. Connie always had Tom on duty out front. As soon as he saw their carriage, he was instructed to have them pull over to the side of the road. Then he went inside, told Connie and waited for her to get ready. Then he and Connie drove her carriage onto the street. Teenie, Betsey and Connie always spent a few minutes hugging each other before Connie jumped into the front of the carriage with Tom, and Tom helped Teenie and Betsey get in the back. Connie got them and their carriage through the redcoat guards every time. She was recognized as General Howe's special friend.

Connie turned to face Betsey. "It's not that I don't think it can work," she said. "It's just that it complicates things, that's all."

"Not too much," Betsey said. "All we have to do is pick up the boxes when they come in."

Connie rolled her eyes at her little sister. "*If* they come in," she said. "If they don't get opened up and stolen."

"Even with your name on them?" Betsey asked.

Connie rolled her eyes again. "Boy, you are naïve," Connie said. "Yes, even with my name on them. My name doesn't carry any weight in some quarters. It carries weight here in Philadelphia, but there's a lot of places a box would have to go through before it gets to Philadelphia, especially if it's coming up from the southern states."

This time, Betsey rolled her eyes. And she frowned. This has to work, she thought. We have to be able to get in some scarves and winter things for Fred and the other boys.

She squinted as she thought.

"Wait, I know," said Betsey. She tapped Connie on the shoulder to get her to turn around again.

"What now?" Connie asked.

"Suppose the boxes didn't have your name on them. Suppose they had the General's name on them?" Betsey asked.

Connie frowned. "Are you kidding me? The General's name? You want to have a bunch of patriots send up boxes and barrels with General Howe's name on them, and then somehow those boxes and barrels are supposed to get to me?"

Betsey smiled, nodded her head, and said, "Yes. Exactly."

"OK, Miss Smarty pants" said Connie. "Explain that to me."

"Certainly," said Betsey. We have the boxes marked for General Howe, but we put a special mark on them, so we know that those are our boxes. Then, when the boxes get in, we have one of our people down there unloading them and putting them aside so we can pick them up when we come down here to get our food."

Connie hit herself in the forehead with the palm of her head. "You've got to be kidding," she said. "The longer this war goes, the harder it is to get anything in that someone doesn't want to scoop up right away. People are hungry. Not enough food is coming in, for the people who live here and for all of those British soldiers. And you think that we can get barrels in that somebody will set aside for me just because there's a mark on them?" She laughed.

Teenie took Betsey's hand. "Wait a minute Connie. Betsey's got something there."

Connie's head snapped around and she stared straight at her mother like her mother had lost her mind, eyes wide.

"This could work Connie," Teenie said, as she stroked Betsey's head. "Here's how," said Teenie.

# CHAPTER 58

# THE VALLEY FORGE

James took his place beside the blacksmith area closest to Washington's quarters. But close wasn't that close. The blacksmith areas were kept away from occupied dwellings and close to the river. An errant spark, a fire that burned out of control, could be deadly. Close to the quarters was close enough to make or fix whatever the General and his generals wanted, but far enough away to keep them safe.

He and Daniel were now used to the routine. Whatever they were given or could scrounge for breakfast, eaten hurriedly by the fire in or near their cabin, an inspiring pep talk from their sergeant and sometimes General Wayne, exhorting them to ignore or endure the cold, the lack of food, and be strong for the cause, before they were dismissed and sent on to their assignments. This morning they were told that they were going to work at their assignments in the morning and start drill training in the afternoons, that was once this general from Germany arrived.

"Good," said Daniel to James as they sat there listening to the sergeant. "Knowing how to shoot critters on the hill is one thing, but knowing how to defend yourself against these redcoats is another."

"Yes," said James. "To hear Fred and the other boys talk, the redcoats are well-trained and know what they're doing."

"Yeah, well, that German better get here soon," Daniel said.

"Right," said James.

But down by the blacksmith area, James had another assignment. Sure, he did the good job that he always did when working. Today, his mind was really on something else. Today, he wanted to meet that beautiful woman who he saw carrying things back and forth between the kitchen and General Washington's headquarters. He saw her just about every day, from a distance, and not close enough and certainly not in any situation where he could say hello. The closest he came was a few days ago when he and Daniel were walking down to their area. Their usual path was blocked with a group of soldiers, so they had to walk around, closer to the back of the cook house. Just as they walked by, she walked out, carrying a large pot. She opened the door, looked at Daniel and James, and quickly diverted her eyes, the way any good slave does when she comes upon a white man she doesn't know, and often even one that she does.

James slowed down and said, "Good morning, Ma'am," as he nodded and tipped his hat. She looked up at the sound of James' voice, just as he touched and tipped his hat.

She smiled at him and said, "It's Miss."

James smiled back and tipped his hat again. "Beg your pardon," he said. "Good morning, Miss." His eyes caught hers for a second. Then he said, "Good day, then."

She nodded and said, "Same to you," as she walked towards the General's headquarters and back inside.


ALL DAY long James thought about this woman. And when he thought about her, he also thought about Ruth. He missed her every day. He missed having Christmas with her. He missed bringing in the New Year with her. He missed walking her to church. He missed holding her hand. He missed sneaking a kiss when he could. He wondered if it was because he missed Ruth so much that he was drawn to this other slave woman. As much as he loved Ruth, he was a man, and most men's heads were turned at the sight of a beautiful woman.

As he worked making tools, he tried to focus on the reason why he was even in this man's army—to make the money to buy Ruth's freedom. But he caught himself looking up more often to try to see this other woman.

One day, he was successful around lunch time. The slaves were shuttling back and forth from the headquarters to the cookhouse with more pots and pans. James sat on a small wooden stool that he had built for himself and ate his lunch rations of hardtack bread baked by the bakers near the blacksmith station. He looked up just as she walked out.

She looked up.

He waved.

She waved back.

He jumped up, held up one finger, and said, "Wait."

She stopped.

James shoved his hardtack in his pocket and brushed crumbs away from his mouth with his hand as he walked towards her. He figured that none of the guards would stop him because he walked by that area every day. He was right. He didn't want to run—he knew they might not stop a black man walking, but they would stop a black man running. He stretched his legs as wide as he could, taking hurried strides.

Watching this man walk towards her, Ernestine wondered what he was going to say to her. She didn't wonder what he wanted; she knew that look in his eyes, even from a distance. She figured that he wanted what most men wanted, black or white, free or slave. The white men could take what they wanted, from her or any other slave. She'd had experience with that, the same as any slave girl. It didn't matter what she looked like—they all had something taken from them; the pretty ones had it taken more often than the plain ones, but they all suffered none the less.

"Good afternoon, Miss," he said.

"Good afternoon," she said, still looking down.

"I thought I'd come and formally introduce myself since I have a few minutes break and since I've walked by you so many times," James said.

Ernestine lifted her eyes up at him.

"Yes, sir," she said.

"You don't have to call me sir," James said. "I'm not your master or one of these white men around here."

She looked up with eyes wide and moving from side to side, not catching his gaze, in fear and reticence.

"Yes, sir," she said, looking up and down. Then she looked up again, staring him straight in the eye, "I mean, yes, if you say so."

James knew the countenance, mannerisms and effect of a slave who lived in fear, and she had that.

He said gently, "You don't have to be afraid of me. I'm not going to hurt you. I just want to introduce myself."

She looked at him, fear still in her eyes. She didn't believe much of what men had to say. They usually said anything to her before they got what they wanted from her, always against her wishes.

"Alright," she said softly.

"I'm James Weldon, a free man, part of the 5th Pennsylvania Regiment," he said. "I'm one of the best blacksmiths in the Pennsylvania Line. That's why they sent me over here to work. My hut is up there on the hill, west of here."

She looked at him again, eyes darting around.

"Well, pleasure to meet you," she said.

"And what's your name?"

She looked up shyly. "My name is Ernestine. I come up here from Virginia with my master, General Washington, and the Mrs.," she said. "I work with the General's cook, Mrs. Hannah Till."

"Well, I'm very glad to meet you, Ernestine," James said.

Ernestine looked at him and flashed a slight smile. "Likewise." She looked around.

"But I best be going now. "

"Right," said James. "I don't want to hold you up and get you in any trouble."

Ernestine shook a bit. "No, don't want to do that."

James looked her straight in the eye, catching it quickly. "I hope we can talk again," he said, smiling slightly.

"Yes, sir," Ernestine said. Then she caught herself, smiled and said, "I mean, yes, perhaps." She looked around, said "Good day then," and walked towards the kitchen entrance.

James said, "Yes, good day," as he watched her push open the door and head into the kitchen. He stood there for a second before turning and walking back towards his post.

"Slavery," he said to himself, bitterly under his breath, frowning and thinking about how so many of his people were ruined just because of the color of their skin.

# CHAPTER 59
# PAOLI

The couriers had returned with good news.

"The messages were delivered to all of their targets," the main courier said to Betsey, Teenie and Orland. "Members of our network in every southern state."

"Great," Betsey said.

"Another group should be down south now, collecting whatever they come up with," the courier said.

"So there should be a shipment soon with scarves, gloves, and sweaters?" Betsey asked, counting each type of good on her finger.

"And food," said Teenie.

"Yes," said the courier, "they should be sending up as much food as we can carry. We think the food should be up here in about two to three weeks."

"Good," said Teenie, "because we're running out of our supplies. We've already taken so much up there, and so has everyone around here. We're all getting hungry."

# CHAPTER 60

# FEBRUARY
# VALLEY FORGE

"Line up men," said Sargent Lawrence as the sun began to shine over Mount Misery.

Daniel, James, and Fred stood next to each other as other soldiers lined up next to them.

"You know that we're suspending your normal work today to start drills with General Von Stueben," the sergeant said. "Baron Von Steuben will start the drills today with General Wayne for all of General Wayne's divisions. We will also be joined by General Nathanael Green who will translate for General Von Stueben, who doesn't speak English."

The men smiled.

"Although," said the Sargent, "We understand that he can drill the hell out of some troops."

The men laughed this time.

"So, we will march over to the open field by Mount Misery, which will be our training field every other day," he said. "Does everyone understand?"

"Yes, sir," the troops shouted in very close to unison.

"Good," he said. "Then forward march."

The men marched towards the open field, past other soldiers who were already engaged in their jobs or on the way. They reached the open field in about 15 minutes.

"Well, this ought to be different," Daniel said to James, after Sargent yelled "At ease."

They stood around for a few minutes before General Wayne's trademark white horse came into view. Riding in next to him were two other men in the distinctive general's uniforms.

The men knew General Green because he was a frequent presence around the camp. But the other general was something different. His brass helmet glinted as the sun shone off of it as he rode in, sitting up rod straight on the horse. His uniform was unlike anything that these men had seen before.

"Fall in," the sergeants yelled in unison as the generals rode closer. Most men were already falling in—the expected action when their general came close.

"Men," said General Wayne, as the men stood at attention. "This is a historic day for the Pennsylvania Line." He smiled from ear to ear. "Today we are going to begin the training that will turn us into an even greater fighting army. The English will have nowhere to run once we are trained by our esteemed guest today." As General Wayne talked, General Nathanael Green repeated what he said to Baron Von Stueben.

"We have with us today, the world renowned general, Baron Von Stueben. He turned the Prussians into one of the finest armies in the world. He is going to do the same thing for us. We do not lack heart. We do not lack passion. We do not lack the will to fight. But we lack discipline. We lack focus. And we lack some of the latest techniques."

"But, have no fail. Baron von Stueben will teach us what we lack," said General Wayne. "Today is the day. Tomorrow is in our hands."

The men yelled approval. Wayne turned to Stueben. "Would you like to address the men now?" Nathanael Green translated.

Von Stueben nodded. He began talking, animatedly and pointedly. He paused. General Green then spoke.

"Men, it is my honor to meet you today and train you for your ultimate victory over the British oppressors," Green said.

The men cheered.

Von Stueben went on. "I tell you that when you follow my training techniques, victory will be yours," he said as he took his sword out of its holder and held it up in the air.

The men cheered.

"I am not one for hyperbole or one to brag. Word of your fighting spirit has traveled all over the world. Know that thousands of people in Prussia, in France, and all over the Continent of Europe stand with you."

More cheers.

"Just follow my techniques. Learn them well. And when you leave this Valley Forge at the end of the winter, you will be prepared to defeat the British scourge."

The men cheered. General Wayne and General Green cheered.

"Now men," yelled General Wayne. "Let's begin. Come closer and fall in in a circle around us," he said, "and let's get started."

The generals jumped off their horses and stood straight. The men surrounded them in a circle.

# CHAPTER 61

# MARCH
# GERMANTOWN

"I have a pick up at the docks today, too," Connie said to the redcoat who was driving her, Tom and Betsey to the market that day, as she climbed into the waiting carriage.

"Which dock, Ma'am?" the redcoat asked.

"2B," said Connie.

"Very good, Ma'am," he said.

Betsey whispered to Connie, "See I told you it would work."

Connie snapped her head around and looked at Betsey as she shot her an evil look and kicked her leg. "Shush," said Connie, in a low voice so as not to arouse the redcoat's suspicions. "It hasn't worked yet."

They rode the rest of the way to the market in silence. The docks were in the back and to the side of the market, and they were controlled by the British, who wanted to be in charge of anything that came into Philadelphia. Connie was banking on her relationship with General Howe to save her here. If things worked the way they were supposed to, her redcoat driver should take them to dock 2B and go with Tom to find the barrels that were shipped in from the southern colonies. There was supposed to be food on the top, since the redcoats were used to her going down and getting food with the General's permission, with warm knitted and sewn clothes and other provisions in the middle, and more food on the bottom, in case that was the side that the redcoats opened up for inspection. If they decided to search the whole barrel and find what else was inside, that would raise questions as to why she was going to the docks. And, even though her sexual prowess had gotten so much out of General Howe, including taming him so that her wishes could be fulfilled, even she was not so confident to think that he would not punish her if he found out that she was a spy, taking advantage of his sexually-infused good graces.

"Do you want to go to the docks or the market first?" the redcoat rightfully asked.

"The docks please," Connie answered.

The redcoat turned the carriage to the left and maneuvered it down the narrow street to the docks. The sails from a few tall ships instantly came into view as they flapped in the wind. Redcoats carried packages off the ships that were docked, and others stood guard by their stashes. Several other ships floated in the distance on the Schuylkill River, waiting their turn to dock.

The redcoat deftly steered their carriage between the piles of goods and walking people, rushing here and there, until they came to a sign that said 2B.

"There it is," Betsey said, lest the eyes of the older people in the carriage weren't as sharp or quick as hers.

"Make way," yelled the redcoat to a few groups of soldiers that blocked his path.

One came over with an angry look on his face, mouth in a frown. "Do you have your papers?" he asked roughly.

"I'm General Howe's man," the redcoat said, as he put his hand into his pocket and pulled out a paper with his name and station.

The redcoat looked at it. Then he looked up at Tom sitting next to him and the women in the back seat. "And who are these people?"

The driver gave the other redcoat a stern look. Then he raised his eyebrow and said, "Friends of General Howe."

The redcoat looked up at Connie with the look that she'd seen a thousand times—hungrily, eyes moving up and down her body—a look that she often despised yet encouraged because that was a look that led to her getting the money that she needed to make the life that she had.

"I see," said the redcoat, smiling at Connie now.

She met his gaze with a heavy and squinted eyelid and a small, upturned curl in her lip, one that would have become a frown, one that definitely showed disdain.

Now the driver got mad. He didn't want Connie to tell General Howe that he had allowed her to be assaulted. "So let us through," said the driver, impatiently. And for good measure he added, "Now and anytime that we should come here by order of or with permission of the General."

"Yes, sir," said the redcoat. He bowed and said sarcastically, "Go on through."

Connie shot him a dirty look with eyelids narrowed. She didn't want any trouble from this man now or ever.

They drove closer to the 2B sign. Tom and the driver jumped down. "Wait here," Tom said. Tom knew who they were looking for. A man in traditional stevedore dress with a cap with a green handkerchief in his right front pocket—the sign of the spy network that the Roberts belonged to. The man's name was William. His cover was that he worked for the British the same as any other loyalist who was lucky enough to get hired by them to help out when needed.

They walked over to where the man stood. The redcoat said, "We are here to pick up a delivery under orders of General Howe. Might you know what order I am talking about?"

Tom looked the man straight in the eyes. He saw the green handkerchief. But, it would never be Tom who would say the man's name. That would blow the cover.

The man looked Tom straight in the eyes and almost, imperceptibly, nodded to him. Then he looked the driver straight in the eye and said,

"Yes, sir. I have an order for General Howe." Then he stuck out his hand to shake the redcoat's hand. "My name is William. At your service."

Then he looked at Tom and stuck out his hand, "William Roberts," he said. Anyone in the Roberts spy network used their first name and the last name of their ring leader which, in this case, was Orland Roberts.

"Pleased to meet you," said Tom. "If you just show us where the order is, we'll get it right up here in the wagon."

William nodded. "Right this way," he said, as he turned and walked a few steps to a collection of three barrels. "Do you have room for all these?" he asked, looking at the redcoat.

"Certainly," said the driver. "General Howe is always prepared."

William looked at Tom and then back at the driver, and said, "Yes, absolutely. I should have known better."

"Yes, you should have," said the driver, with a haughtiness that only a redcoat could carry off. Then he softened as he said, "But no harm done. Now let's get these things on the carriage."

The barrels were about half as tall as the men were. They rolled them down toward the carriage, then bent down with one man on either side, and lifted them up into the carriage.  ·

# CHAPTER 62
# PAOLI

O rland grabbed one end of the first barrel and Betsey grabbed the other.

Teenie turned around and rushed over. "I can get that, honey," she said to Orland. "You get back in the house."

"I'm not helpless," Orland said.

"No," said Teenie, "but you are sick. Too sick to be out here doing any work."

Orland frowned. "Like I said, I'm not that sick." He coughed

"Yes you are," said Teenie. She knew that he was sicker than he cared to admit, to her or to himself. Yes, the doctor talked to him after his last visit, but he talked to her, too, after Orland fell back to sleep, with a body temperature that kept rising every hour and sweat pouring out of his body, causing her to change his sheets almost as frequently. If he wasn't sweating, he was coughing. Teenie didn't like making those trips into the city with just her and Betsey. At first, she thought it was just too unsafe. She would rather have had a man with her. Now, Orland couldn't go with them because he wasn't well. Every time she and Betsey had to make that long, tedious trip in the cold, over rough, rutted and frozen roads, she wished that Orland was with them, but she understood why he wasn't. Yet, as much as she tried to stop him from unloading the barrels, she knew that his pride wouldn't let the women in his life do everything on their own.

Teenie hit his arm. "Don't carry them in," she said, stopping him in his tracks. He took a long breath as he stood there and then coughed almost as long. "They're too heavy. Just roll them in," she said.

Orland carefully let his side of the barrel down, and Betsey followed suit.

"I'll get it, Dad," she said. She bent down and pushed the barrel towards the door.

Orland coughed again.

"Come on, honey," Teenie said, taking his arm gently this time.

He looked at her softly with sad eyes.

"Alright, dear," he said.

Teenie held his arm as they walked towards the house, stopping every few steps while he let out a racking cough. She led Orland over to the chair farthest from the door, away from the cold breeze that blew in whether the door was open or closed. He bent his legs and lowered himself into the seat slowly, holding on to the arms of the chair. Teenie made sure that he was seated comfortably and then walked over to the water jug near the fire. She poured a healthy amount of water into an iron pot and set in on the already open flame. Steaming hot sassafras tea was good for Orland, the doctor said.

"Let me get this water going, and then I'll help you get those other barrels down," said Teenie.

As much as she wanted to spare her mother and say, "No, I'll do it myself," Betsey realized that the barrels were way too heavy for her to take off the wagon. So, instead, she said, "OK, Mom."

Betsey walked over to Orland and picked up the foot stool next to his chair.

"Can I help you get your feet up, Dad?" she asked.

"Thank you, Betsey. That would be nice," he said.

Betsey set the footstool down in front of him and then gently picked up one leg and then the other. Orland winced a bit as she stretched his leg to place it on the footstool. She straightened out both legs and then grabbed another blanket. She laid it on his legs while she carefully wrapped it around his calves. When she had the blanket secure, she looked up into his eyes.

"Is that good, Dad?" she asked.

"Perfect," he said, as he patted her on the head.

Betsey stopped the tears from coming to her eyes. Her Dad was sick. And weak. And she was scared.

Just then, Teenie called out, "OK, the water is starting to heat up." She grabbed her coat. Let's go get those other barrels."

While the water heated up to a nice boil, Teenie and Betsey picked up the barrels from the wagon and carefully set them on the ground. Although they were going to open up the barrels when they took them inside, they didn't want to break them open by setting them down too hard on the rough, frozen ground. Everything was in short supply now because of the war, few goods getting into Philadelphia or anywhere else for that matter, and they couldn't afford to waste anything.

Once they brought the barrels inside, Teenie went to make Orland's tea. Betsey went out back to get her father's tools to open the barrel.

"I can help you with that," Orland said, when he saw Betsey coming in with a few tools.

"Roll the barrel over here."

Betsey knew that she was strong enough to open the barrels herself, but she did as her father asked. She rolled the first barrel over next to him. Then she bent down, tilted it, and steadied it so that it stood straight. Orland leaned forward in the chair, and she handed him one of the tools. He shimmied the thin blade of the crowbar between the barrel lid and the barrel. Then, with all the strength that he could muster, he leaned the weight of his arms on the other side of the crowbar. The nails holding the lid down came loose.

"Turn it around a little, and I'll get the other side," he said to Betsey.

She smiled at him and said "Yes Dad." She turned the barrel. He found the right spot and applied his strength until the lid raised up.

Teenie walked over with a steaming mug of hot sassafras tea, carefully strained, taking out as many of the sassafras leaves as possible. Orland leaned back, coughed, and then steadied himself as he took the mug from Teenie's hands.

Betsey carefully lifted the lid off the barrel. The first thing she saw was a layer of dried fruit and herbs. Whoever packed the barrel had followed their instructions—food on the top.

"Dried peaches," said Betsey happily, as she reached inside and lifted out the fruit. "And some kind of herbs," she said, as she sat them on a nearby table.

"Good," said Teenie as she ran over to take a look. "The boys will appreciate having some fruit up there."

Then Betsey reached down into a layer of worn and dirty clothes, nothing that any of the British opening the barrel would find too appetizing or interesting, even with the shortages. They had clothes to wear, either their uniforms or something else. She lifted out the old dirty clothes and then gasped. "Wow. Now that's much better."

Underneath the top layer was a layer of clean, freshly knitted and crotched woolen goods. She put her hand in and lifted out scarves, hats, socks, sweaters, mittens. Layer after layer. Then when she reached to about the middle, she pulled out carefully wrapped packages that contained dried meat, dried fruit, and dried vegetables. She carefully set those things aside as she bent further over the barrel and stuck her hand further in. She pulled out the next layer of wool goods.

"They came through," she said happily to Orland and Teenie. She clapped her hands.

"I knew they would."

The word that went out to the networks was that the women who were knitting and crocheting these things couldn't put any notes in the barrel identifying them as patriots or letting anyone who might come upon them understand that the goods were headed towards the boys at Valley Forge. The women, desperately missing their men—their husbands and fathers—wanted them to know that they were back home, doing something to support the war effort. The Roberts' spy group, then, made one concession. The women could put a small letter in any garment that they sent up, identifying the state where the garment came from.

"Where are they from?" Orland asked.

Betsey held up a few garments and carefully examined them. The letters were not to be too large, just large enough so that anyone who was looking for them would see them.

"Here's a G, so that must be Georgia," Betsey said. "And a SC, so that must be South Carolina."

Teenie picked up some and looked. "This one here has a V on it, so that must be Virginia."

"Good," said Orland, as he smiled.

Betsey clapped her hands. "The whole southern states did come through," she said.

And she smiled broadly. "Just like I said they would."

THE NEXT morning, Betsey and Teenie packed the goods into smaller barrels and containers so they would be easier to carry and handle. Rochelle came over to sit with Orland while they went on this most important errand.

"How's he doing today?" Rochelle asked.

"Same," said Teenie. "That's all I can say."

Rochelle nodded. "I understand," she said, as she patted Teenie on the shoulder. "I'll take good care of him."

Teenie wiped a tear from her eye. Rochelle gave her a hug.

Betsey pulled her skirt up and climbed into the driver's seat. Teenie unloosened the horse from the hitching post and then pulled up her skirt and climbed up next to Betsey. She pulled her woolen cap down tighter on her head as the wind blew cold and steady. She looked over at her brave daughter.

"Are you ready?" Teenie asked.

"Ready," Betsey said, as she tightened her grip on the reins.

"Then let's head out," Teenie said.

"Here we go," said Betsey as she smiled at her mother.

BETSEY HELD the reins tightly as she directed the horses down the road on their property and on to the Lancaster Road. The wagon twisted and turned as Betsey pulled the reins first one way and then the other, steering the horses and the wagon around the many ruts in the road. Luckily, there was no snow covering the ruts so she could see the deepest ones that would definitely leave them stuck. It was also thankfully cold enough that the road and its ruts hadn't turned to mud. She also had to make sure that their wagon didn't crash into any of the other wagons that were doing this intricate dance to avoid the large ruts. Thankfully, the roads weren't all that crowded these days. Family after family had left the area as the war dragged on and their food for the winter dwindled. Even the families that were patriots started to starve after they gave the Continental Army half of the food they had on hand. Every time soldiers came out looking for half, the family's stores shrunk. For some families, no matter how patriotic, they couldn't keep going like that. So, they joined the steady stream of people still coming out of Philadelphia and making their way up the Lancaster Road to Lancaster or Reading or York or Bethlehem, where there was more food because there were fewer soldiers. But, as Orland said, "We'll never leave as long as our boys are here. They need us."

So they continued the ride. Every so often, Betsey stopped the wagon and pulled her wool coat tighter. Teenie patted her on the arm. "You're a good girl, Betsey," she said.

She drove the horses down the Swedesford Road, closer to the encampment. The pickets knew Betsey and Teenie by now, so they weren't searched as thoroughly as some wagons that came close to camp. And, the pickets knew that whenever these two women appeared, they were likely carrying much needed food and supplies.

When they reached the last picket, he said, "Good afternoon, ladies. What do you have here today?"

"Woolen goods and dried meat and fruits from the Southern states," Betsey said proudly.

"And how did you get all of that?" the picket asked.

This time Teenie spoke up. "That's for us to know, young man," she answered smiling. "You know we can't reveal how. Just suffice it to say that we got it."

The picket nodded. "Yes, Ma'am. Then we're mighty glad that you did." Teenie nodded, proudly.

The picket stepped aside. "You can take it on up to General Wayne's area," he said. "But be careful. Stay on the main road. I think that the General's men are in marksmanship training today, and we wouldn't want you to get caught in the middle of that."

Teenie smiled. "We wouldn't either."

Betsey drove on.

AS THEY drove further up the hill, Betsey said excitedly, "That must be them," pointing to a group of soldiers in an open field. They drove closer, and the uniforms of the Pennsylvania line came into view.

"Yup, that's them," she said, loudly.

The men were lined up for drills. Betsey and Teenie heard orders shouted. All of the men made movements in unison. They raised their rifles. They pointed them in the same direction. Then they turned in another direction in response to another order. Then they bent down on a knee. Then one group walked in one direction and another group walked in another direction as they made one formation after another.

The wagon reached the top of the hill where one of Wayne's men was on guard.

"Good afternoon," he said, recognizing Betsey and Teenie. "It's the Roberts family." He smiled.

"Yes," said Betsey, "and we've got a great delivery today. Woolen goods and dried meat."

The soldier grinned. "Then let me get your brother and his friends up here right away to help you unload." He turned to the soldier next to him and said, "Please go tell Captain Bartholomew to tell Fred Roberts that his family is here. And he should bring his hut mates to help them unload."

The other soldier took off while Betsey and Teenie waited. Soon, they saw that familiar group of four break away from the drilling soldiers and walk their way.

"Mom! Betsey!" Fred yelled.

"THERE SHE is," James said to Daniel, poking him in the side with his elbow.

Daniel was already smiling. He started smiling as soon as Fred told him that his sister was here. Daniel didn't have too many eyes for the women who hung around the camp. Most of them were as dirty and disheveled as the men, although he appreciated their commitment to the war the same as the men. But, there was something about Fred's little sister. She was committed to the war effort, as committed as anyone, willing to do what she could to help, even being part of the spy network, but she didn't have that hardness about her that many of the women at camp did. And she smelled clean, cleaner than any of them could usually get.

So, Daniel said to James, "Yes, there she is. My woman."

"Your woman?" James said, laughing. "Now how is that when we're here, and she's there?"

"I don't know," said Daniel, shrugging his shoulders. "I don't know. But I do know that one day, I'm going to marry that woman."

"Whoa,'" said James, laughing. "You've never even had a conversation with her that lasted more than the time it took to unload that wagon."

"It doesn't matter," said Daniel. "In due time." He patted James on the shoulder. "And sometimes you just know. And even though I can't remember where or when, her face is familiar."

They joined Fred up at the wagon. He had already begun to unload. Daniel walked right up to Betsey.

"Good afternoon," he said, smiling. "It's nice to see you."

Betsey smiled back and said, "Yes, good afternoon. It's good to see you as well."

Daniel looked at her with a gaze that lasted a little longer than was normal or polite. But, Betsey held his gaze. She looked at him a little longer than was considered polite, too.

Daniel then smiled. And Betsey smiled, too.

Teenie looked on, and then she smiled, catching for just an instant, that look that she knew all too well. That look that passed between man and woman. That look that she had for Orland. That look that she had never seen in Betsey's eyes. But, that look that she knew she was going to have to get used to seeing now that her daughter was a full grown woman.

JAMES AND Daniel were walking on the path to the blacksmith area when Ernestine, as she usually did, walked out of the door of the kitchen area carrying a basket full of bread for the people in General Washington's headquarters. She looked down as if she needed to see where she was going, on a path that she walked on several times a day. James called out, "Good morning, Miss Ernestine."

Instead of her turning her head towards James voice, as she usually did when he gave her his morning greetings, she turned her head in the opposite direction.

"Maybe she didn't hear you," Daniel said.

"Miss Ernestine," James called out again, this time, walking a little faster to get closer, right up on her. When he did, he tapped her on the arm to get her attention. She turned her head but still looked down.

"Miss Ernestine," said James. "Here I am. Up here."

"I hear you," she said softly.

James didn't like the sound of her voice. But he said softly, "Then why won't you look at me?"

She sighed and slowly raised her head.

James gasped when he saw her face, which she also obviously was trying to hide with the scarf that was on her head pulled down the sides of her face and knotted about as tight around her face as it could get. But even as tight as she tried to pull it, she couldn't hide the black and blue marks on her cheek from her nose to her chin.

James tried to control himself. "What happened here, Miss Ernestine?"

She looked at him with sadness and deceit in her eyes. "I fell," she said.

"When?" he asked.

"Last night," she said, softly.

He looked her straight in the eyes, knowing that if she truly fell, she wouldn't be embarrassed nor feel the need to hide that. "Really?" he asked.

She lowered her eyelids and said, "Really."

James just looked at her. He knew she was lying. He knew that look. He knew that women hung their heads when they felt shame. He wanted to ask her to tell him who did this to her, what man hit her with his hand, what happened—really. But what could he say? Even more paralyzing, what could he do? The answer to both questions was nothing. So he just looked Ernestine in the eye, touched her arm, and said. "Alright, Miss Ernestine. You be careful."

She looked at him, nodded her head, and walked towards the headquarters, head held down.

THE IMAGE of Ernestine's face and the look in her eyes stayed with James all morning. At lunch time, he didn't sit down and eat his hard tack lunch as usual. He put down his tools and walked over to the back of the kitchen, near the stove area where the slave men gathered to cook the meats for General Washington and the men in his headquarters. He knew that Ernestine would be inside with the rest of the women, serving the noonday meal while the men started cooking and smoking the meat for the evening meal.

As he approached, one of the slave men looked up. "Good afternoon," he said to James.

"Good afternoon, Tom," James said.

"How are you doing today?" Tom asked.

"Oh, me," said James. "I'm fine as usual," he said as he got closer. Then he said in a lower tone of voice, "But I'm worried about Miss Ernestine."

Tom stopped turning the meat. He looked at James. And he looked around.

"With good reason," said Tom.

"What's going on?" James asked. "What really happened to her face?"

Tom sighed and looked around again. "What do you think?"

James closed his eyes and said, "You know what I think. The only thing I don't know is who."

Tom put down the tools he was using and looked around again. "One of those Virginia crackers in there," he said, pointing towards Washington's Headquarters.

"Which one?" James asked.

"The one with the scar on his face today," Tom said. "He's been looking at Ernestine ever since we came up here and saying all kinds of things to her when she was passing by. Last night he came by our quarters late, looking for her. He pulled her out of bed and took her outside. Next thing we knew, we heard him yell out 'Bitch' and her scream. Then nothing. Then a few minutes later, he comes walking by, and she come running back to her quarters, crying. The other ladies in her cabin got up and did what they always do—drew some water, lit a fire, and cleaned her up."

James swallowed hard. Just what he thought. Every slave woman's curse. Even here. Nowhere to hide. Even here.

He shook his head, and he looked around at the soldiers walking around. He had to find out who it was. He didn't know how he was going to protect Ernestine, but he was going to try.

WHEN HE went back to his area to have his lunch, James sat next to Daniel.

"Where were you?" Daniel said.

James filled him in.

Daniel said, "My God. What's wrong with that man? How could he do that to a woman?"

James shook his head and rolled his eyes. "He doesn't see her as a woman," James said. "Not really. Not like a woman who deserves to be treated with respect. But like a woman who is his property to use as he sees fit."

Daniel said, "Well, he should be made to pay for that. We can't be having that here."

"We shouldn't," said James. "But we do."

"So what can we do about it? Can't we report that to someone?" Daniel asked.

James said, "And say what? One of the esteemed officers in General Washington's headquarters raped one of his slaves last night?" James shook his head. "Who would care about that? So many of them in there have slaves. And they all probably have one of their women slaves that they've done the same thing to."

Daniel sighed and said, "OK, but there must be somebody in there who thinks that slavery is wrong, and that raping women is even more wrong. They're Christian men in there, after all."

"They're all Christian in there," said James. "But that doesn't seem to make a difference."

"Well, maybe it will to one of them," Daniel said.

"Maybe," said James, "but I'm not holding my breath." He looked down at the ground himself. Then he looked up at Daniel. "I'm trying not to think about Ruth over there and what might be happening to her because it drives me crazy that I'm not there to protect her, but it's hard not to think about it."

Daniel looked at James and said, "I know, man." He patted him on the back. "I know."

James looked up. He watched the officers walking back and forth from the General's Headquarters to the kitchen, to the horses, doing their rounds. He wished he had a magnifying glass so that he could find the one with the fresh scar on his face.

## CHAPTER 63
# APRIL
# GERMANTOWN

Connie, Betsey, Teenie and Tom readied for another pickup of goods and clothes. The general's carriage came around at the usual time, and they all got in. They kept their conversations to a minimum as they rode down the Germantown Road. Spies were everywhere. As they reached the docks, they followed the usual actions to get in. They looked around for their connection, spotted him, and drove their wagon over to him where he stood surrounded by a few barrels. The driver halted the carriage, and he and Tom jumped down and walked over towards the connection.

"Good day," said the redcoat.

"Good day," said the connection.

"Good day," said Tom.

"So this is what you have for us today?" the driver said.

"Yes, it is," said the connection, holding his arms out, pointing them to a nice collection of four or so barrels.

They loaded the barrels in the carriage like any other day, and then they went to the market, picked up some other goods, and headed back up the Germantown Road to Connie's house. When they arrived, they unloaded the carriage and sent the driver on his way. Then, they loaded the barrels bound for the troops and a few other barrels of food into the Roberts wagon. Teenie took the reins and Betsey hopped up beside her.

"We'll see you later," Teenie said, waving as they drove away.

Connie and Tom walked back in the house and started putting the goods away. Only a few minutes passed before the yelling started.

"Open this door," someone yelled, knocking hard. "Open right now."

Connie looked at Tom.

"Open this door before we break it down," the voice yelled.

Tom ran over to the door. He pulled back the window curtains.

"Redcoats," he said to Connie.

"Let them in," she called back.

Tom opened the door and fell back against the wall with the force of the redcoats pushing the door open.

"What's this about?" Connie asked.

"You're under arrest!" one of the redcoats yelled.

"What? Arrest?" Connie yelled back. "What are you talking about?"

A few redcoats had picked Tom off the floor and held his arms tight.

"For being a traitor. For treason. For conspiring against the crown. For smuggling goods in from the colonies to support the traitors who are now encamped up by the Valley Forge," said a redcoat.

Connie thought fast. "What are you talking about? Don't you know who I am? I am a good friend of General Howe's, and he's not going to be pleased when I tell him that you've mistaken me for some traitor and caused all kind of upset in my house."

The redcoat walked over to Connie and grabbed her arm. "We know who you are. You're the General's whore."

Connie looked at the man with hate in her eyes. She raised the other hand to slap him, but the redcoat caught it.

He laughed. "We all know who you are," he said. "And, imagine how surprised we were to find out that the traitor that we were supposed to follow back from the docks was you, indeed. The general's whore."

He held both of Connie's arms tight as she squinted her eyes at him. If she could have shot venom out of them at him, she would have.

"And wait until the General finds out," the redcoat said, as he looked Connie in the eyes and up and down her face. "Your pretty face might not remain so pretty after he's done with you."

"What are you talking about?" she said.

"You'll see what we do to traitors," the redcoat said. He laughed. "You'll see."

That particular officer took his hands off Connie and said to one of his men. "Here, you come and hold her. " And he looked at his other men. "And the rest of you hold that man there. Two of you go upstairs and round up the rest of the people in this house and bring them down into the parlor here."

The men did as they were told. The girls walked down the stairs with redcoats holding bayonets behind them. Connie caught the eye of every one as they walked down the steps past her and Tom. She tried to say to them silently that everything would be all right, that she would straighten this out with the general, that they were to keep their cool.

When the girls were in the parlor, the lead officer said, "Three of you stay here and watch these ladies, if you can call them that." Then he looked at Connie. "I have the distinct honor of taking this traitor and the other one here to see the general." He walked up close to Connie and got right up in her face. "I wonder if he's going to be so happy to see you this time." Connie squinted her eyes in hate at the redcoat. She wanted to spit at him, but she knew that she didn't hold the cards in her hand like she used to.

The officer said to his men holding Connie and Tom, "Come on. Put them in the carriage. Let's go see the general."

TEENIE AND Betsey rode up the Germantown Road. Teenie said, "It sounds like there's a ruckus behind us, Betsey. Do you see anything?"

Betsey turned around. She saw more dust coming up the road than usual.

"It looks like a few horses are riding up the road faster than usual."

"I wonder why," said Teenie.

"I don't know," said Betsey.

"How far back do you think they are?" Teenie said.

"Maybe about a quarter of a mile, maybe a half," Betsey said.

Teenie thought to herself. "I don't like it," she said. "No telling what's going on back there." She took a deep breath. "With all that we have in this carriage, I need to stay out of anybody's way." She thought for a few seconds. "Hold on Betsey. I'm going to speed up and see if we can't put some distance between us and them."

Betsey turned back around and put her hands on the front railing.

Teenie hit the horse with the hand whip, and he picked up speed. The carriage jumped a bit in the air as it did.

"It still sounds really noisy back there," Teenie said.

Betsey turned around. "Oh my God," she said. "I see them now."

"See what?" Teenie said. "See who?"

"Redcoats," Betsey said. "Looks like there's about six of them. They're riding fast and headed our way." She turned back around to face her mother, eyes wide and scared.

"Darn," said Teenie. "I don't know anywhere to hide along here, so we'll just have to keep going. I have to get us out of Germantown and into patriot territory."

She hit the horse again.

"Alright, Betsey, what I'm going to try to do is to get up the Germantown Road as fast as I can and hope they don't stop to shoot, and then get us to those pickets in Whitemarsh."

"OK, Mom," Betsey said as she turned around to see the redcoats riding up after them. She turned back around and said, "Hurry."

Teenie looked at Betsey and said, "Hold on, honey."

Teenie hit the horse with the whip, again and again, and yelled, "Get on now." The horse ran faster and faster. The carriage hit a few bumps and the barrels flew up in the air.

"I hope none of those barrels fall out," Teenie said.

"Me, too," said Betsey. But then she thought. "But maybe we might be better off if they did, Mom," Betsey said. "Maybe we should throw one of them back there and hope it stops them."

Teenie kept heading forward. "How are you going to do that Betsey? You'd have to get back there and throw it, and those barrels are too heavy for you to lift by yourself."

"I don't have to lift them, Mom," said Betsey. "I just have to tilt it to the side and give it a big push. It will fall over all on its own."

"But you have to get back there to do that," Teenie said. "That's not safe."

"No I don't," said Betsey. "One of the ones we got from the food market is right behind me. If I can just turn around and maneuver my body right, I can push it out. Maybe that will stop them or get them to stop and look."

Teenie kept riding. It seemed to her that the noise behind her was getting closer.

"Alright then," she said. "But only if you can do it while sitting in this seat. I don't want you to fall out same as the barrel."

"I won't," said Betsey. She kept one hand on the front rail and turned her body so that her right hand reached the barrel behind her. She held onto the front rail tight with one hand and cupped her right hand so that it lay right under the rim of the barrel. She could get a good hold on the barrel at that rim. She pushed the barrel with her right hand. She felt it tilt over slightly, but it wasn't far enough. She knew she'd have to use both hands. She looked straight ahead and saw that Teenie would soon be taking the curve near Barren Hill in Whitemarsh. Maybe when she takes the curve, the barrel will lean enough on its own, so my one-handed push will be enough.

She looked back around and saw the redcoats coming closer now. No matter what, she had to try. As Teenie held tight to the reins and pulled the horse to the left to take the Barren Hill Road, Betsey gave the barrel a good push as it leaned to the right. The bottom of the barrel rose up, and Betsey kept pushing. Suddenly, the barrel lifted up, and Betsey gave it one more good push out of the wagon. The barrel careened onto the road and down the hill, straight into the path of the redcoat horses.

Teenie made the turn and hit the horse with her spurs now. The Continental Pickets were just down the road at the bottom of the hill. She rode faster and faster. As they rode toward the bottom of the hill, Teenie pulled the reins hard to slow the wagon down. She didn't want to run into the patriot soldiers. As the patriots saw her wagon approaching, they moved into formation and blocked the roadway. Teenie pulled hard to stop the wagon as the soldiers cried out, "Halt. Who goes there?"

Betsey yelled, "We're patriots! We're patriots! We're being chased by redcoats. We're being chased by redcoats."

A few of the pickets rode up to the wagon as Teenie slowed it to a stop.

"The redcoats," she yelled. "They've been chasing us all the way up the Germantown Road. We think we stopped them when we pushed a barrel out into the road."

The patriot pickets looked at Teenie and Betsey. "We just smuggled in provisions for the men up at the Valley Forge."

The pickets looked at each other quickly and said, "Redcoats? Behind you?"

"Yes," Betsey yelled.

The men yelled, "Go on down to the next pickets and wait there." One picket said to the other, "Come on," as they hit their horses and hurried down towards the Germantown Road.

# CHAPTER 64
# GERMANTOWN

"The General will have your head," Connie said with as much indignation as she could muster to the redcoat sitting in the back of the carriage with his bayonet pointed directly at her.

The redcoat laughed. "No, I'm afraid it will be your head, Miss." Then he moved the bayonet a few inches to the left so that it was pointed directly at Tom. "And his head, too."

"Just what is your name, soldier?" Connie asked, as if she had a right to.

"That'd be none of your business, Miss," he said.

"Well, that doesn't matter," said Connie. "The General will know who you are."

Tom said nothing. He only wished that Connie's charms would work again as they always had. But he had his doubts this time.

The ride from Connie's house to the General's wasn't that long, so Connie didn't have much time to think. That was fine, though. She'd been lying to men her whole life, so coming up with another one wasn't so hard, even in straits that even she would consider to be desperate.

The wagon stopped at the first guard on the Germantown Road on the approach to the General's headquarters. They were waved through to the next checkpoint. As they got closer to the headquarters, Connie looked directly at Tom and tried to communicate with him. He already knew to stay silent and let her talk and work her magic. She wanted to smile to reassure him, but she didn't. She was using her energy to reassure herself.

The wagon came to a complete stop. The redcoat guarding them jumped out and down. He pointed the bayonet at Tom first and said, "Get out." Tom rose and jumped down. Then he pointed at Connie and said, "Now you. Get out."

Connie raised her head and held it high. "You'll watch how you talk to me," she said.

"Just get out," the redcoat said.

Connie rose, and said, "I can't step down in this skirt and with handcuffs," holding her bound and useless hands up behind her back.

"Blimey," said the redcoat as he stuck out one hand and grabbed Connie's arm with it.

"Ouch," she said, glaring at him.

"My God," he said. "Just shut up and get down!" he yelled. He applied force and pulled Connie out of the wagon.

"You'll be sorry," she said, as she glared at him again.

"I doubt it," he said, as he waited for another soldier to walk over.

Another redcoat walked over and looked Tom and Connie up and down. "So these are the traitors," he said, with a mouth-twisting snarl on his face.

"These are them," the other soldier said.

"So I understand that this one," he said, pointing to Connie, "needs no introduction to our commanding officer."

"No," said the other soldier. "She's the general's whore."

Connie held her head high and said, "Like I said. You'll be sorry," as she looked at him. Then she looked at the other soldier and said, "You will, too."

"I doubt it, whore," said the soldier as he took Connie's arm. "Come on," he said as he walked her down the stone walkway to the General's home away from home.

The other soldier grabbed Tom and dragged him behind Connie.

The soldier held Connie's arm in a tight grip as he led her into a room off the left of the entry parlor. It was beautiful, as befitting a General. There were overstuffed chairs with red and gold tapestry, a large sparkling crystal chandelier in the center of the room, and ornately carved wooden furniture with gold trim. Connie refused to look at the other soldiers. She looked at the bucolic scenes in the oil painting on the walls. She calmed herself as she imagined that she was the lady in the painting, sitting next to the flowing stream, having a picnic with her lover. She kept her eyes stayed on that picture until she heard his voice behind her.

"They told me it was you, but I didn't believe them," the General said.

Connie turned around. She could see the hurt in the General's eyes. She could see that his face was drained. Where he would normally be standing straight up, shoulders straight, he looked slumped over, a weight on his shoulders, defeated.

"They're lying," Connie said as she let her face and eyes soften. "They don't know what they saw." She called forth the tears that she had been holding back. "I would never betray you," she said, tears welling up in her eyes. "I love you," she said, softly. "You must know that."

The General just looked at her. He took it in. She had never said that she loved him before. He wanted to believe it, but he found it hard to. He walked over towards her and looked her closely in the eyes. He'd looked into those eyes so many times before. He loved those eyes. And he loved her, too. He'd never said it before, either. But now, even as she stood before him, a lying, handcuffed traitor, he wanted to say it. He put out his hand and gently touched her cheek. He took some more time to look into her dark eyes. "You've never said that to me before," he said.

"I know," said Connie, as she held his gaze. "But I should have."

He took his hand off her cheek and walked around her. He looked at the thin waist that he liked to put his hands around as he entered her from behind. He looked at the hands that stroked him delicately when he wanted that and with power and force when he wanted that, now bound together with round pieces of metal. He walked back around to the front and looked at the mouth that gave him so much pleasure in so many ways. He raised his other hand, gently put it around her cheek, and then squeezed it hard as he looked her straight in the eyes and said, "You're lying," as he roughly snatched his hand from off of her cheek.

"I'm not," Connie said, raising her voice.

"You're lying to save yourself," the General said, as he looked at her, compassion and softness leaving his face with every word.

Connie let all of her stored up tears flow. "No, I'm not lying. You know I'm not."

The General's eyes narrowed as he watched her cry. He wanted to go to her. He wanted to hold her in his arms and comfort her. He knew that her girls were whores, but he thought, wished, and hoped that she was different. He didn't think that she could make love like she did if she didn't have some feeling for him. He had known enough women to know when he was being fooled; he was convinced of that. He knew that this woman had feelings for him, even though her relationship with him made every aspect of her life almost normal and comfortable in a world that had been upended by war. He knew that he wanted his men to be wrong and that he wanted to believe her. But, he also knew that he couldn't appear to be weak to his men. He was their commander-in-chief, after all.

"Well, my dear," he said sarcastically, "if you are not lying, you are going to have to prove it."

Connie looked at him, wondering what he meant. She hoped that he wasn't going to humiliate her. She tried to muster up every bit of tenderness that she could as she looked into his eyes for answers.

Howe walked over to her, brought his face close to hers, grabbed her arm, roughly, and said, "Come with me." He dragged her towards the door, out of the room.

"Sir," one of the soldiers called out. "Shall I unlock the handcuffs?"

The General looked at Connie, smirked and said, "No. She won't be needing her hands this time."

For the first time since she walked in the room, Connie was worried.

THE GENERAL held Connie's arm as he dragged her out the door, through the parlor, and up the stairs, past guards at every level who tried to keep their eyes straight ahead as they were trained, but who, Connie saw, looked at her out of the corners of their eyes. They reached a room at the end of a long hallway on the second floor, and the guard opened the door and stepped aside. It was the General's bedroom. Connie had been having sex with him for months but she had never seen this room before. A large, four-poster brass bed was pushed up against the far wall. Marble-topped side tables were on either side. The wooden floor was polished so that the light that came in the lace-curtained windows bounced off of it. He pulled her over to the bed and pushed her shoulders to make her sit down. She let more tears flow, hoping that would help her.

The General stood over her, no more than a few inches between where she was sitting and where he was standing. "You're at my mercy, you know," he said, angrily.

"I didn't do anything," she cried out, between her tears. "You must believe me."

"Must? Why?" he asked.

She cried some more, and then said softly, "Because you love me, too."

He cast his eyes down, looking at her, knowing that he should say something to hurt this woman who had hurt him so much. He was the commander of His Majesty's army, for Christ's sake, and this woman was a traitor who had made a fool out of him, as far as he knew.

The vile words come to his mind, but he didn't let them fall from his mouth. The vile thoughts came, too. He thought that he could stop her lying and humiliate her at the same time by standing even closer, unhooking his trousers, and sticking his dick in her mouth. Her hands were cuffed behind her, and she couldn't push him away. That would show her that he was the boss, the one in charge of this relationship. He thought about it, but he didn't do it.

He looked down on her, his beautiful woman, here crying and fearful of him, vile words and thoughts ready to burst out, and he said, "Yes, you're right. I love you, too," as he collapsed on the bed next to her, put his head in his hands, and let his tears flow.

Connie moved her body closer to him.

"Can you take off my handcuffs?" she asked softly.

The general sniffed and wiped the tears from his eyes with his hand. "Why should I?" he said, regaining some of the composure that he had lost.

"So I can hold you and make love to you," Connie said. "Really make love to you," she added, again softly.

Howe turned his head and looked at her.

Connie saw the questioning look in his eyes. He squinted them together a bit as his face hardened.

"You made a fool out of me," he said, angrily. "Imagine what my men think?" He stood up and started pacing the room. "No, I don't have to imagine. I heard what they were saying. 'Well look who it is. The General's whore. How did she get away with that? A traitor right under his nose. Or his body. What kind of general is he if his own whore can pull one over on him?"

Connie sighed softly. "I can only tell you that the only thing that I was guilty of was sharing some of my food, the food that you thankfully make sure that I have, with my family," she said. "That's all. I was sharing the food with them and nothing else. I didn't know anything else was going on."

He looked at her again with the same hardened face. "And I'm supposed to believe that? First you tell me you did nothing wrong and that my men were lying, and now you tell me that yes, something else was going on except you getting food for yourself and your girls, that you were also getting food for your family," he said as he paced the room. "And no telling how large that family is."

Connie let the tears flow again. "I had to get some food for my family," she said between tears. "My Dad is sick," she cried out. "In fact, we're sure that he's dying," she said. "So now do you see?" she said, crying and pleading.

He turned again to look at her. This time his face had softened. The hard lines around his mouth had disappeared.

"Dying, you say?" he asked.

"Yes," Connie said. "Dying," as she kept crying.

Howe walked over to her, sat down next to her, pulled her body up straight and hugged her to him as she continued to cry.

"What's wrong with him?" Howe asked.

Connie said, "We think he has the cancer," she said. "He's getting thinner and thinner, weaker, and is in so much pain."

Howe rubbed her shoulders. "I'm sorry to hear that. Watching a parent waste away is a painful thing."

"Yes it is," Connie said.

Howe rubbed her shoulders and arms some more as she cried. This time the tears were real. She wasn't lying. From what her mother and sister told her, it seemed like it would only be a few more months before the disease had its way.

"So you see why I had to let them come and get some food? Why I had to share it with them?" she said. "I couldn't let them starve and not have what they need."

He looked at her, all traces of hardness having now left his face. "No you couldn't," he said. "So that is all that you were picking up for your family?"

"Yes," she said, adamantly.

"You didn't know that they were picking up other things in those barrels?" he asked.

"No," she said loudly. "Not at all. What other things are you talking about?"

Howe looked at her. "Things that lead us to believe that whoever picked up that barrel was a traitor and a spy for that army of traitors."

"No," said Connie, trying to act surprised. "Not my family," Connie lied. "They're not spies or traitors. They're just farmers, like everybody else out where we live."

"Well, that may be, but someone who was getting that barrel is a traitor and a spy," he said. "But now we know," he added, "and we'll catch them next time."

Connie thought briefly about how she was going to warn the family but quickly turned her thoughts back to how she was going to get back on the general's good side, out of those handcuffs and back to her home.

"I hope you do," she said. Then she nuzzled her head against his shoulder. "And now can you take off these handcuffs so I can properly take care of you," she said, as she looked up into his eyes with as much passion and seriousness as she could muster up.

Howe looked at her hungrily as he reached his free hand into his pocket and pulled out a small silver key. "I can't wait," he said.

"Neither can I," she said, which wasn't really a lie.

Howe slipped his other arm from around her, turned her slightly to the side, and put the key in the handcuffs. He twisted it and then maneuvered the handcuffs until they fell off her wrists. Once they did, Connie didn't rub her wrists to get rid of the pain like she wanted to. Instead, she flung her arms and hands around the general's neck, pulled him close, and kissed him with all of the passion that she had ever used to kiss a man. She drew on the genuine passion that she felt when she was just a young teenager kissing her first real boyfriend. Yes, she thought to herself. That's the feeling that I have to keep in mind right now if I am to truly get back the privileges that I've had.

Her thoughts must have worked. Howe put his strong hands around her lower waist and pulled her close as he luxuriated in her kisses. He returned the kisses with passion, too. He realized how much he missed the woman he knew who truly loved him, his wife. He realized how much he wished that it was she that he was kissing instead of this woman who he loved but whose love he couldn't be really sure of. So, as they both thought of partners they truly loved and love that was pure and innocent, they made love to each other for hours in a way that they never had before. Even Connie enjoyed the reality that was created by their fantasies. When they finished with each other for the second or third time, they both fell back on the bed, tired, happy and satisfied, wondering if what had just happened had turned a corner in their relationship. Connie hoped that it had. The general hoped that it hadn't.

As he dressed, Connie planted soft kisses on his neck, hands, face, lips, and whatever part of his body remained exposed. She was anxious to hear him speak and to see just what he was going to do with her now.

Howe finished buttoning his jacket and putting back on all of the decoration that a general wore. He straightened his sash and wiped the brass buttons and epaulets until they shone. Then he turned and faced Connie.

"Very good, darling," he said. He walked over and sat on the bed next to her.

"So," he said, "I'm going to take you home."

Connie stifled a smile.

He looked for a reaction. She had none. She was smarter than that.

"But I'm not going to leave you home alone," he said.

Connie just looked, still no reaction.

"You will have company, around the clock."

Connie frowned and asked, "What?" like she was confused.

"You tell me that you are not a traitor or spy and that you were just getting food for your sick father," he said, somewhat haughtily, "and I believe you. You tell me that your family members are not traitors or spies and, because you tell me, I'll believe you on that one, too. "But," he said, as he started pacing again, "someone around you is a spy and a traitor."

"No one that I know of," she said, shocked. "I don't get in to all that. You know that I'm just running a business."

"Oh, yes, and about that," he said. "That's going to have to change, too," he said.

Connie furrowed her brow and looked even more puzzled, which she was.

"What are you saying, dear?" she asked. "I wish you would come right out with it."

"Fine," he said. "Here it is. You may not be a spy and traitor, but someone around you is. And, I can't afford to let that spy and traitor run around and out to the Valley Forge or anywhere else, giving away our secrets. So, I've already put a guard on your place, and I've cut back your business."

"What?" Connie called out, a bit indignant this time.

"There are a few guards already up there at your place. Your girls are still there, but your regular customers are banned. The only customers that they can have are members of my army, men who are preapproved to visit and use your women for the comfort that they need," he said.

"Wait a minute," Connie said, getting a little mad now. "What are you saying?"

"You heard me, dear. Your girls can only service members of His Royal Highness' Army, and no one goes or comes from your house without my approval."

Connie's eyes widened. Now she truly was shocked. "You don't trust me," she said.

"No, my dear, it's not you I don't trust," he said. "It's everyone around you."

Connie shook her head. She was incredulous. This man, who she just made love to with tenderness, ferocity, passion, and whatever else he wanted, was taking over her life, her business, her everything.

"So, you're just taking over my life and my business?" she asked.

"Yes," he said, the hardness returning to his eyes as he squinted them. "Surely you must understand why."

"I don't," she said, sounding like a hurt child. "All I understand is that you don't trust me."

"No," he said, walking closer to her. "I trust you. It's everyone around you, or who might be, that I don't trust," He held her face in his hands. "I love you. Remember?" he asked, stroking her cheek.

She wanted to say something smart, but she realized that she wasn't holding the cards any more. What's done is done. He'd already taken over. So she said, "Yes, I remember," softly.

Then she kissed him softly on the lips and said, "And I love you, too. " Then she added, making sure that it sounded nothing like the threat that it was, "Remember that," because if it's one thing that Connie cherished above all else, it was her independence and her insistence that she was not going to let any man ever again tell her what to do and hold her life and her future in his hands, especially not this general who she suddenly believed would burn down the house with her and everyone else in it if he ever found out that her sick father was the head of the area's largest spy ring, and her mother and sister were some of best spies.

# CHAPTER 65

# PAOLI

Teenie drove the horses hard the whole way home to Paoli. The carriage jumped up in the air as they ran over the ridges in the road, and Betsey stretched out her arm to keep the barrels from falling out. When they reached the Lancaster Road, which was more open and dotted with lights from the houses and shops that lined the street, Betsey called out to her mother, "Mom, can you slow down now? There's nobody following us, and I'm having a hard time holding these barrels in."

"How do you know no one is following us? You can't see everything," Teenie yelled back.

"Now I can," Betsey said. "I've been looking back ever since we turned on the Lancaster Road. No one followed us. No one has turned on to this road behind us in a long time."

Teenie hit the horse with the reins again. "I don't care," she said. "I want to get home. Then I'll be sure that no one has followed us," as she held tight as the carriage jumped up in the air again. "Or at least we can get to the Tavern. Yes, that's it. We'll turn in there and then have Norman ride back with us."

Betsey had seen her mother like this before. Stubborn and determined. There was very little that she could say to convince her that she was right, so she might as well save her breath and her strength to keep the barrels from falling off the carriage. At least the Tavern was only a few miles down the road now.

"Fine," Betsey said, angrily.

"I know what I'm doing, young lady," Teenie shot back.

"I said fine," Betsey said, sarcastically.

"But I don't like your tone of voice," Teenie said.

"Ok," Betsey said, with even more attitude. Then she thought better of herself and her mother and said measured and even, "Fine." She looked at her mother and said nicely, "Is that good?"

"Don't get smart with me Betsey," Teenie said. "Let's just get to the tavern so I can make sure that we're safe."

Betsey felt bad for ever criticizing her mother. They both had a horrifying experience with the redcoats chasing them out of Germantown. "I'm sorry, Mom," she said. "You've been nothing but great and so brave tonight," as she finally relaxed her shoulders a bit and let the tears brought on by fear finally fall.

"You've been great, too, baby," Teenie said. Then she laughed. "Who would have thought? The two of us ladies outrunning the redcoats," she said, as she gave the horse another hit with the whip.

"Yes," said Betsey. "Paoli girls one, redcoats nothing!"

"You've got that right," Teenie said, as she laughed.

They hightailed it down Lancaster Avenue in virtual silence until the Paoli Tavern came into view. "There it is," Betsey yelled, as she saw the light from the tavern down the road.

"Thank God," Teenie said, as she rode on. "My arms are getting tired." But she kept the horse and the carriage steady as they flew down the road. When they reached the intersection where the Tavern was, she turned left, steered left onto their grounds, and pulled the carriage around the back. "Go on and get Norman," Teenie said to Betsey. "I'll stay out here with the wagon."

Betsey jumped off the wagon and ran inside. The tavern was almost full. Betsey didn't look at the patrons' faces to see if it was the usual crowd, like she usually did. She just took a quick look at the bar and never felt happier when she saw Uncle Norman standing behind it.

She ran right over to him. "Uncle Norman, Uncle Norman," she called out as she ran.

Norman looked up the second he heard his name. He saw Betsey running toward him, face red, hair loose, and coat dirty. "Betsey," he called out, running towards her. "What's wrong?" he asked, as the men at the bar put down their mugs ready to run outside if Norman asked them to.

"Mom's outside with the wagon and the barrels," she said. "Some redcoats chased us up the Germantown road, so we had to fly out of there, and we lost them, but we've been riding hard ever since."

Norman dropped his rag on the bar and ran out to where Betsey had just come from. A few of the regulars ran out behind him. When they got outside, they saw Teenie sitting in the front of the carriage, head slumped over, crying.

Norman ran over calling out, "Teenie!" She raised her head and held her hands to her eyes as she alternately cried and wiped tears from her eyes. Norman held out his hand and helped her down out of the carriage. Teenie slumped over and collapsed in his arms. The hard ride had taken its toll. Norman held her tight against him, but then he scooped up her legs, whispered to her, "put your arms around my neck," and carried her inside, where Rochelle waited for them with a cool rag to run across Teenie's hot brow.

# CHAPTER 66

# GERMANTOWN

Connie paced around the parlor like a panther trapped in a cage, ready to strike, which of course, she was. It had been two weeks since the family's cover was blown and she was confined to the house. Two weeks of her so-called British lover treating her like a prisoner-of-war, which, of course, she was. Two weeks since her every move was under scrutiny by the British guards that sat outside her house and the one that sat in the parlor for good measure. No one in the house could go anywhere except in the yard for some spring air or in their bedrooms to service the British officers who never stopped coming, literally and figuratively. Even her so-called lover, General Howe, paid her his usual visit, twice a week. At first, she mentioned nothing of the guard. She just told him how much she loved him and wanted to make him happy. She made love to him like she really cared about him, all the while seething inside. She didn't bring up the fact that she and her girls were trapped, going stir crazy, and wondering just how long they were going to have to endure this capture. When she was returned to her house, she offered him all of the money that her girls would make their first week as a gesture to show him how grateful she was for him. He eagerly accepted the offer. Then he said that he had an offer for her. He would allow her to keep all of the money that her girls made from then on, but that he would have his guards hold it. That way, there'd be no way for her, her girls, or her man Tom to bribe anyone to let them out of the house.

He trusted her, he said. It was the others that he was leery of. She objected to that the way she objected to everything that he was doing now, but she told him, "Fine. As long as you trust your guards."

He laughed. "Of course I trust them," he said. "I am their Commander- in-Chief. They dare not go against my orders."

She said, "I hope not."

He patted her head and said, "Dear, don't you worry. You're completely under my care now." She looked up at him and smiled with her mouth as she hoped that he couldn't see the daggers that her eyes were shooting straight to his heart.

# CHAPTER 67

# MAY
# VALLEY FORGE

The hills and fields around the camp looked like one of the patchwork quilts that his mother loved making. Pink, yellow, red, orange, and white flowers were in bloom on the trees and on the grounds. The long winter had finally come to an end. Nature's vibrant display was in stark contrast to the general conditions of the camp. Winter had taken its toll. Too much green grass had been trampled, never to grow again. Nearby trees had been cut down for firewood. And, no matter how much the men were exhorted and commanded to keep their huts and the general camp area clean, months of hardship had resulted in discarded and threadbare clothes strewn all around, along with rotten food, bare animal carcasses, and the occasional areas of human waste.

Fred couldn't wait to break camp. All of the men knew that they would break camp soon because spring was here. The roads would unfreeze and be smooth enough for the army to drag their wagons and weapons across the roads and fields. The trumpet sounded. Fred stopped cleaning his rifle and reassembled it. He walked toward the lineup with the rest of his hut mates.

General Wayne greeted his troops, still looking resplendent in the uniform that he kept clean, even through the harsh winter. He tried to keep his men looking as resplendent, but he wasn't as successful. Even though their families were close buy and could more easily repair and clean their uniforms than other soldiers, the times were still hard for everyone. A lot of families had to put more of a focus on finding enough food to eat during the winter than on keeping their clothes clean.

"Men," said the General. "Today is a great day. A day of celebrating. A day that will go down in history. Today," he said, "our Commander-in-Chief has received notice that the countrymen of our General the Marquis de Lafayette have formed an alliance with our new nation against the British."

The men took a minute to take it in and then cheered.

"Our mighty cause is no doubt near the end," Wayne said. "Soon, we will be on the march, engaging the British again and winning yet another battle for our liberty."

The men cheered.

"So be ready, men," Wayne said. "We believe that we will be on the march any day now, reclaiming our capitol city, and sending those redcoats back across the sea."

The men cheered again.

"Stay strong, men. Stay strong," he said to their cheers.

As he rode off, their Sargent moved into place, and another day at Valley Forge began.

Fred looked at Daniel. "So that's great news, isn't it?" Fred asked.

"Sure is," said Daniel.

Fred wrapped his hand around his head before he lifted it at the sound of what seemed to be louder than usual trumpets blowing revelry.

"Damn," he said, closing his eyes again.

"What cruel joke is this?" Daniel asked, rubbing his eyes. "General Washington allows us to drink and party all night to celebrate the French Alliance, makes sure we all have at least a gill of ale, or more, and then we still have to wake up at the same time the next morning?"

"That's not right," said James, as he slowly lifted his arms above his head.

The trumpet sounded louder.

"My God, they're serious," Fred said as he stretched his arms out in front of him. He stretched his legs and then swung them over so that they touched the floor. Even those slight movements caused his head to ache.

"How the hell are we ever going to get through this day?" he asked his bunk mates, who were also making slow and slight movements of their bodies with much pain.

"Very carefully," said James, laughing. "Very carefully."

They all laughed as he slowly walked towards the fireplace to start their day.

The cabin mates moaned and groaned as they splashed water on their faces to wake up and get ready for their day. One by one, they walked outside where the other men in camp were also moaning and groaning and holding their aching and hung over heads in their hands. They all lined up for daily orders and then walked towards their various stations.

When Fred finished the seemingly endless steps to get to his area, he noticed more guns lying around than usual. "Shit," he said to himself as he kept walking. "Don't tell me we are going to have to fight today."

He looked at his friend, Sidney, who was joining him from the 2nd Virginia.

"There's more guns there than we need for our daily work," Sidney said.

"I know," said Fred as they walked towards the pile of guns. "I think we better shake off the effects of the ale pretty quick. It looks like we've got some kind of special assignment today that's going to take a clear head."

"I'd agree with you, there," Sidney said.

They reached the gun pile and just waited.

Brigadier General Henry Knox and his lieutenants rode in, dressed in clean uniforms and shined brass.

"Oh, God," said Fred. "What the hell? We are going to battle today," he said, rolling his eyes and looking at Fred. Generals always dressed for battle.

General Knox called his men to attention. "Men," he said. "Today is a special day. A day that is almost as special as the days we have had for the last two—the news of the French Alliance and our celebration of the same."

"What now?" Fred silently asked himself.

General Knox continued. "Yesterday we celebrated our alliance with the nation of France," he said. "Today we will celebrate our alliance with another nation. A nation that is right here on the same continent."

The men looked puzzled.

"That nation is one that is composed of our Indian brothers. That nation is the Oneida nation, from the great state of New York," he said. "Yes, that nation has agreed to help our new nation win its freedom from the tyranny of the British."

Some men started yelling, "Huzzah!" Fred joined in cheering in excitement, even though the loud noise hurt his still delicate constitution.

"These men who are coming to join us are warriors in the greatest sort, yet peaceful. They defend what is theirs and usually do not seek to take from others," General Knox said.

"They are coming to help us in every way. And, a group of them are coming to join us, to learn how to become even better warriors by learning from our best shooters, which are you all."

He looked at his men, who he knew were hung over, take it all in. He wished they could start their training on a different day, but he knew, as everyone did, that their days at the camp at Valley Forge were numbered, and that they must be ready for battle at any moment. He looked over the horizon and saw the feathers flying off tall poles first.

He pointed his gun towards the ridge behind them. "Here they come now," he said. "Turn around men, and welcome the great warriors of the Oneida nation."

Fred and the rest of the men pivoted and looked at the group advancing towards them. Poles and spears could be seen in the air for about a half mile away, with feathers of all colors attached to the top of them and flying in the wind. As the group advanced closer, the rest of their regalia came into view. There were feathers everywhere. In the headdress that the men wore. Flying in the wind from the back of their moccasins and leather and suede and calfskin britches. A group of about 50 men sat straight up in their horses as they approached. When they reached the camp, the man leading the group, the man with the headdress with the most feathers, held up his staff, and the rest of the men behind him stopped. Except Fred noticed that not all of them were men. There was a small group of women in the back of the group with their long black hair flying out loose, instead of braided like the men, and their skirted legs slung over one side of the horse, riding side saddle like the white women did. He later found out that the women rode that way out of respect for their first time seeing these men. Normally, Oneida women rode their horses just like the men did. They were equal to the men in many ways, and even superior in others.

As they rode closer, the Indians dismounted. They followed their leader in rows, three across. As the Indians paraded by the patriots, the patriots stood at attention. Fred looked at the men with respect, the same respect that he gave the Lenape Indians that he often encountered in Paoli. Just because their skin was darker and their clothes were different didn't mean that they weren't men deserving of respect, just like the white people. He wasn't raised to think of them as anything different, like many others were. As the men approached and walked by, he also kept his eyes trained on the row of beautiful women, one in particular. She was a bit taller than the rest, and her features were striking. Her eyes seemed to shine in the morning sun, just like her long, jet black hair did. She had black, white, and grey feathers sticking out of a headband that was as brightly decorated as a spring field. There were orange, turquoise, green, yellow, red, navy blue, and white beads and stones all over the headband. The leather dress-like garment that hugged her body was a creamy white that set off her black hair and dark skin even more. He stared at her as long as he could, hoping to catch her eye. As she walked by him, head held high and proud, her eyes turned towards his slightly. He nearly melted from the heat that he felt in his groin with that one look.

Once the group walked by, the general ordered the men to turn and face their new fellow soldiers. The men turned, and now Fred could look at this woman face-to-face.

The general and the Oneida leader shook hands. The Oneida leader gave the general one of the bows that he had been carrying on his back. The general smiled and gave the general one of the guns that had been stacked on the ground. The two men then shook hands and ceremonially hugged, patting each other on the back.

General Knox called out, "Huzzah!"

Fred and the rest of the men followed suit.

The Oneida leader called out something, and his men, and women followed suit.

General Knox led the rest of the Oneidas to the gun pile. He then turned to his men. "Men," I am assigning one of these men to you. He will be your partner. You will drill with him and show him what you know. You will turn him into a great marksman, just like you. He will be your brother and your friend."

With that, he called his men to come forward, and the Oneida leader called his forward. One by one, the men from the two groups were paired up. When he reached Fred, General Knox said, "Fred Roberts," pointing to Fred. The Oneida leader said, "Chetan".

Fred and Chetan nodded at each other, shook hands, and walked to stand together. When all of the patriots and the Oneidas were matched, General Knox announced that the Oneida women now were going to perform a short ceremony to bless the work of the men. The three women walked to their leader, and each presented him with something from the bag they had been carrying. Fred couldn't see everything clearly, but it looked like they presented the leader with three different pieces of fruit. Then each woman walked by the Oneida soldiers and presented each man with a piece of fruit. The men nodded at the women and then turned and gave the fruit to their patriot companion.

"Acha," the men said.

General Knox called out to his men that Acha means friend and that the Oneida's were acknowledging that the patriots were now their friends and brothers. The beautiful woman came close to Fred's companion, Chetan. She gave the fruit to Chetan, and she smiled at him. Chetan smiled back, then turned, smiled at Fred, and gave him the apple. Fred nodded and smiled at Chetan, and then at the beautiful woman, who was still looking at him.

ERNESTINE STIRRED the big cast iron soup pot and looked across the grounds as a group of Indian women walked towards her. She admired their bright headbands and leather garments decorated with feathers and stones. The sun glinted off the silver and turquoise bracelets and necklaces that the women wore in multiples on their arms and around their necks. Their appearance was in stark contrast to hers. A brown homespun dress with no decoration. Her dry and worn hair hid underneath a greasy grey headscarf. She always wished that she had some of the jewelry like the white women had, but she didn't have any, and neither did any slave that she knew of.

The Indians stopped to talk with Hannah Till, the free black woman who cooked for General Washington and who managed the slave women who worked in the kitchen.  Miss Hannah hugged the first, older, woman, and then the other women in the group of five.  Then they turned and headed towards Ernestine.  Ernestine stopped stirring the pot full of that day's supper, stood up, wiped her hands on the apron that laid over her dress and waited.  Miss Hannah approached, smiling.

"Ernestine," said Miss Hannah, "this here is Miss Polly Cooper, of the Oneida Nation, come down to help General Washington and the troops."

Ernestine nodded respectfully and said, "Welcome Miss Polly."

Ernestine flinched with surprise at first when Miss Polly reached out and hugged her, but she smiled as she let herself enjoy the warm friendly human touch that she rarely felt as opposed to the skin-curdling touch of her rapist.

Miss Hannah stuck her arm out toward the group.  "And these here are her girls who have also come to help us.  Let me see if I remember their names.  We have here Adsila, Talise, Onata and Sora."

Ernestine smiled at all of them and nodded as each one was introduced.

"They will be helping us out here with the cooking, helping us cook what we have here, and also teaching us some things about how they cook," Miss Hannah said, as Miss Polly nodded.

"Sora here will be working with you," Miss Hannah said, as she put her hand out to Sora and gently took her hand and led her to Ernestine.  Sora walked forward to Ernestine and smiled at her.  Ernestine immediately felt at ease with this woman who exuded brightness and light.  Ernestine smiled back, opened both arms, as did Sora, and they hugged.

Ernestine then looked at Miss Hannah and said, "I'll go get Sora an apron," as she ran her hand across her apron.  "We can't have her ruining her pretty clothes." Ernestine didn't wait for Hannah to answer. She turned and ran into the cookhouse and came out with the cleanest apron she could find. She handed it to Sora, who smiled as she put it over her head.

"Thank you," said Sora.

"You're welcome," said Ernestine.

"Now you go on and let Sora help you get that soup together," Miss Hannah said.

"Yes, Ma'am," said Ernestine, as she turned to Sora and said, "I look forward to working with you."

Sora smiled, nodded and said, "Yes, I do, too. I want to learn."

With that, the two new friends walked back to the cook stove.

OVER THE next few weeks, Sora helped Ernestine with her work during the day. As the Oneida women and the slave women cooked together, the Oneidas taught the slaves how to use certain foods the way the Oneidas did. The Oneidas especially had many ways to make corn that the slaves didn't. They taught the patriot men not to eat the corn raw because it would make them sick. They taught them many ways to cook the corn.

Sora and Ernestine worked well together. Ernestine was happy that she had a friend, someone her own age who wasn't dragged down by the circumstances of a life that she didn't want to live. Sora wasn't anyone's property. She was a free woman, and everything about how she carried herself showed that. While she enjoyed her days working with Sora, Ernestine dreaded her nights more and more. It seemed like almost every other day now, her tormenter from Virginia would call her out of the slave quarters and take her out back or to the cabin by the stream. Ernestine hated every moment that she was with him, but she resigned herself to it. She knew that she couldn't stop him. She knew that she couldn't fight him off or else she would be beaten or maimed or worse. She didn't want any more black eyes or bruised arms or scratches or bleeding. The only person who suffered was her, not him. In fact, it seemed like he liked the sex with her even more if she fought him or struggled. So she stopped, thinking that maybe that would stop him from coming for her. But, that didn't work. So, she just laid there and let him do his business in her like every slave woman did when a white man decided that he wanted her.

The only man she felt anything for like a normal man was James. The time of the day when she saw him, or usually two or three times, when he came to and left from his work and when he took his lunch break, started to brighten her day. They exchanged the usual pleasantries, and sometimes they had time to say more than a word or two. She knew that he had that look in his eye that he liked her, too. She hadn't seen it much before, but she knew what it looked like, and she certainly knew what it felt like. Just looking at him made her body feel differently than it did when she looked at most men. Most nights when she laid in bed, hoping that her tormenter wasn't going to come, she thought of James, and wished that she could have the normal life with him that she saw Mrs. Washington and the other white women in the camp had with their men. She was a flesh and blood woman, too, just like Mrs. Washington, but she wasn't allowed to feel like Mrs. Washington felt, and she wasn't allowed to love like Mrs. Washington loved. Sometimes the thought of that made her sad, but most times, the thought of that settled on her like it was normal, like fog settling in, a normal part of life, a normal part of a day that was not a bright one.

At night, when the slaves who didn't have to work had time to relax, she'd sit around the campfire with them. She had no interest in any of the other slave men who were there, and, most of them were too tired and beat down to be too interested in her, too. They all were worked hard every single day. She wished that James could come and sit with them someday, sit with her and talk with her, at this time when she had some free time. But, most soldiers had to stay with their regiments at night and couldn't be out roaming around the camp at all hours of the night. The only soldiers who were down at the headquarters area at night were the ones who were assigned down there, like her tormenter. If any other soldiers were down there, it was for a special occasion, like dinner with General Washington and the other generals to celebrate something or the other.

So, this night, like every night, she would take whatever joy she could find from the day and hold on to it as best as she could even if she heard that familiar voice of her tormenter calling her to come out through her cabin door.

OVER THE next three days, Fred and his group of expert marksmen taught the Oneidas a lot of what they knew about shooting and the weapons that they used. The Oneidas were expert with hitting their target, having honed their skills with bows and arrows, which were less precise in the hands of most of the patriots, but just about as precise and deadly in the Oneida's hands.

Fred enjoyed working with Chetan. He spoke some English and understood more words of English than Fred originally thought. Chetan was a quick study with the guns, so much so that when they had finished their drills and Chetan hit all his targets, there were always a few minutes a day where Chetan could teach Fred how to improve his own skills on the bow and arrow. As much as Fred liked learning about weapons and hunting, that was not the high point of his day. That came when the Oneida women walked up with the men's noon day meal.

Fred took his eyes off his assignments as much as he could when he caught a glimpse of the women walking up the open field. The silver jewelry that they had draped around their necks, waists, wrists, and hanging from their hair and ears glistened in the sun when they approached. Even the slightest wind would blow their long, dark hair, so that it fanned out behind them as they walked. Most of the women were beautiful, Fred thought, but Sora was the most beautiful of all. And, good for Fred, she brought lunch to Chetan every day.

As he was going through yet another drill with Chetan, Fred caught that familiar glistening coming across the field. He said to Chetan, "You've done well again, my friend. I think we are finished for now. Besides, here comes your lunch."

Chetan turned around to see the women walking across the field. He had noticed the smile on Fred's face when he said "lunch".

The women walked to the edge of the practice area and waited until the head of the Oneida contingent raised his hand and motioned for them to come closer. The women acknowledged the raised hand and walked towards the men that they were serving.

Sora walked over towards Chetan and Fred. Chetan smiled and greeted her in the Oneida language. Fred smiled at Sora and said, "Hello." Sora smiled back.

Fred said, "Nice day that we're having today."

Sora smiled and said, "Yes, it is."

Then she nodded her head as if almost bowing and walked away with the rest of the women. Fred leaned on his musket and watched her intently as she walked away.

Fred thought about her the rest of the day, as they drilled and drilled. Even when everyone—the Oneidas and the patriots—hit all of their targets, they continued to drill. That was unusual. Even though he enjoyed the sun and warm air that day, he couldn't help but think that winter had ended and soon would their respite from war.

"LOOKS LIKE we have little more meat in the stew tonight," Fred said, as he watched the soldier spoon stew into his bowl.

"Maybe we got some food in from the French," his hut mate said.

"Viva la France," said Fred, laughing.

They sat down and quickly devoured the stew, savoring the taste of the beef.

As soon as they finished, which didn't take them long, Captain Bartholomew called them all together.

"Men," he said. "I trust you ate hearty tonight."

The men called out, "Sure did." "Yes, sir."

"Good," said the captain. "You will need your strength, at least most of you."

Oh no, thought Fred. Before he could finish his thought, even to himself, there was commotion in the camp.

"Make way. Make way," various soldiers yelled.

The sound of horses grew louder. The men looked towards them and again saw the familiar white horse of General Wayne. Joining him this time was another general. Fred normally couldn't tell which one until he got closer, but the louder the horse hoofs sounded, so did the louder the sound of "Vive la France."

"Lafayette," Fred said out loud to no one in particular.

"It must be," said Daniel as they both stood at attention.

General Wayne held his musket up in the air and said, "Evening Men."

The men called back, "Evening General".

General Wayne said, "Men. I am pleased to have with me today one of our finest generals and a true friend of the patriot cause, the General the Marquis de Lafayette."

"Vive la France." "Huzzah!" The men cheered.

General Lafayette smiled and took in the cheers. After about a minute or two, he raised his hands and gestured for them to quiet down. They did.

"Merci. Thank you," Lafayette said.

General Wayne said, "Men, you know as well as I do that we all owe General Lafayette a debt for all that he has done for our cause on the ground here and in his correspondence, convincing his government to also join our cause."

The men clapped. Wayne hushed them with his hands.

"And, we know that General Lafayette distinguished himself with a strong show of bravery on September 11, 1777, when we fought the British in the Battle of the Brandywine. He took a bullet in his leg for us, men," Wayne said, as he shook Lafayette's hand. "And now, General Washington has seen fit to assign General Lafayette to lead an important mission." Wayne paused for a moment to let that sink in. "We all know that our army will be on the march soon since winter is over. But, we have gotten some intelligence that the British Army is already on the march. We need to have better intelligence of what those dirty, filthy redcoats are doing." He paused to let that sink in, too. "So, General Washington has asked General Lafayette to lead a party of men to go closer to the British camp and report back. We believe that they may be forming to attack us here at Valley Forge or leave our precious national capital and high tail it on back to that traitorous city of New York." Wayne looked around. "And, since you men know the area, many of you will be assigned to go with General Lafayette. He needs the best of the best—scouts, shooters, everything."

Wayne continued, "You will join General Lafayette and some of the finest troops in the Continental Army and the Militia. And, you will be joined by some of our allies from the Oneida Indian nation."

"Oh," said Fred to himself. "That explains it."

"So," said General Wayne, "when the captain calls your name, I want you to go to your huts, grab your gear, and then line up behind General Lafayette. Then you will go with him, spy on those damnned redcoats, and help turn the course of this war," he said, lifting his musket up in the air.

"Huzzah!" the men cheered.

Captain Bartholomew stepped forward. He started calling the names. "Fred Roberts. Daniel Welburn. James Weldon."

Fred and his hut mates walked away from the line one-by-one.

"Well, we knew something was coming," Fred said.

"Yeah," said Daniel.

"We knew we'd have to leave here one day," James said, "and it looks like today is the day."

"I guess that's what all that drilling with the Oneida Indians was all about last week that my group was involved in," Fred said.

"Sounds like it," said Daniel. "So, whatever else is going on, it sounds like it's happening on grounds that we know something about."

"Sure does," said James.

"That could be anywhere around here," Fred said, as they walked inside their hut.

They gathered up their backpacks and filled them with the provisions that they were taught to fill them with any time that they went out on patrol. They picked up their muskets and quickly checked them to make sure that everything was working.

"I guess we'll get the musket balls and buck shot later," James said, knowing that none of them really had enough if they encountered any redcoats.

"I'm sure the generals won't send us out there unprepared," Daniel said.

"Let's hope not," James said.

Fred paused to look around at the hut. "This hut isn't much but it's been our home for the past three months," he sighed. "As much as I wanted to get out of there, I sure hope that I get to return here," as slight tears welled up in his eyes with the realization of what they were all leaving behind and what they might all be walking into.

"You've got that right," said James, as he looked around. A chill came over him, and he closed his eyes.

Daniel felt the mood in the hut change, and he knew that his mood changed, too.

He looked at James, who had already meant so much to him, and then at Fred, who grew to mean so much to him. "Before we walk out there, fellows, can we just say a short prayer? I couldn't wait to get the hell out of here, either, but now I think we need to pray to God that we come back."

"Go right ahead," Fred said.

They all took their caps off and bowed their heads.

"Dear Lord," Daniel said. "Thank you for keeping us safe thus far as we undertook this journey of freedom. Please continue to keep us safe in your arms as we leave this place, our home away from home, and continue our quest for freedom." Daniel wiped his eyes. "Amen," he said softly.

"Amen," said James, as he wiped his eyes and put his cap back on his head.

"Amen," said Fred, as he opened his eyes and looked up to the heavens.

FRED, DANIEL, and James joined the other men from the Pennsylvania regiments behind Lafayette. General Wayne shook all of his men's hands, going down the line one-by-one, until Captain Bartholomew confirmed that they were all lined up.

Then Wayne said, "Men, I couldn't be more proud of you than if I was leading you into battle myself. I know that you will bring honor and glory to the Pennsylvania regiments." He looked at Lafayette. "General, these are some of our finest men. They will do you proud. I know that you will command them with great skill and honor."

Wayne paused to look at all of his men lined up, ready to enter God knows what might await them, in service of their new country. Wayne looked at his troops and said, "Men, today, I salute you," and he raised his arm in salute. He looked at Lafayette and saluted him. "God speed my friend," he said.

The General the Marquis de Lafayette saluted Wayne and turned to the men who were now his men. "Men," he said, "Attention."

The men stood up straight at attention.

"Let us go collect the rest of your compatriots."

They saluted the General and walked behind him as he rode off toward the next regiment.

LAFAYETTE STOPPED by Poor's New Hampshire Brigade, Captain McLean's Light Troops, the West Virginia regiments, and the Pennsylvania Militia as the scene with General Wayne was played out with the other generals that commanded the other regiments that would make up Lafayette's reconnaissance army. Then they reached the part of camp where the Oneida nation held camp.

Lafayette rode up to the edge of the camp where Han Yerry, leader of the Oneida contingent, was waiting. But not waiting alone. What looked to be the entire Oneida compliment of fifty soldiers stood at attention, watching Lafayette—the general representing not just one, but two, nations—riding up to greet the leader that was representing their nation. The silver, feathers, leather of all colors, and turquoise gleaming in the sun was a bright and beautiful sight.

"Wow," Fred said to James, as they marched along. "They sure know how to show out."

"Beautiful," said James, as he admired his brown brothers and sisters in their silver, turquoise-colored leather, and feathers blowing in the wind and glistening in the sun.

The men were lined up in rows in the middle, and the few women were lined up in a row on the side. Fred lengthened his neck so he could see Sora. He figured that Chetan and the other Oneidas they trained would be a part of their group. He wanted to see Sora again, and he wanted Sora to see that he was a great soldier, or warrior, selected by their great warriors for this great responsibility. As they marched closer, Fred saw her. On the end. Luckily, the men from the Pennsylvania regiments were the first ones picked up, so Fred and his friends were in the front.

As they marched behind Lafayette, Lafayette saluted Han Yerry. Yerry nodded and saluted back.

Yerry said, "General, we have 50 of our finest men to go with you today. These men were already our finest with the bow and arrow. Thanks to the training of your men, these men are now the finest with the musket."

"Thank you, Monsieur Yerry," said Lafayette, "on behalf of General George Washington."

Yerry nodded. Then he stepped to the side and held his arm out. One warrior stepped forward. "This is Daniel Teouneslees, the son of our great Chief Shenandoah. He will lead our men under your command."

Daniel nodded at Lafayette and saluted him. He turned towards his men and said something to them in their language. As he did, the men walked forward and took their place in line behind the other soldiers.

Chetan caught Fred's eye as he marched past him, and both nodded and smiled. Then Fred looked up and over at Sora, who was looking at them. He nodded and smiled at her. She smiled back. Fred looked at her directly in the eyes and felt their souls connect.

He smiled slightly and then said softly, "I'll be back." He knew she couldn't hear him, but he sensed that she understood him. She raised her hand to her lips, touched the middle of a few fingers with her lips like she was kissing them, turned her hand so that her fingers and wrist faced him, and then tenderly placed her fingers over her heart and left them there for a few seconds.

Fred felt a shiver move through him. He smiled at her again. He raised his fingers to his lips as if he were kissing them, turned his hand towards her, and then laid his fingers across his heart.

They smiled at each other once again as Fred marched on with the rest of his group.

# CHAPTER 68
# GERMANTOWN

Connie opened her eyes and immediately sighed. Another day of being a prisoner in her own house. She stretched both arms and swung her feet around to touch the floor.

"At least the birds are happy," she said to herself as she heard the sounds outside of her window.

Then she heard the sounds that she had come to dread. The British accents of the redcoats who stood outside, day and night, right under her window.

"Hell," she said as she stretched her legs and walked over to the window. She looked down at them, standing there, at ease, chatting among themselves, not caring that their loud voices would wake up her or any of her girls who worked just as hard as they did before "the home invasion," as they called it.

Connie stuck her head out of the window and yelled down, "Good morning." She smiled as they turned around to face her in the window. She always leaned over some so that the cleavage and her bountiful breasts were on full display. She leaned her elbows on the window sill, put her head between her hands and said, "Beautiful day, isn't it?"

The soldiers called back, "Yes, good morning, ma'am. Yes, it is a beautiful morning."

Connie stretched her arms out fully to either side, which made her breasts separate and point upward, and faked a yawn.

The soldiers smiled.

"Well, I'd better get out of these bedclothes and change into something decent," she said as she smiled and flipped her hair. "I'll see you when I get down there," she said, as she waved goodbye and turned. She sighed softly and rolled her eyes. Even though she hated everything British now more than she ever did, she still had to be friendly to the guards. She truly believed that one day her captors would soften, including the general, because every man she ever wanted to soften eventually had. This was just taking a little longer than usual, but one day without her freedom was long enough.

Connie walked over to her wardrobe, opened it, and looked at all of her beautiful dresses. "Which one will do the trick?" she asked herself. Surely one dress would cause the general to change his mind or one of those guards to slip up for long enough for her to get out of there and get home and warn her family that the British were on to them so that they didn't come back into Germantown or Philadelphia again.

She had worn just about every red dress since the occupation began, but to no effect. Sure, she received the usual compliments from the general when he came to visit. But she couldn't get him to loosen up or call off the guards. She fingered some other dresses, thinking that she'd never seen a tight red dress not get her what she wanted. She stopped when she came to a light blue dress with ivory silk. It was beautiful, like all of her dresses, and, of course, she looked good in it.

"What the hell," she said, as she pulled it out of the wardrobe and held it up on a hanger to examine it. "Maybe blue will be my lucky color." She dropped down the straps on her night gown and let it fall to the floor. She lifted it up gently and laid it on the bed. Then she gently took the blue dress off the hanger. She unbuttoned the small white pearl buttons in the front and stepped into the full skirt. She pulled the skirt up past her ample hips and started buttoning the buttons. A lot of women liked the buttons in the back, but Connie never did. She liked them in the front. She was as independent about her dressing as she was about anything else. She could button her own dress when the buttons were in the front. And, she could unbutton them easily, too, when she wanted to. Or, if she wanted one of her clients to unbutton her dress, he could do that while her eyes, hands, or lips also engaged him in any way that she wanted. She didn't want to have to depend on a man for anything.

When she buttoned the last button, she put her hands on the outside of her breasts and arranged them just the way she liked it. Tight cleavage with a little spillage over the top. She walked over to her vanity and picked up her tortoise shell hairbrush and ran it through her hair a few times. Then she bent over and flipped her head back up to separate the strands. She fluffed the ends with her hands, looked into the mirror, smiled, and said, "Perfect."

"Good morning, ladies," she said as she stepped in to the hall. The guards had awakened her girls, too. They were walking from room to room in various stages of dress or undress, getting ready for the day.

"Maybe today will be the day," Connie said, whispering and smiling. She said that every day since the invasion began.

"Maybe, Miss Connie," one of the girls said. "Here's hoping."

They were all tired of the occupation. Besides their usual work of fulfilling men's fantasies and desires, all they could do was walk outside and sit in the garden. They were getting as tired of just looking at each other and their customers as Connie was. But, all Connie could say was, "Be patient. This can't last forever."

Connie walked down in to the kitchen and knocked on the back door. Tom rose from where he sat outside, watching the carriages and horses ride by down the hill on the road by the Wissahickon.

"Good morning, Miss," he said, as he walked inside. "How are you this morning?"

Connie shrugged and raised an eyebrow. "Same as always. They're still here," she said.

"Yeah, that's right," Tom said. Then he walked closer to her and said, "I don't know what's going on, but there sure is a lot more activity on the road by the Wissahickon today."

"Already?" Connie said. "It's not even 9 o'clock."

"I know," said Tom. He whispered, "I don't know what those redcoats have in mind, but it looks like more of them are on the move today."

Connie looked into Tom's eyes, searching for answers. Not finding any, she walked outside herself. The view to the road wasn't as clear as it used to be because many of the spring leaves had filled in, but Connie could still see large swaths of the road. And, Tom was right. There were more groups of redcoats on the move than she had seen in quite some time. They were on foot, on horse, in carriages and in wagons. She watched and grew worried as everybody on the road seemed to be moving north— towards the Valley Forge.

Connie turned and hurried back inside. She looked at Tom. "You're right. Something's going on."

Tom looked back at her, equally serious. "I'm going to say a prayer for our boys."

Connie threw her hands up in the air and said, "It seems like that's all that we can do. Pray for them."

She wrung her hands on her dress. "I came down here to eat and get this godforsaken day started, and now, this." She paced around the kitchen. "I can't concentrate. And, I sure as hell can't eat." She paced around the kitchen a few times. She felt like a caged animal, which she was. "I can't stand to be cooped up in this house one more minute" she said. She took Tom's hand, "Come on, let's go outside. At least we can walk around."

Connie practically pulled Tom through the house and to the front door. She threw opened the front door and looked to the right, by the lamp post, where the guards stood. They weren't there. She looked to the left, by the rose garden, where they liked to stand, too, and they weren't there. She looked at Tom. "Where are they?" she asked, like he knew.

"I don't know," said Tom. He looked way down the walkway and the front yard to the gate by the Germantown Road. There were no patches of red to be seen, at least not in their yard. They weren't there either, guarding the front gate like they often did.

"Maybe they went around the back while we were walking through the house," she said.

"They'd have to be moving pretty fast," said Tom, "but I'll go back there and look."

Tom ran back down the side of the house. He looked around and ran around, even close to the edge of the property where the woods began, but he didn't see them. He ran around to the front to Connie.

"I don't see them," Tom said.

Connie's eyes widened. "They're not here? Do you think they've left us?"

Tom turned his body around, turning his head and looking from side to side. "I think so, Miss. I don't see them."

"Go look in the barn with the horses and carriage," Connie said, getting excited.

Tom ran over to the small barn where they kept their horses and carriage. He looked around, and even called out, "Sirs? Sirs? Are you here?" When he heard and saw nothing but four-legged animals, Tom ran back to Connie.

"They're not there, Miss," he said.

Connie lifted up her skirt and ran towards the front gate. Tom ran right beside her.

She stopped at the gate and looked at either side. No redcoats there. No guards anywhere. She opened the gate and ran out into the Germantown Road. She looked down the road, and then she saw it. A sea of redcoats moving in her direction from a few miles down. They stirred up the dirt on the street into a cloud of dust. And the noise.

Connie turned towards Tom. "They're headed towards the Valley Forge," she said. "And by the looks of what's coming up the street, it looks like it's just about all of them."

Tom frowned and said, "I think you're right, miss."

Connie looked down the street again as the dust cloud caused by an army on the march came closer.

"This is my chance," she said. "I've got to get out of here and warn them."

Tom squinted. He knew there was no stopping her, but he wondered how she was going to make it up the road fast enough to avoid the redcoats seeing and capturing her.

"I'll get the horses," he said.

"Horse," said Connie. "I'm going alone."

Tom grabbed her arms. "Miss, you can't do that yourself. I'll go with you. You'll need my help."

"No," said Connie. "You stay here with the girls and watch the place."

"Suzie can take care of it," Tom said. "She's done it before."

"I know," said Connie, "but this is different."

"Not as far as I'm concerned," said Tom. "You need me."

Connie looked Tom straight in the eyes. As confident as she was and felt, she couldn't deny that she might need Tom's help to get up the street.

"Fine," she said. "You can go with me, but let's get going. I just need to let Suzie and the ladies know what's going on and grab my bag and get some money. You go get the horses." She grabbed his arm, and they both ran.

Connie flung open the front door. "Girls! Suzie!" she called out. "Come on down here now! The guards have left, but the redcoats are coming en masse."

One by one, the girls ran into the parlor. "Wait here until I grab my bag," she said to them as they gathered. Connie ran up the stairs to her bedroom. She lifted up a loose floor board and flung open the small trunk that she kept hidden there. She reached in and grabbed a leather pouch where she kept the money that she worked so hard to earn. Then she reached into her dresser drawer and took out the cloth pouch that she could strap under her dress and hide everything she was carrying. Years of walking the rough streets of Philadelphia when she first started working for Madam taught her how to hide everything she wanted to carry. She put the leather pouch in to the cloth pouch and then quickly strapped the pouch around her middle section and secured it. Then she ran down the steps.

All of the girls were gathered.

"Ladies," said Connie. "Our guards have just left us, but that's because the redcoats are on the march. They're a few miles down the Germantown road, but it looks like the whole redcoat army is headed up the street. I'm sure they're headed up towards the Valley Forge where our boys are."

"Now, I know that you all hate the redcoats as much as I do," she said. The girls nodded.

"Tom and I are going to make our way up the Germantown Road and warn our boys. And, you know I've been wanting to get out of here and go to Paoli and warn my family to not come down here."

"So, that's what we're going to do," she said as she looked around. "Suzie," she said, "I'm leaving you in charge," she said, as she took Suzie's hand. "You girls know what to do," she said, looking at all of them. "But," she said, "I don't know when I'll be back. " She waited a few seconds as she let her eyes go from woman to woman who had become like her family. "You all are welcome to stay, but if any of you want to go, now or later, I understand," she said.

The girls all looked at her. She felt a tear coming to her eyes. "I've never known a finer group of ladies," she said. "If you leave, let Suzie know where I can find you. And, Suzie, you know how to contact me."

Tom ran inside, "Miss, we've got to go. They're getting too close."

Connie looked at him and said, "Yes." She moved from girl to girl, giving each a quick hug. By the time she got to Suzie, the tears that she had tried to hold back were falling.

"Stay safe," Suzie said, as her tears flowed. "I'll be here when you get back. Whenever that is."

Connie hugged her. "I know you will," she said. "I love you, Suzie."

Suzie said, "I love you, too," as she hugged her. "Now go and warn our boys."

Connie stepped back and ended the hug, took a good look at Suzie, turned and looked at all of the girls, and said, "Till we meet again."

"Till we meet again," yelled the girls, as they let their tears flow, too.


Tom had two of their strongest horses right outside the door, saddled and ready. He helped Connie climb on top of hers, and she got herself situated for a long, hard ride. Tom jumped on top of his horse, turned towards Connie, and said, "Ready, Miss?"

Connie said, "Ready."

Tom handed her one of the two pistols that he was carrying. "Here," he said.

"Thanks," said Connie.

"We'll stay on the road as much as we can," said Tom, "but if we see any of their pickets, we'll have to go through the woods."

"Got it," said Connie.

"So just follow me," Tom said.

They kicked the horses with their spurs, and the horses took off through the open gate onto the Germantown Road.  They both looked down the road, saw the dust clouds and the sea of red and white, and kicked their horses even harder as they tore off up the Germantown Road.

CONNIE AND Tom rode hard up the Germantown Road.  Luckily, the redcoat pickets weren't hard to spot.  And luckily, Tom had traveled up and down that road and the woods in between so many times that he knew the road and the trails.  As they rode closer to the edge of Germantown, they had to turn off the road and go through the horse trails hidden deep in the woods.  That slowed them down a bit, but they made steady progress until they came to the stream that basically separated Germantown from Whitemarsh.  Luckily, the May showers had been few so far, so the stream wasn't that high.  Still, Connie grabbed the skirt of her dress and shoved it under her behind so that it didn't get too wet.

"Let's go," said Connie, once she was ready.

They kicked their horses, which flew across the stream as fast as they could.  Tom had picked a crossing that wasn't so full of riverbed stones.

Once they crossed the stream, Tom said, "I think we should stay on these back trails, Miss, until we get to the road leading to the Matson Ford."

"Fine," Connie said, as she followed Tom and his horse.

Tom and Connie rode hard but carefully.

"Here we are," Tom said, as he led his horse out of the woods and onto the road leading to the road that led to the Matson Ford and the Continental Army pickets.  Just as they were emerging from the woods and ready to get onto Barren Hill Road, they saw them.  A group of pickets in blue uniforms.  And brown uniforms.  And Indians in war dress.

Tom and Connie looked at each other.  They had already reached the outer line of the Continental Army.

"Let me approach first," Connie said. "They're not as likely to shoot a woman."

Connie maneuvered her horse in front of Tom's and slowly came out of the woods.

"We are patriots!" she yelled. "We come to warn you!" she yelled. "The British Army is coming up the Germantown Road, and it looks like there's thousands of them."

As she yelled, a few of the pickets approached on their horses, muskets drawn.

"I said we are patriots, coming to warn you that thousands of redcoats are on their way up the Germantown Road."

Three of the soldiers surrounded Tom and Connie with their horses. One of them said, "What did you say?"

Connie repeated herself, "I said that thousands of redcoats are on the march up the Germantown Road, right now."

Two of the pickets took off and headed down the road.

The other three looked at Tom and Connie and said, "Where did you come from?"

"Further down the Germantown Road, in Germantown. I live there," she said.

"And you're patriots?" one asked.

"Yes," said Connie. "My name is Connie Roberts. I'm from Paoli. My brothers Fred and Allen fought with General Wayne's 5th Pennsylvania Regiment. My brother Allen was killed in the Paoli Massacre last year. My brother Fred was still fighting with General Wayne, as far as I knew, last year."

Both men squinted as they looked over Connie and Tom.

One of the soldiers said, "Come with me." He turned his horse in the opposite direction as he rode off towards the church that was a few hundred yards behind him.

Connie and Tom followed behind him.

When they reached the stone fence surrounding St. Peter's Lutheran Church, there was another group of soldiers there, milling about, some looking towards the road, at the ready, others loading and cleaning their guns. The soldier who they followed called out, "Fred Roberts, 5th Pennsylvania."

Fred heard his name, called out and raised his hand before he could turn around. "Here," he answered. He turned around, as the soldier asked, "Is this your sister?"

Fred looked up and saw Connie, sitting straight up in her horse, hair flying in the wind, looking worn but as beautiful as he had ever seen her.

"Yes, it is. Connie," he said. Fred ran over to Connie, and lifted her out of her saddle. He hugged her and spun her around.

"So you're alive!" Connie said, as she buried her head into the crook of his neck.

"We didn't know," she said, as she cried.

Fred stepped back, "Yes, yes. I'm alive and fine. You are a sight for sore eyes" he said. "But what are you doing here?"

"We were on our way to the Valley Forge to warn our boys that the redcoat army is marching up the Germantown Road. We think they're going to attack you boys."

Fred said, "My God." He noticed other men in his group riding back and forth in front of the church and up and down the road.

"Get in here," he said, to her as he took her horse's reins and headed behind the fence.

"And my house man, too," Connie said, as she pointed to Tom.

"Him, too," Fred said, as Tom jumped off his horse and followed Fred.

"What are you doing here?" Connie asked. "Why aren't you at the Valley Forge?"

"Because I'm in this special group led by General Lafayette that was sent out to see if what our intelligence had heard was truly true. That the redcoats were going to attack our army at Valley Forge," he said.

By now, the pickets had verified what Connie and Tom had said. The redcoats were truly headed in their direction.

"Everyone in position," their commander yelled. "Wait for further orders."

The soldiers around them were running here and there, loading their guns, putting cannons in place, and fortifying the church.

"Sharpshooters, get inside," a sergeant yelled.

"You come with me," Fred said, as he gathered a few more guns and ammunition and headed inside the church.

Once they were inside, Connie noticed that there was quite a collection of different uniforms with colors even more different than what they saw outside with the pickets. There was blue, green, brown, tan homespun and the coonskin caps that men wore in the wilderness.

"The men in this group come from all over," Fred said, as he noticed Connie looking around, eyes wide. "West Virginia, Pennsylvania, New Hampshire, Delaware. We're the best in our regiments at sharpshooting, strategy, everything."

"Oh," said Connie, the fear in her voice evident.

"Don't be afraid, Connie," Fred said. "We are the best of the best. And, you know I'm not going to let anything happen to you. Especially now that I've found you again. Or should I say, that you've found me," he said with a smile.

Connie squeezed his hand. "I know," she said. "I feel safe with you. My, look how my little brother has grown up."

Fred smiled. "And my other bunk mates are here, too," he said, pointing over at James and Daniel. "They grew up in this area, down near Matson's Ford. They know these hills like the back of their hands. They're not in the top sharpshooter group like me, but they're pretty good, and they know all the hiding places around here," he said. Then he pointed over at the Oneidas. "And over there we have the Oneida Indians. They are some of the finest warriors I've ever met, and they know how to track and hunt and get around outdoors better than we could even hope to," he said. He patted Connie on the shoulder. "So don't worry," he said. "The best of the best is here."

Connie looked around at all of the soldiers now filling the church. The men's uniforms looked well-worn and somewhat rag tag, but one man stood out. He wore clean blue and white with the shiny brass buttons of an officer. He was talking with other men, some in clean uniforms, most with more decoration on them than the men around them. She noticed that he looked up and over at her and Tom often. She looked over, too, hoping to catch his gaze. She could see that he was an attractive man. He conferred with the other men, and then he dispersed with the rest of them. She just sat there with Tom and Fred, still. The man approached them.

Fred jumped up on his feet and stood at attention. "General," he saluted.

"At ease," General Lafayette said.

"What is this soldier?" Lafayette asked. "Who is this beautiful lady and this man?"

"This is my sister, Connie," Fred said. "And this is her house man, Tom. They rode up the Germantown Road from their house in Germantown to warn the army at Valley Forge that thousands of redcoats were marching towards us up the Germantown Road."

"Is that true?" said Lafayette, as he looked at Connie.

"That's true, General," said Connie, with a serious tone, not yet sure that a smile was in order.

"Then we thank you for your patriotism and dedication to our cause," Lafayette said.

"But I must ask you and your man to stay in one of these interior rooms," he said, as he pointed to a small group of rooms, "while your brother and our men here figure out what we need to do to fight off these redcoats."

Fred looked at Connie, who was looking at him. "I beg your pardon, General, but my sister and her man are good shooters, too. And, I just promised her that I would protect her," Fred paused for a minute while Lafayette looked at them both. "We lost our other brother at Paoli, and she just found out that I'm alive. I will keep us all safe, General, and do my duty, but I know my head will be clearer if she can stay near me."

Lafayette looked over at Connie. "I can't risk this beautiful lady's life, now that she is under my charge here," he said.

"General," said Connie. "I beg your indulgence. But, I know how to take care of myself, and I've done so in many situations. And my man, Tom here, has done the same. I think we can be helpful to Fred and to you."

Lafayette looked Connie up and down. "So you say you know how to take care of yourself?"

"I do," said Connie, confidently.

"Well, then, if you are anything like your brother, I believe you," he said.

"Thank you, General," said Connie.

Lafayette smiled and looked Connie straight in the eyes. "You can thank me later," he said.

Connie smiled. "I look forward to that."

"I do, too," said Lafayette, as he took her hand and kissed it, in that French way. And then he walked off.

Fred laughed. "You've still got it," he said.

"Thank God," said Connie. "Sometimes it comes in really handy."

"Well, let's see if you have to use that against these redcoats or if you have to use one of these muskets," he said, pointing to one lying on the floor.

"Either one," said Connie. "I'm prepared."

"I know you are," said Fred, "now let's listen for our orders," he said, as the lieutenant in charge of their division stepped forward to give orders.

CAPTAIN ALLEN McLane, commander of McLane's Partisans, looked out over the group of brave soldiers gathered in the church basement. If any group of soldiers could keep the British army at bay, it was this group, he thought. But it wouldn't be easy. Their scouts now said that some 8000 redcoats, the bulk of the British Army in Philadelphia, were at the edge of and all along the Germantown Road, waiting to strike. Those redcoats could easily over run the 2000 patriots who were holed up in the church and on the roads and woods nearby. If the British overran those patriots, they would be on to Valley Forge in no time. General Lafayette thought that the best thing they could do was to make the British think that there were more patriots around the church than there were, create a diversion to hold them off, and buy some time so they could retreat back to Valley Forge and alert General Washington and the rest of the army to prepare for an attack.

"Alright men," Captain McLane said. "General Lafayette wants the sharp shooters to line the perimeter of the church, behind the stone fence, and be prepared to shoot as many rounds as possible and as fast as possible. We need to make them think that there's more of us than there are."

He continued, "The sharpshooters will have to stay in place all night. In the meantime, James and Daniel, you will plan an escape route since you know these hills, and you will have a division of the West Virginia boys with you."

James and Daniel said in unison, "Yes, sir," and looked over at the West Virginia soldiers that were huddled close to them.

"Now," said the Captain, "if all of this fails, the Oneidas will create a diversion with their war whoops, drums, and screams that would curdle the blood of even the most hardened man. We hope that would scare some of the redcoats off or at least cause them to think twice about attacking and at least slow them down."

"Any questions men?" McLane asked.

The men just looked straight ahead. No one had any questions. They understood their orders. They understood the situation that they were in. They understood that this could be their last day on earth.

Fred looked over at Connie. "Look Connie," he said, touching her hand. "I know I said that you could stay with me, but I don't think you should be outside with us all night. I think you should stay inside here."

Connie shook her head and said, "Absolutely not." She squeezed his hand. "I'm going where you're going. I lost you once, and I'm not going to lose you again. And, whatever happens out there, tonight or any time, we'll be together."

Fred looked at her as his eyes watered. "You're also as stubborn as ever, and I know it's pointless to try to change your mind."

Connie said, "You're right." Then she looked over at Tom and said, "And besides, Tom is one of the best shooters I know. Why do you think I've kept him on all of these years?"

Tom looked at Connie and smiled. "Yes, missus. You're right." He knew that she kept him on for so many reasons, not the least of which was his skill with a musket, and he also knew that if the evening was going to put either of them in death's path, they'd also want to be together.

Captain McLane looked around at the group and realized that he might never see any of them alive again. He said, "Men, you are some of the finest soldiers that we have at Valley Forge. That's why you are here. Now let's go on out there and make General Washington proud." He saluted the men, and they saluted him back. He turned his back and led his men outside.

FRED, CONNIE and Tom took up position behind the stone fence. The quartermaster on site gave Connie and Tom extra ammunition, for themselves and for Fred. He knew Fred from their sharpshooter training, and he knew that he was one of the fastest and best marksmen, so he knew that if anyone could shoot off extra rounds, it would be Fred.

Luckily, the May air was slightly warm. Connie let her shawl hang loosely from her shoulders as she sat cross legged on the ground behind Fred. Tom took up position right next to Fred. And Fred sat on the ground, knees up, but gun aimed straight ahead.

They sat like that all night, ready to shoot or run at the slightest movement or order. But neither happened. No warnings that the redcoats were approaching. No orders to retreat. The sun rose in the east like any other day, and they were still in position, tired and sore from sitting out all night, but still alive.

The quartermaster's soldiers came around shortly after sun rise with a cup of water and a hardtack biscuit for everyone. The soldiers hurried up and gulped down the water and swallowed the biscuit. Everyone went back to waiting on high alert.

# CHAPTER 69

# REBEL HILL/THE GULPH

James and Daniel had spent the night on the hill, near James' cabin at the Gulph. That was the farthest most point of the escape path that they made sure was clear between the Barren Hill church and the patriot pickets at their post at the bottom of the hill by the Gulph Mill.

The West Virginians lined the path back towards the church as pickets.

James watched the sun rise from the top of the hill, turned to the east, toward the Matson Ford. Daniel was on post right beside him.

"Well, I guess the Brits didn't attack last night," James said.

"Thank God," said Daniel. "Let's hope that we can get our boys out of there before they do."

"Yeah," said James. "I think this will be a busy day."

Daniel looked at his old friend and laughed. "You think?"

James laughed, too. Just as he was about to say something, James heard the hooves of what sounded to him like ten to twenty horses riding quickly down the still hardened road by the Gulph Mill. He jumped up and ran over to the edge of the hill and looked down. He was right. And he was surprised. He ran back over to where Daniel was now standing up, hair on edge, wondering what was going on.

"You're not going to believe it," James said to Daniel as he ran over to him.

"What?" Daniel asked.

"You'll see," James said.

Daniel pulled his musket closer. James put his hand up.

"You won't need that," James said, as the sound of the horses hooves grew louder.

Both James and Daniel stood and watched the first soldiers ride up. It was an advance guard of three soldiers. Behind them was another guard of three. And, then, behind them, there he was. General Washington, resplendent in his blue and white uniform, on a white horse.

James and Daniel stood at attention and saluted as the advance guard approached, led by Lieutenant Colonel Aaron Burr, commander of the picket post at the bottom of the hill.

"At ease men," Commander Burr said. "I understand that you are James Weldon and Daniel Welburn."

"Yes, sir," they both said.

"Very good," said Burr. "I understand that you men lived right here in these hills."

"Yes, sir," they both said again.

"Yes," said Burr, "and that you've used your knowledge of these hills to lay out an escape path for our boys holed up at Barren Hill."

"Yes, sir," they said again, in unison.

"Very good," said Burr. Then he added, "Well, what you boys have done is very important, and we thank you for your service. "

"Yes, sir," they said, both watching General Washington over Commander Burr's shoulder as Washington's horse halted behind him.

"General Washington is very concerned about General Lafayette and all of our boys over there. So much so that he felt it necessary to come here himself and see what was going on over there as best as he could since it was he who sent General Lafayette and the boys over there to spy on the British," Burr said.

"Yes, sir," James and Daniel said, not knowing what else to say or think.

Burr continued. "Yes, and what we need you boys to do is to escort General Washington to the highest spot in these hills where he can see over to Barren Hill, the Matson's Ford, and this entire area, so he can see if our boys are safely retreating or if the redcoats are coming," he said. "This particular mission is so important to the General, he did not want to depend on our regular network of pickets to see and report back to him. He wants to see for himself."

James and Daniel looked over at Washington. "Yes, sir," they said.

"Now, can you lead our party?"

James and Daniels looked at each other. "Yes, sir," they said.

Daniel continued, "Yes, Lieutenant Burr, we will have to lead you on foot because we don't have our horses."

Burr said, "Yes, our intelligence has told us that." Then he pointed behind him. "We've brought two horses for you."

"Come forward," Burr yelled. A soldier leading two horses slowly road forward, past General Washington. James and Daniel moved forward and jumped up on the horses. They looked at Burr, and Daniel said, "Commander, please follow us." James and Daniel looked at each other as they pulled on the horses' reins and rode off.

James and Daniel led their important party down the path that they had selected. The West Virginia boys who lined the path were as surprised as James and Daniel were when they saw General Washington as part of the party. The path first went down the hill slightly until it turned to the left and led up to the high points of the hills. The view from the hills was as spectacular and wide-ranging as always.

The West Virginia boys sent one of their own to go ahead of James and Daniel, and he told each one along the path to clear a wider path so the tree limbs didn't hit General Washington and his party. After about ten minutes of slow and steady riding, it was clear that they reached the highest point on the Hills.  Daniel turned to Commander Burr behind him and James and said, "This is it, sir.  The highest point."

Burr held up his hand to stop the party behind him, and said as he turned his horse around so he could see all directions around him, "Yes, I see that it is."  Then he rode back to General Washington.  James and Daniel watched as Burr and Washington engaged in a short conversation.  Then Burr rode back towards Daniel and James, with Washington right behind him.  James and Daniels' eyes widened as General Washington rode his horse and stopped right in front of them.  They both saluted, and Washington saluted them back.

"At ease, men," General Washington said, as he smiled at James and Daniel.

"I want to thank you for fashioning this escape route for our men," Washington said.

"It is our honor and privilege," Daniel said.

"Yes, sir," James said.

"And, pray, tell me your names and ranks." Washington said.

"I am Daniel Welburn, private, 5th Pennsylvania, under the command of General Wayne."

"And I am James Weldon, private, also 5th Pennsylvania, also under the command of General Wayne."

"Well," said General Washington.  "I will tell General Wayne about your honorable service."

"Thank you sir," James and Daniel said.

"Now," said Washington, "we will wait here and see what is happening over at Barren Hill.  I wanted to be here personally because of the importance of this mission.  Depending on what we see today, if we need to, I want to personally give the order to bring the Continental Army here to beat back the redcoats."

James' and Daniels' eyes widened again.  "Yes, sir," they said.

Washington nodded his head. "So, we wait," he said, as he turned his horse to the right and looked out over the highest point in the Hills, ready to call the Continental Army to fight, right there in James' and Daniels' back yard.

GENERAL WASHINGTON, Commander Burr, James, Daniel, and the West Virginia boys waited there, atop the Hills, until the sun was just about to set. There had been no movement at Barren Hill.

Burr rode up to James and Daniel, who stood at attention. "Men," he said. "The advance guard is going to escort General Washington back to Valley Forge before it gets dark."

James and Daniel said, "Yes, sir."

"You two should remain here, on lookout," Burr said.

"Yes, sir," said James and Daniels.

"I know that you are still under the command of General Lafayette, but I want you to know that if you feel that you need the assistance of any of the men at our picket post, all you have to do is send a man down to our post, and they will come to your aid," Burr said.

Daniel said, "Yes, sir. We appreciate that sir."

Burr saluted them both, turned his horse and rode over to General Washington. General Washington looked over at James and Daniel, smiled, and saluted them.

James and Daniel nodded and saluted back. Then, General Washington, Burr, and their guards rode away.

James and Daniels watched as General Washington and his entourage rode out of sight.

When they were gone, they looked at each other and laughed.

"Wow," said James. "Can you believe it?"

Daniel laughed as he said, "No, I sure can't. To meet General Washington again. To have him twice on our hills?"

"Who would have thought that our hills were that important?" James asked.

"Not me, that's for sure," Daniel said. "After all this time living here, being unimportant, we all of a sudden are so important that the Commander in Chief of the Continental Army is turning to us for help?" he laughed. "Who would have thought?"

Suddenly, they both heard a loud boom coming from the direction of Barren Hill. They both looked over, and they saw the smoke rising from far down below in the valley.

They looked at each other. "Looks like something's starting," James said.

"Yeah," said Daniel. "It looks like General Washington left too early."

They both moved closer to the edge of the ridge to look at what was going on.

"Alright," said Daniel. "We just need to follow our orders, stay put, and make sure that our boys can get out if they need to."

"Right," said James, as he squinted his eyes, hoping to see everything that was happening over at Barren Hill.

# CHAPTER 70

# BARREN HILL

"**M**ove out," yelled Captain McLean to the shooters along the stone fence.

Right on cue, the Oneidas started their war dance and their war whoops.

Fred grabbed his musket and stuffed extra ammunition into his back pack. Connie and Tom stood up and slung extra ammunition over their shoulders.

"Come on," Fred said, as he grabbed Connie's hand with his free hand. They started running away from the church with the rest of the sharp shooters. The three of them took off, Connie and Fred running like they used to when they were children running from farm to farm through the fields in Paoli. Tom kept right up with them. They ran through the woods in back of the church, through the escape route that James, Daniel and the West Virginia boys had made. Hundreds of soldiers ran as fast as they could as the Oneida's war sounds became more distant.

"Are you alright?" Fred yelled to Connie.

"I taught you how to run through the woods, remember baby brother?" Connie said, as she ran right alongside Fred.

They ran past the West Virginia soldiers in their coon skin caps, pointing the way along the path. They ran besides the trees until they reached the Matson Ford. Then Connie hitched up her dress as she ran across the river, right next to Fred and Tom and the other soldiers. They ran past the few shops still remaining near the Ford and then back into the woods along the windy path through the hills. They ran up the hill with the other fleeing soldiers, dodging whatever had been dropped in their path by the soldiers that were ahead of them. They got a little breathless as they ran up the last few hundred feet to the top of the hill. When they reached the top, Fred smiled as he looked around. There was James and Daniel, moving the soldiers on, giving a helping hand to any soldier who needed it, helping them to gather right there at the top of the hills where they had spent many a day as children and as adults.

Fred and Connie ran towards them as Fred yelled, "James! Daniel!"

James and Daniel looked over, smiling, as they saw their cabin mate and friend running towards them.

"There's Fred," James said, as he saw him.

"Yes!" Daniel yelled.

"Yes, with a woman," James said, as he looked over and saw Fred holding tight to the hand of a beautiful dark-haired woman.

Fred ran over to James and Daniel, let go of Connie's hand, and gave them a brotherly hug.

"Good job guys," Fred said.

"You made it out," Daniel said.

"Thank God," said Fred.

James and Daniel looked quizzically at Connie.

"Oh, my God," Fred said. "This is my sister, Connie."

James and Daniel squinted their eyes, confused.

"My sister Connie, the one who was living in Philadelphia," Fred said.

Connie stepped forward and stuck out her hand, "Glad to meet you two," she said, "Fred has told me about you."

James and Daniel looked at Connie. They stuck out their hands and shook her hand.

"Pleased to meet you," said Daniel, looking at this beautiful woman who again looked familiar to him. No time to think of how right now, Daniel thought to himself. He had to focus on getting 2000 soldiers away from the British.

"Me, too," said James.

"And this is or should I say, was, my house man, Tom," Connie said, pointing to Tom.

"Pleased to meet you," Tom said, as he bent over, held his hand on his knees and caught his breath.

"Likewise," James said.

Daniel looked at the little party and said, "Glad you all made it out. Now go on and sit down while we get the rest of our boys in." He pointed to an area where the quartermaster on duty there gave the soldiers water. "Head on over there. We'll find you once everyone gets up here."

Connie, Fred and Tom went over, got some water, and feel down on the ground, exhausted.

James and Daniel continued helping soldiers up the hill and into the clearing at the highest point until the last soldier, and then the last Oneida Indian, had made it up the hill, safely away from the clutches of the British army, which, to the Continentals surprise, never advanced any further than the perimeter of the church at Barren Hill.

# CHAPTER 71

# REBEL HILL

The bunkmates plus Connie settled in and caught their breath with the rest of those who had survived the Battle of Barren Hill. They drank the water and ate the small bits of food that they were offered. It seemed like everyone who participated in the battle was there, falling out or sitting on the ground, waiting.

As the bunkmates looked out across the hill, General Lafayette rode towards them, along with an entourage of officers on horseback. They went from group to group, talking to the men as the men slowly stood up at attention. As General Lafayette and his group rode closer to theirs, Fred stood up slowly. Then he stuck his hand out and offered it to Connie. She held out her arm, and he lifted her to her feet.

They stood at attention as the general rode towards them. When he came within a few feet of them, Gen. Lafayette said, "Men," looking out across the group, and then, as he looked directly at Connie, "and beautiful lady."

Connie looked Lafayette directly in the eyes and smiled. Then she let her gaze roam to the other officers in his entourage. Even as tired as she was, she felt a surge of heat and energy as she looked at one of the officers whose handsome and striking features were very evident, even in the now dimming light.

"Good work, men," Lafayette said. "You helped hold the entire British army at bay with your marksmanship, your orienteering skills, and your bravery. I just wanted to come over and thank you and to tell you that I know General Washington will thank you when he learns of your bravery."

He looked out over the men. "I know that you're tired, but I also know that you're some of the strongest men, and women," he said, looking directly at Connie, "that I know. Because we don't want to give those redcoats another chance to reorganize, we're going to march back to the Valley Forge right away. So, please, organize your belongings and fall in behind your commanding officer." Then he bent down closer to Connie and said, "Ma'am, I know that you are strong and brave like your brother here," he said, pointing at Fred. "But, I would not be the gentleman that I am if I also didn't recognize you as the fair lady that you are."

Connie smiled as he went on.

"Please allow me to offer you a ride on a horse with one of my officers. The men may have to walk back to the Valley Forge, but I must insist that you ride back," he said.

Connie looked at Lafayette, and then at Fred. Fred nodded yes. Connie looked back at Lafayette, held her hand out, and said, "Why General, if you insist, how I can object? I'd be pleased to ride back with one of your officers."

Lafayette took Connie's hand, lowered his head, kissed her hand, all the while looking Connie straight in the eyes. "Very good, madam," Lafayette said. Then he tightened his grip on her hand as he led her towards him. Lafayette turned and looked at an officer behind him. "Major DuPree," he said. "Would you be so kind as to carry this beautiful woman on your horse back to the Valley Forge?"

The handsome man who had already stirred something inside of Connie said, "Oui, General," and held out his hand. Lafayette led Connie to Major Dupree. Connie took Dupree's hand, looked directly in his eyes and said, "Thank you for the ride."

Dupree smiled and looked directly at Connie and said, "The pleasure is all mine."

Connie smiled and thought, "You don't know the half of it," as she lifted her skirt, stepped up on the stirrups and sat on the horse.

"Please put your arms around my waist," Dupree said. "I wouldn't want you to fall off."

Connie put her arms around his waist and smiled. She said, "Don't worry. I won't fall off. I'm used to rough riding."

Dupree turned around and looked at her. Connie raised one eyebrow, and he said, smiling "Good."

Connie tightened her arms around Dupree's waist as they rode off.

# CHAPTER 72
# VALLEY FORGE

Fred, James, Daniel and all of those who fought at Barren Hill were welcomed back to the Valley Forge like conquering heroes. Soldiers and generals lined the road into camp as they returned to cheers. At the end of the line was General Washington himself, personally saluting every man—and woman—who marched back in with the group. When the last man marched in, Washington addressed the group.

"Men, your bravery is well-established. You fought off the entire British army, held them back, and stopped them from coming towards the Valley Forge to attack the rest of the Continental Army," he said. "General Lafayette has told me tale after tale of your bravery and courage. We are indebted to you," he said, as he took off his hat and bowed.

The men cheered for their commander-in-chief.

"We are so indebted to you," Washington said, "that I want to show you how much. I want you to return to your cabins and rest up and freshen up. Then, I want you to report to my headquarters at 5 p.m. tomorrow evening for a celebration with eating, drinking and music. You are heroes," he said.

The men cheered again.

Washington rode off, and Fred and his bunkmates started marching back to their bunk. Major Dupree rode Connie over to where Fred was and helped her off the horse. "So you will be in the bunk with your brother?" he asked.

Connie said, "For a few days," she said. "Then I'm going back to my family in Paoli, about five miles from here."

Dupree took her hand. "May I visit you while you are here?"

Connie shook her head and said, "Yes. I'd like that."

Dupree kissed her hand. "Then look for me soon," he said. "And, I will look for you at the fete tomorrow."

Connie said, "Yes, I'll be there." She pulled on her skirt and said, "Cleaned up and looking better than I look today."

"You look beautiful," he said. "If you can do any better, I can only imagine."

Connie smiled and thought to herself that the reality of her whole self had exceeded many a man's imagination. But, she played it cool and said, "Until then."

Dupree kissed her hand and said, "Until then."


**THE BUNKMATES** took advantage of the day off from chores and drills to boil enough hot water to wash themselves in the tub that one of the men had built. James, Daniel, Fred, and Connie all took turns taking a bath in the tub that they put in the back of their cabin. Connie made Fred get some tree limbs with leaves to shield curious eyes while she lay in the tub. She found some talc somewhere, mixed it with some flower petals, and dusted on herself. Then she found some honeysuckle and early blooming rose petals to use to rub behind her ear, between her décolleté and on her wrists. She took off her dirty dress and washed it the night before and spent most of the day in a spare shirt that Fred had. Her dress had dried in the sun just enough for her to wear it for the party. The men shaved and changed into their spare set of clothes. James wanted to look especially nice.

A party at Washington's Headquarters meant that he would be able to see Ernestine again, and see her as a conquering hero. He missed her and worried about her safety as he spent just a few days at Barren Hill away from her.

At about 4:45, they were ready. Daniel patted James on the back, "You clean up pretty well, old friend," Daniel said.

"I hope Ernestine likes it," James said, running his hand down his clothes.

"She will," Daniel said. "She will."

Connie walked out of the bunk, dark hair having been curled on flexible green tree branches and blowing in the slight wind.

"You look beautiful, sis," Fred said.

"And you look very handsome," Connie said, "for a little brother."

They both laughed.

"Shall we?" Fred asked, bending his arm at the elbow and holding it out for Connie to take it.

"Certainly," said Connie, as she took his elbow.

They turned in the direction of General Washington's headquarters and walked off towards the only victory party they had ever attended.

THE PATRIOTS who had fought in the Battle of Barren Hill walked down hills and across fields in a steady stream to Washington's Headquarters. There was an explosion of colors because so many men had different colored uniforms representing their various units. Fred, Daniel and James and most of the men were in the blue and white of the Continental Army; Hundreds more were in the brown and white of the Pennsylvania Militia; the West Virginia patriots wore their coon skin caps with their brown, white and black fur; and the Oneidas were in full victory dress with multicolored feathers running from one side of their headdress to the other, green and blue turquoise decorating their belts, sashes, and everything else, and, of course, all of that being reflected in their polished silver that shone like a mirror. Some of the camp women that followed the men had, like Connie, cleaned themselves up and washed their clothes in honor of a party at Washington's Headquarters to which the various men that they were either married to or attached to had been invited.

"It smells real good down here," Daniel said, as they reached the general vicinity of the Headquarters.

"Sure does," said James. "It smells like the ladies have been cooking all day and," he said, pointing down towards the cook house near the headquarters, "it looks like they still are."

The fires raged full blown from pots of all types that were set out in the open area next to the cook house. People scurried back and forth from the cook house to the main house to the rows of wooden tables were set out next to the headquarters.

James looked hard to see if he could pick Ernestine out of the crowd, but he wasn't so lucky. He could see some of the Oneida women in the group, so he looked closely at them. He thought that Ernestine might be working near Sora, since they had become good friends.

As they reached the level field where the tables were set up, there was a receiving line. General Lafayette and the other generals of the Continental Army were first in the line, shaking hands with all of the warriors. Then next in the line were the other officers who were at Barren Hill.

The bunkmates took their spot in line.

"Ladies first," said Connie as they lined up.

Connie smiled as she led the bunkmates. As they reached General Lafayette, he smiled at Connie.

"Ah, Madam," he said, as he leaned down, took her hand, and kissed it.

"So nice to see you again, General," Connie said, as she nodded in recognition to him kissing her hand.

"You look beautiful," he said, smiling.

"Thank you," said Connie. "And you look very handsome."

Lafayette laughed. "That's not the usual greeting I get from one of the people who has joined me in battle, but I'll take it," he said.

Connie smiled, and said, "Well, I'm not one of the usual patriots."

Lafayette laughed again and said, "No, you certainly are not usual." Then he smiled and added, "Thank God."

Connie laughed as she curtsied and moved down the line. The other generals were equally moved by seeing her as evidenced by the time that they held her hand and tried to keep her talking to them. The line behind her grew longer with every officer she met. As she reached the other officers who had fought at Barren Hill, she was pleased to see Lt. Dupree.

"I can't tell you how nice it is to see you again," Lt. Dupree said.

"Likewise," said Connie.

"And I see that you are causing your usual commotion," Dupree said.

"That I cannot help, Lieutenant," Connie said.

"Yes, I know," said Dupree. "Well, perhaps we can get together later during the party and see if there's anything that I can do to calm things down around you."

Connie laughed. "Many men have tried to do that, Lieutenant," she said. "Let's see if you will be the successful one."

Dupree laughed. "I have many skills that other men do not," he said.

"I'm sure you do," said Connie, as she curtsied and moved down the line to the end where she, Fred, Daniel and James were escorted to one of the waiting tables.

When all of the Barren Hill warriors had passed through the receiving line and were seated at the tables, there was a flourishing sound of trumpets. One of the Generals called out, "Attention!", and they all scrambled to their feet. The door to Washington's Headquarters opened, and out came General Washington with his wife, Martha, on his arm. He was followed by Han Yerry, the highest ranking Oneida male, with the highest ranking Oneida woman, Polly Cooper, on his arm. The two leaders of their great nations walked to the table at the head of all of the other tables and stood there facing the Barren Hill patriots. General Washington spoke first.

"I am honored to welcome all of you to my headquarters. You are valiant soldiers and patriots. Your performance at the Battle of Barren Hill saved all of your compatriots here at Valley Forge, and it sent the British running back to Germantown and to Philadelphia. I thank you for your service, and Martha and I hope that you have a wonderful time here. We have food and entertainment, and we hope that this one night, in some small measure, gives you strength and comfort as we carry on our war for freedom."

The men and women yelled, "Huzzah! Huzzah!" as they clapped and cheered for their Commander in Chief.

"At ease," yelled General Lafayette, as the men sat back down. Then, a commotion of sound and activity came from the cook house. A line of men and women carrying bowls, trays, and baskets filled with food marched towards the tables.

James turned in his chair and strained his neck and head every which way to find Ernestine in the group. This time, he was successful. Ernestine carried a tray of food and was in the middle of the line of servers. Sora was right behind her, carrying another tray,

Come this way, James said to himself, as if in a prayer. Come this way.

Ernestine and Sora turned and headed towards their table.

"See," Daniel said, as he hit James on the arm. "Looks like this is your lucky day."

"About time," James said, as Ernestine came closer.

"And yours," said Daniel, as he kicked Fred, who sat directly across from him, under the table.

"I see," said Fred, happily, as Sora came closer to their table.

James let his eyes roam over every inch of Ernestine's face and body as she walked closer. And, he became alarmed at what he saw. Ernestine's face was fuller. She had clearly gained weight. Even though it had only been a few days since he had seen her, she looked different. His eyes immediately focused on her stomach and, when he did, almost all of the joy that he felt that day left him. She had gained weight. She was beginning to show. She was with child.

As she walked closer, he tried to catch her eye, but Ernestine kept her eyes straight ahead. For James, that would never do. Ernestine came closer, walking between his table and the row behind him towards the front where those ahead of her were already beginning to serve the seated patriots. James knew that he couldn't let her walk by without trying to catch her attention. He whispered loudly, "Hello Ernestine."

Ernestine looked down at him and smiled slightly.

In an instant, James' searched Ernestine's eyes with his eyes, wanting to say more, but Ernestine had already turned her head back and was headed towards the top of the table. She and Sora were in the row of servers who were serving the side opposite from James. As they came closer to where Fred and Connie sat, James kept looking at Ernestine. Yes, he thought to himself, she is definitely pregnant. He never doubted or questioned Ernestine's integrity. He never doubted or questioned who it was who made Ernestine pregnant. He knew that it was that officer from Virginia who had inflicted upon Ernestine every slave woman's nightmare and, for far too many, their daily reality.

Fred smiled at Sora and touched her hand as she served him the meat from the tray that she was holding.

James kept his eyes trained on Ernestine as she served Connie and Fred. Ernestine looked over at him with eyes downturned and mixed with sadness.

"I'll come look for you later, Ernestine," James said, as Ernestine continued serving.

Ernestine looked up at James and just nodded. James knew why there was no smile this time. She was close up. He had plenty of time to look at her. She knew that he knew.

THE VICTORY celebration went on. The Barren Hill crowd ate more food that night than they had for weeks. Having a few different meats, even though no one had large portions, was also a huge treat. While they ate, a small band played the familiar songs that they all grew up singing. They even had a few extra portions of wine each. As the sun set, other soldiers lit fires around the tables to illuminate the area. Some soldiers got up to dance, alone, with each other, or with the camp women. Fred and Connie joined the dancers, and then General Dupree joined them. At one point, it was just Connie and General Dupree, dancing and talking, getting to know each other. Fred talked with the other warriors, Continental Army, militia and Oneida. He danced with some of the camp women as they came by and grabbed him. Daniel did the same. James stood back, watching everyone have a good time, waiting for his opportunity to sneak away and talk to Ernestine. As the party went on and it seemed like everyone who had been engaged in battle just days before was dancing, laughing and drinking, James got up and walked towards the cook house.

As he approached, he saw that the workers and servants were in various stages of cleaning up. Some of them had finished already and were sitting around, taking much deserved rests, eating and drinking themselves.

"Hey there, James," said Cephas, one of the older slave men who he had come to know. "Congratulations on the battle and escaping the British. You boys did a great job."

"Thank you," said James, as he tipped his hat to the few slaves sitting there.

He looked around at everyone. He didn't see Ernestine. He walked closer to the old man and said, "I'm looking for Ernestine. Do you know where she is?"

Cephas sighed, as he put down his fork. "She probably went back to her cabin," he said. Then he added softly, "She's been mighty tired these days, and we've all been working real hard getting ready for this here celebration."

James looked at him. He knew what the man was trying to say—she's been tired because she's pregnant. James just patted the man on the shoulder, "Thanks Cephas. I understand."

Cephas looked up at James and said, "It's a shame, man. Again."

James shook his head and said, "Yes, it is."

James walked off towards the cabins. He didn't see hardly anyone as he walked quietly yet quickly towards Ernestine's cabin. Most of the slaves were still over at the celebration doing clean up duty and thankful for a break in their usual daily drudgery. It was unusually quiet near the cabins. Yet, not as he approached Ernestine's cabin. As he approached her cabin, he heard crying. And the sound of wood hitting wood. And he heard moaning. He ran towards Ernestine's cabin now. He stood at the window for an instant, confirmed that he heard what he heard, and then looked in the window. He paused for a minute as he saw Ernestine crying on the bottom, hands down at her side, with the Virginia officer on top of her, pants down to his ankles, thrusting into Ernestine, the top of the bed hitting the cabin wall every time that he did.

James threw open the door and rushed in. The officer looked over at him and cried out, "Get out of here!"

Ernestine looked over at James and cried out, "Help!"

James ran over, hauled back and punched the Virginia officer dead in the jaw as he pushed him off of Ernestine. He grabbed Ernestine's arm as he pulled her off the bed and helped her to her feet.

Eyes wild with rage, he looked at Ernestine and said, "Go and get my friend Daniel and the other men from my bunk," he said. "They're the only ones who will stop me from killing this man."

Ernestine, eyes wide, looked at James. She pulled her underpants up as James turned his back. He lunged toward the Virginia officer, who had now pulled up his pants and was coming towards James, trying to pull out his gun with one hand. James ran faster than the officer could draw. He punched the officer dead in the face once again. Then he punched him again and knocked him down. James reached for the officer's gun. He wasn't able to get it as he and the officer rolled around on the cabin floor, punching each other.

"I'll kill you, nigger," the officer said.

"Not if I kill you first," said James, as he landed another punch.

"How dare you assault an officer?" the officer asked, as he punched James.

"How dare you rape a woman?" said James, as he hit the officer again.

"She's not a woman," the officer said, as James held him down. "She's property. A nigger slave, just like you."

James punched him again. "I'm a free man," James said, as he punched the officer.

The officer spat blood at James. "Free or slave, you're just a nigger to me."

James hauled back his hand and was ready to hit the officer again. Just then, Daniel yelled out, "James, don't!" as he ran in the cabin. There was scuffling at the door as Fred ran in after Daniel. Both of them ran over to James and pulled him off the officer.

James yelled out, "And you're just a rapist to me," as Fred and Daniel held him back.

The officer was standing now, blood streaming down his face. He wiped some blood off his face as he said, "You're lucky your friends are here now. But, I'll have you court-martialed for striking an officer."

James spat at him. "You're the one who ought to be court martialed for raping a woman, time after time, and for making her pregnant."

The officer laughed. "Rape? You can't rape property. And I certainly won't be court-martialed for that as an officer. Whose word will our generals take? Your's? That piece of property?" he said pointing at Ernestine, who had now arrived, running back more slowly than Daniel and James. "Or mine?"

As he said that, there was more noise at the cabin door. Lieutenant Dupree ran in, sword drawn. Connie ran in close on his heels. When Ernestine ran to get Daniel, he was sitting at the table drinking with Fred, Connie and Lt. Dupree. They had all heard Ernestine's plea for help for James.

DuPree ran over to the Virginia officer. "I think the generals will take my word," he said. "My word about your despicable conduct and your deplorable violation of this woman," he said, pointing to Ernestine, who stood there crying as Connie put her arm around her.

The officer laughed. "She's not a woman. She's property. Free for me to do with as I wish," he said. "This is America, not France. We do things differently here," he said, with contempt.

Dupree walked over to the officer. "I know," said Dupree, as he held his sword to the officer's neck. "But one thing is no different here than in France. And that is the chain of command. You, sir, are merely a Sargent. I am a Lieutenant. So, you must follow my orders," he said, emphasizing the word "my." "And my order is that you stay right here so I can make sure that you are held accountable for your conduct."

Dupree turned towards Fred. "Monsieur Fred, would you please go and get General Lafayette and tell him what has transpired here, and ask him to please join us."

Fred squinted his eyes together as he looked at the sergeant with disdain. "Absolutely Lieutenant," he said, as he saluted Dupree and ran towards and out of the front door.

The officer looked at Dupree with his eyes squinted, shooting arrows at him.

Dupree looked at James, now held just by Daniel. "Are you alright now soldier?" Dupree asked, as he gave James a handkerchief to wipe the blood off his face.

"I am now," James said, as he looked at the Virginia officer with a smile on his face.

James said calmly to Daniel, "Daniel, you don't have to hold me now."

Daniel said into James ear, "Are you sure?"

"I'm sure," said James, "now that I know that something is going to be done about this rapist."

Daniel said, "Ok. Don't do anything stupid now if I let you go."

"I won't," said James.

Daniel took his strong hands off James. James looked at the officer and rolled his eyes. Then he walked over towards the bed, where Ernestine and Connie now sat. Ernestine had laid her head on Connie's shoulder as Connie stroked her head and arms, calming her down.

"Can I talk to her?" James said to Connie as he approached.

Ernestine looked up. She nodded her head yes.

Connie stood up, warmly grabbing James hand and shaking it.

James looked Connie in the eyes and said, "Thank you."

Connie took his other hand and said, "No, thank you. If there's anything that's lower than a snake, it's a man who takes a woman against her will." Then she looked closer at James and said, "Any woman."

James nodded and walked over to the bed where Ernestine sat, head looking down, still crying. James knelt on the floor in front of her. He just said softly, "He won't be bothering you anymore."

Ernestine sniffled, wiped her eye with her dress sleeve, and said, "I hope not."

"I'm sure of it," James said.

She looked straight into James eyes and said, "I'm a slave. I can't be sure of anything."

James said, "The lieutenant said it was the officer who was going to get the court martial for this, not me."

Ernestine said between tears, "That's what he says. We'll see what he does. You know I'm not the only slave woman who's had one of these soldiers come to her."

"I know," said James, softly.

"And nobody does anything about it. They keep coming," Ernestine said. "And us?" she said, with a mixture of sadness and hysteria, "We keep getting used and used. And they don't even stop when we get with child," she said, putting her hand on her belly. "Some of them even seem to like it better then," she said, as she let the tears flow.

James looked over at Dupree and then back at Ernestine. "It's different now," he said.

"Is it? Is it?" she asked, crying loudly. "Is he ever going to have to pay for what he did to me?" she said, rubbing her belly.

"Yes, he is," a voice called loudly from the cabin door.

James turned his head around quickly and then he hurriedly stood on his feet. "General," he said, as he saluted General Lafayette, standing in the doorway.

Gen Lafayette strode in, accompanied by a few other officers. He walked over to where Daniel, Lieutenant DuPree and the Virginia officer were standing, now all at attention, and now all saluting Lafayette.

"General," the Virginia rapist called out, "this isn't what it seems."

Lafayette said, "I know what it seems like to me. I know what I've been told. So what is going on here officer?" Lafayette asked.

Before the Virginia officer could speak, there was another voice booming from the front of the cabin door. "Yes, what is going on here, officer?"

The entire group turned towards the door and gasped. Then they saluted.

"At ease," said General Washington.  He walked towards the group of soldiers and got right up in the face of the Virginia officer.  "I said, officer, so what is going on here?"

"Nothing but a case of me having relations with that slave woman over there," he said, pointing at Ernestine.  "She begged me to.  She begs me just about every day."

General Washington looked at the officer.  Then he turned and looked at Ernestine, who still sat on the bed crying.  Then he looked back at the officer.

"That is not what I heard happened here, officer," Washington said.  "What I heard when I was having a cup with General Lafayette, enjoying the Barren Hill victory celebration, when this man here," he said, pointing to Fred, "interrupted him and told him what was going on here and to come quickly at the request of Lieutenant Dupree, was that an officer in the Continental Army, the Virginia regiment at that, had brutally and repeatedly raped this woman here," he said, pointing to Ernestine.

"He's lying," the Virginia officer said.

Washington closed his eyes briefly and looked around at the people inside the now crowded cabin.

"Oh, is he now?" Washington said, as he started pacing.  He walked over towards Fred and looked in his eyes.  "Were you lying, son?"

"No, sir," said Fred.

Then Washington walked to Daniel.  "Were you lying, son?"

"No sir," said Daniel.

Then Washington walked to James.

"Were you lying, son?" Washington asked.

"No, sir," James said.

Washington paused and looked more closely at James.  "I never forget a face," he said.  "Didn't I see you on the top of the Rebel Hill while we were waiting for the men to return from Barren Hill?"

"Yes, sir," said James.

"I thought so," said Washington. "Good work there, mapping out a route to bring our boys back safely."

Then he walked over to Ernestine. She started to stand. Washington put his hand out.

"No, no. Stay seated," he said.

She looked up at him.

"Are you lying, Ma'am?"

"No sir," Ernestine said softly.

Washington nodded and said, "Thank you."

He looked over at Connie and nodded.

"Are you lying, Ma'am?" he asked.

"No general, I am not," Connie said.

"Thank you," said Washington. Then he turned on his heels and walked over to the Virginia officer.

"Officer? What did you say your name was?" Washington asked.

"Reston," he said.

"Officer Reston," Washington said. "All of these people say that they are not lying, so could it be that you are?"

"No," said the officer loudly. "It's not me. They're all in cahoots. They're all lying."

Washington sighed. "Well, Officer Reston, there's only one way to tell whether you are telling the truth or whether all of these other people," he said, stretching his arm around the room, "are lying." Washington looked straight at Reston, and said, "And that is to put you before a court of your peers and theirs, and let everyone tell their story and let all of the evidence come out."

Washington looked at Reston. "Do you know what I'm talking about officer?"

Reston frowned and looked worried. "A court martial, sir?"

"There you have it," Washington said. "A court martial. You're not as dumb as you look."

Then Washington turned his back towards Reston and addressed the rest of those gathered in the cabin. "I want everyone to understand that I do not tolerate what has been reported to me as occurring here tonight. Officer Reston has no right to violate this woman here, no matter what her status. And, like any officer of the Continental Army who engages in conduct that is unbecoming of an officer, Officer Reston will be called to account for himself," he said. Washington walked over to Ernestine. "Ma'am, there will be a court-martial for what happened here."

Ernestine just nodded her head in acknowledgment of what Washington had just said.

Washington turned to General Lafayette. "General, please have one of your men take this man into custody, where he will stay until the court martial concludes."

"Absolumon," Lafayette said, as he saluted Washington. Lafayette pointed to one of his men to get Reston. A few men walked over to Reston, held both arms, put those arms behind his back, and then put him in handcuffs.

Washington watched that and then said, "Take him away," as the men led Reston away.

Washington then turned to the group, saluted them, turned on his heels and walked out of the small cabin door.

# CHAPTER 73

# JUNE 19, 1778
# VALLEY FORGE

James walked quickly as he headed towards the slave quarters by General Washington's Headquarters. Even though it was early morning, the whole camp was awake and in motion, carrying and moving guns, cooking equipment, clothes, and all types of equipment. Today was move-out day. The army was marching out of Valley Forge after months of joy and pain all the way around. James never thought that he would be going on with them when he signed up six months ago. Even though he had earned just about enough to buy Ruth's freedom, because the Continental government was in turmoil and exile and all available funds were needed for the war effort, he didn't have all of his earnings in gold or silver, but in the Continentals that some considered not even worth the paper that they were printed on. So he signed up for a tour of duty with the Continental Army, planning to leave and go home and get Ruth as soon as he got his money. He asked one of the men who were stationed at the picket post at the Gulph Mill to ride down the road a few miles and deliver the message to Ruth to hold on just a little while longer until he could return and buy her freedom.

Even though his mind was on Ruth today, his intentions were set on Ernestine. As he approached the quarters and the cookhouse, the slaves were as busy as everyone else, carrying things and packing them up.

"How're you doing this morning?" James asked of one of the slave men that he had come to know and call a friend.

"As well as can be expected for a day when we're leaving six months of relative peace for God knows what we'll find when we meet those redcoats again," the man said, as he packed some cast iron cookware into a wagon.

"I know what you mean," said James as he hurried past.

He waved and greeted the other slaves as he walked along. After a few minutes, he reached Ernestine's cabin. He knew not to look inside but to go around the back. He found her standing around, talking with and hugging the other slaves. Even though they all worked and lived together at Valley Forge, they would be split up and assigned to different regiments on the road. Those generals who had brought their slaves with them would take them with them like the rest of their property, and there was no telling, once they left the Valley Forge, that all of the regiments would stay together.

James walked over and got in line. The sadness that he felt descended on him like an anvil. When it was his turn, he put his arms out and pulled Ernestine as close to him as he could for a woman who was five months pregnant.

"Take care of yourself," he whispered in her ear.

"I'll miss you so much," she whispered back.

Then they pulled back from each other and looked as deeply into each other's eyes as any two people could.

Ernestine kept holding both of his hands. "I can't thank you enough for everything you've done for me."

"I did what any decent man would do," he said.

Ernestine continued looking at him deeply. "Your woman, Ruth, is very lucky," she said.

James closed his eyes for a few seconds and said, "If it wasn't her, it would have been you."

Ernestine said, smiling, "Then I would have been the lucky one." She squeezed his hand. "You take care of yourself out there," she said, turning her head. "I hope that you make it back to her."

James continued looking at Ernestine, and said, "I hope I do, too. I hope that all of that drilling and shooting and training that we did here pays off the next time we run into those redcoats."

"Yes," said Ernestine. "That is my prayer."

As everyone else clamored around them, a horn sounded. That was the sign for the men to line up with their regiments.

James looked at Ernestine and said, "Well, I've got to go now."

Ernestine said, "Me, too."

They pulled each other into their arms and hugged as hard as they could.

"I'll never forget you," James whispered into her ear as tears came to his eyes.

"Same here," she whispered back as her tears came.

They pulled back from each other, squeezed their hands tight, and then James turned and walked away, leaving behind another woman that he loved, wondering when this kind of madness would end.

# CHAPTER 74

# JUNE 19, 1778
# PAOLI

The Roberts family woke up earlier than usual. They all knew that they had to get over to the Valley Forge early in the morning before the Continental Army marched out.

Betsey put on the dress that she had just made out of one of her mother's old dresses. There wasn't enough fabric floating around to buy and make something new, so she had to make do.

Connie put on one of the dresses that she was able to get Tom to bring her from her house in Germantown before the British blocked off the Germantown Road. The night before, she had neatly folded several of the dresses into a cloth bag that she had made out of one of the old carpets that he also took from the house.

Teenie put on one of her usual dresses made out of plain old homespun. After she did, she dressed her still ailing husband, fed him a light breakfast, and gently led him to their wagon.

The girls were already waiting there.

"Ready?" said Betsey to her mother once she and Connie helped their father into the wagon.

"Ready," said Teenie, as she held her husband's hand and arranged the pillows around him for his maximum comfort.

"Then let's go," said Betsey, as she picked up the reins and slowly drove the carriage away from their house.

# CHAPTER 75

# VALLEY FORGE

The road to the Valley Forge was already crowded with locals who wanted to send their boys off with prayers and whatever food and goods they could give them. When their carriage reached the Valley Forge and they cleared all of the pickets and guards, they headed towards the 5th Pennsylvania Regiment's cabins. Betsey jumped out first and ran over to the cabin where Fred waited for them.

"Good morning brother," she said, as she grabbed his arm and pulled herself into his waiting arms.

Fred smiled and said, "And good morning little sister," as he gave her a big hug.

They walked over to the carriage arm in arm.

Connie jumped down first and gave Fred a big hug. "You be careful out there, little brother," she said.

"I always am," Fred said, as he hugged her back.

Then Fred turned towards his mother. He jumped up on the carriage and hugged her because he knew that she couldn't let go of his father.

"I'm sorry to see you go, son," Teenie said. "At least you were safe here."

"I'll be safe out there, too," Fred said. "You know I'm one of the best shooters in this Army," he said smiling.

"I know that," she said, "but, still, I know you're marching out into another battle."

"Well," said Fred. "You do what you always do, say a prayer for me."

Tears came to Teenie's eyes as she thought of her dead son Allen and how her prayer was not answered that day last September, but she said, "You know I will."

Then Fred turned towards Orland, now a shadow of his former self with his weight and dimmed eyesight and hearing.

"Dad," said Fred. "You take care of yourself and these girls until I return."

Orland smiled weakly, "Of course," he said. He squeezed Fred's hand with a strength that Fred didn't know that he still had. "You watch yourself out there, son."

Fred said, "Absolutely. I'll be back before you know it."

Orland smiled, squeezed his hand again, and said, "I hope so."

Then Fred hugged him as hard as he could without causing pain.

The other men who Fred had shared a cabin with for the past six months, the men who had become like brothers to him, watched as Fred said his private good byes to his family. They all wished that their families had lived close enough to get the news as fast as the Roberts family had gotten it, close enough to ride over and say their own good byes. But they didn't.

When Fred had hugged everyone in his family, he turned towards his cabin mates and waved them over. The men walked over quickly; there wasn't much time before they had to leave.

They all went first to Teenie and Orland, giving them respectful hugs and good bye wishes. Most of them then went to Connie and hugged her and thanked her for her bravery in standing side-by-side with them at Barren Hill. James hugged her the longest and thanked her for standing up for Ernestine.

Connie said, "I might have run a brothel, but no one took advantage of my women, and no woman did anything against her will. I always fought to protect them, and I would fight to protect any woman."

They gave Betsey a quick hug like they would have given their little sister and made way for Daniel, who they knew would not hug Betsey like a little sister.

When it was Daniel's turn, instead of immediately hugging Betsey, he took both of her hands in his. "You look beautiful," he said.

Betsey turned red and said, "Thank you."

Daniel looked deeply into her eyes and said, "I enjoyed getting to know you these past few months."

Betsey returned his gaze and said, "Thank you. I did, too."

Daniel said, "Even though I'm going with the rest of the army now, I'll be coming back." He paused. "And I'll find you," he said, smiling.

Betsey smiled, felt more blood rush to her cheeks, and said, "I hope so." Then she added, "I'll be waiting."

"Good," said Daniel, as he let go her hands and hugged her, longer than anyone else.

When he stepped back and took his arms down, he still gazed into Betsey's face, a face that he thought was the most beautiful one that he had ever seen. He gently laid his hands on both of hers, leaned in, and kissed her softly on the cheek.

Betsey blushed at her first kiss.

The rest of the small group assembled who saw the kiss smiled warmly, thinking of their loves, young and old.

LIEUTENANT DUPREE had gotten a message to Connie that he wanted to see her before they marched out. Of course he did, thought Connie, when the courier delivered the message. The funny thing was that she wanted to see Lieutenant Dupree, too.

So, after the rest of the group said their goodbyes, Connie moved to the outer part of their circle and looked for Dupree. Shortly after she witnessed Betsey's first kiss, Dupree came riding down the road. He wouldn't be giving Connie her first kiss, but truly, the first kiss in a long time that she looked forward to with girlish anticipation.

Dupree was in full uniform. Connie smiled at the sight of him. He rode over and jumped off the horse. He hugged Connie and kissed her passionately on the lips. Connie held on to him tightly and returned his kiss with all of the passion that she could muster, which was a lot.

"Cherie," he said, when they stopped kissing but still embraced. "I will be back for you."

Connie smiled and squeezed his waist, "You better," she said.

"Believe me," he said as he kissed her again. "You will be mine, and we will have a long, happy life together."

"Don't take too long," Connie said. "I'm not the type of woman who likes to wait for what she wants."

Dupree laughed. "I know, mon cherie. I know." He said, "I will be back for you before you know it. It won't take long before we crush those Brits and send them back across the sea."

"I hope so," said Connie.

Dupree laughed. "Now, you believe me."

Connie smiled and kissed him again.

Then, gentleman that he is, Dupree went over to say his goodbyes to the family of the woman who he had fallen head over heels in love with, against everything that he had promised himself.

DOWN AT Washington's headquarters, the Oneidas were lined up in wagons and horses. Their great service to General Washington and the Continental Army completed for now, the tribe was going back to their home in New York.

General Washington had assembled all the generals to join him in seeing the Oneidas march out as they saw them march in. Everyone from both nations, the Oneida and the United States of America, was the worse for wear after a long, hard winter. But, the bonds between the two nations had strengthened to the unbreakable.

Polly sat at the front of her own wagon, a wagon that was packed with blankets, headdresses, jewelry and cookware that the Oneidas had brought with them as well as with gifts that they had been given, like the beautiful shawl that Martha Washington gave Polly. The goods were packed tightly and covered with heavy blankets to keep them from falling out as they rode the many miles and weeks back to New York.

As the Oneida wagon train pulled out, General Washington and the Continental Army assembly saluted them. Each driver nodded at General Washington as he or she rode by.

Polly held her horses with two steady hands. Her cargo was precious, and it was important to get out of the Valley Forge and into New York with everything in there intact.

The wagon train followed the same road that they followed on the way down.

After a few hours of steady riding, the wagon train stopped for fresh water for themselves and their horses. Sora pulled her wagon over and caught Polly's eye. Polly pulled her wagon in front of Sora's and called to another woman to pull her wagon in front of Sora's so that Sora's wagon could not be seen from the road.

Hidden from the road, Sora waited with her wagon until another Oneida woman brought her over a gourd filled with water. Sora looked around, jumped down off the wagon, pulled back one end of the blanket and handed it to Ernestine, giving her the first drink of water that she had as a now runaway slave.

Sora smiled as Ernestine drank it. "When we stop for the night, you will be able to get out," Sora said.

Ernestine smiled.

"And then," said Sora, "in about five nights, we will be home. And you will be, too."

Ernestine smiled again at the thought of freedom and a home with people who believed that all men and women were free and didn't understand how any man could think that he could make another man his property.

FRED, DANIEL, James, and the other members of the Pennsylvania Line were lined up, all of their belongings rolled up into a sack that they carried on their backs, muskets at their side.

General Wayne rode up while the bugles played. His white horse gleamed in the bright June sun. As he approached, the men stood at attention.

Wayne held his musket up in the air with one hand and his horse with another. "Huzzah," he shouted as he brought his nag to a gentle stop.

"Huzzah," the men shouted back, hoisting their muskets in the air with one hand, too.

"Men, we have come to a great day. The day that we will leave this, our home for the past six months, as an army that has been battered but not beaten, pressed in on every side but not destroyed, an army that is better trained and better disciplined," he said.

"You men have my eternal gratitude and the gratitude of General Washington and every general who has worked with you over the past six months," he continued. "When the generals speak of the Pennsylvania Line, they speak of a well-trained, committed fighting force."

He went on. "These generals know that you men were near your home and could have deserted, left here for the comforts of home when things got rough here at the Valley Forge." He smiled. "But you didn't. You stayed here. You endured the hardship the same as the men from Maine who couldn't run home over the snow-covered roads. You trained, and for some of you, fought, side-by-side with men from all over the continental United States.  And for that, you have the undying gratitude of our commanders."

"Huzzah," the men yelled out.

"So, today," Wayne said, "we march out.  We leave here.  We head towards New Jersey to confront the redcoats.  And I have no doubt that when we see their bloody red and white, the Pennsylvania Line will continue to distinguish itself and outshine them all."

The men cheered.

"So now," Wayne said, "attention."

The men stood even straighter.

General Wayne turned his horse towards the north and said, "Head out," as he lifted his musket in the air and marched out of Valley Forge with his men.

THE END

*Also by The Elevator Group*


If you liked *Becoming Valley Forge,* you might be interested
in these books by The Elevator Group:

*Patriots of African Descent in the Revolutionary War,*
a children's book, by Marion Lane

*Six Days in December: General George Washington's and the Continental
Army's Encampment on Rebel Hill,* December 13 - 19, 1777, by Sheilah Vance
(an ebook prequel to *Becoming Valley Forge)*


Read about these and all other books published by The Elevator Group at
www. TheElevatorGroup.com
or contact us at PO Box 207, Paoli, PA 19301, 610-296-4966,
info@TheElevatorGroup.com.